LOVE STORIES FOR THE REST OF US

LOVE STORIES

FOR THE REST OF US

―――――――――――――

PUSHCART

EDITED BY

GENIE D. CHIPPS & BILL HENDERSON

For information address
Pushcart Press,
P.O. Box 380
Wainscott, NY 11975

ISBN: 0-916366-90-1
        0-916366-93-6 (paperback)
LC 94-67424

Distributed by W.W. Norton & Co.
500 Fifth Ave., New York, NY 10110

Grateful acknowledgement is given to the authors
of these stories for permission to reprint them
in this anthology and to the following:
"Jack of Diamonds" © 1986 Elizabeth Spencer, from
Jack of Diamonds and Other Stories. Used by permission
of Viking Penguin, a division of Penguin Books USA Inc.

Again, For Lily

WITH THANKS...

The editors would like to thank the following literary magazines and small presses for originally publishing these stories: *New England Review, Iowa Review, Ontario Review, Callaloo, Ploughshares, ZYZZYVA, Georgia Review, Boulevard, Missouri Review, Antaeus, The American Voice, TriQuarterly, Kenyon Review, Shenandoah, Crazyhorse, Threepenny Review, Partisan Review, Grand Street,* Ecco Press, Seal Press, Graywolf Press.

CONTENTS

ISLAND
    Alistair MacLeod   1
THE HAIR
    Joyce Carol Oates   31
MY MOTHER AND MITCH
    Clarence Major   46
NOSOTROS
    Janet Peery   57
SAME OLD BIG MAGIC
    Patricia Henley   78
AN EMBARRASSMENT OF ORDINARY RICHES
    Martha Bergland   82
CRAZY LIFE
    Lou Mathews   100
THE COLUMBUS SCHOOL FOR GIRLS
    Liza Wieland   113
OTHER LIVES
    Francine Prose   127
HOUSEWORK
    Kristina McGrath   141
TELL ME EVERYTHING
    Leonard Michaels   153
YUKON
    Carol Emshwiller   177
THE MIDDLE OF NOWHERE
    Kent Nelson   185
WAITING FOR MR. KIM
    Carol Roh-Spaulding   203
JACK OF DIAMONDS
    Elizabeth Spencer   217
HUSH HUSH
    Steven Barthelme   248

"BY LOVE POSSESSED"
    Lorna Goodison   264
ASTRONAUTS
    Wally Lamb   270
GREEN GROW THE GRASSES O
    D.R. MacDonald   289
WAR
    Molly Giles   314
ACTS OF KINDNESS
    Mary Michael Wagner   324
ROSE
    Andre Dubus   334
LYRICS FOR PUERTO RICAN SALSA
AND THREE SONEOS BY REQUEST
    Ana Lydia Vega   368
JOHNNIERUTH
    Becky Birtha   374
LAWNS
    Mona Simpson   380

INTRODUCTION

How much jabber there is in the name of love! A best-selling author tops the list with a book interchangeable with the last. Spin the radio dial and try to distinguish one lyric from the next; channel surf and the images fly by with titillating commercials, identical soap plots, and a surfeit of slick passion with little joy. We live in a throw away love culture where the very nature of the thing we hunger for most is served up to us packaged in Styrofoam like fast food. Love is for sale everywhere; it keeps the cash registers ringing, the bottom line solidly in the black.

Ok, so that's *them*. What about the rest of us? Do we seek happy endings or the beginnings of understanding? Who can voice for us the complexity of love in all its guises and illusions? Who will grapple with love's betrayals and losses and preposterous fantasies? Who will get us through the night? Over the past eight years, the stories collected in this volume were selected as among the best from our literary writers and reprinted in the annual *Pushcart Prize* series, an anthology publishing the best of our literary magazines and small presses. In *Love Stories For the Rest of Us* they have been picked again, out of hundreds, because they speak of love, all kinds of love — and they are terrific.

Small press writers tend to speak honestly. They do not write for the jingle of coins. These tales did not spring from a commercial cookie cutter. They come from the experience and imaginations of today's most talented writers. Consequently, the tales we have collected here are an unpredictable lot describing love as tragic, joyous, excruciating, ridiculous, crazy, blissful: in other words, all the emotions that the rest of us know love to be.

The rest of us, be we young, old, straight, gay, urban, suburban, black, white, oriental, hispanic, rich, poor (or in between), married or single will find our hearts here. These writers are not the usual suspects. The love they speak of is told in unsentimental often unsparing ways. Like love, these fictions will enthrall you, hurt you, enrich you and make you cry or laugh or pound the desk in outrage, but they will never bore.

In 1987 we edited and published *Love Stories For the Time Being*, gleaning its selections from the first ten years of *The Pushcart Prize: Best of the Small Presses*. It was welcomed by readers and lovers worldwide. In the small press universe, where the bottom line is often equated with staying afloat, this was gratifying indeed and certainly signaled that we should follow through with a subsequent edition. The last eight years have produced a stunning wealth of fiction in our literary subculture. Perhaps it is because commercial literary outlets for serious writers have narrowed so alarmingly — perhaps, it is because good writing must proliferate to keep the grim world of glib at bay. Whatever the reason, we feel we can deliver on this promise: these stories are literally the best of the best.

We suspect that these fictions carry the voice of truth, and we also conjecture that truth is what the rest of us would like to enjoy.

Genie D. Chipps
and Bill Henderson

LOVE STORIES FOR THE REST OF US

ISLAND

by ALISTAIR MACLEOD

ALL DAY THE RAIN FELL upon the island and she waited. Sometimes it slanted against her window with a pinging sound which meant it was close to hail, and then it was visible as tiny pellets for a moment on the pane before the pellets vanished and rolled quietly down the glass, each drop leaving its own delicate trickle. At other times it fell straight down, hardly touching the window at all, but still there beyond the glass, like a delicate, beaded curtain at the entrance to another room.

She poked the fire within the stove, turning the half-burned lengths of wood so that they would burn more evenly. Some of the wood lengths were old fence posts or timbers which had been hauled from the shore before being cut into sizes which would fit the stove. Some of them contained ancient nails which were bent and twisted deep into the wood's core. When the fire was very hot, they glowed to a cherry red, reminiscent of a blacksmith's shop or, perhaps, their earliest casting. They would glow in the intense heat while the wood was consumed around them and, in the morning, they would be shaken down with the ashes, black and twisted but still there in the grayness of the ashpan. On days when the fire burned with less intensity because the wood was damp or the drafts poor, they remained a rusted brown while the damp wood sputtered and hissed reluctantly before releasing them from the coffins in which they were confined. Today was such a day.

She went to the window and looked out once more. Beneath the table the three black and white dogs followed her with their eyes but

1

made no other movement. They had been outside several times during the day and the wetness of their coats gave off the odor of damp woolen garments which have been hung to dry. When they came in, they shook themselves vigorously beside the stove, causing a further sputtering and hissing, as the water droplets fell against the heated steel.

Through the window and the beaded sheets of rain she could see the gray shape of *tir mòr,* the mainland, more than two miles away. Because of her failing sight and the nature of the weather she was not sure if she could really see it. But she had seen it in all weathers and over so many decades that the image of it was clearly in her mind, and whether she actually saw it or remembered it, now, seemed to make no difference.

The mainland was itself but another large island although most people did not think of it in that way. It was, as many said, larger than the province of Prince Edward Island and even some European countries and it had paved roads and cars and now even shopping centers and a fairly large population.

On rainy or foggy evenings such as this, it was always hard to see and to understand the mainland but when the sun shone it was clearly visible with its white houses and red or gray barns, and with the green lawns and fields surrounding the houses while the rolling mountains of dark green spruce rose behind them. At night the individual houses, and the communities they formed, seemed to be magnified because of the lights. In the daytime if you looked at a certain spot you might see only one house and, perhaps, a barn, but at night there might be several lights shining from the different windows of the house, and perhaps a light at the barn and other lights shining from hydro poles in the yard, or in the driveway or along the road. And there were the moving lights caused by the headlights of the travelling cars. It all seemed more glamorous at night, perhaps because of what you could not see, and conversely a bit more disappointing in the day.

She had been born on the island at a time so long ago that there was now nobody living who could remember it. The event no longer lived in anybody's mind nor was it recorded with accuracy anywhere on paper. She had been born a month prematurely at the beginning of the spring breakup when crossing from the island to the mainland was impossible.

2

At other times her mother had tried to reach the mainland before her children were born. Sometimes she would cross almost a month before the expected delivery because the weather and the water in all seasons, except summer, could never be depended upon. She had planned to do so this time as well but the ice that covered the channel during the winter months began to decay earlier than usual. It would not bear the weight of a horse and sleigh or even a person on foot and there were visible channels of open water running like eager rivers across what seemed like the gray-white landscape of the rotting ice. It was too late for foot travel and too early for a boat because there was not, as yet, enough open water. And then too she was born a month earlier than expected. All of this she was, of course, told much later. She was also told that when the winter began her parents did not realize that her mother was pregnant. Her father was sixty at the time and her mother close to fifty and they were already grandparents. They had not had any children for five years and had thought their child-bearing years were past and the usual signs were no longer there or at least not recognized until later in the season. So her birth, as her father said, was "unexpected" in more ways than one.

She was the first person ever born on the island as far as anybody knew.

Later she was brought across to the mainland to be christened. And still later when the clergyman was sending his baptismal records to the provincial capitol he included hers along with those of the children who had been born on the mainland. And perhaps to simplify matters he recorded her birthplace as being the same as that of the other children and of her brothers and sisters or if he did not intend to simplify perhaps he had merely forgotten. He also had the birthdate wrong and it was thought that perhaps he had forgotten to ask the parents or had forgotten what they had told him and by the time he was ready to send in his records they had already gone back to the island and he could not contact them. So he seemed to have counted back a number of days before the christening and selected his own date. Her middle name was wrong too. Her parents had called her Agnes but he had somehow copied it down as Angus. Again perhaps he had forgotten or was preoccupied and he was a very old man at the time, as evidenced by his shaky, spidery handwriting. And, it was pointed out, his own middle name was Angus. She did not know any of this until years later when she

3

sent for her official birth certificate in anticipation of her own marriage. Everyone was surprised that a single document could contain so many errors and by that time the old clergyman had died.

Although hers was thought to be the only birth to have occurred on the island there had been a number of deaths. One of them was that of her own grandfather who died one November from "a pain in the side" after pulling up his boat for the winter—thinking there would be no further need for a boat until the spring. He was only forty when it happened, the death occurring only two weeks after his birthday. His widow and children did not know what to do as there was no adequate radio communication and they were not strong enough to get the boat he had so recently hauled up, back into the water. They waited for two days hoping the sullen gray waves would subside, and stretching his body out on the kitchen table and covering it with white sheets—afraid to put too much fire in the kitchen stove lest it might hasten the body's decay.

On the third day they launched a small skiff and tried to row across to the mainland. They did not know if they would be strong enough to make it so they gathered large numbers of dried cattails and reeds from one of the island's marshes and placed them in a metal washtub and doused them with the oil used for the lamp at the lighthouse. They placed the tub in the prow of the skiff and when they rowed out beyond the shape of the island they set the contents of the tub on fire hoping that it might act as a signal and a sign. On the mainland someone saw the rising funnel of gray-black smoke and the shooting flames at its base and then the skiff moving erratically—rowed by the desperate hands of the woman and her children. Most of the mainland boats had already been pulled up for the winter but one was launched and the men went out to what looked like a burning boat and tossed a line to it and towed it in to the wharf after first taking off the woman and her children and comforting them and listening to their story. Later the men went out to the island and brought the man's body over to the mainland so that although he died on the island, he was not buried there. And still later that evening someone went over to light the lamp in the lighthouse so that it might send out its flashing warning to possible travellers on the nighttime sea. Even in the face of her husband's death, the woman, as well as her family, harbored fears that they might lose the job if the Government realized the lightkeeper was dead. They had already purchased their supplies for the winter and there was no other place to go so late in the season, so they decided to say nothing until the spring and returned to the island after the funeral accompanied by the woman's brother.

The original family had gone to the island because of death or rather to aid in death's reduction. The lighthouse was established in the previous century because of the danger the island represented to ships travelling in darkness or in uncertain weather. It was thought that the light would warn sea travellers of the danger of the island or, conversely, that it might represent hope to those already at the sea's mercy and who yearned so much to reach its rocky shore. Before the establishment of the light there had been a number of wrecks which might or might not have been avoided had there been a light. What was known with certainty was that survivors had landed on the island only to die from exposure and starvation because no one knew that they were there. Their skeletons being found, accidently by fishermen in the spring—huddled under trees or outcrops of rock in the positions of their deaths. Some still had the remains of their arms around one another. Some still with tattered, flapping clothes covering their bones although the flesh between the clothing and the bones was no longer there.

When the family first went they were told that their job was to keep the light and to offer salvation to any of those who might come ashore. The Government erected buildings for them which were better than those of their relatives on the mainland and helped them with the purchase of livestock and original supplies. To some it seemed they had a good job—a Government job. In answer to the question of the isolation, they told themselves they would get used to it. They told themselves they were already used to it, coming as they did from a people in the far north of Scotland who had for generations been used to the sea and the sleet and the wind and the rocky outcrops at the edge of their part of Europe. Used to the long nights when no one spoke and to the isolation of islands. Used to seeing their men going to work for the Hudson's Bay Company and the North West Company and not expecting them back for years. Used to seeing their men going to the vast ocean-like tracts of prairie in places like Montana and Wyoming to work as sheepherders. Spending months that sometimes stretched into years, talking only to dogs or to themselves or to imaginary people who blended into ghosts. Startled by the response to their own voices when they appeared, strange and unexpectedly, at the camp or at the store or at the rural trading post. In demand as sheepherders, because it was believed, and because they had been told, that they did not mind the isolation. "Of course I spoke to ghosts," a man was supposed to have said once upon his returning. "Wouldn't you if there was no one else to speak to?"

In the early days on the island, there was no adequate radio communication and if they were in trouble and unable to get across they would light fires on the shore in the hope that such signs would be visible on the mainland. In the hope that they who had gone to the island as part of the business of salvation, might they themselves be saved. And when the Great War was declared, it was said, they did not know of it for weeks, coming ashore to be told the news by their relatives, coming ashore to a world which would be forever changed.

Gradually, with the passage of the years, the family's name as well as their identity became entwined with that of the island. So that although the island had an official name on the marine and nautical charts it became known generally as MacPhedran's Island while they themselves became known less as MacPhedrans than as people "of the island." Being identified as "John the Island," "James the Island," "Mary of the Island," "Theresa of the Island." As if in giving their name to the island they had received its own lonely designation in return.

All of this was already history by the time she was born and she had no choice in any of it. Not choosing, for herself, to be born on the island (although the records said she was not) and not choosing the rather surprised individuals who became her parents after they had already become the grandparents of others. For by the time she was born the intertwined history of her family and the island was already far advanced. And when she was later told the story of the man who died from the pain in his side, it seemed very far away to her although it was not so for her father who had been one of the children in the skiff, rowing with small desperate freezing hands at the bidding of his mother. By the time of her early memories, the Government had already built a wharf at the island which was superior to any on the mainland. The wharf was built "to service" the lighthouse but it also attracted mainland fishermen who were drawn to its superior facilities. Especially during the lobster season months of May and June, men came to live in the shacks and shanties they erected along the shore. Leaving their shanties at four in the morning and returning in the early afternoon to sell their catches to the buyers who came in their big boats from far away. And returning to their mainland homes on Saturday and coming back again on Sunday, late in the afternoon or in the early evening, their weekly supplies of bread and provisions in burlap bags lying at the bottom of their boats. Sometimes lying in the bottoms of the boats there were also yearling calves with trussed feet and eyes bulging with fear who were brought to the island for summer pasturage and would be taken off half-wild in the cold, gray months of fall. Later in the summer the energetic, stifled rams would be brought in the same way, to spend monastic, frustrated months in all-male company before returning to the mainland and the fall fury of the breeding season.

He came to the island the summer she was seventeen. Came before the rams or the young cattle or the buyers' boats. Came at the end of April when there were still white cakes of ice floating in the ocean and when the family's dogs still ran down to the wharf to bark at the approaching boats and to snarl at the men who got out of them. In the time before such boats and men became familiar sights and sounds and odors. Yet even as the boat came into the wharf the dogs seemed to make less fuss than was usual and whatever he said quietened them and caused them to be still. She saw all this from the window of the kitchen. She was drying the dishes for her mother at the time and she wrapped the damp dish towel around her hand as if it were a bandage and then she as quickly unwrapped it again. As he bent to loop the boat's rope to the wharf, his cap fell off and she saw the redness of his hair. It seemed to flash and reflect in the April sun like the sudden and different energy of spring. She and most of her people were dark-haired and had dark eyes as well.

He had come, she learned, to fish for the season with one of the regular men from the mainland. He was the nephew of the man's wife and came from a place located over the mountain. From a distance of some twenty-five miles which was a long distance at the time. He had come early to make preparations for the season. To work on the shanty and repair the winter's damages, to repair the man's lobster traps and to make a few new ones. He told them all of this in the evening when he came up to the lighthouse to borrow oil for his lamp. He brought them bits and scraps of news from the mainland as well although they did not have that many people in common. He spoke in both Gaelic and English although his accent

7

was different from theirs. He seemed about twenty years of age and his eyes were very blue.

They looked at one another often. They were the youngest people in the room.

In the early madness of the lobster season they did not speak to one another although they saw each other almost every day. The men were often up at three in the morning brewing their tea by the flickering lamps, casting their large shadows eerily upon the shanties' walls as they moved about in the semi-darkness. At night they sometimes fell asleep by eight. Sometimes still sitting on their chairs, their heads tilting suddenly forward or backward and their mouths dropping open. She worked with her mother, planting the garden and the potatoes. Sometimes in the evening she would walk down by the shanties but not very often. Not because her parents openly disapproved but because she felt uncomfortable walking so close to so many men. Sometimes they nodded and smiled as all of them knew her name and who she was and some of them were her distant relatives. But at other times she felt uneasy, hearing only bits of the comments and remarks exchanged among them as they stood in their doorways or sat on their homemade chairs or overturned lobster crates. The remarks seemed mainly for themselves, to demonstrate their wit and masculinity to each other. As if they were young schoolboys instead of being mostly beyond middle age. Sometimes they reminded her of the late summer rams, playful and friendly and generally grazing contentedly in *achadh nan caoraich*, the field of the sheep, although sometimes given to spontaneous rages against those who would trespass into their territory or sometimes unleashing their suppressed fury against one another. Rearing and smashing against one another until their skulls thundered and reverberated like the growling icebergs of spring and their pent-up semen ejaculated in spurting jets, leaving them stunned and weak in the knees.

She and her mother were the only women on the island.

One evening she walked to the back of the island, down to the far shore which did not face the mainland but only the open sea. There was a small cove there which was known as *bagh na long bhriseadh*, bay of the shipwreck, because there were timbers found there in the long ago time before the lighthouse was established. She sat on *creig a bhoird*, the table rock which was called so because of its shape, and looked out across the seeming infinity of the sea. And then he

8

was standing beside her. He made no sound in coming and the dog which had accompanied her gave no signal of his approach.

"Oh," she said, on realizing him so unexpectedly close. She stood up quickly.

"Do you come here often?" he said.

"No," she said. "Well yes, sometimes."

The ocean stretched out flat and far before them.

"Were you born here?" he asked.

"Yes," she said. "I guess so."

"Do you stay here all the time? Even in the winter?"

"Yes," she said, "most of the time."

She was defensive, like most of her family, on the subject of the island. Knowing that they were often regarded as slightly eccentric because of how and where they lived. Always anticipating questions about the island's loneliness.

"Some people are lonely no matter where they are," he said as if he were reading her mind.

"Oh," she said. She had never heard anyone say anything quite like that before.

"Would you like to live somewhere else?" he asked.

"I don't know," she said. "Maybe."

"I have to go now," he said. "I'll see you later. I'll come back."

And then he was gone. As suddenly as he had come. Seeming to vanish behind the table rock and the water's edge. She waited for a while, sitting down once more upon the rock to compose herself and then walking up the island's rise towards the lighthouse. Later when she looked down from the kitchen window towards the shanties, she could see him hammering lathes onto a broken lobster trap and readying the bait buckets for the morning. His cap was pushed back upon his head and the evening sun caught the golden highlights of his burnished hair. He looked up once and her hand tightened upon the cloth she was holding. Her mother asked her if she would like some tea.

It was into the next week before she again walked down by the shanties. He was sitting on a lobster crate splicing rope. As she went by she thought she heard him say *Àite na cruinneachadh*. She quickened her step as she felt her color rise, hoping or perhaps imagining that he had said "the meeting place." She went there immediately, down to the bay of shipwrecks and the table rock and waited. She faced out to the sea and sat in such a way that she could not see him *not* coming if that was the way it was supposed to be. The dog sat at her feet and neither of them moved when he came to stand beside them.

"I told you I'd come back," he said.

"Oh," she said. "Oh yes. You did."

In the weeks that followed they went more frequently to the meeting place. Standing and later sitting on the table rock and looking out across the vastness of the sea. Talking more and sometimes laughing and, in retrospect, she could not remember when he asked her to marry him but only that she had burst into tears when she said "Oh yes" and they joined their hands on the flatness of the table rock which was still warm from the retained heat of the descending sun. "Oh yes," she had said. "Oh yes. Oh yes."

He planned to work in a sawmill, he said, after the lobster season was done; and then in the fall or early winter, after the snows began to fall and the ground became frozen, he would go to work in the winter woods of Maine. He would return to fish with the same man the next spring and then in the summer they would marry. They would go then, he said, "to live somewhere else."

"Oh yes," she said. "Oh yes, we will."

It was in the late fall, on the night following a day of cold and slanting rain that she was awakened by the dog pulling at the blankets that lay so heavily upon her bed. She sat up, even as she shivered and pulled the blankets about her shoulders, and tried to adjust her eyes to the darkness of the room. The rain slanted against the window with a pinging sound which meant that it was close to hail and even in the darkness she could see the near-white pellets visible for a moment before they vanished on the pane. The eyes of the dog seemed to glow in the dark and she felt the cold wetness of its nose when she extended her hand beyond the boundary of the bed. She could smell the wetness of its coat and when she moved her hand across its head and down its neck the water filmed upon her palm. She got up then, throwing on what clothes she could find in the darkness of the room, and followed the clacking nails of the dog as it moved down the hallway and past the closed door behind which her parents snored, sometimes snoring regularly and at other times with fitful catches in their sound. She went down through the kitchen and through the tiny puddles caused by the rain slanting through the opened door. Outside it was wet and windy although nothing like a gale and she followed the dog down the darkened path. And then in the revolving cycle of the high lighthouse light the pale beam shone in a straight but moving path. In a single white instant she saw the dark shape of the boat bobbing at the wharf and his straight but dripping form by the corner of the shanties.

The creaky door of the summer shanty yielded easily to his familiar shoulder. Inside it was slightly musty although the wind persisted through some of the unsealed cracks. Their eyes adjusted to the gloom and the few sticks of basic furniture that still remained. The primitive mattresses had been stored away to protect them from mice and the dampness of the sea. They held one another in their urgency and lay upon the floor fumbling with the encumbrances of their clothes. She felt the wet burden of his garments almost heavy upon her although the length of his body seemed light within them.

"Oh," she said, digging her fingers into the dampness of his neck, "when we are married we can do this all the time."

At the moment of explosion their breaths bonded into a single gasp that bordered on a cry.

She thought of this later as she passed the closed door of her parents' room. Thought of how her breath and his had become one and contrasted it with the irregular individual snoring which came from beyond her parents' door. She could not imagine them ever being young.

The same wonder was there the next morning as she watched her father in his undershirt preparing the fire and later going to polish the thick glass of the lighthouse lamp. She watched her mother washing the dishes and then reaching for her knitting needles and the always present ball of yarn.

She went outside and walked down towards the shanties. The door was pulled tight and she had a hard time getting it to move. Inside it all seemed different, probably, she thought, because of the daylight. She looked at the gray boards of the floor thinking she might see the outline of their bodies or even a spot of dampness but there was nothing. She went outside and walked to the wharf, to the spot where the dark boat was moored, but again there was no sign. He had "borrowed" the boat of the man he had fished with and had to have it back before dawn.

The wind was rising as the temperature was dropping. The hail-like rain had given way to stinging snow and the ground was beginning to freeze. She touched her body to see if it had been a dream.

11

As the winter began she was alive with the prospect of marriage. She sent for her birth certificate without ever revealing why and helped her mother with the knitting. As the winter deepened she looked at the calendar more often.

When the ice began to rot and break in the spring she looked out the window more frequently. It seemed like a later spring than usual although her father said there was nothing unusual about it. One day the channel would be clear of ice but the next day it would again be solid. The wind shifted and blew from inconsistent directions. On the mainland they could see, or imagined they could see, men moving about and readying their gear for the opening of the season. Because of the ice they were still afraid to launch their boats into the water. They all looked very small and far away.

When the first boats finally came, the dogs ran down to the wharf barking and snarling and her father went down also, calling to the dogs and welcoming the men and telling them not to be afraid. She looked out the window but did not see him in the boats or on the wharf nor moving about the familiar shanties. But neither did she see the mainland man he fished with nor his boat.

When her father came in he was filled with news and carried some fresh supplies and a bundle of newspapers and a bag of mail.

In the midst of all the newness it was a long time before he mentioned the mainland fisherman's name and added, almost as an afterthought, "That young man who fished with him last year was killed in the woods this winter. Went to Maine and was killed on a skidway. He's looking for another man right now."

When her father spoke he was already looking at a marine catalogue and had put on his glasses. He raised his eyes above the rims of his spectacles as he lowered the catalogue and looked towards them. "You remember him," he said without emotion, "the young fellow with the red hair."

"Oh poor fellow," said her mother. "God have mercy on his soul."

"Oh," was all she could say. Her hands tightened so whitely on the metal knitting needles that the point of one pierced and penetrated the ball of her thumb.

"Your hand is bleeding," said her mother. "What happened? You'll have to be more careful or you'll get blood on your knitting and everything will be ruined. What happened?" she asked again. "You'll have to be more careful."

"Nothing," she said, rising quickly and going to the door. "Nothing at all. Yes I'll have to be more careful."

She went outside and looked down towards the shanties where the newly arrived men were busy preparing for the new spring season. The banter of their voices seemed to float on the current of the wind. Sometimes she could hear their actual words but at other times they were lost and unknown. She could not believe the magnitude and suddenness of change. Could not believe the content of the news nor the method of its arrival. Could not believe that news of such outstanding impact could arrive in such a casual manner and mean so little to all of those around her.

She looked down at her bloodied hand. "Why didn't he write?" she asked herself and considered going back in to recheck the contents of the mailbag. But then she thought that both of them were beyond letters and that in the instant of his death it was already too late for that. She did not even know if he could read or write. She had never thought to ask. It had not seemed important at the time. The blood was beginning to darken and dry upon her palm and between her fingers. Suddenly last winter, although it was barely over, seemed like a long, long time ago. She pressed her hand against her stomach and turned her face away from the mainland and the sea.

When it became obvious that she was expecting a child there was great wonder as to how it came to be. She herself was rather surprised that no one had ever seen them together. It was true that she had always walked "over" or "across" the island while he had walked "around": seeming to emerge suddenly and unexpectedly out of the sea by the table rock of their meeting place. Still the island was small and, especially during the fishing season, there was little opportunity for privacy. Perhaps, she thought, they had been more successful, in some ways, than they planned. It was as if he had been invisible to everyone but herself. She was struck by this and tried to relive over and over again their last damp meeting in the dark. Only the single instant of his dark silhouette in the lighthouse beam was recallable to vision. All the rest of it had been touching in the dark. She remembered the lightness of his body in his dark, wet clothes but it was a memory of feeling rather than of sight. She had never seen him with all his clothes off. Had never slept with him in a bed. She had no photograph to emphasize reality. It was as if in

13

vanishing from her future he had also vanished from her past. It was almost as if he had been a ghost, and as she advanced in her pregnancy she found the idea strangely attractive.

"No," she kept saying to the pressure of their questions. "I don't know. I can't say. No, I can't tell you what he looked like."

She wavered only twice. The first time was a week before her delivery at a time when the approximate date of the conception was more than obvious. They were all on the mainland and the late August heat shimmered in layers above the clear deep water. The shape of the island loomed gray and blue and green across the channel and she who had wished to leave it now wished she might return. They were at her aunt's house and she would remain there until her baby would be born. She and her aunt had never liked each other and it bothered her now to be dependent upon her. Before her parents left to return to the island they came into her room accompanied by the aunt who turned to her father and said, "Well go ahead. Tell her what people are saying."

She was shocked to see the pained embarrassment on his face as he twisted his cloth cap and looked out the window in the direction of the island.

"It is just the way we live," he said. "Some say there was no other man."

She remembered the erratic snoring coming from her parents' room and how she could not imagine that they ever had been young.

"Oh," she said. "I'm sorry."

"Is that all you have to say for yourself?" said her aunt.

She wavered a moment. "Yes," she said. "That's all. That's all I have to say."

After the birth of her daughter, with the jet black hair, she received a visit from the clergyman. He was an old man although not as old as she imagined the one who had confused her own birth records, it seemed to her, so very long ago.

At that time it was in the power of clergymen to refuse to christen children unless they knew the identities of both parents. In cases such as hers the identities could be kept as confidential.

"Well," he said. "Can you tell me who the father is?"

"No," she said. "I can't say."

He looked at her as if he had heard it all before. And as if it were an aspect of his job he did not greatly like. He looked at her daugh-

14

ter and back at her. "We wouldn't want innocent people to burn in hell because of the willfulness of others," he said.

She was startled and frightened and looked towards the window.

"Tell me," he said quietly. "Is it your father?"

She thought for a flash of her own unexpected birth and of how her father was surprised again although the situation was so very much different.

"No," she said firmly. "It isn't him."

He seemed vastly relieved. "Good," he said. "I didn't think he would ever do anything like that. I will stop the rumors."

He moved towards the door as if one answer were all answers but then he hesitated with his hand upon the knob. "Tell me then," he said, "one more thing. Do I know him? Is he from around here?"

"No," she said, gaining confidence from seeing his hand upon the knob. "He isn't from around here at all."

That fall she stayed on the mainland until quite late in the season. It seemed as if her daughter were constantly sick and each time the journey was planned a new variation of illness appeared to stifle the departure. Out on the island her parents seemed to grow old all at once or maybe it was just that she saw them in a different light. Of course they had always seemed old to her and she had often thought of having grandparents for parents. But now they seemed for the first time to be almost afraid of the island and the coming of winter. Never since the first year of their marriage had they been there without a child. When her father fell from the ladder leading up to the lighthouse lamp it was almost as if the fall and the resulting broken arm had been expected.

Ever since her grandfather's death from "a pain in the side," the Government had more or less left them alone. It was as if the officials had been embarrassed by the widow's reluctance to tell them of her husband's death and by her fear that she might lose, in addition to her husband, the only income the family possessed. It was as if the officials had understood that "some MacPhedran" would always be on the island that bore the name and that no further questions ever would be asked. The check always arrived and the light always shone.

But when her father fell it brought a deeper seriousness. He could neither climb to the light nor navigate the boat across the channel, nor manage, quite, to look after the house and buildings

15

and the animals. It seemed best that they should all try to stay on the mainland for the winter.

Her brother came home from Halifax, reluctantly, and manned the light deep into fall. He was a single man who worked on construction crews and who drank quite heavily at times and was given to moods of deep depression. He was uneasy about the island although he understood it and was regarded as "an excellent man in a boat." At the beginning of the winter he said to his father who stood in the departing boat, "I don't want to stay here. I don't want to stay here at all."

"Oh," said his father, "you'll get used to it," which was what they had always said to one another.

But it seemed he did not get used to it. Deep in the blizzards of February one of the island dogs crossed on the ice to the mainland and came to a familiar door. It was impossible to see or move for three days because of the severe temperatures and the force of the wind-driven snow. Impossible for a man to stand upright in the wind or, as they said, for one "to see the palm of his hand in front of his face." When the storm abated four men started across the vast white landscape of the ice. They could feel parts of their exposed faces freezing and the exhaled moisture of their breath froze upon their eyebrows and they could see their eyelashes drooping heavily with ice. As they neared the island's wharf they could see that it was almost buried under gigantic pans of ice. Some of the pans had been pushed so far up on the shore that they almost tilted against the doors of the summer shanties. There was no smoke from the chimney of the house. The dogs came down snarling and circling at first, but the one who had crossed to the mainland had returned and had a calming effect upon the others. The door of the house was open and the stove was cold. The water in the crockery teapot had frozen causing the teapot itself to split into two delicate halves. There was nobody in any of the rooms and no answer to their calls. Outside, the barn doors were open and swinging in the wind. The animals were all dead, still tied and frozen in their stalls. The frozen flesh of some of them had been gnawed on by the dogs.

It seemed his coat and cap and winter mitts were missing but that was all. A loaded rifle and a shotgun were hanging in the porch. The men started a fire in the stove and made themselves something to eat from the store of winter provisions. Later they went outside again. Some walked across the island and some walked around it.

They found no tracks other than their own. They looked at the dogs for a signal or a sign. They even spoke to them and asked them questions but they received nothing in return. He had vanished like his tracks beneath the winter snow.

The men remained for the night and the next day crossed back to the mainland. They told what they had found and not found. The sun shone and although it was a weak February sun it was stronger than it had been a week earlier. It melted the ice upon the window panes and someone pointed out that the days were getting longer and that the winter was more than half way over.

Under the circumstances they decided to go back but to leave the baby behind.

"There seems almost more reason to go back now," said her father, looking through the melting ice on the windows. His broken arm had healed although he knew it would never be the same.

She was often to think of why she went back although at the time there seemed little conscious thought surrounding the decision. While her parents were willing to leave the island to the care of their son they were not willing to abandon it to others. They had found life on the mainland not as attractive as it sometimes seemed when viewed from across the water. They also seemed bothered by complicated shafts of guilt concerning their lost son and their headstrong daughter and while these shafts might persist on the island there would be no people to emphasize and expose them. She, herself, as the child of their advanced years seemed suddenly willing to consider herself old also and to identify with the past now that her future seemed to point in that direction.

She went back with almost a bitter gladness. Glad to leave her carping aunt and her mainland family behind although worried about leaving her sickly daughter in their care. Still, she knew they were right to say that the winter island was no place for a sick child and she felt also that if she did not go her parents could not manage.

"Who will climb up to the light?" asked her father simply. They viewed her youth as their immediate salvation and thought of her as their child rather than as someone else's mother.

It seemed a long time since the red-haired man had asked her to marry him and to share his life in the magical region of "somewhere else." In her persistent refusal to identify him she had pushed him so far back into the recesses of her mind that he seemed even more ghostly than before. She thought sometimes of his body in the dark and of his silhouette by the sea. She was struck by the mystery of his age—if he had an age she thought it had suddenly "stopped" and he had become part of a kind of timelessness—unlike the visible deterioration she witnessed in her father.

In the winter cold of February they returned with a certain sense of relief, each harboring individual reasons. Because of her youth she did most of the work, dressing in her father's heavy, shapeless clothes and following easily the rituals and routines that had become part of her since childhood. More and more her parents remained close to the stove, talking in Gaelic and sometimes playing cards

When March came in with its howling blizzards it seemed that they had been betrayed by the fickle promise of the February sun and although her father's will was strong his aging body seemed also to contribute to a pattern of betrayal. He was close to eighty and it seemed that each day there was another function which his body refused to perform. It was as if it had suddenly grown tired and was in the process of forgetting.

One day when there was a lull in the storms some of their relatives crossed the ice with a horse and sleigh. They were shocked at the condition and appearance of her father, seeing him changed "suddenly" after an absence of weeks while those who were with him had seen him change but gradually. They insisted that he return with them while the weather was good and the ice still strong. Reluctantly he agreed on the condition that his wife go with him.

After years of isolated permanence he was aware of all the questionable movement.

"Sometimes life is like that," he said to his daughter as he sat bundled in the sleigh at the moment before departure. "It goes on and on at a certain level and then there comes a year when everything changes."

Suddenly a gust of wind passed between them, whipping their faces with fine, sharp granules of snow. And suddenly she knew in that instant that she would never ever see him again. She wanted to tell him, to thank him or perhaps confess now that their time was vanishing between them. The secret of her own loneliness came down upon her and she reached towards his bundled body and his face which was muffled in scarves except for his eyes which were filled with water converting to ice.

"It was," she said, "the red-haired man."

"Oh yes," he said but she did not know with what degree of comprehension he said it. And then the sleigh moved off with its runners squeaking on the winter snow.

Although she was prepared for the death of her father she had not anticipated the loss of her mother who died ten days behind her husband. There was no physical explanation for her death and it seemed not unlike that of certain animals who pine away without their mates or who are unwilling or unable to adjust to new surroundings. As wild birds die in captivity or those who have been caged die from the shock of unexpected freedom or the loss of familiar boundaries.

Because of the spring breakup she was unable to attend either of their funerals and on the respective days she looked across the high gray waves and the grotesque icebergs that rolled between. From the edge of the island she saw the long funeral processions following the horse-drawn coffins along the muddy roads to the graveyard by the mainland church. She turned her face into the wind and climbed up towards the light.

That spring and summer she continued to tend the light although she had little to do with the mainland fishermen and never walked down by the shanties. She began to sign the requisition slips for government supplies with the name "A. MacPhedran" because her initial and that of her father were the same. After a while the checks came in the name of "A. MacPhedran" and she had no trouble cashing any of them. No one came to question the keeper of the light, and the sex of A. MacPhedran seemed ambiguously unimportant. After all, she told herself, wryly, her official birth certificate stated that her given name was Angus.

When the fall came she decided to remain on the island for the winter. Some of her relatives approved because they wanted "some MacPhedran" to remain on the island and they cited her youth and the fact that she was "used to it" as part of their reasoning. They were interested in "maintaining tradition" as long as they were not the ones to maintain that specific part of it. Others disapproved and towards them she was, secretly, most defiant. Her aunt and her aunt's family had grown attached to her daughter, had "gotten used to her" as they said and regarded the child as their own. When she visited them she experienced a certain fearful hostility on their part, as if they feared that she might snatch the child and flee while they were busy in another room.

Most of her relatives, however, either willingly or unwillingly, agreed to help her with the island, by assisting her with supplies, by doing some of the heavier autumn work or even by visiting occasionally. She settled into the life with a sort of willful determination tempered by the fact that she was still waiting for something to happen and to bring about the change.

Two years later on a hot summer afternoon, she was in the light-house tower when she saw the boat approaching. She had been restless all day and had walked the length and width of the island twice. She had gone to its edge as if testing the boundaries, some-what as a restless animal might explore the limitations of its cage. She had walked out into the cold salt water feeling it move gradually up and through and under the legs of her father's coveralls which had become, for her, a sort of uniform. She walked farther out feeling the water rise as she felt the rocks turning beneath her feet. She looked downward and saw her coveralled limbs distorted in the green water, shot through by the summer sun. They seemed not to be a part of her but to have become disembodied and convoluted and to be almost floating away from her at a horizontal level. When she closed her eyes she could feel them intensely but when she looked at them they did not appear the way they felt. The dogs lay on the shore, just above the water line, and watched her. They were pant-ing in the summer heat and drops of water fell from the extended redness of their tongues.

She returned to the shore, still dripping, and walked among the shanties. The lobster fishermen had departed at the end of the season leaving very little of themselves behind. She walked among the deserted buildings looking at the few discarded objects, some-times touching and turning them with her toes: a worn woolen sock, a length of spliced and twisted rope, a rusted knife with a broken blade, tobacco packages with bleached and faded lettering, a rubber boot with a hole in it. It was as if she were walking through the masculine remnants of an abandoned and vanished civilization. She went back to the house to put on dry coveralls and to hang the wet ones on the outside clothesline. As she left to climb to the light-house she looked over her shoulder and was startled by the sight of the vertical coveralls. Their dangling legs rasped together with the gentlest of frictions and the moisture had changed their color up to the waist. Droplets dripped from them onto the summer grass which was visibly distorted by their own moving shadow.

There were four men in the approaching boat and she realized that they were mackerel fishing and did not have the island in mind as a specific destination. The boat zigzagged back and forth across the stillness of the blue-green water stopping frequently while the men tossed their weighted lines overboard. They jerked their lines up and down rhythmically hoping to attract the fish by the movement of the lures. Sometimes they dipped their hands into pails or tubs of *gruth*, dried cottage cheese, and flung the white handfuls onto the surface of the water, waiting and hoping for the unseen fish to strike. She turned her head and looked towards the back of the island. From her high vantage point she could see, or thought she could see, pods or schools of mackerel breaking the surface, beyond the meeting place and the table rock, and beyond the bay of the shipwreck. They seemed like moving, floating islands, changing the clear, flat surface into agitated areas that resembled boiling water.

She hurried down from the lighthouse and shouted and gestured to the men in the boat. They were still far offshore and, perhaps, saw her before they heard her but were still unable to comprehend her message. They directed the boat towards the island. As they approached she realized that the movement of her arm, which was intended as a pointing gesture to the back of the island, was also a beckoning gesture, as they might understand it.

When they were within earshot she shouted to them, "The mackerel. At the back of the island. Go around."

They stopped the boat and leaned forward trying to catch the meaning of her words. One of the younger men, probably the one with the best hearing, understood her first and relayed the message to the others.

"Behind the island?" shouted the oldest man, cupping his hands to his mouth.

"Yes," she shouted back. "By the bay of the shipwreck."

She almost added, "By the meeting place" before realizing that the phrase would be meaningless to them.

"Thank you," shouted the oldest man. He took off his cap and tipped it to her and she could see the whiteness of his hair. "Thank you," he repeated. "We'll go around."

They changed the course of the boat and began to go around the island.

She rushed up to the house and changed out of her coveralls and put on a summer dress which she found in the back of a closet. She

21

walked across the island accompanied by the dogs and went down to the meeting place where she sat on the table rock and waited. The rock was hot from the heat of the day's sun and burned her thighs and the backs of her legs. She could see the floating islands of frenzied mackerel beyond the mouth of the bay. They were deep into their spawning season and she hoped they would still be there when the men in the boat arrived.

"They seem to be taking an awfully long time," she said to no one in particular. And then she saw the prow of the boat rounding the island's end.

She stood up and pointed to the boiling, bubbling mackerel but they had already seen them and even as they waved back they were in the process of readying all their available lines. The boat glided silently towards the fish and by the time the first one struck it was almost completely stilled. The mackerel seemed to surround the boat, changing the water to black by their own density. Their snapping mouths fastened on anything thrown their way and when the men jerked up their lines there were sometimes two or three fish on a single hook. Sometimes they broke the surface as if they would jump into the boat and sometimes their bodies were so densely packed that they became "snagged" as the hooks went into their bellies or their eyes or their backs or their tails. The scent of their own blood spreading within the water spurred them to an even greater frenzy and they fell upon their mutilated fellows, snapping the still living flesh from the moving bones. The men moved in their own frenzy as if to keep pace. Hooks snagged in their thumbs and the singing, sizzling lines burned through the calluses on their hands. The fish filled the bottom of the boat and began to rise in a blue-green, flopping, snapping mass to the level of the men's knees. And then, suddenly, they were gone. The hooks brought back nothing but clear drops of water or shreds of mutilated seaweed. There was no indication of them anywhere either on the surface of the sea or beneath. It was as if they had never been, apart from the heaving weight which caused the boat to ride so low within the water. The men wiped the sweat from their foreheads with swollen hands, sometimes leaving other streaks behind. Some of the streaks contained a mixture of fishblood and their own.

The men looked towards the shore and saw her rise from the table rock and come towards them until she reached the water's edge. They guided the boat across the glass-like sea until its prow grounded heavily on the gravelly shore. They tossed the painter rope to her and she caught it with willing hands.

All afternoon they lay on the table rock. At first they seemed driven by the frenzy of all that had happened and not happened to them. By all the heat and the loneliness and the waiting and all the varied events that had conspired to create their day. The clothes of the men were sprinkled with blackening clots of blood and the golden spawn of the female fish and the milky white semen of the male. She had never seen fully aroused men before, having known only one man at one time, and having experienced in that damp darkness more of feeling than of sight.

She was to remember, for the rest of her life, the oldest man with the white hair. How he took off his cap and then pulled his heavy navy-blue jersey over his shoulders and folded it neatly and placed it on the rock beside her. She was to remember the whiteness of his skin and arms compared with the bronzed redness of his face and neck and that of his bleeding and swollen hands. As if, without clothes, his upper body was still clothed in a costume made of two different materials. The whiteness of his skin and the whiteness of his hair were the same color but totally different as well. After he had folded his jersey he placed his cap neatly upon it. It was as if he were doing it out of long habit and was preparing to lie down with his wife. She almost expected him to brush his teeth.

After the first frenzy they were quieter, lying stretched beneath the sun. Sometimes one of the younger men got up and skipped flat stones across the surface of the sea. The dogs lay above the waterline panting and watching everything. She was later to think how often she had watched them in the fury of their own mating. And how she had seen their surplus young placed in burlap bags, weighted down with rocks, and tossed over the boat's side into the sea.

The sun began to decline and the tide began to fall, the water receding from the heavy boat which was in danger of becoming beached. The men got up and adjusted their clothes. Some walked some distance away to urinate. They came back and all four of them put their shoulders to the prow and prepared to push the boat back into the water.

"One, two, three, heave!" they said, moving in concentrated unison on the last syllable. Their bodies were stretched out almost horizontally as they pushed, the toes of their rubber boots scrabbling in the loose beach gravel. The boat began to move, grudgingly

23

at first, and then more rapidly as the water took its weight. The men scrambled over the prow and over the sides. Most of them were wet up to their waists. They seized their oars to push the boat farther out so there would be room to turn it around and face it towards home.

She watched them leave, standing on the shore. As the boat moved out, she noticed her undergarment crumpled and discarded by the edge of the table rock. The boat moved farther out and farther away and the men waved to her. She felt her arm rising in a similar gesture, almost without her willing it. The man with the white hair tipped his cap. She knew in one of those intuitive flashes that they would never say anything to anyone or scarcely mention the events of the day among themselves. She also knew that they would never be back. As the boat rounded the island's end, she scrunched up her undergarment and threw it into the sea. She began to walk up towards the lighthouse. She touched her body. It was sticky with blood and fishspawn and human seed. "It will have to happen this time," she thought, "because there was so much of it and it went on so long." Comparing the afternoon to her one previous brief encounter in the dark.

When she reached the lighthouse she heard the cries of the scavenging gulls. She looked in the direction of the sound and saw the boat cutting a "v" in the placid water on its way to the mainland. The men were bent double grasping their fishforks and throwing the dead mackerel back into the sea. The gulls swooped and screamed in a whitened noisy cloud.

Two years later she was in a mainland store ordering supplies to take back to the island. Usually she made arrangements with one of her relatives to take the supplies from the store to the water's edge and then ferry them across to the island but on this day she could not find the particular young man. One of the items was a bag of flour. As she stood paying her bill and looking out the door in some agitation, she saw, out of the corner of her eye, the white-haired man in the navy-blue jersey.

"This is too heavy for you," he said. "Let me help," and he bent down and picked up the hundred pound flour sack and threw it easily onto his shoulder. When it landed some of the flour puffed out, sprinkling his blue jersey and his cap and his hair with its fine white powder. She remembered the whiteness of his body beneath

24

the blue jersey and the frenzied afternoon beneath the summer sun. As they were going out the door they met her young relative.

"Here, I'll take that," he said, relieving the man of the bag of flour.

"Thank you," she said to the man.

"My pleasure," he said and tipped his cap towards her. The flour dust fell from his cap onto the floor between them.

"He is a real nice fellow," said her young relative as they moved towards the shore. "But of course you don't know him the way we do."

"No," she said. "Of course I don't." She looked across the channel to the stillness of the island. Her expected child had never arrived.

The years of the next decade passed by in a blur of monotonous sameness. She realized that she was becoming more careless of her appearance and that such carelessness was regarded as further evidence of eccentricity. She came ashore less frequently preferring to try to understand the world through radio. She found her teen-age daughter to be foreign and aloof and embarrassed by her presence. Her aunt's family harbored doubts about their decision to rear the girl and, one day, when she was visiting, suggested that she might want to live on the island with her "real mother." The girl laughed and walked into another room.

Gradually during the next years things changed even more, but so quietly that, in retrospect, she could not link the specific events to the specific years. Many of them had to do with changes on the mainland. The Government built a splendid new wharf and the spring fishermen no longer came to inhabit the shanties which began to fall into disrepair, their doors banging in the wind and the shingles flying from their roofs. Sometimes she looked at the initials carved by the absent men on the shanties' walls but his, as she knew, would never be among them.

Community pastures were established, with regular attendants, and the bound young cattle and the lusty rams no longer came to the summer pasturage. The sweeping headlights of cars became a regular feature of her night vision, mirroring in a myriad manner the beam from her solitary lighthouse. One night after a quarrel with her aunt's family, her daughter left in such a car, and vanished into the mystery of Toronto. She did not know of it until weeks later when she came ashore for the purchase of supplies.

The wharf at the island began to deteriorate and the visitors came less often. She found herself often dealing with members of a newer generation. Many of them were sulky and contributed to the maintaining of island tradition with the utmost reluctance and only because of the badgering of their parents.

Yet the light still shone and the various missives to and from "A. MacPhedran" continued to travel through the mails. The nature of such missives also changed, however gradually. When the first generation of her family went to the island it had been close to the age of sail when captains were at the mercies of the winds. In her own time she had seen the coming of the larger ships and the increasing sophistication of their technology. There had not been a wreck upon the island in all her time of habitation and no freezing, ice-caked travellers had ever knocked upon her midnight door. The "emergency chest" and its store of supplies remained unopened from one inspection to the next.

One summer she realized with a shock that her child-bearing years were over and that that part of her life was past.

Mainland boat operators began to offer "trips around the island," taking tourists on circumnavigational voyages. Very often because of time limitations they did not land but merely circled or anchored briefly offshore. When the boats approached the dogs barked, bringing her to her door or sometimes to the water's edge. At first she was not aware of the image she presented to the tourists with their binoculars or their cameras. Nor was she aware of how she was described by the operators of the boats. Standing at the edge of the sea in her dishevelled men's clothing and surrounded by her snarling dogs, she later realized, she had passed into folklore. She had, without realizing it, become "the mad woman of the island."

It was on a hot summer's day, some years later when, in answer to the barking of the dogs, she looked out the window and saw the big boat approaching. The men wore tan-colored uniforms and the Canadian flag flew from the mast. They tied the boat to the remnants of the wharf and began to climb towards the house as she called off the dogs. The decision had been made, they told her quietly, while sitting in the kitchen, to close the lighthouse officially. The light would still shine but it would be maintained by "modern technology." It would operate automatically and be serviced by supply boats which would come at certain times of the year or, in emergency, they added, by helicopter. It would, however, be maintained in its present state for approximately a year and a half. After that, they said, she would have "to live somewhere else." They got up to leave and thanked her for her decades of fine service.

After they had gone she walked the length and width of the island. She repeated all the place names, many of them in Gaelic, and marvelled that the places would remain but the names would vanish. "Who would know?" she wondered that this spot had once been called *achadh nan caoraich,* or that another was called *creig a bhoird.* And who she thought, with a catch in her heart, would ever know of *Àite na cruinneachadh* and of what had transpired there. She looked across the landscape repeating the phrases of the place-names as if they were those of children about to be abandoned without knowledge of their names. She felt like whispering their names to them so they would not forget.

She realized with a type of shock that in spite of generations of being people "of the island" they had never really owned it in any legal sense. There was nothing physical of it that was, in strict reality, formally theirs.

That autumn and winter her rituals seemed without meaning. There was no need of so many supplies because the future was shorter and she approached each winter task with the knowledge that it would be her last. She approached spring with a longing born of confused emotions. She who had wanted to leave and wanted to return and wanted to stay felt the approaching ache of those who leave the familiar behind. She felt, perhaps, as those who leave bad places or bad situations or bad marriages behind them. As those who must look over their shoulders one last time and who say quietly to themselves, "Oh I have given a lot of my life to this, such as it was, and such was I. And no matter where I go I will never be the same."

That April as the ice broke, for her the final time, she was drying the dishes and looking through the window. Because of her failing eyesight she did not see the boat until it was almost at the remains of the wharf and the dogs did not make their usual sound. She saw the man bending to loop the boat's rope to the wharf and as he did so his cap fell off and she saw the redness of his hair. It seemed to flash and reflect in the April sun like the sudden and different energy of spring. She wrapped the damp dish towel around her hand as if it were a bandage and then she as quickly unwrapped it again.

27

He started up the path towards the house and the dogs ran happily beside him. She stood in the doorway uncertainly. As he approached she realized that he was talking to the dogs and his accent was slightly unfamiliar. He seemed about twenty years of age and his eyes were very blue. He had an earring in his ear.

"Hello," he said, extending his hand. "I don't know if you recognize me."

It had been so long and so much had happened that she did not know what to say. Her hand tightened on the cloth she was still holding. She stepped aside to let him enter the house and watched as he sat on a chair.

"Do you stay here all the time?" he asked, looking around the kitchen, "even in the winter?"

"Yes," she said. "Most of the time."

"Were you born here?"

"Yes," she said. "I guess so."

"It must be lonely," he said, "but I guess some people are lonely no matter where they are."

She looked at him as if he were a ghost.

"Would you like to live somewhere else?" he asked.

"I don't know," she said. "Maybe."

He raised his hand and touched the earring as if to make certain it was still there. His glance travelled about the kitchen, seeming to rest lightly on each of the familiar objects. She realized that the kitchen had hardly changed since that other April visit so long ago. She could not think of what to say.

"Would you like some tea?" she asked after a moment of awkward silence.

"No thank you," he said. "I'm pressed for time right now but perhaps we'll have it later."

She nodded although she was not certain of his meaning. The dogs lay under the table, now and then thumping the floor with their tails. Through the window she could see the white gulls hanging over the ocean which was still dotted with cakes of floating ice.

He looked at her carefully, as if remembering, and he smiled. Neither of them seemed to know just what to say.

"Well," he said getting up suddenly. "I have to go now. I'll see you later. I'll come back."

"Wait," she said rising as quickly, "please don't go," and she almost added the word "again."

"I'll be back," he said, "in the fall. And then I will take you with me. We will go and live somewhere else."

"Yes," she said and then added almost as an afterthought, "Where have you been?"

"In Toronto," he said. "I was born there. They told me on the mainland that you are my grandmother."

She looked at him as if he were a genetic wonder which indeed he seemed to be.

"Oh," she said.

"I have to go now," he repeated, "but I'll see you later. I'll come back."

"Oh yes," she said. "Oh yes we will."

And then he was gone. She sat transfixed not daring to move. Part of her felt that she should rush and call him back and another fearful part told her she should not know what she might see. Finally she went to the window. Halfway across to the mainland there was a single man in a boat but she could make no clear identification. She did not say anything to anyone about the visit. She could think of no way she could tactfully introduce it. After years of secrecy it seemed a dangerous time to bring up the subject of the red-haired man. Perhaps, again, no one else had seen him? She did not wish to add further evidence to her designation as "the mad woman of the island." She scanned the faces of her relatives carefully but could find nothing. Perhaps he had visited them, she thought, and they had told him not to come. Perhaps they considered themselves in the business of not disturbing the disturbed.

Now as the October rain fell she added yet another stick to the fire. She was no longer bothered by the declining stock of wood because she would not need it for the winter. The rain fell turning more to the consistency of hail and she knew this by its sound as well as by her sight. She looked away from the door as she had so many years ago, the first time at the table rock. Deliberately not looking in the direction of his possible coming so that she could not see him *not* coming if that was the way it was supposed to be. She waited, listening to the regular pattern of the rain, and wondered if she were on the verge of sleep. Suddenly the door blew open and the hail-like rain skittered across the floor. The wet dogs moved from beneath the table and she heard them rather than saw. Perhaps she should mop the wet floor she thought but then she remembered that they planned to tear the house down anyway and its cleanliness seemed like a minor virtue. The water rippled across the floor in rolling little wind-driven waves. The dog came in, its nails clacking across the floor even as little spurts of water rose from beneath its padded paws. It came and lay its head upon her lap. She got up not daring to believe. Outside it was wet and windy and she followed the dog down the darkened path. And then in the revolving cycle of the high lighthouse light she saw in a single white instant the dark shape of the boat bobbing at the wharf and his straight but dripping form by the corner of the shanties.

They moved towards each other.

"Oh," she said, digging her fingers into the dampness of his neck.

"I told you I'd come back," he said.

"Oh," she said. "Oh yes. You did."

She ran her fingers over his face in the darkness and when the light revolved again she saw the blueness of his eyes and his red hair darkened by the dripping water. He was not wearing any earring.

"How old are you?" she asked, embarrassed by the girlish triviality of the question which had bothered her all these years.

"Twenty-one," he said. "I thought I told you."

He took her hands and walked backwards while facing her, down to the darkness of the bobbing boat and the rolling sea.

"Come," he said. "Come with me. It is time we went to live somewhere else."

"Oh yes," she said. "Oh yes we will."

She dug her nails into the palms of his hands as he guided her over the spume-drenched rocks.

"This boat," he said, "has to be back before dawn."

The wind was rising as the temperature was dropping. The hail-like rain had given way to stinging snow and the ground they left behind was beginning to freeze.

A dog barked once. And when the light revolved, its solitary beam found no MacPhedrans on the island or the sea.

THE HAIR

by JOYCE CAROL OATES

THE COUPLES FELL in love but not at the same time, and not evenly.

There was perceived to be, from the start, an imbalance of power. The less dominant couple, the Carsons, feared social disadvantage. They feared being hopeful of a friendship that would dissolve before consummation. They feared seeming eager.

Said Charlotte Carson, hanging up the phone, "The Riegels have invited us for dinner on New Year's," her voice level, revealing none of the childlike exultation she felt, nor did she look up to see the expression on her husband's face as he murmured, "Who? The Riegels?" pausing before adding, "That's very nice of them."

Once or twice, the Carsons had invited the Riegels to their home, but for one or another reason the Riegels had declined the invitation.

New Year's Eve went very well indeed and shortly thereafter—though not too shortly—Charlotte Carson telephoned to invite the Riegels back.

The friendship between the couples blossomed. In a relatively small community like the one in which the couples lived, such a new, quick, galloping sort of alliance cannot go unnoticed.

So it was noted by mutual friends who felt some surprise, and perhaps some envy. For the Riegels were a golden couple, newcomers to the area who, not employed locally, had about them the glamour of temporary visitors.

31

In high school, Charlotte Carson thought with a stab of satisfaction, the Riegels would have snubbed me.

Old friends and acquaintances of the Carsons began to observe that Charlotte and Barry were often busy on Saturday evenings, their calendar seemingly marked for weeks in advance. And when a date did not appear to be explicitly set Charlotte would so clearly—insultingly—hesitate, not wanting to surrender a prime weekend evening only to discover belatedly that the Riegels would call them at the last minute and ask them over. Charlotte Carson, gentlest, most tactful of women, in her mid-thirties, shy at times as a schoolgirl of another era, was forced repeatedly to say, "I'm sorry—I'm afraid we can't." And insincerely.

Paul Riegel, whose name everyone knew, was in his early forties: he was a travel writer; he had adventures of a public sort. He published articles and books, he was often to be seen on television, he was tall, handsome, tanned, gregarious, his graying hair springy at the sides of his head and retreating rather wistfully at the crown of his head. "Your husband seems to bear the gift of happiness," Charlotte Carson told Ceci Riegel. Charlotte sometimes spoke too emotionally and wondered now if she had too clearly exposed her heart. But Ceci simply smiled one of her mysterious smiles. "Yes. He tries."

In any social gathering the Riegels were likely to be, without visible effort, the cynosure of attention. When Paul Riegel strode into a crowded room wearing one of his bright ties, or his familiar sports-coat-sports-shirt-open-collar with well-laundered jeans, people looked immediately to him and smiled. There's Paul Riegel! He bore his minor celebrity with grace and even a kind of aristocratic humility, shrugging off questions in pursuit of the public side of his life. If, from time to time, having had a few drinks, he told wildly amusing exaggerated tales, even, riskily, outrageous ethnic or dialect jokes, he told them with such zest and childlike self-delight his listeners were convulsed with laughter.

Never, or almost never, did he forget names.

And his wife, Ceci—petite, ash-blond, impeccably dressed, with a delicate classically proportioned face like an old-fashioned cameo—was surely his ideal mate. She was inclined at times to be fey but she was really very smart. She had a lovely whitely glistening smile as dazzling as her husband's and as seemingly sincere. For years she had been an interior designer in New York

32

City and since moving to the country was a consultant to her former firm; it was rumored that her family had money and that she had either inherited a small fortune or spurned a small fortune at about the time of her marriage to Paul Riegel.

It was rumored too that the Riegels ran through people quickly, used up friends. That they had affairs.

Or perhaps it was only Paul who had affairs.

Or Ceci.

Imperceptibly, it seemed, the Carsons and the Riegels passed from being friendly acquaintances who saw each other once or twice a month to being friends who saw each other every week, or more. There were formal dinners, and there were cocktail parties, and there were Sunday brunches—the social staples of suburban life. There were newly acquired favorite restaurants to patronize and, under Ceci's guidance, outings to New York City to see plays, ballet, opera. There were even picnics from which bicycle rides and canoe excursions were launched—not without comical misadventures. In August when the Riegels rented a house on Nantucket Island they invited the Carsons to visit; when the Riegels had houseguests the Carsons were almost always invited to meet them; soon the men were playing squash together on a regular basis. (Paul won three games out of five, which seemed just right. But he did not win easily.) In time Charlotte Carson overcame her shyness about telephoning Ceci as if on the spur of the moment—"Just to say hello!"

Ceci Riegel had no such scruples, nor did Paul, who thought nothing of telephoning friends—everywhere in the world; he knew so many people—at virtually any time of the day or night, simply to say hello.

The confidence born of never having been rejected.

Late one evening the Carsons were delighted to hear from Paul in Bangkok, of all places, where he was on assignment with a *Life* photographer.

Another time, sounding dazed and not quite himself, he telephoned them at 7:30 A.M. from John F. Kennedy Airport, newly arrived in the States and homesick for the sound of "familiar" voices. He hadn't been able to get hold of Ceci, he complained, but they were next on his list.

Which was enormously flattering.

33

Sometimes when Paul was away on one of his extended trips, Ceci was, as she said, morbidly lonely, so the three of them went out for Chinese food and a movie or watched videos late into the night; or impulsively, rather recklessly, Ceci got on the phone and invited a dozen friends over, and neighbors too, though always, first, Charlotte and Barry—"Just to feel I *exist*."

The couples were each childless.

Barry had not had a male friend whom he saw so regularly since college, and the nature of his work—he was an executive with Bell Labs—seemed to preclude camaraderie. Charlotte was his closest friend but he rarely confided in her all that was in his heart: this wasn't his nature.

Unlike his friend Paul he preferred the ragged edges of gatherings, not their quicksilver centers. He was big-boned with heavy-lidded quizzical eyes, a shadowy beard like shot, deep in the pores of his skin, wide nostrils, a handsome sensual mouth. He'd been an all-A student once and carried still that air of tension and precariousness strung tight as a bow. Did he take himself too seriously? Or not seriously enough? Wild moods swung in him, rarely surfacing. When his wife asked him why was he so quiet, what was he thinking, he replied, smiling, "Nothing important, honey," though resenting the question, the intrusion. The implied assertion: *I have a right to your secrets*.

His heart pained him when Ceci Riegel greeted him with a hearty little spasm of an embrace and a perfumy kiss alongside his cheek, but he was not the kind of man to fall sentimentally in love with a friend's wife. Nor was he the kind of man, aged forty and wondering when his life would begin, to fall in love with his friend.

The men played squash daily when Paul was in town. Sometimes, afterward, they had lunch together, and a few beers, and talked about their families: their fathers, mainly. Barry drifted back to his office pale and shaken and that evening might complain vaguely to Charlotte that Paul Riegel came on a little too strong for him, "As if it's always the squash court, and he's always the star."

Charlotte said quickly, "He means well. And so does Ceci. But they're aggressive people." She paused, wondering what she was saying. "Not like us."

When Barry and Paul played doubles with other friends, other men, they nearly always won. Which pleased Barry more than he would have wished anyone to know.

And Paul's praise: it burned in his heart with a luminosity that endured for hours and days and all in secret.

The Carsons were childless but had two cats. The Riegels were childless but had a red setter bitch, no longer young.

The Carsons lived in a small mock-Georgian house in town; the Riegels lived in a glass, stone, and redwood house, custom-designed, three miles out in the country. The Carsons' house was one of many attractive houses of its kind in their quiet residential neighborhood and had no distinctive features except an aged enormous plane tree in the front which would probably have to be dismantled soon—"It will break our hearts," Charlotte said. The Carsons' house was fully exposed to the street; the Riegels' house was hidden from the narrow gravel road that ran past it by a seemingly untended meadow of juniper pines, weeping willows, grasses, wildflowers.

Early on in their friendship, a tall cool summer drink in hand, Barry Carson almost walked through a plate glass door at the Riegels'—beyond it was the redwood deck, Ceci in a silk floral-printed dress with numberless pleats.

Ceci was happy and buoyant and confident always. For a petite woman—size five, it was more than once announced—she had a shapely body, breasts, hips, strong-calved legs. When she and Charlotte Carson played tennis, Ceci was all over the court, laughing and exclaiming, while slow-moving premeditated Charlotte, poor Charlotte, who felt, in her friend's company, ostrich-tall and ungainly, missed all but the easy shots. "You need to be more aggressive, Char!" Paul Riegel called out. "Need to be *murderous!*"

The late-night drive back to town from the Riegels' along narrow twisty country roads, Barry behind the wheel, sleepy with drink yet excited too, vaguely sweetly aching, Charlotte yawning and sighing, and there was the danger of white-tailed deer so plentiful in this part of the state leaping in front of the car; but they returned home safely, suddenly they were home, and, inside, one of them would observe that their house was so lacking in imagination, wasn't it? So exposed to the neighbors? "Yes, but you wanted this house." "No, you were the one who wanted this

35

house." "Not *this* house—but this was the most feasible." Though sometimes one would observe that the Riegels' house had flaws: so much glass and it's drafty in the winter, so many queer elevated decks and flights of stairs, wall-less rooms, sparsely furnished rooms like designers' showcases, and the cool chaste neutral colors that Ceci evidently favored: "It's beautiful, yes, but a bit sterile."

In bed exhausted they would drift to sleep, separately wandering the corridors of an unknown building, opening one door after another in dread and fascination. Charlotte, who should not have had more than two or three glasses of wine—but it was an anniversary of the Riegels: they'd uncorked bottles of champagne—slept fitfully, waking often dry-mouthed and frightened not knowing where she was. A flood of hypnagogic images raced in her brain; the faces of strangers never before glimpsed by her thrummed beneath her eyelids. In that state of consciousness that is neither sleep nor waking Charlotte had the volition to will, ah, how passionately, how despairingly, that Paul Riegel would comfort her: slip his arm around her shoulders, nudge his jaw against her cheek, whisper in her ear as he'd done once or twice that evening in play but now in seriousness. Beside her someone stirred and groaned in his sleep and kicked at the covers.

Paul Riegel entranced listeners with lurid tales of starving Cambodian refugees, starving Ethiopian children, starving Mexican beggars. His eyes shone with angry tears one moment and with mischief the next, for he could not resist mocking his own sobriety. The laughter he aroused at such times had an air of bafflement, shock.

Ceci came to him to slip an arm through his as if to comfort or to quiet, and there were times when quite perceptibly Paul shook off her arm, stepped away, stared down at her with a look as if he'd never seen the woman before.

When the Carsons did not see or hear from the Riegels for several days their loneliness was almost palpable: a thickness in the chest, a density of being, to which either might allude knowing the other would immediately understand. If the Riegels were actually away that made the separation oddly more bearable than if they were in fact in their house amid the trees but not seeing the Carsons that weekend or mysteriously incommunicado with their telephone answering tape switched on. When Charlotte called, got the tape, heard the familiar static-y overture, then Paul Riegel's cool almost hostile voice that did not identify itself but merely stated *No one is here right now; should you like to leave a message please wait for the sound of the bleep*, she felt a loss too profound to be named and often hung up in silence.

It had happened as the Carsons feared—the Riegels were dominant. So fully in control.

For there was a terrible period, several months in all, when for no reason the Carsons could discover—and they discussed the subject endlessly, obsessively—the Riegels seemed to have little time for them. Or saw them with batches of others in which their particular friendship could not be readily discerned. Paul was a man of quick enthusiasms, and Ceci was a woman of abrupt shifts of allegiance; thus there was logic of sorts to their cruelty in elevating for a while a new couple in the area who were both theoretical mathematicians, and a neighbor's houseguest who'd known Paul in college and was now in the diplomatic service, and a cousin of Ceci's, a male model in his late twenties who was staying with the Riegels for weeks and weeks and weeks, taking up every spare minute of their time, it seemed, so when Charlotte called, baffled and hurt, Ceci murmured in an undertone, "I can't talk now, can I call you back in the morning?" and failed to call for days, days, days.

One night when Charlotte would have thought Barry was asleep he shocked her by saying, "I never liked her, much. Hotshit little Ceci." She had never heard her husband utter such words before and did not know how to reply.

They went away on a trip. Three weeks in the Caribbean, and only in the third week did Charlotte scribble a postcard for the Riegels—a quick scribbled little note as if one of many.

One night she said, "*He's* the dangerous one. He always tries to get people to drink too much, to keep him company."

They came back, and not long afterward Ceci called, and the friendship was resumed precisely as it had been—the same breathless pace, the same dazzling intensity—though now Paul had a new book coming out and there were parties in the city, book signings at bookstores, an interview on a morning news program. The Carsons gave a party for him, inviting virtually everyone they knew locally, and the party was a great success and in a

37

corner of the house Paul Riegel hugged Charlotte Carson so hard she laughed, protesting her ribs would crack, but when she drew back to look at her friend's face she saw it was damp with tears.

Later, Paul told a joke about Reverend Jesse Jackson that was a masterpiece of mimicry though possibly in questionable taste. In the general hilarity no one noticed, or at least objected. In any case there were no blacks present.

The Riegels were childless but would not have defined their condition in those terms: as a lack, a loss, a negative. Before marrying they had discussed the subject of children thoroughly, Paul said, and came to the conclusion *no*.

The Carsons too were childless but would perhaps have defined their condition in those terms, in weak moods at least. Hearing Paul speak so indifferently of children, the Carsons exchanged a glance almost of embarrassment.

Each hoped the other would not disclose any intimacy.

Ceci sipped at her drink and said, "I'd have been willing."

Paul said, "*I* wouldn't."

There was a brief nervous pause. The couples were sitting on the Riegels' redwood deck in the gathering dusk.

Paul then astonished the Carsons by speaking in a bitter impassioned voice of families, children, parents, the "politics" of intimacy. In any intimate group, he said, the struggle to be independent, to define oneself as an individual, is so fierce it creates terrible waves of tension, a field of psychic warfare. He'd endured it as a child and young adolescent in his parents' home, and as an adult he didn't think he could bear to bring up a child—"especially a son"—knowing of the doubleness and secrecy of the child's life.

"There is the group life, which is presumably open and observable," he said, "and there is the secret inner real life no one can penetrate." He spoke with such uncharacteristic vehemence that neither of the Carsons would have dared to challenge him or even to question him in the usual conversational vein.

Ceci sat silent, drink in hand, staring impassively out into the shadows.

After a while conversation resumed again and they spoke softly, laughed softly. The handsome white wrought-iron furniture on which they were sitting took on an eerie solidity even as the human figures seemed to fade: losing outline and contour, blending into the night and into one another.

Charlotte Carson lifted her hand, registering a small chill spasm of fear that she was dissolving, but it was only a drunken notion of course.

For days afterward Paul Riegel's disquieting words echoed in her head. She tasted something black, and her heart beat in anger like a cheated child's. *Don't you love me then? Don't any of us love any of us?* To Barry she said, "That was certainly an awkward moment, wasn't it? When Paul started his monologue about family life, intimacy, all that. What did you make of it?"

Barry murmured something evasive and backed off.

The Carsons owned two beautiful Siamese cats, neutered male and neutered female, and the Riegels owned a skittish Irish setter named Rusty. When the Riegels came to visit Ceci always made a fuss over one or the other of the cats, insisting it sit in her lap, sometimes even at the dinner table, where she'd feed it on the sly. When the Carsons came to visit, the damned dog as Barry spoke of it went into a frenzy of barking and greeted them at the front door as if it had never seen them before. "Nice dog! Good dog! Sweet Rusty!" the Carsons would cry in unison.

The setter was rheumy-eyed and thick-bodied and arthritic. If every year of a dog's age is approximately seven years in human terms, poor Rusty was almost eighty years old. She managed to shuffle to the front door to bark at visitors but then lacked the strength or motor coordination to reverse herself and return to the interior of the house so Paul had to carry her, one arm under her bony chest and forelegs, the other firmly under her hindquarters, an expression of vexed tenderness in his face.

Dryly he said, "I hope someone will do as much for me someday."

One rainy May afternoon when Paul was in Berlin and Barry was in Virginia visiting his family, Ceci impulsively invited Charlotte to come for a drink and meet her friend Nils Larson—or was the name Lasson? Lawson?—an old old dear friend. Nils was short, squat-bodied, energetic, with a gnomish head and bright malicious eyes, linked to Ceci, it appeared, in a way that allowed him to be both slavish and condescending. He was a "theater person"; his bubbly talk was studded with names of the famous and near-famous. Never once did he mention Paul Riegel's name,

39

though certain of his mannerisms—head thrown back in laughter, hands gesticulating as he spoke—reminded Charlotte of certain of Paul's mannerisms. The man was Paul's elder by perhaps a decade.

Charlotte stayed only an hour, then made her excuses and slipped away. She had seen Ceci's friend draw his pudgy forefinger across the nape of Ceci's neck in a gesture that signaled intimacy or the arrogant pretense of intimacy, and the sight offended her. But she never told Barry and resolved not to think of it and of whether Nils spent the night at the Riegels' and whether Paul knew anything of him or of the visit. Nor did Ceci ask Charlotte what she had thought of Nils Larson—Lasson? Lawson?—the next time the women spoke.

Barry returned from Virginia with droll tales of family squabbling: his brother and his sister-in-law, their children, the network of aunts, uncles, nieces, nephews, grandparents, ailing elderly relatives whose savings were being eaten up—invariably the expression was "eaten up"—by hospital and nursing home expenses. Barry's father, severely crippled from a stroke, was himself in a nursing home from which he would never be discharged, and all his conversation turned upon this fact, which others systematically denied, including, in the exigency of the moment, Barry. He had not, he said, really recognized his father. It was as if another man—aged, shrunken, querulous, sly—had taken his place.

The elderly Mr. Carson had affixed to a wall of his room a small white card on which he'd written some Greek symbols, an inscription he claimed to have treasured all his life. Barry asked what the Greek meant and was told, *When my ship sank, the others sailed on.*

Paul Riegel returned from Berlin exhausted and depressed despite the fact, a happy one to his wife and friends, that a book of his was on the paperback bestseller list published by *The New York Times*. When Charlotte Carson suggested with uncharacteristic gaiety that they celebrate, Paul looked at her with a mild quizzical smile and asked, "Why, exactly?"

The men played squash, the women played tennis.

The Carsons had other friends, of course. Older and more reliable friends. They did not need the Riegels. Except they were in love with the Riegels.

Did the Riegels love them? Ceci telephoned one evening and Barry happened to answer and they talked together for an hour, and afterward, when Charlotte asked Barry what they'd talked about, careful to keep all signs of jealousy and excitement out of her voice, Barry said evasively, "A friend of theirs is dying. Of AIDS. Ceci says he weighs only ninety pounds and has withdrawn from everyone: 'slunk off to die like a sick animal.' And Paul doesn't care. Or won't talk about it." Barry paused, aware that Charlotte was looking at him closely. A light film of perspiration covered his face; his nostrils appeared unusually dark, dilated. "He's no one we know, honey. The dying man, I mean."

When Paul Riegel emerged from a sustained bout of writing the first people he wanted to see were the Carsons of course, so the couples went out for Chinese food—"a banquet, no less!"—at their favorite Chinese restaurant in a shopping mall. The Dragon Inn had no liquor license so they brought bottles of wine and six-packs of beer. They were the last customers to leave, and by the end waiters and kitchen help were standing around or prowling restlessly at the rear of the restaurant. There was a minor disagreement over the check, which Paul Riegel insisted had not been added up "strictly correctly." He and the manager discussed the problem and since the others were within earshot he couldn't resist clowning for their amusement, slipping into a comical Chinese (unless it was Japanese?) accent. In the parking lot the couples laughed helplessly, gasping for breath and bent double, and in the car driving home—Barry drove: they'd taken the Carsons' Honda Accord, and Barry was seemingly the most sober of the four of them—they kept bursting into peals of laughter like naughty children.

They never returned to the Dragon Inn.

The men played squash together but their most rewarding games were doubles in which they played, and routed, another pair of men.

As if grudgingly, Paul Riegel would tell Barry Carson he was a "damned good player." To Charlotte he would say, "Your husband is a damned good player but if only he could be a bit more *murderous!*"

Barry Carson's handsome heavy face darkened with pleasure when he heard such praise, exaggerated as it was. Though afterward, regarding himself in a mirror, he felt shame: he was forty

41

years old, he had a very good job in a highly competitive field, he had a very good marriage with a woman he both loved and respected, he believed he was leading, on the whole, a very good life, yet none of this meant as much to him as Paul Riegel carelessly complimenting him on his squash game.

How has my life come to this?

Rusty developed cataracts on both eyes and then tumorous growths in her neck. The Riegels took her to the vet and had her put to sleep, and Ceci had what was reported to the Carsons as a breakdown of a kind: wept and wept and wept. Paul too was shaken by the ordeal but managed to joke over the phone about the dog's ashes. When Charlotte told Barry of the dog's death she saw Barry's eyes narrow as he resisted saying Thank God! and said instead, gravely, as if it would be a problem of his own, "Poor Ceci will be inconsolable."

For weeks it wasn't clear to the Carsons that they would be invited to visit the Riegels on Nantucket; then, shortly before the Riegels left, Ceci said as if casually, "We did set a date, didn't we? For you two to come visit?"

On their way up—it was a seven-hour drive to the ferry at Woods Hole—Charlotte said to Barry, "Promise you won't drink so much this year." Offended, Barry said, "I won't monitor your behavior, honey, if you won't monitor mine."

From the first, the Nantucket visit went awkwardly. Paul wasn't home and his whereabouts weren't explained, though Ceci chattered brightly and effusively, carrying her drink with her as she escorted the Carsons to their room and watched them unpack. Her shoulder-length hair was graying and disheveled; her face was heavily made up, especially about the eyes. Several times she said, "Paul will be so happy to see you," as if Paul had not known they were invited; or, knowing, like Ceci herself, had perhaps forgotten. An east wind fanned drizzle and soft gray mist against the windows.

Paul returned looking fit and tanned and startled about the eyes; in his walnut-brown face the whites glared. Toward dusk the sky lightened and the couples sat on the beach with their drinks. Ceci continued to chatter while Paul smiled, vague and distracted, looking out at the surf. The air was chilly and damp but wonderfully fresh. The Carsons drew deep breaths and spoke admiringly of the view. And the house. And the location. They were wondering had the Riegels been quarreling? Was something wrong? Had they themselves come on the wrong day or at the wrong time? Paul had been effusive too in his greetings but had not seemed to see them and had scarcely looked at them since.

Before they sat down to dinner the telephone began to ring. Ceci in the kitchen (with Charlotte who was helping her) and Paul in the living room (with Barry; the men were watching a televised tennis tournament) made no move to answer it. The ringing continued for what seemed like a long time, then stopped and resumed again while they were having dinner, and again neither of the Riegels made a move to answer it. Paul grinned, running both hands roughly through the bushy patches of hair at the sides of his head, and said, "When the world beats a path to your doorstep, beat it back, friends! *Beat it back for fuck's sake!*"

His extravagant words were meant to be funny of course but would have required another atmosphere altogether to be so. As it was, the Carsons could only stare and smile in embarrassment.

Ceci filled the silence by saying loudly, "Life's little ironies! You spend a lifetime making yourself famous, then you try to back off and dismantle it. But it won't dismantle! It's a mummy and you're inside it!"

"Not *in* a mummy," Paul said, staring smiling at the lobster on his plate, which he'd barely eaten, "you *are* a mummy." He had been drinking steadily, Scotch on the rocks and now wine, since arriving home.

Ceci laughed sharply. " 'In,' 'are,' what's the difference?" she said, appealing to the Carsons. She reached out to squeeze Barry's hand, hard. "In any case you're a goner, right?"

Paul said, "No, *you're* a goner."

The evening continued in this vein. The Carsons sent despairing glances at each other.

The telephone began to ring, and this time Paul rose to answer it. He walked stiffly and took his glass of wine with him. He took the call not in the kitchen but in another room at the rear of the house, and he was gone so long that Charlotte felt moved to ask if something was wrong. Ceci Riegel stared at her coldly. The whites of Ceci's eyes too showed above the rims of the iris, giving her a fey festive party look at odds with her carelessly combed hair and the tiredness deep in her face. "With the meal?" she

43

asked. "With the house? With us? With *you?* I don't know of anything wrong."

Charlotte had never been so rebuffed in her adult life. Barry too felt the force of the insult. After a long stunned moment Charlotte murmured an apology, and Barry too murmured something vague, placating, embarrassed.

They sat in suspension, not speaking, scarcely moving, until at last Paul returned. His cheeks were ruddy as if they'd been heartily slapped and his eyes were bright. He carried a bottle of his favorite Napa Valley wine, which he'd been saving, he said, just for tonight. "This is a truly special occasion! We've really missed you guys!"

They were up until two, drinking. Repeatedly Paul used the odd expression "guys" as if its sound, its grating musicality, had imprinted itself in his brain. "OK, guys, how's about another drink?" he would say, rubbing his hands together. "OK, guys, how the hell have you been?"

Next morning, a brilliantly sunny morning, no one was up before eleven. Paul appeared in swimming trunks and T-shirt in the kitchen around noon, boisterous, swaggering, unshaven, in much the mood of the night before—remarkable! The Riegels had hired a local handyman to shore up some rotting steps and the handyman was an oldish gray-grizzled black and after the man was paid and departed Paul spoke in an exaggerated comical black accent, hugging Ceci and Charlotte around their waists until Charlotte pushed him away stiffly, saying, "I don't think you're being funny, Paul." There was a moment's startled silence; then she repeated, vehemently, *"I don't think that's funny, Paul."*

As if on cue Ceci turned on her heel and walked out of the room.

But Paul continued his clowning. He blundered about in the kitchen, pleading with "white missus": bowing, shuffling, tugging what remained of his forelock, kneeling to pluck at Charlotte's denim skirt. His flushed face seemed to have turned to rubber, his lips red, moist, turned obscenely inside out. "Beg pardon, white missus! Oh, white missus, beg pardon!"

Charlotte said, "I think we should leave."

Barry, who had been staring appalled at his friend, as if he'd never seen him before, said quickly, "Yes. I think we should leave."

They went to their room at the rear of the house, leaving Paul behind, and in a numbed stricken silence packed their things, each of them badly trembling. They anticipated one or both of the Riegels following them but neither did, and as Charlotte yanked sheets off the bed, towels off the towel rack in the bathroom, to fold and pile them neatly at the foot of the bed, she could not believe that their friends would allow them to leave without protest.

With a wad of toilet paper she cleaned the bathroom sink as Barry called to her to please hurry. She examined the claw-footed tub—she and Barry had each showered that morning—and saw near the drain a tiny curly dark hair, hers or Barry's, indistinguishable, and this hair she leaned over to snatch up but her fingers closed in air and she tried another time, still failing to grasp it, then finally she picked it up and flushed it down the toilet. Her face was burning and her heart knocking so hard in her chest she could scarcely breathe.

The Carsons left the Riegels' cottage in Nantucket shortly after noon of the day following their arrival.

They drove seven hours back to their home with a single stop, silent much of the time but excited, nervously elated. When he drove Barry kept glancing in the rearview mirror. One of his eyelids had developed a tic.

He said, "We should have done this long ago."

"Yes," Charlotte said, staring ahead at dry sunlit rushing pavement. "Long ago."

That night in their own bed they made love for the first time in weeks, or months. "I love you," Barry murmured, as if making a vow. "No one but you."

Tears started out of the corners of Charlotte's tightly shut eyes.

Afterward Barry slept heavily, sweating through the night. From time to time he kicked at the covers, but he never woke. Beside him Charlotte lay staring into the dark. What would become of them now? Something tickled her lips, a bit of lint, a hair, and though she brushed it irritably away the tingling sensation remained. What would become of them, now?

MY MOTHER AND MITCH

by CLARENCE MAJOR

He was just somebody who had dialed the wrong number. This is how it started and I wasn't concerned about it. Not at first. I don't even remember if I was there when he first called but I do, all these many years later, remember my mother on the phone speaking to him in her best quiet voice, trying to sound as ladylike as she knew how.

She had these different voices for talking to different people on different occasions. I could tell by my mother's proper voice that this man was somebody she wanted to make a good impression on, a man she thought she might like to know. This was back when my mother was still a young woman, divorced but still young enough to believe that she was not completely finished with men. She was a skeptic from the beginning, I knew that even then. But some part of her thought the right man might come along some day.

I don't know exactly what it was about him that attracted her though. People are too mysterious to know that well. I know that now and I must have been smart enough not to wonder too hard about it back then.

Since I remember hearing her tell him her name she must not have given it out right off the bat when he first called. She was a city woman with a child and had developed a certain alertness to danger. One thing you didn't do was give your name to a stranger on the phone. You never knew who to trust in a city like Chicago. The place was full of crazy people and criminals.

46

She said, "My name is *Mrs.* Jayne Anderson." I can still hear her laying the emphasis on the Mrs. although she had been separated from my father twelve years by 1951 when this man dialed her number by accident.

Mitch Kibbs was the name he gave her. I guess he must have told her who he was the very first time, just after he apologized for calling her by mistake. I can't remember who he was trying to call. He must have told her and she must have told me but it's gone now. I think they must have talked a pretty good while that first time. The first thing that I remember about him was that he lived with his sister who was older than he. The next thing was that he was very old. He must have been fifty and to me at fifteen that was deep into age. If my mother was old at thirty, fifty was ancient. Then the other thing about him was that he was white.

They'd talked five or six times I think before he came out and said he was white but she knew it before he told her. I think he made this claim only after he started suspecting he might not be talking to another white person. But the thing was he didn't know for sure she was black. I was at home lying on the couch pretending to read a magazine when I heard her say, "I am a colored lady." Those were her words exactly. She placed her emphasis on the word lady.

I had never known my mother to date any white men. She would hang up from talking to him and she and I would sit at the kitchen table and she'd tell me what he'd said. They were telling each other the bits and pieces of their lives, listening to each other, feeling their way as they talked. She spoke slowly, remembering all the details. I watched her scowl and the way her eyes narrowed as she puzzled over his confessions as she told me in her own words about them. She was especially puzzled about his reaction to her confession about being colored.

That night she looked across at me with that fearful look that was hers alone and said, "Tommy, I doubt if he will ever call back. Not after tonight. He didn't know. You know that."

Feeling grown-up because she was treating me that way, I said, "I wouldn't be so sure."

But he called back soon after that.

I was curious about her interest in this particular old white man so I always listened carefully. I was a little bit scared too because

I suspected he might be some kind of maniac or pervert. I had no good reason to fear such a thing except that I thought it strange that anybody could spend as much time as he and my mother did talking on the phone without any desire for human contact. She had never had a telephone relationship before and at that time all I knew about telephone relationships was that they were insane and conducted by people who probably needed to be put away. This meant that I also had the sad feeling that my mother was a bit crazy too. But more important than these fearful fantasies, I thought I was witnessing a change in my mother. It seemed important and I didn't want to misunderstand it or miss the point of it. I tried to look on the bright side, which was what my mother always said I should try to do.

He certainly didn't sound dangerous. Two or three times I myself answered the phone when he called and he always said, "Hello, Tommy, this is Mitch, may I speak to your mother," and I always said, "Sure, just a minute." He never asked me how I was doing or anything like that and I never had anything special to say to him.

After he'd been calling for over a month I sort of lost interest in hearing about their talk. But she went right on telling me what he said. I was a polite boy so I listened despite the fact that I had decided that Mitch Kibbs and his ancient sister Temple Erikson were crazy but harmless. My poor mother was lonely. That was all. I had it all figured out. He wasn't an ax murderer who was going to sneak up on her one evening when she was coming home from her job at the factory and split her open from the top down. We were always hearing about things like this so I knew it wasn't impossible.

My interest would pick up occasionally. I was especially interested in what happened the first time my mother herself made the call to his house. She told me that Temple Erikson answered the phone. Mother and I were eating dinner when she started talking about Temple Erikson.

"She's a little off in the head."

I didn't say anything but it confirmed my suspicion. What surprised me was my mother's ability to recognize it. "What'd she say?"

"She rattled on about the wild west and the Indians and having to hide in a barrel or something like that. Said the Indians were shooting arrows at them and she was just a little girl who hid in a barrel."

I thought about this. "Maybe she lived out west when she was young. You know? She must be a hundred by now. That would make her the right age."

"Oh, come on, now. What she said was she married when she was fourteen, married this Erikson fellow. As near as I could figure out he must have been a leather tanner but seems he also hunted fur and sold it to make a living. She never had a child."

"None of that sounds crazy." I was disappointed.

"She was talking crazy, though."

"How so?"

"She thinks the Indians are coming back to attack the house any day now. She says things like Erikson was still living, like he was just off there in the next room, taking a nap. One of the first things Mitch told me was his sister and he moved in together after her husband died and that was twenty years ago."

"How did the husband die?"

"Huh?"

"How did he die?"

She finished chewing her peas first. "Kicked in the head by a horse. Bled to death."

I burst out laughing because the image was so bright in my mind and I couldn't help myself. My pretty mother had a sense of humor even when she didn't mean to show it.

She chewed her peas in a ladylike manner. This was long before she lost her teeth. Sitting there across the table from her I knew I loved her and needed her and I knew she loved and needed me. I was not yet fearing that she needed me too much. She had a lot of anger in her too. Men had hurt her bad. And one day I was going to be a man.

When I laughed my mother said, "You shouldn't laugh at misfortune, Tommy." But she had this silly grin on her face and it caused me to crack up again. I just couldn't stop. I think now I must have been a bit hysterical from the anxiety I had been living with all those weeks while she was telling me about the telephone conversations that I wanted to hear about only part of the time.

49

It was dark outside and I got up when I finished my dinner and went to the window and looked down on the streetlights glowing in the wet pavement. I said, "I bet he's out there right now, hiding in the shadows, watching our window."

"Who?" Her eyes grew large. She was easily frightened. I knew this and I was being devilish and deliberately trying to scare her. "You know, Mister Kibbs."

She looked relieved. "No he's not. He's not like that. He's a little strange but not a pervert."

"How'd you know?"

By the look she gave me I knew now that I had thrown doubt into her and she wasn't handling it well. She didn't try to answer me. She finished her small, dry pork chop and the last of her bright green peas and reached over and took up my plate and sat it inside of her own.

She took the dishes to the sink, turned on the hot and cold water so that warm water gushed out of the single faucet, causing the pipe to clang, and started washing the dishes. "You have a vivid imagination," was all she said.

I grabbed the dishcloth and started drying the first plate she placed in the rack. "Even so, you don't know this man. You never even seen him. Aren't you curious about what he looks like?"

"I know what he looks like."

"How?"

"He sent me a picture of himself and Temple together.,"

I gave her a look. She had been holding out on me. I knew he was crazy now. Was he so ugly she hadn't wanted me to see the picture? I asked if I could see it.

She dried her hands on the cloth I was holding then took her cigarettes out of her dress pocket and knocked one from the pack and stuck it between her thin pale lips. I watched her light it and fan the smoke and squint her eyes. She said, "You have to promise not to laugh."

That did it. I started laughing again and couldn't stop. Then she started laughing too because I was bent double, standing there at the sink, with this image of some old guy who looked like The Creeper in my mind. But I knew she couldn't read my mind so she had to be laughing at me laughing. She was still young enough to be silly with me like a kid.

50

Then she brought out two pictures, one of him and the other one of his sister. She put them down side by side on the table. "Make sure your hands are dry."

I took off my glasses and bent down to the one of the man first so I could see up close as I stood there wiping my hands on the dishcloth. It was one of those studio pictures where somebody had posed in a three-quarter view. He had his unruly hair and eyebrows pasted down and you could tell he was fresh out of the bath and his white shirt was starched hard. He was holding his scrubbed face with effort toward where the photographer told him to look, which was too much in the direction of the best light. He was frowning with discomfort beneath the forced smile. There was something else. It was something like defeat or simple tiredness in his pose and you could see it best in the heavy lids of his large blank eyes. He looked out of that face at the world with what remained of his self-confidence and trust in the world. His shaggy presence said that it was all worthwhile and maybe even in some ways he would not ever understand, also important. I understood all of that even then but would never have been able to put my reading of him into words like these.

Then I looked at the woman. She was an old hawk. Her skin was badly wrinkled like the skin of ancient Indians I'd seen in photographs and the westerns. There was something like a smile coming out of her face but it had come out sort of sideways and made her look silly. But the main thing about her was that she looked very mean. But on second thought, to give her the benefit of the doubt, I can say that it might have been just plain hardness from having had a hard life. She was wearing a black iron-stiff dress buttoned up to her dicky which was ironically dainty and tight around her goose neck.

All I said was, "They're *so* old." I don't know what else I thought as I looked up at my mother who was leaning over my shoulder looking at the pictures too, as though she'd never seen them before, as though she was trying to see them through my eyes.

"You're just young, Tommy. Everybody's old to you. They're not so old. He looks lonely, to me."

I looked at him again and thought I saw what she meant.

I put the dishes away and she took the photographs back and we didn't talk any more that night about Mitch and Temple. We

51

watched our black-and-white television screen which showed us Red Skelton acting like a fool.

Before it was over, I fell asleep on the couch and my mother woke me when she turned off the television. "You should to go bed."

I stood up and stretched. "I have a science paper to write."

"Get up early and write it," she said, putting out her cigarette.

"He wants me to meet him someplace," my mother said.

She had just finished talking with him and was standing by the telephone. It was close to dinner time. I'd been home from school since three-thirty and she'd been in from work by then for a good hour. She'd just hung up from the shortest conversation she'd ever had with him.

I'd wondered why they never wanted to meet then I stopped wondering and felt glad they hadn't. Now I was afraid, afraid for her, for myself, for the poor old man in the picture. Why did we have to go through with this crazy thing?

"I told him I needed to talk with you about it first," she said. "I told him I'd call him back."

I was standing there in front of her looking at her. She was a scared little girl with wild eyes dancing in her head, unable to make up her own mind. I sensed her fear. I resented her for the mess she had gotten herself in. I also resented her for needing my consent. I knew she wanted me to say go, go to him, meet him somewhere. I could tell. She was too curious not to want to go. I suddenly thought that he might be a millionaire and that she would marry the old coot and he'd die and leave her his fortune. But there was the sister. She was in the way. And from the looks of her she would pass herself off as one of the living for at least another hundred years or so. So I gave up that fantasy.

"Well, why don't you tell him you'll meet him at the hamburger cafe on Wentworth? We can eat dinner there."

"We?"

"Sure. I'll just sit at the counter like I don't know you. But I gotta be there to protect you."

"I see."

"Then you can walk in alone. I'll already be there eating a cheeseburger and fries. He'll come in and see you waiting for him alone at a table."

52

"No. I'll sit at the counter too," she said.

"Okay. You sit at the counter too."

"What time should I tell him?"

I looked at my Timex. It was six. I knew they lived on the West Side and that meant it would take him at least an hour by bus and a half hour by car. He probably didn't have a car. I was hungry though and had already set my mind on eating a cheeseburger rather than macaroni and cheese out of the box.

"Tell him seven-thirty."

"Okay."

I went to my room. I didn't want to hear her talking to him in her soft whispering voice. I'd stopped listening sometime before. I looked at the notes for homework and felt sick on the stomach at the thought of having to write a science paper.

A few minutes later my mother came in and said, "Okay. It's all set." She sat down on the side of my bed and folded her bony pale hands in her lap. "What should I wear?"

"Wear your green dress and the brown shoes."

"You like that dress don't you."

"I like that one and the black one with the yellow at the top. It's classical."

"You mean classy."

"Whatever I mean." I felt really grown that night.

"Here, Tommy, take this." She handed me five dollars which she'd been hiding in the palm of her right hand. "Don't spend it all. Buy the burger out of it and the rest is just to have. If you spend it all in that hamburger place I'm going to deduct it from your allowance next week."

When I got there, I changed my mind about the counter. I took a table by myself. I was eating my cheeseburger and watching the revolving door. The cafe was noisy with shouts, cackling, giggles and verbal warfare. The waitress, Miss Azibo, was in a bad mood. She'd set my hamburger plate down like it was burning her hand.

I kept my eye on the door. Every time somebody came in I looked up, every time somebody left I looked up. I finished my cheeseburger even before my mother got there, and, ignoring her warning, I ordered another and another Coca-Cola to go with it. I figured I could eat two or three burgers and still have most of the five left.

Then my mother came in like a bright light into a dingy room. I think she must have been the most beautiful woman who ever entered that place and it was her first time coming in there. She had always been something of a snob and did not believe in places like this. I knew she'd agreed to meet Mister Kibbs here just because she believed in my right to the cheeseburger and this place had the best in the neighborhood.

I watched her walk ladylike to the counter and ease herself up on the stool and sit there with her back arched. People in that place didn't walk and sit like that. She was acting classy and everybody turned to look at her. I looked around at the faces and a lot of the women had these real mean sneering looks like somebody had broke wind.

She didn't know any of these people and they didn't know her. Some of them may have known her by sight, and me too, but that was about all the contact we had with this part of the neighborhood. Besides, we hardly ever ate out. When we did we usually ate Chinese or at the rib place.

I sipped my coke and watched Miss Azibo place a cup of coffee before my mother on the counter. She was a coffee freak. Always was. All day long. Long into the night. Cigarettes and coffee in a continuous cycle. I grew up with her that way. The harsh smells are still in my memory. When she picked up the cup with a dainty finger sticking out just so, I heard a big fat woman at a table in front of mine say to the big fat woman at the table with her that my mother was a snooty bitch. The other woman said, "Yeah. She must think she's white. What she doing in here anyway?"

Mitch Kibbs came in about twenty minutes after my mother and I watched him stop and stand just inside the revolving doors. He stood to the side. He looked a lot younger than in the picture. He was stooped a bit though and he wasn't dressed like a millionaire which disappointed me. But he was clean. He was wearing a necktie and a clean white shirt and a suit that looked like it was about two hundred years old but one no doubt made of the best wool. Although it was Fall he looked overdressed for the season. He looked like a man who hadn't been out in daylight in a long while. He was nervous, I could tell. Everybody was looking at him. Rarely did white people come in here.

Then he went to my mother like he knew she had to be the person he'd come in to see. He sat himself up on the stool beside her and leaned forward with his elbows on the counter and looked in her face.

She looked back in that timid way of hers. But she wasn't timid. It was an act and part of her ladylike posture. She used it when she needed it.

They talked and talked. I sat there eating cheeseburgers and protecting her till I spent the whole five dollars. Even as I ran out of money I knew she would forgive me. She had always forgiven me on special occasions. This was one for sure.

She never told me what they talked about in the cafe and I never asked but everything that happened after that meeting went toward the finishing off of the affair my mother was having with Mitch Kibbs. He called her later that night. I was in my room reading when the phone rang and I could hear her speaking to him in that ladylike way—not the way she talked to me. I was different. She didn't need to impress me. I was her son. But I couldn't hear what she was saying and didn't want to.

Mister Kibbs called the next evening. But eventually the calls were fewer and fewer till he no longer called.

My mother and I went on living the way we always had, she working long hours at the factory and me going to school. She was not a happy woman but I thought she was pretty brave. Every once in a while she got invited somewhere, to some wedding or out on a date with a man. She always tried on two or three different dresses, turning herself around and around before the mirror, asking me how she looked, making me select the dress she would wear. Most often though she went nowhere. After dinner we sat together at the kitchen table, she drinking coffee, and smoking her eternal cigarettes. She gave me my first can of beer one night when she herself felt like having one. It tasted awful and I didn't touch the stuff for years after that.

About a day or two after the meeting in the hamburger cafe I remember coming to a conclusion about mother. I learned for the first time that she did not always know what she was doing. It struck me that she was as helpless as I sometimes felt when con-

55

fronted with a math or science problem or a problem about sex and girls and growing up and life in general. She didn't know everything. And that made me feel closer to her despite the fear it caused. She was there to protect me, I thought. But there she was, just finding her way, step by step, like me. It was something wonderful anyway.

NOSOTROS

by JANET PEERY

IT WAS ALWAYS hot in the little house, her mother's house, even in December. Licha, lying on the floor, arms above her head and braced against the mirrored bedroom door, thought how cool it was here, in Madama's house where the big air conditioners hummed, pumping cold air through all the louvered vents in the spacious rooms. Madama's son Raleigh strained above her, drops of his sweat pooling on her breasts and belly like warm coins, his movements grinding her hips into the wool carpet until they stung, but it was cooler. Licha drew up her knees and curled her toes; even the carpet was cool, and she wondered how far down the coolness went.

All the houses in the Valley were slab houses, built on concrete. There were no basements; hurricanes came this far inland. Few peaked roofs: there was no snow here. Ever. Under the slab, Licha knew, and in the space between the walls, lived thousands of lizards: stripebacks, *chalotes,* green anoles. They came out to bask on the hot packed dirt around the foundation, to crawl up the screens. Madama hated them. If she saw too many she called the exterminators down from McAllen. Then Licha's mother Camarena was set to draping the furniture in sheeting, removing dishes, food and clothing from the house so the pesticide wouldn't contaminate Madama and Raleigh. When the exterminator's immense plastic tent was pulled from the house and all the lizard carcasses were shoveled into bushel baskets, her mother would come back in to give the house a thorough cleaning:

Pine-Sol the terrazzo, scrub the pecky cypress walls, shampoo the carpets. Then she would move everything back in, washing each dish and glass and fork in hot detergent water while Madama supervised, giving orders in her tight rough voice.

At the little house behind Madama's, her mother's house, lizards entered and departed through the gap between the screen door and the flagstone sill, unremarked. Geckos made their way around the walls, eating insects, spatulate toepads mocking gravity. But it was so hot there. Licha thought about the house she and Raleigh could have when she finished high school and moved from the Valley, a little college house with a peaked roof and an air conditioner in the window, a Boston fern hanging above the table, her biology texts and notes spread out beneath it.

"Squeeze your titties together," Raleigh said. "I want to see them that way."

She braced her feet against the floor and took her hands from the door. She tried to place them on the sides of her breasts, but his movements inched her too far up. "I can't. I'll hit my head."

Raleigh balanced on one arm, pushing his glasses farther up on his nose. She didn't understand how he could sweat so, when it was as cool in the room as it was in the stores downtown. The lenses of his glasses were fogged. She wondered why he wore them, what he saw as he watched, if he saw the two of them as a watery image, the edges of their bodies blurred and running together. She wondered what it was he wanted to see in the mirror, with his glasses. She looked up at him, under the rims, at his eyes, and their blue startled her. It was an uncommon color, she thought, a surprise of a color, a color she marveled the human body, with its browns and tans and pinks, could produce. She couldn't look at it long without imagining it was from another place—foreign, vaguely holy, like the blue of the Blessed Virgin's mantle at the church of San Benito; cool and infinite, like the blue of the sky when the heat lifted and the haze that sealed the Valley blew away in the wind of a norther. It was a blue like ice and snow.

It snowed sometimes in Austin, even in San Antonio. Where her brother Tavo had gone—to Fort Dix, New Jersey—it was probably snowing now, great fat flakes floating and floating, covering the barracks until they looked like rows of sugared cakes, and Tavo, inside with other soldiers, maybe some from other warm places, laughed from the surprise of it. As much as she hoped Tavo wouldn't have to go to Vietnam, she envied him his chance to be away, to open a window and draw the coolness in. She closed her eyes and imagined she could smell the snow. It must be sweet and powdery, she thought, like coconut. She looked again at Raleigh, his neck cords straining, watching in the mirror. "Have you ever seen snow?"

"Don't talk," he said. "I'm almost there." He clenched his jaw, and Licha knew her question had irritated him.

Raleigh went to school in Tennessee, to Vanderbilt. He was home for winter break. Madama had picked him up at the Brownsville airport, taking the yardman Perfilio along to drive the big car. She refused to drive the road alone. Raleigh's father, called Papa by everyone in the little towns along the highway, had been killed on this road, on an inspection tour of his groves. As he pulled out of the Donna off-ramp, he was struck by one of his own trucks, the driver drunk and running with no lights, a load of stolen television sets concealed by cotton bales in the truck bed. On the day of Raleigh's return Licha had seen Perfilio pull the car into the driveway, Raleigh and Madama in the back seat. When Perfilio piled Raleigh's red plaid luggage on the *porche* beside the tall white poinsettias, Licha thought they looked like Christmas packages from another country, from England or Scotland, not like they should belong to Raleigh, whom Licha and Tavo had grown up with, the three of them playing in the shell-flecked dirt around the roots of the live oaks in the backyard, none of them wearing a shirt, Raleigh's hair bleached almost white with the sun, tanned until he was nearly as brown as Licha and Tavo.

Licha was nine when she overheard Madama's order: the children were not to play together any longer. Madama stood by the laundry shed, her mother at the clothesline. "Camarena," she said, "that girl of yours isn't mine to boss, but she's about to bust out of herself."

Her mother pretended she didn't understand Madama's English, and it irritated Licha; her mother smiling, nodding, an impassive, half-comprehending look in her eyes, wiping her hands on a dish towel or patting little balls of dough into flat round tortillas: pat-pat-pat, smile, nod, shuffle around the big *cocina* in her starched blue work dress and apron, her backless sandals.

She had lived in the little house eleven years, since Licha was five, but still she pretended she didn't understand, or understood only dimly, forcing Madama into a fractured mixture of languages: "Camarena, *deja* all that laundry *sucio en el* whatchamacallit."

Licha and Tavo had laughed about it, about their mother getting the best of bossy Madama in such a sly, funny way, but it made Licha angry that her mother could let Madama think she was stupid; her mother understood everything Madama said. After Madama's bridge-club meetings she entertained Tavo and Licha with stories and imitations until they collapsed on their beds in the little house, wrung out from laughing at the dressed-up stupidity of Madama and her henna-rinsed friends. On the day of Madama's order, she had pretended not to understand, but she complied, keeping Tavo and Licha from Raleigh. Licha remembered how unfair it seemed, and that Madama saw it as her fault: *that girl.*

"Hurry, Raleigh," she said. "They'll be back."

"Maybe if you did something more than lie there," he said. "Move a little."

She tried moving her hips in a small circle. She wasn't sure if it was the right way, the way he expected or was used to, or if there was a right way. Their first time, two days before, when they stood behind the closed door of Raleigh's bedroom, she hadn't had to move at all, and it had been over sooner. Madama and her mother had gone to the grocery store. Raleigh came around the side of the big house to the clothesline where Licha was hanging towels. He held a radio to her ear, as though the years they spent avoiding each other had been no more than a few weeks. She heard a raspy female voice.

"Janis Joplin," he said. "Great, isn't she?"

He lowered the radio when Licha nodded. "Bobby McGee," she said. "I heard it at school."

Raleigh looked the same as he had in high school, when Licha would see him in the halls or at a football game, surrounded by other boys in the same kind of clothing: madras shirts, wheat jeans, loafers they wore without socks. They dressed as if they were already in college, and everyone knew it was where they would end up. The other Anglo boys—those who would stay in the Valley to work and marry, to hunt whitewing dove in the fall, *javelinas* and coyote the rest of the year—wore blue jeans and white T-shirts. Raleigh's hair was still cut in Beatle bangs, but he had grown sideburns, the earpieces of his new wire-rim glasses cutting into them. "Are you at Consolidated?" he asked.

She looked at him, trying to decide if he was joking. She reached for a clothespin to clip the corner of a towel over the line. He should know she wouldn't be at Blessed Sacrament; she was the daughter of a maid, and the public high school was her only choice. When she nodded, he asked her what she was taking.

She wanted to tell him about the frog dissection they had done the week before in biology, how she had cut into the pale, pearlescent belly to expose the first layer of organs, the ventral abdominal vein like a tiny, delicately branching river, the torsion of the small intestine giving way to the bulk of the large intestine and how both of them, when held aside, revealed the deeper viscera, the long posterior vena cava, the testes, kidneys and adrenal bodies; how the heart and lungs lay over the perfect fork of the aortic arch; how surprisingly large the liver was, its curves, its fluted edges, and how she could hardly catch her breath, not because of the formaldehyde or out of revulsion, like some of the other students, but from awe, for joy at the synchrony and mystery of the workings of the body laid out before her, its legs splayed on the cutting table, the fragile mandible upturned and yielding to her touch. She wanted to tell him how she felt as her probe and scalpel moved through the frog's body, about the sacred, almost heartbreaking invitation of it, but she couldn't. "I'm taking biology," she said.

"Does Mohesky still teach it?"

She nodded. "I really like him." She became aware of Raleigh looking at her breasts, and when she stooped to pick up another towel from the basket she checked the buttons of her blouse. She hoped he didn't notice the downward glance that meant she knew he was looking at her.

"Come in the house a minute," he said. "I want to show you something."

When they were just inside his bedroom he closed the door, telling her how beautiful she was, how sweet. She was all he thought about his first semester away at school. Her breasts were beautiful; titties, he called them, and he'd bet they'd grown— would she show him? She was surprised to feel her nipple tighten when he took it into his mouth, the whole breast seem to swell

61

around it. He lifted her skirt and eased his fingers past her panties until the middle one was inside her. "You know all about it," he said. He unzipped his pants.

"It hurts," she said, and he stopped moving his fingers. "A little."

"You don't act like it," he said. He slid his fingers out and guided himself into her, knees bent, his hand pressing against her hip.

"That doesn't mean it doesn't."

"You like it, though." It wasn't a question, and Licha didn't bother to answer. She did like it. She liked it that he wanted her. She liked the push of it, the tip of him pushing past the part of her that felt like a small, rugate tunnel into a bigger part that had less feeling, more like a liquid cave that seemed to swallow him. She worried that she was too big. Anglo boys said Mexican girls were built for breeding. She wondered if Raleigh was small. She had seen other men; several times she had surprised Tavo, and she had seen *braceros* relieving themselves in the groves after *siesta*. She hadn't looked closely, but it seemed that most of these were more substantial, their color fuller, more nearly like the rest of their skin. Raleigh's was the color of sunburn, almost purple at the tip.

When it was over he had gone into the bathroom. She heard the tap running, a flush. She cleaned herself with her panties, not wanting to use the lacquered box of tissues beside Raleigh's bed. She noticed only a slight pink tinge, no more blood than from a paper cut. She tucked the panties into the waistband of her skirt and pulled down her blouse to conceal them.

Now, two days later, he had come up behind her as she emptied trash from the little house onto the burn pile at the back of the property. "*Nalgas,*" he said, patting her bottom. She laughed at the *pachuco* word for buttocks, at the growling, mock-salacious way he said it, the furtive waggle of his eyebrows behind his glasses, and she had gone with him again to the big house, this time to Madama's bedroom where he locked the door and showed her the full-length mirror behind it. Facing it, with Raleigh behind her, Licha watched his hands, nervous and more intent this time, move up her body, the tips of his fingers tapered, almost delicate, nails bitten to the quick. She could see ragged cuticles and dark flecks of dried blood as his fingers worked at buttons, at the elastic of her shorts. He pressed himself closer, sweating already, his breathing shallow and uneven, and when they were on the floor, Licha on her hands and knees, Raleigh upright, kneeling behind her, she looked at their image in the mirror, at Raleigh watching, his head thrown back and arms extended so his hands grasped her hips, his movements regular and insistent. She thought of the mice they had mated in biology lab, of the male, a solid black, his motions powerful and concentrated in mount, of the female, a pink-eyed white, hunched and holding her ground to help him, her neck at an angle of submission, and she knew they were more alike than different, the mating mice, herself and Raleigh; that this impulse shot through all of life, through male and female, and made them do the things they did, made men and women lie down together. We are mating, she marveled.

He seemed to go deeper this time, deeper than when they stood against his bedroom wall. She felt her belly swell from him, a soft, cramping fullness like her menstrual cycle, pleasant at first, then almost painful. She asked him to stop, and he had waited while she turned over to face him, her arms braced against the door. Then he had continued. Again she tried to hold her breasts for him and to move her hips at the same time. "You have to take it out," she said. "Before." She had forgotten to tell him the first time.

He said nothing, concentrating on their image in the mirror. Finally he moaned, withdrawing, and Licha felt slow, warm spurts against her thigh. She squirmed beneath his weight, and when he rolled over she got up. "We'll leave a spot."

She went into the bathroom, looking for a cloth for the carpet. She didn't want to use the pale yellow towels folded in a complicated way across the bar, so she tore a length of paper, setting the roller spinning, and hurried to dab at the wetness where they had lain. The paper pilled and shed, leaving lint on the close shear of the wool. She tried to pick it off with her fingers, but it stuck here, too. Raleigh laughed and got up to go to the bathroom. "Don't worry so much," he said. He closed the door. "Camarena will get it."

His mention of her mother startled Licha; she and Madama would be back soon from McAllen. She dressed quickly, tucking the wad of paper into her pocket. She was halfway down the *galería* to the stairs when she heard the bathroom door click open and Raleigh call out, but she didn't want to risk the time to answer.

The little house felt hot and close after the expanse of the big rooms. Even before she opened the door she smelled the heat inside, the dust, warm *cominos* simmering into the beans in the big cast-iron *olla* on the hot plate. As she crossed the room to her bed she compared what she had seen upstairs in the big house with her mother's attempts to brighten things: a scattering of secondhand bathroom rugs across the dull linoleum, knickknacks cast off from Madama, paper flowers at the single window. Licha's bed was the lower bunk of a government-issue set, curtained with a sheet tucked under the mattress of Tavo's top bunk where boxes of clothing and household things were stored now that Tavo had gone. The beds were white, but the paint had chipped, exposing leopard-spots of army green. At the head and foot the letters US were carved into the wood. When Licha was learning to read, she thought the letters meant herself and Tavo; us, *nosotros,* and she felt special, good, tracing the letters with her fingers, with a purple crayon, lucky: no one else had a bed that told of herself and her brother, of their place in the world. She didn't want to believe Tavo when he laughed and told her what the letters stood for. Her mother slept on a daybed in the opposite corner, behind a partition made of crates and a blue shower curtain with a picture of an egret wading among green rushes. Licha lifted her sheet curtain and lay down, letting the heat and dimness envelop her.

She heard the car pull into the driveway, the sound of its doors closing and Madama's voice telling Perfilio to wash the car. She heard the slap of her mother's sandals on the flagstone path, coming toward the little house. She wished she had washed; the girls at school said other people could tell by your smell if you had been with a boy. In the stuffiness of the room her mother would notice it. She lay still and hoped her mother would think she was asleep.

Through the thin sheet Licha saw her come in, silhouetted in the light streaming through the doorway. She could see well enough to tell her mother still wore her apron. Madama insisted on it, especially when they went to town. Licha watched as she took it off and folded it over a wooden chair, then began taking dishes and pots and pans from the crates stacked to form shelves, wisps of hair springing from the bun at the back of her neck.

She tried to remember how her mother looked when her skin wasn't glistening with sweat, when her hair wasn't escaping from the bun: Saturday before church, sometimes for whole days in winter if a norther came in and work at the house was light. Even through the screen of the sheet Licha could see the patches of darker blue under her mother's arms, around her waist, between her shoulder blades. They were as much a part of her mother as the starched workdress, as the apron, as the low song she sang while she worked, a song that irritated Licha for its persistence, its quality of being a song yet not a song, more a droning, melodic murmur made low in the throat that had the power to remove her mother, lift her beyond Licha's reach and back into the time before Licha, a song from her mother's earlier life in the *barrancas* of the East Sierra Madre, the place she had left to come here, first to work for Papa in the fields, then for Madama in the house, a place she never talked about.

When Tavo and Licha asked about it she said little. All they knew was that Papa had found her walking along the road, fifteen, pregnant with Tavo, on one of his trips below the border to find workers. He didn't like the migrant teams, preferring whole families who wanted to come across, to live in the block houses at the bend in the levee until they found something better, or even asked about something better, and then he would help them, with papers, by getting their children into school, with medicine and food. Her mother had been alone on the road, in the last months of pregnancy, but Papa had idled the truck alongside her, asking questions in Spanish, inviting her to join the families in the truck bed. Tavo had been born in the block house by the levee. Licha was born three years later. Her father was a *Latino* from Las Cruces working a few months with the Army Corps of Engineers on an irrigation project before he moved on. This was all she knew. She and Tavo had stopped asking; their mother didn't welcome questions about the other life.

A stack of Melmac plates clattered to the floor, causing Licha to jump. Her mother stooped to pick them up, her eyes on Licha's curtain. "*¿Estás aquí?*"

Licha swung her legs over the edge of the bed. "I'm here, Mama." She made it a practice to answer her mother's Spanish with English, as though she were talking to a toddler just learning the words for things. "What are you doing?"

Her mother ignored her and continued picking up the scattered plates. Licha sighed and repeated the question in Spanish. Her mother was stubborn enough to ignore the question all day if it was a matter of will.

Her mother smiled at her, setting the stack of plates on the wooden table. She told Licha she and Madama had gone to an appliance store in McAllen. She described the shining rows of silver and white, and a new color for stoves and refrigerators called avocado green. They had picked out a new stove for the *cocina* in the big house. It was to be delivered tomorrow. And guess who, as a gift for Christmas, was to have the old one? Licha smiled in spite of herself. "We are!"

Her mother crossed the room and stood behind the big chair next to the window. "*Ayudame, chica.*"

Licha helped her move the chair. They placed it at an angle by Licha's bed, then lifted the table from the corner where the new stove would go. They put it by the window. While her mother dusted the tabletop, Licha went outside to get one of the potted aloes that lined the step. She arranged it in the center of the table.

"*Mira,* Mama," she said, gesturing grandly toward the plant. "*Better Homes and Gardens.*" They laughed, and Licha felt good, good and happy, like Licha-nine-years-old, Licha-of-no-secrets, her mother's *chula niña* in a ruffled skirt and braids stretched tight for church. She watched her mother poke the broom into the cleared corner and shoo a lizard along the baseboard toward the door, her throaty song rising in the heat, happy with so little, and suddenly she was angry.

"A stove," she said. "An old stove. How much did the new one cost?"

Her mother continued sweeping, the hem of her work dress swaying stiffly with the motions of the broom. "*No importa.*"

She felt like grabbing the broom away and forcing her mother to listen. "We don't need a stove. Let her sell the old one and give us the money. Let her buy us an air conditioner. She has enough. She has everything." She thought of nights in the little house, trying to sleep with only the old black fan to cool her, its woven cord stretched from chair to chair, tripping her if she got up to get a drink of water, the frayed fabric encasing it reticulated like the backs of the water snakes she sometimes saw in the arroyo. "It will only make it hotter in this place!" She pushed against the screen door hard enough to wedge the flimsy frame against the bump on the far edge of the step and walked out.

She cut through the live oaks, through the rows of oleander set out like railroad tracks to shield the little house from view, around to the back of the property to the overgrown area she and Tavo and Raleigh had called the jungle when they were little. It was mostly scrub pecan choked with ololiuque vines, avocado trees, crotons and yucca, but a few banana and papaya trees survived, making it seem exotic and lush. Saw palmetto slashed her legs as she ran past the boundaries. She looked down to see the thin lines like razor cuts across her thighs. She darted through the algarroba thicket and came out on the other side, to Grand Texas Boulevard. A fine name, she thought, for the rutted road that led to the highway toward Reynosa.

She slowed down, thinking about what had just happened, thinking that she now knew what made people run away. It wasn't a simple matter of not liking home, it was far more complicated than that, and at the point when things became too complicated to even think about any longer, people ran away. For whatever reasons they had that were too entwined to sort out. She imagined her mother, a pregnant girl from the *barrancas*, walking along a road, and she imagined a man in a truck, a man in khaki workpants and a Panama hat, a smiling, red-mustached man. She would have climbed inside the truck bed, too. She saw herself riding away from the Valley to a different place, any place, maybe a place with snow. To Fort Dix where Tavo was, a soldier in uniform, able to be what he was without people thinking they *knew* what he was just by looking at him, by knowing where he came from, where there was more to get excited about than avocado appliances, where he made his own money and didn't have to depend on a bossy old woman like Madama, where he didn't have to care what such a woman thought of anything he did. Tavo would understand how she felt. He had been glad to leave the Valley.

She picked up a stone and threw it at an irrigation pump. She knew what Tavo would think of what she and Raleigh did. He would spit, and make the jerking, upward jab with his wrist, like stabbing. He would stab Raleigh if he knew. He wouldn't see that Raleigh wasn't like the others; he was more like Papa. Tavo would see only his side of it, the *pachuco* side that hated all Anglos. He wouldn't see that it was different with Raleigh, that they were what they were, male and female, Licha and Raleigh. He wanted her, he found her beautiful. The feeling made her stomach tighten as she walked along, slower now. She held her shoulders straighter and began to sway her hips the way she had seen other girls do, feeling the heads of her femurs articulating deep in her pelvis. She knew now why those girls walked like this: a man wanted them.

She stopped to watch the sun go down behind a grove of Valencias. The heavy fruit hung full and brilliant, orange as the sun, as the bright new tennis balls Madama kept in canisters on the laundry-shed shelf. She heard the big trucks start up, loading *braceros* for the trip back to the *colonia*. Traffic on the highway quickened and Licha turned to go home, the trucks rumbling by. When she heard the clicking noises the men made, their high-pitched yips of appreciation, she toned down her walk, but she thought: let them look, let them want.

He didn't come for her the next day, or the next, though she made many trips between the house and the laundry shed, the laundry shed and the burn pile, watching the back door of the big house. She began to think she had been a fool, that Tavo's version of the way things were with Anglo boys and Mexican girls might be right. She could hardly bear her mother's excitement about the stove, and she snapped at her to stop polishing it so often—she'd polished it every day for eleven years—to speak English, to pick up her feet when she walked and stop shuffling around like a cow. Her mother stared at her when she said this, and Licha had seen her face close down.

On Saturday Perfilio brought two chickens and her mother baked them, filling the house with a rich yellow smell that made Licha queasy. She couldn't touch the chicken and she didn't go with her mother to church. She knew it was far too early, improbable, given the dates of her cycle, but she began to worry beyond reason that she was pregnant.

At sundown Saturday a norther blew in, rattling the rickety door and filling the house with random pockets of cold air. Licha pulled a sweater from the box under her bed and put it on. She slid the shutter panel across the window and shut the heavy storm door. She sat at the table in the dark, not bothering to pull the string on the overhead light. When the first knock came she thought it was the wind, but it kept up and finally she opened the door.

Raleigh wore a zippered red windbreaker and his hair blew up behind his head like a rooster's tail. He was smiling. "Did you miss me?"

She wanted to slap his glasses away so they skittered across the flagstone into the potted plants and he would never find them. She wanted to tear off her blouse and sweater and show him her breasts, press them into his chest so hard they burned him. "No," she said.

"You're mad at me." He tried to look around her to see inside the house. "Can I come in?"

She looked behind her into the dark room, at the silly rugs and the shower curtain and the stove in its corner like a squat white ghost. "I'll come out.

They walked around the house to the jungle, Licha with her arms folded across her chest, her hands tucked into the sweater sleeves, Raleigh with his hands jammed into the pockets of his windbreaker, neither of them speaking. Licha sat on the rim of a discarded tractor tire where Tavo had once found a coral snake. She shivered, glad it was too cold for snakes. Raleigh sat beside her, quiet. He bent to flick an oleander leaf from the toe of his loafer.

Alarm surged through her. He had found someone else, she wasn't good enough. Madama had found out. She wanted Licha gone—that girl, her mother, gone.

"I'm busted at Vanderbilt," he said. He looked at her. "Kicked out."

Licha hoped she kept a straight face, kept from smiling: this is all?

"Mother's been hauling me all over south Texas for the last two days, throwing her weight around." He laughed, but Licha could tell he didn't think it was funny. "She thinks she can get me into

San Marcos or Pan American. They're piss-poor schools, but I guess it's better than getting drafted." He laughed again.

Licha waited to see if he had anything else to say, but he was quiet, drumming his knuckles on the thick black tread of the tire. "Maybe it's not so bad," she said. She thought about telling him what Mr. Mohesky had told her—that if she continued to work hard he would help her apply for a scholarship to San Marcos— but she didn't.

He shrugged, then pulled a jeweler's box from his pocket. "Anyway, I got you these." He handed her the box. "For Christmas."

"Not yet," she said.

"You don't want it?"

"I mean, it's not Christmas yet." She held the box, stroking the nap of the black velveteen.

"Soon enough," he said. "Open it."

Inside was a pair of earrings, tiny gold chains with filigree hummingbirds at the ends, red stones for each eye. In the moonlight she could make out the store name on the inner lid: Didde's of San Marcos. She imagined him on the streets of the college town, going into the jewelry store while Madama waited in the car, poring over hundreds of boxes until he chose these, for her. "Thank you," she said, and when he stood and held his hand for her she went with him through the jungle to the laundry shed. He waited while she removed the silver hoops she wore, then he inserted the posts of the new earrings into her lobes. She tilted her head to each side to help him, and she was reminded of the female mouse. The thought came to her that staying still was just as powerful an act as moving, just as necessary, and she again felt linked to the everlasting, perfect cycle of things.

They made love on the floor of the laundry shed, her hips lifted, supported by a pile of towels. They were damp against her skin and smelled of Lifebuoy soap and Clorox. Her carotid artery throbbed from the rush of blood to her head, but she didn't complain, and she didn't tell him to withdraw. She wanted to give him this, a sign of trust, of utter welcome. It would be all right, no matter what. What they were doing, this act, was a promise of that, a pact. She felt the earrings slide back and forth against her neck.

She made it back to the little house and into bed before her mother returned from church, and when she woke up Sunday morning, the first things she felt were the hummingbird earrings. She thought of Raleigh. Was he waking up just now in his room in the big house, remembering what they had done? She moved her hands down her body to the warm pocket between her legs and wondered how she felt to him. How could they ever know, male and female, what each felt like to the other? She heard her mother stirring and she sat up to part the curtain. Her mother was tying her apron on over her work dress.

"¿Café?"

"Coffee," Licha repeated automatically. Sunday mornings they usually sat at the table drinking coffee. It was her mother's day off. "Why are you wearing that?"

There was no answer. Licha sighed, repeating the question in Spanish. Her mother explained that Madama needed her to help with a party. She had to clean, prepare food, set things up. She would come home in the middle of the afternoon to rest, then she would go back in the evening to serve.

"On Sunday?" Licha pulled out a chair and sat down at the table, pouring coffee into a Melmac cup, adding sugar.

Her mother shrugged, and the helpless gesture irritated Licha.

"Why didn't you tell her no? You always do everything she says. 'Sí, Madama, no, Madama, ¿algo más, Madama?'" She rose from her chair and went to the small refrigerator for the milk.

Her mother stood at the sink, calmly tucking wisps of hair into her bun with bobby pins, her back to Licha, saying nothing. Licha thought she may as well have been talking to the stove, for all the effect it had. Even her mother's back looked obstinate, her hips wide and stolid, square and stupid, the apron bow at her back as ridiculous as the daisy garland around the ear of the cow on the milk carton she took from its shelf. She stirred the milk into her coffee and looked at the older woman. She knew her mother's life would always be the same, shuffling back and forth between houses, going to church, easing her knees and elbows with salve she made from Vaseline and aloe, waiting on others, obsequious, stubborn in her obsequiousness, forcing Madama into pidgin silliness, and all of it because of stubbornness, because she wanted nothing more, because she thought no further

71

than the day after tomorrow. Licha banged her cup onto the table, sloshing coffee over the edge and onto her cotton shift. "Why didn't you get papers when Papa offered? You could get a better job."

Her mother turned, and Licha saw her face, hurt, defiant.

"You could *learn* to read, Mama." She felt suddenly defeated; there was nothing she could do. "It's your only day off," she said weakly.

She watched her mother rinse her own cup and dry it; she took it with her to work because Madama believed disease was spread by sharing dishes with the help. She left the house, closing the screen door gently, leaving Licha alone at the table sipping coffee she could barely swallow for her welling sense of injustice. Licha got up and ran after her mother, catching up with her along the flagstone path. "Don't do it, Mama. Say no. Say it for once in your life. Show her what you think of her."

Her mother shook her head. "I think nothing. I only work." She resumed her walk.

"You work for nothing. For a house too little and too hot. For a stove!" She grabbed her mother's arm and shook it. Her mother looked away, across the yard toward the laundry shed.

"*Dejame en paz.*"

"English, Mama, your English is good. Use it. Make her *see* you!"

Her mother looked at her hard, and Licha felt suddenly exposed in her cotton shift, as though she was standing naked on the path. Her mother shook off Licha's hand. "No."

Perfilio came around the corner of the house with a wheelbarrow full of sand and a box of candles. He began placing the *luminarias* around the patio. Licha stood still, watching her mother walk toward the service entrance. Her mother had almost reached the door when she whirled, throwing her coffee cup to the ground. She started back down the path toward Licha, her face dark and angry. She reached out and with a violent flick at Licha's ear set one earring spinning wildly. "*Éstos son de Madama!*"

Licha's hand flew to her ear, to the sting. She was dumbfounded by her mother's anger until she realized she thought Licha had stolen the earrings from the big house. "They are mine," she said, proud that they were, glad her mother was wrong. "Raleigh gave them to me."

Her mother's eyes widened. Licha watched as she took in the information, as she looked at her daughter for clues. She felt her mother's eyes on her body, looking through the thin shift at her breasts which seemed in that moment huge and bobbing, giving away her secret. Her mother slapped her.

"Fool!" She slapped her again and Licha reeled. "It is worse!"

Licha ran to the little house, to her bed, where she cried until her eyes were red and swollen and her throat was raw. She got up to dress. Her hands felt limp as she pulled her skirt up over her hips. She didn't want to be home when her mother returned for her nap, but she didn't know where to go. She didn't want to go for a walk, and the few girls at school she could call her friends were just that, school friends; they rarely saw each other outside, and if they did they only teased Licha about studying so hard and taking everything so seriously. When she opened the refrigerator to look for something to eat she realized it was Raleigh she wanted to talk to. She sat at the table most of the afternoon, pushing cold rice around her plate with the tines of a fork, watching the activity at the big house, Perfilio arranging the *luminarias*, raking palm trash from the drive, pulling the car around. When she saw her mother come out the service entrance, she left the house and hurried to the laundry shed.

The pile of towels was still on the floor, flattened slightly from the weight of her body and Raleigh's. She fluffed them up with her foot to make them look more natural. She looked out the window to see her mother going into their house, then she took a tennis ball from the shelf. She planned to stand behind the poinsettia bush outside Raleigh's window and throw the ball against the screen.

Her first throw fell short of the window, and her second, thumping against the wire mesh, was louder than she imagined it would be. The ball bounced into a plot of white azaleas. Its presence there looked miraculous and unreal, like one fully ripened orange in a grove of trees still in blossom. Licha thought of leaving it there and giving up, but she wanted to see Raleigh. As she crossed the front yard to retrieve the ball, she heard the heavy, carved door swing open on its wrought-iron hinges.

73

Raleigh stood on the *porche*, the fingers of his right hand kneading his left bicep, the blue stone in his class ring glinting in the sun. He stepped from the *porche* and walked toward her. His face looked fuller, younger, somehow; he had shaved his sideburns. She remembered her mother's slap. She couldn't make herself meet his eyes.

"What's the matter?"

She still couldn't look at him. "My mother knows," she said. She felt bad and stupid, as though she alone was responsible for what they had done. It was her fault her mother knew. "I'm sorry." She hoped he would tell her it was all right, that he didn't care, that he was glad: now they could be together.

He laughed. "Is that all?"

She looked at him, relieved beyond words.

"It's not like she hasn't done the same thing," he said. "She's been around the block."

She was puzzled. "What?"

He waved his hand, dismissing it. "It was a long time ago." He winked at her. "You know. When we were kids."

Licha never thought of her mother in that way. Her mother was just what she was—aproned, blue-dressed, patting tortillas, sweeping: working. She started to ask him what he meant, but all of a sudden she knew. She remembered when they had first come to live in the little house, her mother—younger, thinner— had sat on the floor with them, showing them how to cut circles of colored paper and twist them into the shapes of bougainvillea, oleander, the blue trumpets of jacaranda, her hair loose and fragrant from the Castile shampoo she kept on the shelf above the sink. Laughing, she had tucked one of Licha's flowers behind her ear, and in the hollow of her throat a small vein pulsed. Licha had reached up to place her fingers on it, moved to joy, to longing at the happy mystery of her mother's beauty. Her mother had scooped her up and hugged her with a strength that surprised her. In the hot still nights after she and Tavo were in bed, her mother would leave the house. Just for a walk, she said, just to cool off. Licha would try to stay awake until she came back in, but the hum of the fan would always put her to sleep. In the morning her mother would be at the sink, running water for coffee, draining the soak water from the beans, and Licha would forget. But it was Papa who brought the fan, Papa with the red mustache that fascinated her, taking off his Panama before he entered the little house, patting the top of her head, "*Qué chula niña.*" Papa who brought the beds.

"Come inside," Raleigh said. "You can see the preparations for Mother's big to-do." From his tone Licha could tell what he thought of Madama's party, but she hesitated.

"She's not here. She's at the club getting a bag on."

She followed him into the house. As they passed through the big hall she caught a glimpse of the *sala* with the grand Spanish windows she had seen only from the outside. At the far end of the room stood an enormous fir, its branches flocked with white, shimmering with gold and silver birds. She thought of the plastic Santas she and her mother would hang on the potted Norfolk pine they brought in from its place among the other plants that rimmed the little house, the red suits nearly pink from sun and age, the white of the beards and fur trim gone yellow.

"She's got it all decked out," he said, starting up the stairs to the *galería*. Licha followed him. She nodded though she knew he couldn't see her. When they were inside his bedroom he locked the door and took a mirror from the wall. He propped it on the floor against the bed. He fingered one of her earrings. "Beautiful," he said.

She pushed his hand away, but then stood still, her arms lifted as he pulled her blouse over her head. He kissed her, unhooking her bra. She felt her nipples draw and tighten. "My mother isn't what you think," she said. The words surprised her; she felt her knees weaken, almost buckle.

He eased himself down and took her nipple in his mouth, but she drew it back. "She speaks English. She only pretends she doesn't so your mother will look like a fool." She felt the beating of her heart, shuddering and rapid, almost hot, astonishing as sudden anger.

He laughed, nuzzling her, pulling at the elastic of her skirt. "I know," he said. "It's been a joke for years. I used to spy on Mother's bridge club just to hear her do the Camarena imitation."

Licha stared at him as he unbuckled his belt and stepped out of his jeans. "Lie down, *chula.*" His hands on her shoulders, he pressed her down with him until they were kneeling beside the mirror. She looked at him, at the dark triangle of pubic escutcheon against his pale skin, at his penis rising, then to the mirror where she saw the flexion at the side of his buttock where the gluteus inserted, where she saw herself, smaller, a fool looking up at him, a fool somehow more beautifully made, browner, smoother, more round. She tried to meet his eyes, fixed on his own, but couldn't, and she had the feeling each of them was seeing something different in the framed rectangle, like two people looking at the same slide under a microscope, trying to adjust the focus to accommodate both their visions, failing. She removed his hands from her shoulders and stood up, gathering her clothes. "I have to go," she said.

She walked out into the early dark of December. Light shone from the little house, and as she got closer she saw her mother's form moving back and forth against it. Licha knew she would be eating her supper, standing over the *olla* eating beans rolled into a flour tortilla, alternating beans with bites of pepper, waiting to go back to work. She looked up when Licha entered, but didn't meet her eyes.

"Café," she said, gesturing toward the pot on the stove. Licha saw that the light came from behind the pot, from a small bulb under the hood of the stove that cast the shadows of the *olla* and the coffee pot onto the floor. She sat down at the table. Her mother took cups from their hooks, poured them full and placed them on the table. She sat down across from Licha, and Licha looked at her, at the crease from her nap across the smooth brown of her cheek, her hair freshly brushed and fastened back, in her eyes the sleepy distance of the saints, the prophets. Her mother lifted the lid of the sugar bowl. "*¿Azúcar?*"

Licha nodded. Her mother spooned the sugar into their cups. They were small things—not objecting to her Spanish, letting her mother serve her—but Licha could tell they pleased her. The low song began in her throat, obscuring for a while the faint metallic buzz of the stove light rattling under its enameled hood. Then it trailed away. They sat for a long time at the table, speechless, beyond apology. Even the presence of a small green anole emerging from behind the stove to skitter across the top and bask briefly in the harsh white glare, the ruby throat it expanded when threatened now a flaccid sac, was not enough to disturb the silence between them. When her mother scraped her chair back on the linoleum and left for work Licha sat for a long time afterward, drained and still, stunned by the complex living heart of grace.

SAME OLD BIG MAGIC

by PATRICIA HENLEY

He kept the maps. They'd had a cardboard Kahlúa box of maps, forest service maps, topo maps, road maps, some of them from the early sixties when his parents had taken him and his brothers on road trips in the summers. She had to admit they were mostly his maps, though she'd grown to love them, their gift of anticipation, their memory of blind stabs at settling down, of wilderness euphoria. After thirteen years the Kahlúa box was soft as dish towels along the corners.

"That's my favorite boulder in the Cascades," she told her sister. They were both on the wagon, drinking cranberry tea and talking early marriages. "We camped under it in February one year and walked up into the mountains and hugged trees." Her sister said, "You were stoned, right?" "Yeah," she said, smiling and shaking her head yes and flipping the photo album page. "And we lived to tell the tale."

Hitchhiking can make you hate one another—or forge a link between you that can't be broken. They had taken two major trips by thumb: one from Oregon to Arizona in the middle of winter and one from Lumby, British Columbia, to Seattle, also in the winter. During these trips, life went on. They made love in the A-frame North Face mountain tent; she complained about how cramped she was on top. She sometimes cried at night, missing her sisters. They fed fragile, hopeful camp fires, drinking brandy and talking, weaving the toughest cloth of their fears and desires, finding out what they believed in. They fought over

78

whether to eat in a restaurant or cook over a camp fire. They never had any money to speak of, but there was a stamina to their love. They prided themselves on having endured. Seventeen below; Nevada; camping in an arroyo among cages of snowy sagebrush. That's love of a different color, her girlfriends said. Hardcore. They did it to see Monument Valley in the winter, rime like crystal sugar everywhere. They did it because they thought they were both born to the road.

Once they had a cabin with a big black Monarch cookstove. This was in the beginning. Lightning pinwheeled into their bedroom and he leaped from the bed and found a book of poems and read her a poem in the storm. They carried water from the creek and shared a zinc tub of steaming bathwater. She scrubbed his back with a loofah. They made love in the parsnip patch in broad daylight. At night there were always the stars and he knew them by name. At a garage sale, they bought a cast-iron skillet and an Oriental rug. From secondhand hardbacks, they read short stories aloud to one another. There were always pileated woodpeckers, red whips of willows, evening sunlight only a gold band above the mountain; there were always animal tracks, lichened stones, creeks, applewood, fir, wild plums; there were always, always, the stars, and his arm around her as he named them: *Orion, Cygnus, Sirius.* He smelled like Balkan Sobranie tobacco and wool Woolrich shirts, and his arms were archetypal arms, arms of the woodsman who'd saved her from the wolf within.

The day they moved away from the cabin they stood on the porch and cried in one another's arms. That was the first loss they'd ever shared, shocked at its sweetness.

In town, the first town, the elementary school blazed white as sand in the winter sun. He was a student at the college and she taught at the elementary school. Kites tattered from the cottonwoods beside the playground. Their wantonness required practice. "Talk to me," she said. "You have to have a bit of the ham, the rake, in you to do this. Coax me. Be sly. You know how easy I am." Beyond the shutters an evening snowstorm muffled streets; all the cars had forgotten how to travel; they moved as though forced awry by enchantment, into berms and woodpiles. "The words," she said, "can be about how much you know I'll like it." "How does it feel for you to come?" he said. "It's like stealing something." "Stealing home," he said. She was a marauder, slip of a woman in the flying night, stealing whatever she could, fingers tender and blind, grafting bliss to truancy, crazed absence of self. It was something like an old blues song: that bad, winsome, visceral. She knew how it worked. They found them— the very words—and they became his charm and code, his mojo, sweetbone totem, the rib and thorn in their fenny winter bed.

They each had private dreams and these were difficult to realize together. The first time she talked about moving away, she cried into a brakeman's bandana until her eyes were puffy. Finally he said, "Maybe it's a good idea. Maybe I need to be on my own too." She said no. She said she'd figure out some other way to make her dreams come true. That was in the second year and they had eleven more years to go.

For a long time they took turns moving for one another; the one who followed always felt cheated.

Even now, when she peruses certain maps, she imagines all the places they slept outdoors together. Beside rivers, with that rushing, that glassy green blooming of the waves: Clark Fork, Gallatin, Yellowstone, Lochsa, Columbia, Methow, Okanogan, Entiat, Wenatchee, Skagit, Rogue, Klamath, Williamson, Santiam, Umpqua, Bella Coola, Fraser, Thompson, Quesnel, Chilcotin. Too numerous to mention were the creeks and lakes. And the mountains they ranged: the Cascades, the Rainbows, the Monashees, the Purcells, the Selkirks, the Tobacco Roots, the Big Belts. Field mice; blackened pots; woodsmoked sleeping bags zipping together; their breath visible in the mornings; aspens shimmering; cutthroat winds. They were caught in the bite of the mother's moon tooth.

At shi-shi beach near Neah Bay, they slept together outdoors for the last time. To the Indians, *shi-shi* meant "big magic." The unrestrained Pacific dumped rain on them four days running. Deer cavorted in the surf. They visited a man in a nearby cabin and drank mescal and traded life stories and waited out the weather. He was drunk enough to eat the worm. She has a crescent-shaped scar—petite petroglyph—on the back of her right hand, from falling into a rocky swollen creek on the walk out. She thinks it's a scar that won't fade and that pleases her, to have the mark of *shi-shi*.

Before that particular July, for several years, they practiced moving away from each other. They were getting used to the idea. First there were separate pleasure trips. Then they began going away to work, a month here, two months there, a summer. Finally she took a job in another state, seventeen hundred miles away. They thought they could manage; they were good at reunions.

They broke the rules like pottery, with that little regret. Their letters of breakup crossed in the mail, one of many blessings that befell them over the years. When next they met—after the divorce was final—they were rife with happy grief, a blessing in itself they realized. He lived in a small wooden house beside a gang of McIntosh trees. The apples were nearly ripe. The whole tiny house smelled of fresh pocket bread; he baked bread so often that the muslin curtains gave off the odor of yeast and sugar. They cried, made love, slept. They had left an open bottle of Polish vodka on the kitchen table. Once, in the middle of the night, she went out to the screened-in porch. An inverted yellow kayak glowed under the clothesline. She couldn't deny feeling free, a kind of joy in the soles of her feet. The night had grown frost on the dull grass; smudge pots tilted under the trees. Stars stirred above them like fading fires, trying to focus through mottled clouds. This is how she thought of the stars: blurry, a little drunk, still there.

AN EMBARRASSMENT OF ORDINARY RICHES

by MARTHA BERGLAND

W HEN YOU ARE AWAY, most of what happens to me happens in the supermarket. I like it. I wouldn't like it all the time, but sometimes I love to let myself go to seed, live unwashed, uncombed. I read in the sun on our unmade bed, eavesdrop, go to the Grand Union several times a day. And I eat too much—probably for want of talking and kissing on these long days in this apartment in this brand new suburb. The little tree trunks are still wrapped in tape and the scalp still shows through the grass. We are new here too, so I can't connect one name with one face in this town, except the names and faces of our neighbors—J. G. and C. E. Mazza, according to the mailbox. But when I hear them I never see them, and when I see them they never speak.

My days here when you are on the road selling are usually broken into two parts: (1) sinking, and then (2) hauling myself up out of my petty squalor. The first half of each day is disintegration, self-indulgence, slovenliness; the last half, furious reform, listmaking, housecleaning. In the mornings I go to the supermarket for white cake; in the afternoons, for vegetables. I try not to let myself go later than 3:00 or 4:00. If I disintegrate beyond late afternoon, the downward curving of the day and the weight of the falling light pull me down too far and I am in way over my head. So when the day begins to curl under, I have to act fast. I quickly wash and dress and clean up the place. I go to the supermarket, buy food for a healthful meal, cook the food carefully, set myself a place at the table, and try to eat slowly while I watch the news. Then I wash the dishes, make sure each room is in order, make a list for tomorrow, select some classic to read while I wait for you to call.

Occasionally I wake up organized, in a secular state of grace, but not usually. More often, there is something I go after in silence, indolence, eavesdropping, inaction. There is something I am waiting to hear or feel or come to. But I have never actually found out what it is. I lose my nerve (or maybe it's nerve I find) and I reform myself every day.

I woke up early this summer morning into the bird song and the chilly air with your pillow at my back instead of you. When you go away, this little domestic sea calms, and some other self of mine slowly floats to the surface. Instead of jumping out of bed at the first touch of light, I lie still, wait for more sun, conserve my warmth. I remember your warming me. I slow my breathing and sift carefully through each breath for smells of your hair, your mouth, your skin. I breathe in to see pictures of you—both all of you and parts of you. As the summer sun moves into our sparsely furnished bedroom, over the white walls, the bureau, the bed, a sweet breeze moves the Sears curtains. Oh love, where will we *be* next year? I *try* to remain calm and light on my feet. I do like traveling light. I calm down. In every city on earth there is a bedroom with a window facing east. I lie still and wait for the sun or the birds or the clock radio to wake the Mazzas.

Because I don't turn on the TV or stereo when you're gone, I hear all the sounds of the Mazzas living next door. When they make love or fight in their bedroom, I eat cake on our bed a yard or so away from them. When they are in their kitchen, I sit on our kitchen counter and listen. The female voice when they argue is low, sometimes inaudible, drones on and on; the male voice is more infrequent and louder and clearer: "I don't know what the fuck you're talking about," "I'm sick of hearing all this shit," and "What kind of a schmuck do you think I am?"—things on that order. Their arguments are dreary, but I love to hear them. Their walls are probably white as ours are. They fight in the same light we do. Their door slams have the same ring to them. In the lulls, she probably stands at the window and stares out at what I see: the parking lot and cars and vans; the little trees; the building just like this one facing us; and, at sunset, the great wide grey and salmon

83

blazes in the sky—nutty to me above the mercury vapor lights' wan green glow, the false mansard roofs, and the electric-green subdivision grass.

This morning as I was waiting for them to wake up, I remembered last Wednesday when you were so frustrated and enraged at the committees and the shitheads who thwart your plans. When you came home, you could no longer hold back your invective and you paced and pointed from the time you walked in the door until supper. Even after supper when you sat down and let me rub your back and shoulders, your arms were still untamed. They jumped and tensed like horses under my palms. So when you finally went to sleep on the couch in my arms, my breathing, too, relaxed as I was released from your battering consciousness. As you slid jerkily into sleep, we began to trade places in the air of the room around us. I expanded up into the room as you receded into the sleeping body that I love so much. I was relieved, but I also missed you, as I miss you now. Waiting this morning for the Mazzas to come to, I was regretting my relief at that small loss of you to sleep.

Our neighbor, J. G. Mazza, is, as we have both remarked, an aristocratic-looking young man. He carries his head as though he alone feels with his face the currents of air we earthlings walk through. His straight and severe bearing, his large, light eyes, his high cheekbones and thin nose, his light hair all seemed to mark him as a WASP prince, but from listening I know he's Italian. We thought him a poet, a musician, a scholar, but, get this, he's an assistant manager in one of those stereo stores in the shopping mall. And I know that he's an angry man with a nasty temper. C. E. Mazza always looks to be in his tow when they walk to their Datsun in the parking lot. She looks like a lot of other women: medium-color hair, average weight for her average height, neither very pretty nor unattractive. Both Mazzas come from large families—his Italian, hers WASP—and neither one can stand the other's. She wanted to live near the family, but, since he's up-and-coming in the stereo-selling business, his career ladder brought them here. She's an unemployed high school music teacher. Her name is Cindy; his is Jerry.

When he goes to work at 9:00 after either hard words or politeness or horseplay or silence at breakfast, she goes back to bed and cries herself back to sleep, I think. I read magazines and novels in bed on the other side of the wall until she wakes up, washes and dresses, does the breakfast dishes. I think of her with fondness living her life parallel to mine—with almost the same views out the windows, in the same light at dusk, on the same carpet—though I am exasperated at her inability to make herself understood, at her ability to choose consistently the wrong metaphors and wrong tone of voice to make a point with him. She feels sorry for herself in this new place without her mother, her sisters, her career, her own money, without a house to take care of, and she doesn't like their friends here who are his friends. She talks out loud to herself. She asks herself questions: "What next? What am I going to do? Why does he have to be like that? What am I going to fix for supper?"

This morning before eight one of the teenagers who works here at Marshridge Acres began mowing the lawn right underneath our—and the Mazzas'—bedroom windows. I felt J. G. hit the floor, felt their window flung open, and probably all the other neighbors heard, too, J. G. above the sound of the mower call the boy down there a Goddamned little cocksucker who didn't even have the brains or the courtesy. . . . His voice—suddenly too loud—trailed off when the lawnmower turned without comment around the corner of the building. J. G. got back in bed.

After a few minutes of silence, I heard C. E. Mazza in a reasonable tone of voice request that he please not talk to the poor kid that way. J. G. then noted in a less reasonable tone that the kid was not a poor kid but a thoughtless putz and why couldn't he start his mowing someplace else. When C. E. observed that somebody would always have to get waked up first and why shouldn't it be them, J. G. requested that she please not use that fucking school teacher tone on *him*. Then there was some more about whether or not it was a fucking issue to be waked up 15 minutes ahead of time and whose fucking fault it was and whether or not they were getting fucked over by the management of this fucking place. After a while of this I heard C. E. get out of her side of the bed and I heard the bathroom door close. When she came out after a flush and a few minutes I could hear very distinctly a sentence which I think she rehearsed in the bathroom: "Jerry, I find your attitude toward the 'working man' very inconsistent." She should have stayed in the bathroom until she got that sentence in better shape.

"What the hell do you know about working man coming from

that big house full of WASP women with table manners? Don't talk to me about working man!"

Now they're slipping into their main argument, the one they've been perfecting for as long as I've been tuning in. And I could hear all the words.

"I wasn't trying to talk about anybody else; I was talking about you. I was making an observation about what I see as an inconsistency in *you*. Please, Jerry, listen to what I *said*." Her voice was wavering; her firm, reasonable tone giving way to something weaker, something guaranteed to lose her the bout. "Jerry," she went on, "I was just trying to . . ."

"I *know* what you were trying to do. I *know*. Don't you think I can tell by now what you are always trying to do to me?"

"I'm not trying to do anything to *you*. It's to us, I mean, *for* us. I'd do anything, say anything to keep us together."

"Really? Then why don't you spend less money on long distance phone calls to your mother to bitch about this place and on dishes to—as you say—make this place seem like a home. It *is* home because we live here and no amount of dishes is going to make it more so."

This caused C. E. to actually raise her voice: "I have *never*, I repeat, *never* bought one fucking dish we didn't need or one fucking dish that wasn't worth more than what I paid for it."

Now J. G. could be reasonable: "Don't you think this discussion of dishes is a bit off the subject? I believe you know what I was getting at."

Then C. E. called J. G. a son of a bitch and a few other things but I couldn't quite hear. Whatever it was made J. G. laugh—an infuriating laugh. Again it was quiet over there.

I think she was standing near the head of the bed, just on the other side of the wall, and I think he was lying on the bed staring at the ceiling. I ran into the kitchen to get a glass to put to the wall so I could hear better. When I came back, they were still in their same places. With the glass I could hear C. E. trying to calm down her breathing.

Then, in a different tone she was trying out, C. E. said, "I want this to work, honey, but I just *hate* it here. I gave up a lot for us."

That last was exactly the very worst thing she could have said. Out of all the possible combinations of words on this earth, she just picked the most inflammatory. J. G. was instantly on his feet. His tone was, as they say in the novels, menacing: "Don't start that fucking list again. Don't remind me again of what you came from down to this. If you know what's good for you, if you start that list one more time, if you begin to mention one item on that list, I will walk out that door and not come back. Do you hear me?"

Haven't they seen the movie? *Everybody* has seen this one at least ten times. This is the one about the pioneer couple in the Klondike or in the Oklahoma oil fields—one of those Godforsaken *raw* places. This is the one where there's money in it for them if they can just stick together. She had chosen to forsake all to support him in his cock-eyed scheme because she *believes* in him; she's left some big house with panelling in St. Louis or a position at a one-room schoolhouse in Ohio. It's all swell at first, but after a while, what with no trees and the dust and all, she gets bitchy and sad and homesick; she wants to bug out. But then the mine caves in and she almost loses him, or the gusher comes in and he is vindicated. So she comes to her senses and chooses all over again for love his choosing money for the both of them. It always works out OK.

Not much more got said. C. E. did not drop the other shoe. J. G. opened and closed the bureau drawers and C. E. cried on the bed. He got dressed and she just cried. Then the front door to the apartment opened and closed. J. G. had gone off to work with the last word but without any breakfast. C. E.'s crying stopped as soon as he was out the door.

But then the door opened again. J. G. came back in the bedroom and I could hear that he stood beside the bed. He had thought of something he wanted to say. C. E. was holding her breath. His voice was cold, cold. He said he changed his mind and that if anyone leaves it will be her since she is the one who hates it here. He pays the rent so if anyone walks out it will be her and she should, once and for all, make up her Goddamned mind. Then she suggested that he should go fuck himself and he left, slamming the door.

I was glad, as I thought of him driving to work, that he was going to a very safe occupation only three miles away. Because in the movies this is when the big accident happens to the man in the plot. But maybe this is the version where his fate arrives in the form of good luck; maybe this is J. G.'s lucky day and he will get promoted to manager in the Tampa, Florida store. In any case, C. E. and J. G. have finally completed a fight they've been working on for more than a year. Not too much mincing of words this time, and no premature apologies, though one could wish for a somewhat fuller expression of feelings and positions. J. G. and C. E. have for the first time pretty good ideas about where the other stands: she wants to leave but loves him and doesn't have the nerve; he can't stand the way she blames him and is not about to go anywhere on account of her. It isn't clear if he loves her or not.

As J. G. was driving to work to meet his fate, C. E. was sobbing on the bed. My ear was pressed to the glass against the wall.

"Oh Jerry, Jerry," she cried, "I love you, you bastard, you prick, you fuck." She cried and cried: "Scumbag. Cocksucker. Jerk. I love you, my Jerry, you shit."

C. E. sobbed on and on. My ear was getting numb. My legs were going to sleep from kneeling on the bed for so long. Finally she got up and blew her nose and went to the bathroom. Then I heard her go to the living room and I think she dialed the phone. This is where she lost me. I can't hear the living room very well. I bet she was calling her mother.

I wonder what you think of all this, of me eavesdropping on their most intimate moments. I venture a guess that you disapprove of my eavesdropping, see it as a feminine weakness. But as long as I know all this stuff, I might as well tell you. Right?

I left C. E. to talk to her mother. I tried to put J. G. and C. E. Mazza out of my mind. I knew that if I hung around here some of the substance of this fight would soak through my thin interest in mainly the form of it. I didn't want to hear apologies or packing or any more crying. When I caught myself beginning to list the fates that could keep you from coming back to me, I dressed fast, grabbed the car keys, and headed for the Grand Union.

I took the longer way, the back road, past the few farm houses, barns, and fields left in this fast-growing "bedroom" community.

I drove slowly with the windows down and the hot air off the asphalt blowing up through the sleeve of my tee shirt. The heat made me contemplative. I drove with one hand like a greaser, a day-dreamer, a teenager. There were plenty of teenagers out this summer morning. I didn't know they got up this early. They were driving or walking or riding bikes everywhere I looked. They're like me, I guess: no place in particular to go, but it's nice to get out

88

of the house. (No, I am not complaining. I have everything I need, though, like most people, not what I've dreamed of. I'm a woman luckier than most. When you are here I have all the kissing and conversation and more that any girl could ask for. And when you're gone, I overhear plenty. What I have is an embarrassment of ordinary riches—you who love me and whom I love, a roof over my head, more than enough to eat, a car that gives me no trouble, a card at a good library, only a little housework to do, and good friends and a loving family—though they are far away.)

Teenaged girls—in twos and threes—walked on the shoulder in the shade of a long row of old maple trees (planted by some long-dead farmer who crosses nobody's mind when they cross his field). They stepped over the beer cans thrown out of cars last night by the boys their pants are hot for. They were heading for the shopping mall. This morning all these undersized females washed their hair and blew it dry. They dressed carefully in tube tops, fake gym shorts, high heels. They have clear skin, small hips, brown legs. They wear pink and blue like babies. Their little bottoms stick out of their tight shorts. They look like baby hookers.

I drove slowly past the teenaged virgins proceeding under the arch of the double line of maples, but even going this long way I still got to the Grand Union before they opened the doors and before I'd thought of a good reason to be there. There was a small clump of people waiting to be let into the Grand Union—serious shoppers with lists and with coupons to redeem, with places to go after this, with reasons and purposes up the ass. In a few minutes, though, the manager (his photo is above the Service Desk) opened the doors and we shoppers fanned out into the aisles, pushing carts with cold handles.

A lot more goes on in the supermarket than you might imagine, though what happens there is surely insignificant in the scheme of things, under the steel and salmon evening sky. I often overhear women speak in anger or in wonder to no one in particular: "So this is the way it's going to be" to the can of beans up nine cents from last week; "Those cocksuckers" the ladies say across the little babies sagging in the carts; "Heads will roll" murmurs a lady in a 200-dollar dress. And, amidst all this wonderful American illusion of choice and plenty, there is always the confusion of comparing apples and oranges, two-ply and one-ply, pitted and unpitted, boneless and boned. Under the Muzak and the green-white light

89

we ladies try to imagine or organize or dream up or just want one more week with its meals. We choose over and over in the aisles—between our time and our money, or between our time and his money. Out of the chaos of plenty offered we try to select what could be significant, what could keep body and soul together and we choose whether to feed body or to feed soul. But the hardest choice of all is who do we feed and who do we choose for.

There in the supermarket, my love, couples and women and children and sometimes men trail like comets' tails the charged electric air of domestic situations, of wanting something they haven't got, of turning what they do have into enough. I am thankful that in all this confusion I don't have to compose my face in case I meet someone who knows me. Because anyone could read on my face that I am trying to read in the writing on the shelves if it is better to get a job or better to make straight the path through the shag, smooth the troubled brow, cook the good food. I try to read there if our strain is financial or neurotic or cultural or just plain cussedness. Should I look harder for work, even though I know we'll be here less than a year? Should I go back to school and become an unemployed something else? Should I introduce myself to my neighbors who do not introduce themselves to me? The practice of which virtues is appropriate in this place? And who should I do them on? My primary virtues are virtues of omission: I don't drink or take drugs; I don't make many long distance calls to my family or friends; I don't shop a lot or buy much or charge things or cost you very much money. I try to keep my bitter tongue in my mouth, though as soon as you come back—even though our voices are sweet when we speak long distance once a day—that mean tongue is the one I will use on you. My main virtues are practiced in bed. There among the cabbages, I wanted you back here, my love, so I could practice and practice on you.

Should I ask you what to do? Should you tell me?

I bought plain yogurt, an artichoke, scallions, Sara Lee pound cake, mushrooms, and the *Times*. As the checker picked up my artichoke she asked, "What do you do with one of them once it's on your plate?" So I told her how to take the leaves off and dip them in butter and how to draw the leaves between your teeth and how to take out the choke, and I told her how to eat the best parts, the hearts and the bottoms. "I guess I wouldn't have much use for one of them after all," she allowed.

90

I drove back here through the heat and put the groceries away. I closed up the windows and turned on the air conditioner to shut out any sounds of the Mazzas, to clear the air of the smells of the former tenant that this heat and humidity were drawing up out of the shag.

I decided to go for a walk. Though we have lived here for several months, I had only driven around the subdivision. I needed to make myself more at home, take a look around and see where it is really that we live.

Do you know that farmhouse right in the center of all these apartment buildings? I decided to walk over there. All of Marshridge Acres must have been at one time farmland, though not good farmland. Whoever owned that house must have owned this land.

I walked across grass and on asphalt. They made no provision here for people afoot, except around the pool and to and from the tennis courts. I breathed slow in the heat. The air conditioners made a terrific enclosing racket, drowning out nature and TVs and traffic.

When I got close to the farmhouse yard, I saw three workmen there clearing away debris—pieces of aluminum siding and pink bats of insulation, ladders, power tools—and putting all this stuff in a panel truck. The house had been re-sided. The old peeling clapboard had been replaced with wider, bright-white aluminum clapboard. I stood beside the fence to look for a minute when a workman came up to me and said, "She's home. Go in on the back porch and holler." I had intended to just walk around the perimeter of the yard, but I went right into the yard and onto the back porch.

A grandmotherly, cheerful old lady met me on the porch and wasn't at all surprised to see me. She was chewing something. "Come in, come in," she said, "come in, come in, come in." And she sort of shooed me through the kitchen, where I could smell something baking, into the dining room where she had evidently been eating her lunch. "Come in, come in, come in," a little too loud. The lady sat me down at her dining table. Then with one hand on my shoulder she poured me a glass of iced tea. I felt as if I had stepped through a looking glass.

In front of me, the dining table was cluttered with half-empty casserole dishes and with little dishes of leftovers. The nice lady set a clean plate in front of me, and, as she put on it a spoonful or two from each of those dishes, she told me what each of those leftovers was, who had made it, when they'd brought it over, and who all she'd given some to. She walked around the edge of the table dishing out for me, and reciting the history of lasagna, macaroni-and-cheese, applesauce, a green bean casserole, chicken-and-rice, pot roast, Swedish meatballs, and more—all cold. When my plate was full she sat down and picked up her fork, then put it down and looked at me: "Who are you anyway? From one of the insurance companies? One of the aluminum siding people?" Before I could say more than no, she started telling me about how they'd decided to sell the place and move south now that they could afford it since they'd sold all the rest of the farm to the developers. They'd decided—her and Jim—to fix it up and sell it. And Jim, being the shrewd businessman he was, called every one of the aluminum siding outfits in the Yellow Pages, *every one,* and had them come out and make him a written estimate. Even though most would have done business based on a word and a handshake, Jim was a smarter man than that. So he picked the lowest bid and she picked the color—white. And the one he picked was the fastest, too; they came out that same week. "But before they could get out here, Jim passed away. I woke up last Tuesday morning and he was dead. Went in his sleep. Simple as that."

She paused and I started to stand up. I said, "Oh no, I'm so sorry."

She said, "Sit down and eat your lunch." She took a few bites and I just sat there.

At the end of the dining room, centered between two long windows, was a big, white freezer which just then began to hum loudly. I noticed that the other end of the dining-room table was covered with newspapers and that the newspapers were covered with cooling cookies. They must have been what I'd smelled when I came in the door. I couldn't think of anything to say or a way to get out of there.

She said she'd given six dozen cookies to the aluminum men, as she called them. "It's my hobby—making cookies. Here, I'll show you."

She got up and opened the freezer and I could see that it was

92

almost full of plastic containers with adhesive tape labels and she said the containers were all full of cookies. "What kind do you like? I got all kinds."

I said I didn't know.

She said, "Sure you do. Chocolate? Chocolate fudge? Chocolate chip? Peanut butter? Sugar? Sugar with walnuts? Oatmeal plain? Oatmeal with raisins? Macaroons?"

"Macaroons."

"Fine. I'll give you some. How many of you at your place?"

I told her one.

"One dozen then." She picked up her empty plate and carried it out to the kitchen, came back carrying a plastic bag from a shoe store and some more plastic containers. She began putting the fresh cookies into the plastic boxes and labelling them. "Taste one of these" or "Try this" she'd say now and then and I ate the still-warm cookies she handed me. Then she took out a box of frozen macaroons and counted out one dozen and put them in the shoe bag. The warm ones she put in the freezer. Finally she was finished and she handed me the bag: "These'll be thawed before you get home."

I started to cry.

"Now, honey, don't cry. You didn't even know Jim, did you? And besides he was an old man, it was his time, and he died a fairly rich man." She gave me a paper napkin off the sideboard to dry my eyes on and she stood beside me and patted me on the shoulder, though not with the same friendliness as before. She wanted this display over with.

"The kids down in Tucson wanted me to call off the aluminum people, but I said, 'No, Jim wanted this done and he signed on it.' I decided we'd just go ahead with it. So they came the day before yesterday, and, I think out of respect, they've finished up in close to no time at all. They're clearing up now. I've already given them their cookies and paid them in full now that the job's done. They got the full amount right away just like Jim would have done. He was a handsome man right up to his dying day. Come here, honey, I'll show you."

She took me by the elbow and led me into the living room where the shades were drawn. She sat me down on the sofa and sat down beside me. In front of us on a coffee table was a slide projector aimed at a white space over the fireplace where usually hung the large picture of cows grazing in a meadow, now propped against a recliner. She turned on the projector and fiddled with it. I watched the white light above the mantel. When the colors finally came on and when she finally got them focussed, what I saw there was a picture of an old hawk-faced man lying dead in his casket. He had on rouge. He was holding a pearl rosary, surely for the first time. I was paralyzed.

She showed me a whole carousel of pictures taken of Jim's wake, his funeral, and the dinner after. There was slide after slide of Jim in his casket from different angles and the flowers and relatives and the limousines. There was one of her standing next to Jim in his casket: one of her hands rested lightly on the casket; the other held her black purse. She was smiling at the camera. There was one of the casket closed and the flowers piled around in front and in front of the flowers stood two scared little children, like Hansel and Gretel, holding hands. There was a picture of her dining room table laden with food no one had yet dipped into—some of the same casseroles I had just eaten a few bites of. She talked all the way through the slides, adding names and details to those weird friezes. I couldn't listen and I couldn't tear my eyes away, though I wanted to get up and run out of the house.

Finally she turned the projector off and opened the shades and then she looked hard at my face. "You have no cause to take it so hard, you know." This was a reprimand. "Death is just a part of life. Are you one of the aluminum people? From the bank? An insurance company?"

Again I said no, but I found myself saying that I had originally come here to see if she had a room to rent, but now that I saw it was out of the question . . .

"Out of the question? Who says? And who said I had a room to rent? Whatever made you think that in the first place? There's no sign out front and no advertisements anywhere and besides that it never occurred to me to *rent*, just to sell. But since you mention it, it might not be a bad idea, that is, until I do make up my mind who to sell to." She took me by the elbow again, "Come on, I'll show you what I've got and we can talk about it; you can choose."

First she showed me her (and Jim's) bedroom just off the living room, told me she didn't think she could rent me that one, even if it was the biggest one in the house and she could probably get the most for it. And anyway, she said I probably wouldn't want to sleep in a room where a man died last week as I looked pretty suggest-ible. She said it didn't bother her in the least because death was just the end of life, you know. I agreed that it was and said I would never even think of asking her to give up her own bedroom. There was a catch in my voice.

She grabbed my arm hard and shook it: "For heaven's sake! Jim was no prize. As a matter of fact, he was a perfect son of a bitch! I won't say I'm glad he's dead, but, frankly, I won't miss him, though he was a provider, I can say that for him. Why, when we moved here as newlyweds, we had nothing but his idea to have a dairy farm. Nothing. Now look at all this. I can go anywhere I want and get just about anything I could ever want. He was a provider. And a looker. Jim was a looker."

(My love, dead, this Jim looked like a wet hawk. Jim who? I didn't know their last name.)

I said, "What was his name, ma'am."

"Want," she said.

"What?"

"Want. Want. Jim Want. Want's our name."

"Oh."

"I know, it's odd. It used to be something else in some other country, but now it's Want. And has been for some time. W. A. N. T. Want." She was tired of having to explain her name. "What's yours?" she asked me.

"Mazza," I said. "Cynthia Elaine Mazza. M. A. Z. Z. A."

"What kind of name is that?"

"Shortened," I said. "It used to be something else too. In some other place."

Mrs. Want took me upstairs, by the arm, and showed me four bedrooms on the second floor and a funny little attic room on the third. The four bedrooms were crammed full of furniture and boxes of stuff, but the attic room, being too hard to get to, was almost empty. There was blue-flowered paper on the walls and moth-eaten white sheer curtains at the little window. I looked out and saw the aluminum men's van run over several of Mrs. Want's peony bushes, then lay some rubber across the parking lot. Mrs. Want was now telling me how she was going to clear out a lot of the junk downstairs, sell it (she offered to sell me a toaster oven, a mixmaster, a meat grinder), and rent out all these empty rooms for the time being. She was going to advertise, and repaper—if she

95

absolutely had to—and get some other clean single ladies (besides me) in here. There were dollar signs in her eyes. She said, "Of course, when I do sell and move south, the deal's off." She named an outrageous sum for rent and I said I'd let her know.

She took me back downstairs and handed me the bag of macaroons and walked with me into the yard to admire her siding. "Never has to be painted," she said, "This is what they like, these young people. I don't blame them at all. Never have to paint. Never."

I started to leave.

"Where's your car?"

"I walked."

By then I was far enough so that she had to almost yell. "Walked?"

"Walked. Walked. Not far," and I pointed in the direction of Building 32.

I walked very fast away from the sound of her voice, toward our apartment, through the heat and the drowning sound of all the cooling systems. On the way, I threw the venal old grandmother's macaroons into a dumpster, and I thought about how to tell you about her so that we would both think this funny. I prayed to never be relieved to lose you, as Mrs. Want was to lose her Jim. I want no release, only grief.

When I got home to our air-conditioned apartment, I closed the curtains, took a bath, straightened each of the rooms, made the bed, made a list, got myself a peach, and got into bed. I turned on the TV to watch one of the soaps. Right away I went to sleep and, probably set off by the blue-flowered wallpaper in Mrs. Want's attic room, I had a very vivid dream of home.

I dreamed about Christmas when I was a girl in New Hampshire. I dreamed that I was lying in the little cherry bed that I slept in until I went away to college. I dreamed that I was breathing in the cold air of my unheated attic room, dreamed the moonlight shining through the frost on the window, and, outside, shining on the snow all around. I felt with my legs and my arms the cold cotton sheets, the heavy wool spread. I dreamed my parents and aunts and uncles and grandparents downstairs laughing. My sisters were in the next room breathing softly, and the mice—descendants of mice that haunted other generations of my family—were busy in the walls. We had lived on this farm in America for a long time, but

96

in this dream, around the house lay the hills of Bethlehem. Out in the moonlight beside their shadows, shepherds and sheep moved slowly across the snow toward a neighbor's yellow light.

When I woke up, it was very cold in our apartment. "Rockford Files" was on the TV. I had slept for hours.

I got up and turned off the TV and the air conditioner and opened the windows. The sun was setting. I stood shivering beside the living room window watching the orange glow in the west. As the sky darkened, I realized that part of the glow was close, not on the horizon, and was getting brighter. There was a fire and it was here in Marshridge Acres. One of the buildings in the complex was burning. I dressed quickly and grabbed a jacket.

In the hallway, I met the Mazzas—also dressed hurriedly for the fire, their faces flushed and excited. As we three—temporarily hooked together by disaster—made our way across lawns and parking lots, past the tennis courts and buildings just like ours, we kept expecting to see the building just beyond in flames. But the fire was not in one of the apartment buildings. Mrs. Want's house was on fire and was surrounded by fire trucks and hoses and men and equipment.

"Oh no," I found myself saying over and over. "Oh no oh no." I had never seen a house on fire. There were great roiling billows of dark smoke and violent orange tongues of flame from the upper windows and the roof. The noise was awful—the shouts of firemen and the sightseers, the pumps, the motors, water rushing, glass breaking, and, worst of all, the terrible roar that was fire consuming.

Mrs. Want's aluminum siding was holding up very well; it was turning her house into a furnace.

After a length of time that I cannot estimate, the flames died down. The streams of water were shut off, the hoses slackened, all pumps shut down. From the blackened shell columns of smoke or steam rose like beams of light into the still night above. Orange sparks glowed and then went out like fireflies here and there on the blackened walls.

I overheard people now in the crowd talking about Mrs. Want and the recent death of Mr. Want. I saw the manager of Marshridge Acres rushing around acting like the host or the head mourner. No one seemed to know Mrs. Want and no one knew if she was in there or not. The firemen began to pack up their equipment. The ambulance left. The sightseers began to go home. In the morning when the ruins have cooled they will come back and sift through the ashes for Mrs. Want. She might be in there or she might not.

As I walked away, I saw ahead of me C. E. and J. G. Mazza walking slowly with their arms around each other. So they've seen the movie.

When I got back to the apartment the phone was ringing. It was you and all this is why I sounded funny and you see why I couldn't begin to go into it on the phone. I love your voice; it has the same textures as your skin. In it I hear the heft of your body.

I didn't sleep all night. I lay in our bed and waited for the sun to come up on another day you will come home. I stayed in bed and waited for the sun to replace my hard words with the lovely wordlessness of your long legs and back, your blue-eyed glance, your arms that are never still, your smile that teases. I teased myself with imagining what it would be like this time, how you would save my days, especially some very sweet hours.

Even though I know you become to me when you are away all my reasons and my refuge, I also know that your coming back and your going away are twin reliefs. I love my solitude but count the hours until you come home. I love you, not more, but better when you're away; my voice clears. Though I planned carefully what to feed you and what to wear, as I was lying there in the sun this morning, I could not keep away the sureness that when I hear your car in the parking lot, your step on the stair, your key in the lock, what will well up in me will be the same old voice and there I will be—the table set nice, all dressed up, and at my very worst.

When I got up and went to the window, I saw that the ground fog was rising in the low places and that the parking lot and the grass sparkled with silver. As I stood there, the street lights went out and the sun came up warm and ripe over this silent and motionless brand-new place.

Oh my love, my sweet difficult love, what resources, what muscles, what skills, what lobes, what ceremonies, what love play or foreplay, what work, what money—*what* can we use that we are not using to keep us together, to keep us—against such odds—loving and loving each other?

I know this: Under this morning sky which is beautiful and through this air which is thick, I see—and maybe it's a lack in my

98

eyes, you tell me—only the buying and selling of barren land and striving, striving on tennis courts. I have tried in my small ceremonies to change what we have into enough, but I can't. You and I have set out across this weird suburban landscape without any supplies but money and love, air and light. I'm afraid and I want to go back.

CRAZY LIFE

by LOU MATHEWS

CHUEY CALLED ME from the jail. He said it was all a big mistake. I said, Sure Chuey, like always, que no? What is it this time, weed or wine? He said it was something different this time. I said, You mean like reds, angel dust, what? Chuey says, No Dulcie, something worse.

I said, So? Why call me? Why don't you call that Brenda who was so nice to you at the party. He said Dulcie. Listen. It's a lot worse. I got to get a lawyer. Then he like started to cry or something. Not crying—Chuey wouldn't cry—but it was like he had a hard time breathing, like he was scared. I couldn't believe it. I didn't do it, Dulcie, he told me. I didn't do nothing. I was just in the car.

I got scared then. Chuey, I said, Can anybody hear you? He said there was a chota—a cop—around and some dude from the D.A.'s office, but not close. I told him, Shut up Chuey. Just shut up. Don't say nothing to nobody. I'll come down. Chuey said, I don't know if they'll let you see me.

They'll let me, I said, Hang on.

I skipped school, fifth and sixth periods, just gym and home wreck, and hitchhiked up to Highland Park. I been there before, the Highland Park cop shop. Chuey's been busted there three or four times. Nothing bad, just drunk and one time a joint in the car.

This time it looked bad. They had a bunch of reporters there. This T.V. chick was on the steps when I come up, standing in

100

front of the bright lights saying about the police capturing these guys. She kept saying the same words, Drive-by murders. Drive-by murders. There was these two kids, brothers, and one was dead and the other was critical.

I walked up the steps and all these people started yelling. This one guy tells me, You can't come up here while we're shooting. I told him, You don't own the steps. The T.V. lights go out and the chick with the microphone says, Fuck. Then she turns around to me, real sarcastic and says, Thanks a lot honey. I told her, Chinga tu madre, Bitch, I got rights too. My boyfriend's in there. I got more business here than you. She gave me the big eyes and went to complain.

I went on inside, up to the desk and said I'm here to see Chuey Medina. Who? he says and he looks at the list, We got a Jesus Medina. That's Chuey, I tell him.

He looks at me, up and down, this fat Paddy with the typical little cop moustache. What's your name, he says. Dulcie Medina, I tell him. It's not, but if they don't think we're related they won't let me see Chuey. Dulcie? he says, does that mean Sugar? Sweet, I tell him it means sweet.

You related? he says. What the hell, I'm thinking, God can't get me till I get outside. I tell him, I'm his wife.

Well, sweetheart, he says, nobody gets to see Jesus Medina until he's been booked. He says it Jeezus, not Hayzhoos the way it's supposed to be pronounced, like he's making a big point.

He's *been* booked, I say. He called me. They wouldn't have let him call me if he hadn't been booked already. The cop looks real snotty at me but he knows I'm right. Just a minute, he says. He gets on the phone. When he gets off he says, You'll have to wait. You can wait over there.

How long? I say. He gets snotty again, I don't know, sweetheart. They'll call me.

Cops, when they don't know what to do, they know to make you wait. I hung out, smoking, for awhile. Outside on the steps, the lights are on and that same blonde T.V. bitch is holding a microphone up to a guy in a suit; he's banging his briefcase against his knee while he talks. I come out the door as the guy is saying about We have to send a message to gang members that we will no longer tolerate—blah, blah, blah, like that—and then all this stuff about the Community.

101

Hey, I tell him, are you the D.A.? They won't let me see my husband, Chuey Medina. He turns around. The blondie is mouthing at me GO AWAY. I tell the D.A. guy, They won't let him talk to a lawyer. Isn't he entitled to legal representation? Those are the magic words. He grabs me by the arm, Mrs. Medina, he says, let's talk inside. The blondie jerks a thumb across her throat and the lights go out. She looks at me and thinks of something. Keep rolling, she says, and the lights go on again. Mrs. Medina, she says, Mrs. Medina. Could we talk with you a moment? The D.A. still has hold of my arm and he pulls me through the door. She gives him a nasty look and then turns around to the lights again, I can hear her as we're going through the door.

In a dramatic development, she says, here at the Highland Park Police Station, the wife of alleged drive-by murderer Jesús-Chuey-Medina has accused the district attorney's office . . . The D.A. says, Goddammit. I don't hear what she says after that, my legs get like water and he has to help me over to the bench. Chuey didn't kill nobody, I tell him, he wouldn't. He looks at me funny and I remember I'm supposed to already know everything. I straighten up and tell him, Chuey wants a lawyer.

That's simply not a problem, Mrs. Medina, he tells me, an attorney will be provided. I *know* Mr. Medina has been offered an attorney.

No, I say, he wanted a certain one. He told me on the phone, but your chingadera phone is such junk that I couldn't hear the name. I have to talk to him.

He gives me another funny look and goes over to the guy at the desk. Look, he tells the cop, I don't know what's going on here, but I don't want *any* procedural fuckups on this one.

The cop says, Big case huh? and the D.A. tells him, This is the whole enchilada, Charlie. Where are you holding Medina?

Second floor tank.

Okay, he says, We'll use the conference room there. Call ahead. The cop looks at me and tells the D.A., We'll need a matron.

I know what that means. One time before, when I went to see my brother Carlos in jail, they gave me a strip search. It was some ugly shit. They put their fingers everywhere, and I mean

102

everywhere, and the lady who did it, she got off on it. You could tell. My ass was sore for a week. I swore to God then that I'd never let anybody do that to me again.

Bullshit, I yell. No strip search. The D.A. guy whirls around. The cop says, If it's a face to face meeting with a prisoner, the Captain says skin search. That's the way we play it.

The D.A. tells him, I'll take responsibility on this one. We'll do a pat search and I'll be with her every step after that. I'm going to walk this one through. He holds the cop on the arm, We got cameras out there Charlie, he says.

The matron is waiting for me in this little room. Undo your blouse, is the first thing she tells me. I already told them, I say, I ain't going to strip. Just the top two buttons, she says, visual inspection, honey. I have to make sure your bra's not loaded.

I undo the buttons and hold the blouse open. Just some kleenex, I tell her. She checks me out and then pats me down. Then she starts poking in my hair. They always do that. Some pachuca thirty years ago supposedly had a razor blade in her beehive and they're still excited about it. They never do it to any Anglo chicks.

The D.A. guy meets me outside and we walk through the first floor jail. It's like walking through the worst party you ever been to in your life. All these guys checking me out. Putting their hands through the bars and yelling. Ola, Chica. Hey, Chica, over here, they keep saying, and worse stuff. This one dude keeps making these really disgusting kissing noises. Guys can be weird. I give the dude making the kissing sounds the finger and make my walk all sexy on the way out, shaking my ass. They all go wild. Serves them right.

Chuey is in this big cell, all by himself except for one other guy. When I see who that is, I know why Chuey's in trouble. Sleepy Chavez is sitting next to him. I don't know why they call him Sleepy. He's wired most of the time. I think he might have been a red freak once. Sleepy is one vato loco. The craziest I know. Everything bad that happens on 42nd Avenue starts with Sleepy Chavez.

There's this guy that shines shoes outside Jesse's Barber Shop. I thought he was retarded but it turns out he got in a fight with Sleepy in like sixth grade and Sleepy kicked him so hard in the

103

huevos that the guy ain't been right since. And what's really sick is that Sleepy *loves* getting his shoes shined there.

Chuey doesn't look so good. He's got bruises on his cheeks, a cut on his forehead and his hand's bandaged up. He looks like what the 42nd Flats, that's his gang, call resisting arrest. He looks sick too, pale and his eyes are all red. Sleepy sees me first. He's chewing on his fingers, looks up and spits out a fingernail. Sleepy can't leave his fingers alone. When he was little, his sister told me, his mom used to put chili juice on them. He's always poking them in his ears or picking his nose or something. You don't want to be alone with him.

Chuey stands up while the cop is unlocking the door. He just looks at me and his eyes are so sad it makes me feel sick. He looks worse than when his father died or even when the guys from White Fence burned his car and laughed at him. Sleepy Chavez looks at me and chucks his head at Chuey. Watch your mouth, Medina, he says.

They take us in this big room. The cop stands by the door. The D.A. guy sits down at the end of this long table and we go down to the other. Chuey reaches out and touches my face. Dulcie, he says, Mi novia. Chuey only calls me that when he's really drunk or sentimental, he never has asked me to marry him. No touching, the cop says. Keep your hands on the table. I figure Chuey needs cheering up so I slip off my shoe and slide my foot up on the inside of his leg and rub him under the table.

Aye, Chuey, I tell him, all happy, que problemas you have, Chuey. My toes are rubbing a certain place, but Chuey surprises me he doesn't even push back.

Dulcie, he says, They think I was the shooter.

Keep your voice down, I say, What did you tell them? Exactamente.

We didn't say nothing. We got to stick together, like Sleepy says. They haven't got any witnesses.

Chuey, I say, one of those guys is still alive.

He sits up when I tell him that.

It doesn't matter, Chuey says, neither of them saw us. All the cops got is Sleepy's car. They ain't got the gun. Sleepy threw it out when they were chasing us. Chuey, I said, were you driving? he just looks at me for awhile and then he says, yeah. I ask, How come you were driving?

104

He had the shotgun, Chuey said, I had to drive.

I can tell when Chuey's lying, which is most of the time; I think he was telling the truth. Chuey, I said, you're crazy. They'll put you both away. You don't owe Sleepy nothing.

Chuey looks mean at me, his eyes get all skinny. It was my fault we got caught, he says. We should have got away. I hit another car and wrecked Sleepy's Mustang. We tried to hide and the cops found us. I owe Sleepy, so just shut up Dulcie.

It's hopeless to argue with Chuey when he gets like this. Muy macho. You can't talk to him about his friends, even the jerks. He won't believe me over them. Chuey says, I'm gonna need a good lawyer. Get me Nardoni.

Tony Nardoni is this big lawyer all the drug dealers in East L.A. use. Chuey I say, I don't think Nardoni does this kind of stuff. I think he just does the drugs.

Yeah he does, Chuey says, he's a lawyer isn't he? Sometimes Chuey can be just as dumb as his friends; it's not even worth telling him. Now he's all puffed up. You call Nardoni, Chuey says, Tell him I'm a compañero of Flaco Valdez. Tell him we're like this, Chuey holds up two crossed fingers, Tight. Flaco Valdez is like the heavy duty drug dealer in Highland Park and Shaky Town. As usual, Chuey's bullshitting. Flaco never ran with 42nd Flats and he deals mostly smack, so Chuey isn't even one of his customers. It's just that Flaco Valdez is the biggest name that Chuey can think of. O.K., I tell him, I'll call Nardoni. Now what about your mom?

Don't call her, Chuey says, all proud, I don't want her to know about this. Chuey, I say, Chuey you big estupido, she *is* going to hear about this. It's going to be in the papers and on T.V.

O.K., Chuey says, like he's doing me this big favor, You can call her. Tell her they made a big mistake. Right Chuey, I'm thinking. Smart, Chuey. Pretend it didn't happen, like always. That's going to be a fun phone call for me. His mom is going to go crazy.

I know better, but I have to ask. Chuey?, I say. Why did you do such a stupid thing?

They was on our turf!, Chuey says. They challenged us. Like we didn't have any huevos, Chica. We got huevos!

And whose smart idea was it to shoot those boys? As if I didn't know. Chuey just looks at me, he doesn't say nothing.

Chuey, I say, was you high? He looks down at the table, when he looks up again, I can't believe it, his eyes are wet. He sees me looking so he closes them. He just sits there, with his eyes closed, pulling on his little chin beard. God, he's such a pretty dude. Ay, Dulcie, he says. His eyes open and he gives me that smile, the one I have to argue to get, the one I love him for. What can I say?, Chuey tells me, La Vida Loca, no? La Vida Loca.

Right Chuey, I think, La Vida Loca. The Crazy Life. It's the explanation for everything on 42nd Ave.

The D.A. knocks on the table. Time, he says. I look right at him, I got to talk to you. Chuey cuts his eyes at me but I don't care. I never done anything like this, I never gone against him but now I have to. Sleepy Chavez could give a shit if Chuey takes the fall. Chuey doesn't get it, he thinks he's tough. If he goes to a real jail, they'll bend him over. They'll fry those huevos of his that he's always talking about.

I walk over to the D.A. and sit down. I tell him, Sleepy Chavez was the shooter. Chuey was driving and he was stoned. If Chuey testifies what will he get? That D.A. sees me for the first time. The numbers turn over in his eyes like a gas pump.

Mrs. Medina, he says, You are not a lawyer, I cannot plea bargain with you. If you were a lawyer I would probably tell you that your client is guilty and that we can prove it.

You got some witnesses? I tell him. He doesn't say nothing but the numbers start rolling again.

Chuey stands up and yells at me, Dulcie you stupid bitch, just shut up. He's all pale and scared. The cop walks over and sits him down.

I'm going to get him a lawyer, I say. The D.A. tells me, If you get a lawyer, we will talk. I would say better sooner than later— he has this little smile—before a witness shows up.

One other thing, I tell him, if I was you I'd put Chuey in a different cell from Sleepy Chavez.

Chuey won't kiss me goodbye. He pushed me away, all cold. He won't look at me. Out in the hall, he won't look at Sleepy Chavez either. Sleepy checks that out good and then when he sees that the cop is taking Chuey someplace else, he starts banging on the bars and screaming in Spanish. Hombre muerto, he's

106

screaming, Hombre muerto. The D.A. looks at me and asks, What's he saying? Dead man, I tell him, he says dead man.

The D.A. walks me back downstairs to the desk and shakes my hand. Thank you Mrs. Medina, he says.

I tell him, Look, don't call me Mrs. Medina no more. O.K.? They're going to check and find out anyway and it doesn't make any difference. It's not Mrs. Medina, I tell him, It's Dulcie Gomez. I'm only married in my mind.

I got what I wanted, I guess. Chuey's lawyer who was this woman from the Public Defender's office, and Chuey's mom, and me, we all worked on Chuey. We worked on him real good. Chuey testified against Sleepy Chavez. We talked him into it.

The D.A. wouldn't make any deals. The brother that was on the critical list recovered but he never came to court. He hadn't seen nothing and they didn't need him anyway. They done this test that showed Sleepy fired a gun and then they found the gun. Some tow truck driver brought it in. It was under a car he towed away. Sleepy's fingerprints was all over it. The only thing the D.A. said he would do, if Chuey testified, was talk to the judge when it was time for the sentencing. Ms. Bernstein, Chuey's lawyer, said it was probably as good a deal as we could get.

Chuey had to stand trial next to Sleepy. Every day Sleepy blew him kisses and told him he was a pussy and a maricon. Ms. Bernstein never complained about it. She said it might help with the jury.

I was surprised at the judge. I didn't think she would let that stuff go on. Every day Sleepy did something stupid. There was all this yelling and pointing, and she never said nothing. The judge was this black chick about forty. She wore a different wig and different nails every day. She sat there playing with her wooden hammer. It didn't seem like she was listening. If you ask me, she was losing it. She called a recess once when one of her nails broke. Ms. Bernstein was real polite to her. She said this was the best judge we could get because she was known for her light sentences.

Ms. Bernstein didn't even try to prove that Chuey was innocent. All she did was show that he didn't know what he was doing. She said that he was stoned that day and she said that he was easily led. Even Chuey's mom got up and said that Chuey was easily led, from when he was a little boy.

It was weird to watch. They talked about him like he wasn't there. Ms. Bernstein would show that Chuey was a fool and then Sleepy's lawyer would try to show that Chuey wasn't a fool. He couldn't do it. Everybody in that courtroom thought Chuey was a fool by the time they got done. Chuey sat at that table listening and he got smaller and smaller, while Sleepy Chavez kept showing off for all the vatos locos and got bigger and bigger.

The jury said that Sleepy Chavez was guilty but they couldn't make their minds up about Chuey. They didn't think he was innocent but they didn't think he was guilty either. They didn't know what to do. The judge talked to them some more and they came back in ten minutes and said Chuey was guilty but with like mitigating circumstances.

The D.A. did stand up for Chuey when it came to the sentencing. The judge sent Sleepy Chavez to the C.Y.A., the California Youth Authority, until he turned twenty-one, and then after that he had to go to prison. The judge said she wanted to give Sleepy a life sentence but she couldn't because of his age. She gave Chuey probation and time served.

The courtroom went crazy. All the gangs from Shaky Town were there. 42nd Flats, The Avenues and even some from White Fence. They all started booing the judge, who finally bangs her hammer. Sleepy Chavez stands up. He makes a fist over his head and yells, Flats! La Raza Unida, and the crowd goes crazy some more.

I couldn't believe it. Sleepy Chavez standing there with both arms in the air, yelling, Viva!, like he just won something and Chuey sits there with his head down like he was the one going to prison.

I go down to kiss Chuey and Sleepy spits at my feet. Hey, Puta, he tells me, Take your sissy home.

I can't stand it. I tell him, Sleepy, those guys in prison are gonna fuck you in the ass and I'm glad.

Sleepy says, Bullshit. I'll be in the Mexican Mafia before I get out of C.Y.A. I'll tell you who gets fucked in the ass, Puta, your sissy, li'l Chuey. He yells at Chuey, Hey maricon. Hombre muerto. Chuey don't never raise his head.

I talked to the D.A. afterward. I said, You saw those guys. Chuey needs help. He helped you, you should help him. What about those relocation programs? The D.A. could give a shit. He cares for Chuey about as much as Sleepy Chavez. He just packs his briefcase and walks away, shaking hands with everybody. The T.V. is waiting for him outside.

Ms. Bernstein says she'll see what she can do about police protection. I tell her that ain't going to make it. The only thing that will make it is if Chuey gets out of East L.A. She says there's nothing to keep Chuey from moving, as long as he tells his probation officer and keeps his appointments. She doesn't understand, the only way Chuey will move is if they make him. She says they can't do that.

I tried to make him move. I tell him, Chuey, they going to kill you. Sooner or later. He doesn't want to talk about it, all he'll say is, Forget it. Flats is my home.

The night he got out, Chuey came to my sister's house where I was babysitting. I wanted him so bad. After I put the kids to bed we made love. He looked so fine, even pale and too skinny, but it wasn't any good. It wasn't like Chuey at all. He hardly would kiss me. It was like I could have been anyone. After we made it all he wanted to do was drink wine and listen to records. Every time I tried to talk he got mad.

On the street, the first month after the trial, the cops were doing heavy duty patrols. It seemed like there was a black and white on every corner. They sent the word out through the gang counselors that Shaky Town was going to stay cool or heads would get broken. They busted the warlords from the 42nd Flats and The Avenues for like jay-walking or loitering.

None of the 42nd Flats would talk to Chuey. They cruised his house and gave him cold looks but there was too many cops to do anything. Chuey went back to work at Raul's Body Shop. Raul said he didn't care about the gang stuff and Chuey was a good worker, but then things started happening. Chuey was getting drunk and stoned every night and then he started smoking at work too. Plus windows got broken at the body shop, then there were fires in the trash cans and over the weekend someone threw battery acid on a bunch of customers' cars. Raul told Chuey he'd have to let him go. He didn't fire Chuey, he just laid him off so Chuey could collect unemployment.

The night that he got laid off I took him to dinner and a movie, Rocky something, I forget the number. I didn't want him to get down. After the movie I took Chuey to the Notell Motel in Eagle Rock. It cost me all my tips from two weekends. They had adult movies there and a mirror over the water bed.

Chuey got into it a little. He'd been smoking weed at the movie and he was real relaxed. He lasted a long time. It wasn't great for me. I was too worried about what I wanted to ask and also he wasn't really there. Maybe because of the weed, but it was like that time when he first got out of jail. I could have been anyone.

When he was done I turned off the T.V. and laid down next to him with my head on his chest. We had a cigarette. When I put it out, I kissed his ear and whispered, Chuey, let's get out of this place. You got a trade, I said. We could move anyplace. We could get married. We could go to San Francisco or San Diego. We could just live together if you want. I don't care. But we got to get out of here.

Chuey sat up. He pushed me down off his chest. Flats is my home, he said. Chuey, I said, They're going to kill you. He looked at me like I was a long way away and then he nodded and his eyes were just like that D.A.'s. With the numbers. That's right, Chuey said. They're going to kill me. The numbers flamed up in his eyes like a match. You did this to me, bitch.

Chuey, I said, I love you. He said it again, You did this to me, bitch, and after that he wouldn't talk. We didn't even spend the night.

After he got on unemployment, he filled up his day with weed and wine. I seen him walking right on the street with a joint in one hand and a short dog of white port in the other. Chuey's color T.V., he calls it. I had to be in school, I couldn't babysit him. On the street, none of his old friends would talk to him and there was no place he could hang out. Even people who didn't know him didn't like him around. White Fence had put out the word that they were going to do him as a favor to 42nd Flats. No one wanted to be near Chuey in case there was shooting.

When I got out of school every day, I'd go find him. I tried to get him interested in other stuff, like school, so he could get his high school diploma, or a car. I was even going to front him some of the money, but he didn't want it. All he wanted was his weed

110

and his wine. I even set him up for a job with my cousin who's a plumber but Chuey said no, unemployment was enough. He just kept slipping, going down, and I couldn't pull him up. There wasn't nothing I could do.

He started hanging out with the junkies. They were the only ones, except his family and me, that would talk to him. The junkies hang out in this empty lot across from Lupé's Grocery Store. A Korean guy owns the store but he's afraid to change the name. He's afraid of the junkies too. They steal him blind and shoot up in his alley. They got some old chairs and a sofa in the lot and they sit there, even when it rains. It wasn't too long before Chuey started doing reds. If you ask me, reds are the worst pill around. Red freaks are like zombies. They talk all slurred and spill things. The only thing that's good about them is they don't fight too much, like a white freak, and if they do, they don't hurt each other.

It was hard to be around Chuey once he started doing reds. He'd want to kiss me and his mouth was always full of spit and then he'd try to feel me up right in front of other guys. I hated it, even if they were just junkies.

Then I heard he was doing smack. Chuey didn't tell me, his uncle did. They were missing money from the house and a stereo. They found out Chuey had done it and they found his kit. The only thing I'd noticed was that he wasn't drinking so much and he was eating a lot of candy bars.

The weird thing was that once he got to be a junkie, the 42nd Flats stopped hassling him so much. Gangs are funny that way. They treat junkies like they was teachers or welfare workers. They don't respect them. It's like a truce or like they're invisible. I don't know now whether they're going to kill him or not. Maybe they think the smack will do it for them or maybe they're just waiting for the cops to go away or maybe they're saving him for Sleepy Chavez's little brother who gets paroled out of Juvie next month. I don't know. They still come by the junkie lot. We'll be sitting there and a cruiser will pull up with like four or five dudes inside and you'll see the gun on the window. They call him names, Calavera, which is like a skeleton, or they whisper Muerto, hombre muerto. But it's like they're playing with him. The other junkies think it's funny. They started calling him Muerto Medina. Chuey don't care.

111

Sometimes I skip sixth period and come down and sit with him. That's the best time of day. He's shot up and mellow by then. I cut out coming by in the morning 'cause he'd be wired and shaky and if he'd just scored he'd want me to shoot up with him. But by late afternoon he's cool. It's real peaceful there in the lot. The sun is nice. We sit on the sofa and I hold his hand. I like to look at him. He's getting skinny but he's still a pretty dude. Chuey nods and dreams, nods and dreams, and I sit there as long as I can. It's what I can do.

THE COLUMBUS SCHOOL FOR GIRLS

by LIZA WIELAND

"It's the oldest story in America," Mr. Jerman says, "only no one seems to know it. When Christopher Columbus went to ask Queen Isabella to bankroll his voyage to the east, she just laughed at him, and she told him it was about as likely he could make that trip as it was that he could make an egg stand on its end. But that Columbus, he said, okay Isabella, watch closely. And he took out an egg—the one he always carried for state occasions just like this—and tapped it ever so gently on one end, not enough to shatter it, but enough to flatten that end just slightly, and there the egg stood, and Isabella gave Columbus the dough, and the rest is history."

We love this story, and we love the teacher who tells it to us and girls like us, year after year at The Columbus School for Girls. We love the way he stands over the lectern at Chapel, right in front of the red-and-white banner that says *Explore thyself!* below the headmaster's favorite words of wisdom, copied from money, IN GOD WE TRUST. We like to sit left of center and close one eye. Half-blind we see Mr. Jerman's face like a hieroglyph in the midst of wisdom, a blessed interruption, and the words say IN GOD WE RUST.

We don't care much for the other teachers, the ones who tell us to spit out our chewing gum, pull up our knee socks, and button our blouses all the way up, the ones who warn us we'll never amount to anything. We know how they fear us—we're walking danger to them, the way we whoop in the halls, the way we dance in slow circles to no music—but still they dream of having us for their daughters, of taking us home and seeing what, given the proper tools and rules, we might become. We smoke cigarettes in the bathroom. We've been known to carry gin in vanilla bottles and have a swig or two after lunch.

Mr. Jerman, though, we would be his daughters in a heartbeat. We would change our names, we would all become Jermans. We would let his wife, Emily Jerman, be the mother of us all. We see her rarely, at wind-ensemble concerts, at dances, and at field-hockey games, standing on the sidelines behind the opposing team. Tiny thin Emily Jerman, always so cold that we'd like to build a fire right at her feet. Emily Jerman, always wearing one of her husband's sweaters, smiling at us, leaning her thin bones against her husband's arm and talking into his ear in a voice we've never heard but guess must sound like baby birds. We want to be like her, so we steal our fathers' sweaters, our brothers' sweaters, our boyfriends'. We let ourselves grow thin. Emily Jerman and Bryan Jerman—we say their names over and over at night into the darkness of the Upper Five Dormitory where the air is already hazy with girls' breath. We pass his name between the beds—*have you had Bryan Jerman yet?*—like he's something you could catch.

In the morning when we wake up, their names are still hanging over us, and it's still November, always November. November is by far the cruelest month at The Columbus School for Girls. By then nothing is new anymore, not the teachers, not the books, not the rules and the bravest ways to break them. November is Indian summer, and then it's rain. November, Mr. Jerman says, is longing, and we agree. We long for Thanksgiving, but we don't know why, because it will only lead to real winter, killer winter when nothing moves. All month, we long to go back to the days when our school uniforms were new and tight across our hips, when our notebooks were empty, when no one had discovered us yet.

"Girls," Mr. Jerman says in the middle of this cruel November, "I have been thinking about you."

We could say the same thing, especially since he has been reading us Emily Dickinson these past weeks. We have come to think of Emily Dickinson as Emily Jerman and vice versa. We whisper about Emily Jerman's closet full of white dresses and her strange ideas about certain birds and flowers and angleworms. We think this must be what Emily Jerman does all day in the bungalow behind Lower Four Dormitory: she writes hundreds of poems on the backs of school memoranda that Mr. Jerman has folded and torn in quarters, just the right size for one of her poems about yellow daisies beheaded by winter, that white assassin.

"I have been thinking," Mr. Jerman says again, "that we need to do a little more exploring. We have been sitting like bumps on logs reading these poems when we could do so much more."

We look at him, making our smiles bright and trusting the way we think he must like them, letting him lead us on.

"I could take you to Emily Dickinson's house," Mr. Jerman says, and we lean forward over our desks. It feels like he's invited us into his own home. "If you're interested, I can call up there this afternoon. We can take one of the school vans. I'm sure my wife would love to come along too. She's always wanted to go there."

We can imagine. We can imagine Emily Jerman going to the home of her namesake, her other, her true self. We can imagine our own selves being the Jermans' daughters for a whole weekend, far away from The Columbus School for Girls, deep in what we think must be the savage jungle of western Massachusetts.

*

Mr. Jerman has a hard time convincing the headmaster to let us go. We listen to them discuss it late the next afternoon while we're waiting for tardy slips.

"Bryan," the headmaster is saying, "think about it. All of *them*. And just you and Emily. What if something happens? What if one of them goes berserk? Or gets arrested? Or smuggles along contraband?"

"Leo," Mr. Jerman says, "nonsense. The girls will be perfect ladies. It will be good for them to get out, see some more of the world. And Emily will be along to take care of any, you know, girl problems."

"I just don't think so," the headmaster says. "I'm not sure these are girls you can trust."

115

"Rust," we say.

"Of course I can trust them," Mr. Jerman says. "That gin at lunchtime business is all a made-up story. They're chafing at the bit a little, that's all. This trip will be just the thing. I've told their parents to call you about it."

"Oh God, Bryan," the headmaster says.

"Oh God," we say.

"Girls," the headmaster's secretary says, "you know there's none of that on school grounds."

The telephone on the secretary's desk rings in a stifled *brrrr*. We're sure it's our parents—all of them making one huge impossible conference call to tell the headmaster to keep us at this school forever, until we grow old and die. We can't stand it anymore. We forge the signatures on our tardy slips and beat it to smoke cigarettes behind Lower Four. From there we can see the Jermans' bungalow, and we keep smoking until Mr. Jerman comes home. We think his shoulders look awfully slumped, and we notice, too, the way the fiery late-afternoon light seems to have taken all the color out of his face. The front door opens, and Emily Jerman is standing there, a yellow halo surrounding her whole tiny body from head to toe. When she reaches up to touch Mr. Jerman's face, we try to look away but we can't. Our eyes have become hard cold points of darkness fixed on them, on their tenderness, and learning it. Emily and Bryan Jerman go inside their bungalow and the door closes. We watch them move from room to room past the windows until it's so dark we have to feel our way back to Upper Five, crawling on our hands and knees, lighting matches to see what little of the way we know.

At night we dream Emily Jerman has come to stand at our bedside. She is putting small pieces of paper under our pillow— Columbus School for Girls memoranda, torn in quarters. *Lie still*, she commands. *If you move, they will explode.*

The next day is Saturday, when we always have detention, and then Sunday, when we have Chapel. The opening hymn is "A Mighty Fortress Is Our God." Mr. Jerman has told us you can sing most of Emily Dickinson's poems to the tune of "A Mighty Fortress Is Our God," so we try it. The headmaster glares at us, but we stare at the word RUST beside his head, rising like the balloon of talk in a comic strip. We sing to him, enunciating like there's no tomorrow, and he watches our mouths move, trying to

116

discover our blasphemies, the mystery of us. Was there ever one of us he understood, he must be asking himself; was there ever one of us who did not have a black heart and carry a knife in her teeth?

*

"Girls," Mr. Jerman says on Monday morning, "grab your coats and hats, pack your bags. It's all set. We leave Friday afternoon. Friday night in Pennsylvania. Saturday at the Emily Dickinson Homestead."

We're stunned, and then we cheer until Mr. Jerman's eyes move from our faces and out to the middle distance. We turn in our desks to see Emily Jerman standing at the window. She waves to us and moves off across the garden.

"She wanted to get a look at you," Mr. Jerman says, his voice strangling in his throat.

We watch her as she gathers wood for kindling: birch, alder, even green pine. Her arms are full of wood and purple thistles, her red hair falling forward to cover her face and throat.

Oh Emily Jerman! Her name rises, almost to our lips. We burn for her, all day long, wherever she goes—our long hair fallen like hers, in flames.

*

By the time we're ready to leave Friday afternoon, it's getting dark. The Jermans are going to drive three hours apiece to get us as far as Harrisburg, Pennsylvania, where we've got rooms in a motel. We look out the windows and watch the back of Emily Jerman's head. She has said hello to us, but nothing after that. She rides up in front next to her husband, and sometimes their arms touch, his right and her left across the space between the seats. We stare at them when this happens, our eyes glittering and hungry, and we play charades. By the time we get an hour out of town, all we can see is night rising on the soft shoulders of the road and our own faces reflected in the windows. The highway is our own hair streaming behind us, and the moon is our eye. For miles and miles, there haven't been any lights. We're all there is in this world, just us and the Jermans.

117

In Zanesville, we stop for supper. Mr. Jerman drives off the highway and through a web of back streets to a Chinese restaurant—the "Imperious Wok," he calls it, glancing over at his wife, who turns to him and smiles. When we get to the parking lot, the marquee says, "The Imperial Wok," and we laugh, even though we don't get the joke and we don't like them having secrets between themselves, a whole history we can never know. Inside, Mr. Jerman explains the menu and shows us how to use chopsticks. He is amazed that we've never had Chinese food before. He toasts us with his tiny bowl of tea.

When the waiter comes, Emily Jerman orders a cocktail. Mr. Jerman looks at her and raises his blonde eyebrows, but doesn't say anything. We realize this is the first whole sentence we have ever heard Emily Jerman say: *I would like a double vodka on the rocks*. Her voice is surprisingly low and sweet. We have always thought she should have a high voice to go with her tiny frail body, but instead it's a voice like being wrapped in a smoky blanket. We hope she'll keep on talking. Right now we want to be Emily Jerman's daughters more than anything else in the world.

The waiter brings our food, announcing each dish quietly, with a question, like he's trying to remind himself what it is. After each name, Mr. Jerman says "ah" and his wife laughs, a low, thrilling laugh, and we know we're going to have to spend all night in our motel room trying to imitate it exactly. She orders another double vodka.

"Dear," Mr. Jerman says, "who's going to help me drive for the next four hours?"

"We will," we say, reaching into our coat pockets for our driver's licenses. We hand them over to Emily Jerman, who looks at the pictures and then up at us, squinting her eyes to get the true likeness.

"Seventeen," she says, "Damn. I remember that." Then she laughs her low laugh—like a car's engine, we think, finely tuned.

Mr. Jerman hands around the dishes of steaming food. We still don't know what any of it is, but the strange new smells are making us not care. We feel a little drunk now, chasing gobbets of meat and snaking onion around on our plates with these wooden knitting needles. A triangle of something bright red flies from someone's plate and lands in Mr. Jerman's tea bowl, and grains of rice ring our placemats where we've let them fall. We lean our

118

heads back and drip noodles into our mouths, noodles that taste like peanut butter. We lick the plum sauce spoon. We take tiny little sips of tea. We watch Emily Jerman get looped.

"Seventeen. Oh God, do I remember seventeen. It was before you," she says to her husband, leaning against him in that way that makes us stare at them with hard bright eyes. "I was at The Columbus School for Girls, can you imagine? Things were by the book then, no drinking gin at lunch, no blouses open down to here, no overnight trips. The goddamn earth was flat then. That's why it's called The Columbus School for Girls, to show how far you could go in the wrong direction."

"Emily," Mr. Jerman says, exactly the way he says the name in class, like he's a little afraid of it.

"Oh don't Emily me, sweetheart," she says thrillingly, her low laugh like a runaway vehicle. "I'm just giving your girls some true history, that's all."

"What was it like?" we ask.

"The same, really. We read Emily Dickinson, too. Or some of us did, 'A narrow fellow in the grass,' " she says, to prove it.

"What house did you live in?" we want to know.

"Cobalt," she says, naming a dormitory we've never heard of. "But the boiler exploded and it burnt to the ground ten years ago. Nobody likes to talk about it."

We glance over at Mr. Jerman, who seems lost to us, shaking his head.

"A girl nearly died," Emily Jerman says, looking us straight in the eye. "And the gardener did die. They were, you know, in her room. It was a big scandal. Hoo boy."

"Emily," Mr. Jerman says in a way that lets us know everything his wife is saying is true.

"He loved Emily Dickinson," Emily Jerman tells us.

"Who did?" her husband says. But we already know who she means.

"The gardener. He'd been to see her house. He had postcards. He gave me one."

"You never told me that." Bryan Jerman stares at his wife. Already we're miles ahead of him, and we can see it all: the girl who is Emily Jerman grown young, and the gardener there beside us, then the two bodies tangled together, singed, blackened by smoke.

119

"Fortune cookies!" Emily Jerman cries, clapping her hands. "We'll play fortune-cookie charades. It's just like regular charades, only when you get to the part about movie, book, or play, you do this."

She brings the palms of her hands together, pulls them in close to her chest, and bows from the waist. Mr. Jerman is smiling again, looking at his wife like he can't believe how clever she is. The fire, the girl, and the gardener drift from the table, guests taking their leave.

"A bit of mysterious East for you," the waiter says. "Many happy fortunes."

Look below the surface, truth lies within. Unusual experience will enrich your life. Positive attitude will bring desired result. Time is in your favor, be patient. The rare privilege of being pampered will delight you. The fun is just beginning, take it as it comes. Beware of those who stir the waters to suggest they are deep.

Our charades make Emily Jerman laugh until tears come to her eyes and run down her cheeks into her mouth. We watch her taste them and she watches us back, holding our eyes just as long as we hold hers. Then Mr. Jerman tells us it's time to get *on the road again*, singing it like Willie Nelson. Out in the parking lot, he takes his wife's hand and presses it to his heart. Light from the Imperial Wok falls on their coats, turning black to tender purple.

"See?" he says, and together they look east to where the lights of Zanesville die away and there's only stars and West Virginia and Pennsylvania and finally the great darkness of western Massachusetts. We stare at them, our eyes going clean through their bodies. Then we look east too, but we can't for the life of us tell what they're seeing.

Hours later, we wake to hear Emily Jerman singing along with the radio. "And when the birds fly south for a while," she sings, "oh I wish that I could go. Someone there might warm this cold heart, oh someone there might know." Her voice breaks on the last line, and we close our eyes again.

At the Holiday Inn in Harrisburg, the Jermans unload us one by one, right into our rooms, right into bed. We stay awake as long as we can listening to Emily and Bryan Jerman in the next room, imagining we can hear the words and other sounds that pass between them when they're all alone.

In the morning, it's Scranton, New York City, Hartford, and on into Amherst. Emily Jerman looks terrible, her hair hanging loose, her skin the color of old snow, but she drives first and Mr. Jerman takes over after lunch. Then she stares out the window. We think something has happened to her during the night. At first we believe it has to do with love, but soon we see how wrong we are, how lost, and for a split second we wish we'd never left The Columbus School for Girls. We've been moving east with Emily Jerman, weightless, like swimmers, but now she's holding on to our uniform skirts, and she's dragging us under. When we get to the Dickinson Homestead in the middle of the afternoon, the air is so wet with snow that we're having to breathe water, like the nearly drowned.

Emily Jerman hasn't said a word all day, but when we're all out of the van, she tells us she's going to stay put. She's been moving too fast, she says, and now she needs to sit for a while. Mr. Jerman hands her the keys, squeezes her knee, and leads us inside the house. We try to catch a glimpse of her out the window as we're standing beside Emily Dickinson's piano, listening to Mr. Jerman make introductions.

The tour guide tell us she is the wife of an English professor who studies Emily Dickinson, and for a whole year when they were first married, he would talk about her in his sleep. That, she explains, is how she learned most of what she knows about the poet, by listening in on her husband's dreams. She looks straight at Mr. Jerman.

"It's how most husbands and wives come to know anything at all," she says.

He stares back at her out of his great blue unblinking eyes, and for the first time ever, we think he looks bullish and stupid. It unhinges us, and we have to sit down on Emily Dickinson's chintz sofa.

The professor's wife keeps talking. She tells us what belongs to Emily Dickinson and what doesn't. She lets us touch a teacup and hold a pair of wine glasses the color of fresh blood. We feel as though they want to leap out of our hands and smash on the floor. We almost want to throw them down to get it over with— the same way we think about standing up in Chapel and shouting out something terrible. Then we wonder if we haven't already done it. At that moment, the back door opens and Emily Jerman walks into the hall. The professor's wife drops the guest book and its spine breaks. Pages and pages of visitors wash over the floor.

"See Bryan," Emily Jerman says to her husband, "I told you I shouldn't have come." As we pick up the pages of the guest book, she walks over to the piano. She stays there with her back to us for a long time, and we can tell that she is crying. We want Mr. Jerman to do something, but he stays with us, listening to the tour guide wander through all her dreamed facts, and we hate him for that.

Upstairs we see the dress and the bed, the writing table, the window that looks out over Main Street, the basket used to lower gingerbread down to children in the garden. We stick our noses inside like dogs and sniff to see if the smell of gingerbread is still there, and we tell each other that it is. When the guide's back is turned, we touch everything: the bed, the shawl, the hatbox, the dress, even the glass over the poet's soft silhouette.

We watch Emily Jerman move down the hall and into this room like she's walking in a trance. We see her eyes are red and her face is swollen. The professor's wife is talking about incontinence, and then about the Civil War, but we don't know how she got there. We watch Emily Jerman, more whisper than woman's body, a sensation in this house, a hot spirit distant from her husband and from us. We stare at the two of them, and all at once we know we will never remember anything Mr. Jerman has taught us, except this: that the world is a blind knot of electric and unspeakable desires, burning itself to nothing.

*

As we're leaving, the professor's wife makes us promise not to miss the graveyard, and we assure her that we won't. We tell her that we have already dreamed of it, just like her husband, and she tells us to button up our blouses. It's cold out, she says.

"We'll save that for tomorrow," Mr. Jerman says. "It's too dark now."

"Oh no," Emily Jerman tells him, the light beginning to come back into her voice, "it's perfect now, perfect for a graveyard."

122

She takes the keys out of her coat pocket, unlocks the van for the rest of us, and gets in behind the wheel.

"I know the way," she says. "I already looked on the map."

Emily Jerman makes three left turns and we're in West Cemetery where it's pitch dark. Mr. Jerman asks if she knows where the grave is and she nods, but then she drives us once around all the graves anyway. When we come back to the entrance road, she pulls a hard left and drives up on the grass. There in front of the van's lights are three headstones behind a black wrought-iron fence.

Emily Jerman climbs down quickly and opens the van doors from the outside. We're surprised at how strong she is, how determined she is for us to be here. She leads us to the graves, pushing us a little from behind, pointing to the marker in the middle. "Called Back," it says. She shows us all the offerings there—dried flowers, coins, somebody's ballpoint pen with its red barrel looking like a swipe of blood.

" 'Just lost when I was found,' " Emily Jerman says behind us, " 'just felt the world go by, just girt me for the onset with eternity when breath blew black and on the other side I heard recede the disappointed tide.' "

"Saved," Mr. Jerman says. "It's *saved*."

"Just lost when I was fucking *saved* then," his wife calls back. " 'Therefore as one returned I feel odd secrets of the line to tell. Some sailor skirting foreign shores.' "

We've turned around to look for her, for Emily Jerman, but she's standing in between the van's headlights, leaning back and against the grille, so we can't see her, only the smoky mist her breath makes in the cold as she speaks.

"Do another one," we say, but she won't.

"That's my favorite," she says. "It's the only one." She tells us to leave something at the grave. She says it doesn't matter what.

There's nothing in our coat pockets but spare change, wrappers from starlight mints, and our driver's licenses. We don't know what to do. We can feel panic beginning to take fire under our ribs, and we look up first at the evening sky, clear and blue-black, then across the street to the 7-Eleven, where the smell of chili dogs is billowing out the doors. We lean over and take hold of the hems of our Columbus School for Girls skirts. We find the seam and pull sharply upward, and then down, tearing a rough triangle out of the bottom of the cloth. Cold air rushes in at our thighs and between our legs.

"Girls!" Mr. Jerman says, but his voice gets lost in the sound of his wife's laughter.

"What a waste," he says, but we tell him it isn't. At school, sewing is compulsory, and we know that with an extra tuck and the letting out of one pleat at the other seam, our skirts will look exactly the same again.

*

At dinner, Mr. Jerman hardly says a word while his wife orders double vodkas and tells us more about her days at The Columbus School for Girls.

"Those graduation dresses you have now," she says, "they were my idea."

We look at Mr. Jerman, who nods his head.

"I just couldn't stand the thought of black robes, and so I drew up a pattern and took it into the headmaster—who's dead now, by the way, and what a blessing *that* is."

"What did he say?" we ask.

"He said absolutely no, he wasn't going to have a bunch of girls traipsing around in their nighties. He wanted us fully covered. But I went ahead and made one dress and wore it every day. Every day for all of March and most of April. I got detention every day, too, and served them all, and finally he gave in."

We wonder why Emily Jerman would now be passing the rest of her life at a place that had treated her so badly. We think she must love Bryan Jerman beyond reason. We can't imagine that she wants to go back tomorrow, not any more than we do.

"It was a beautiful place then," she says. "The gardens were kept up. Outside was like Eden. The gardener could do anything, bring anything back to life. He was a genius."

"Emily," Mr. Jerman says, "I believe you had a crush on that gardener."

"Darling," she says, "we thought you'd never guess—didn't we, girls?"

His laugh dies to a choking sound as his wife stares at him, breathing hard and smiling like she's just won a race. The silence

124

is terrible, beating between them, but we won't break it. We want to watch and see how it will break itself.

"To the new girls," Emily Jerman says finally, toasting us with her third vodka. We can see how, inside the glass, our own faces look back at us for a split second before they shatter into light and fire and gluey vodka running into Emily Jerman's mouth.

*

We don't know how long we've been asleep when Mr. Jerman comes in to wake us up. It's still dark outside. We have been dreaming but we couldn't say about what. Mr. Jerman stands beside our beds and reaches out to turn on the lamp. When he can't find the switch, he takes a book of matches from his pocket, lights one, and holds it over our heads. We think maybe we have been dreaming about that, a tongue of flame hissing above us, or about everything that is going to happen now.

Mr. Jerman tells us to put on our shoes and socks, our coats over our nightgowns, and then he leads us outside, down to the parking lot where the motel's airport van is waiting. The heat inside is on high, so we can barely hear what passes between Mr. Jerman and the driver, except when he says he couldn't very well leave young girls alone in a motel, now could he?

We know they're taking us back to Amherst, and when we pull into West Cemetery, we know why. There, exactly where Emily Jerman had parked it in the early evening, is our school van, the lights on, shining on the wrought-iron fence and the three headstones behind it. Emily Jerman is standing behind the fence, her right hand curled around one of the thin black posts rising up to shoulder height.

Two West Cemetery guards stand off to her left, motionless, watching, their bodies balanced slightly ahead of their feet and their heads hung down as if they had been running and then had to stop suddenly to keep from going over the edge of the world.

"Girls," Emily Jerman says when she sees us standing with her husband. "Look at you, traipsing around in your nighties. How far do you think you're going to get in this world dressed like that? You have to learn how to keep warm. When I was your age, I learned how. When I was your age, I was on fire. On *fire*, do you understand?"

125

We do. We see the two bodies pressed close, Emily Jerman and the gardener who could bring almost anything back to life. We hear his whispering and smell her hair in flames.

Mist rises in front of the van's headlights. The cemetery ground between us and Mr. Jerman looks like it's burning, but this does not surprise us. It only makes us curious, like the night birds that rise now from the leaves to ask *whose fire? whose fire?* and then drop back to sleep.

We know what will happen next. Mr. Jerman will walk through this fire and it won't consume him. He will move past us toward his wife, and we'll feel his breath as he passes, sweet and dangerously cold. This time, we'll look away when they touch. We won't have to see how they do it, or hear what words they use. We know what we need to know. This is the new world.

OTHER LIVES

by FRANCINE PROSE

CLIMBING UP with a handful of star decals to paste on the bathroom ceiling, Claire sees a suspect-looking shampoo bottle on the cluttered top shelf. When she opens it, the whole room smells like a subway corridor where bums have been pissing for generations. She thinks back a few days to when Miranda and Poppy were playing in here with the door shut. She puts down the stars and yells for the girls with such urgency they come running before she's finished emptying it into the sink.

From the doorway, Poppy and her best friend Miranda look at Claire, then at each other. "Mom," says Poppy. "You threw it *out?*"

Claire wants to ask why they're saving their urine in bottles. But sitting on the edge of the tub has lowered her eye level and she's struck speechless by the beauty of their kneecaps, their long suntanned legs. How strong and shaky and elegant they are! Like newborn giraffes! By now she can't bring herself to ask, so she tells them not to do it again and is left with the rest of the morning to wonder what they had in mind.

She thinks it has something to do with alchemy and with faith, with those moments when children are playing with such pure concentration that anything is possible and the rest of the world drops away and becomes no more real than one of their 3-D Viewmaster slides. She remembers when she was Poppy's age, playing with her own best friend Evelyn. Evelyn's father had been dead several years, but his medical office in a separate wing of their house was untouched, as if office hours might begin any minute. In his chilly consulting room, smelling of carpet dust and furniture

127

polish and more faintly of gauze and sterilizing pans, Claire and Evelyn played their peculiar version of doctor. Claire would come in and from behind the desk Evelyn would give her some imaginary pills. Then Claire would fall down dead and Evelyn would kneel and listen to her heart and say, "I'm sorry, it's too late."

But what Claire remembers best is the framed engraving on Evelyn's father's desk. It was one of those trompe l'oeil pieces you see sometimes in cheap art stores. From one angle, it looked like two Gibson girls at a table sipping ice cream sodas through straws. From another, it looked like a skull. Years later, when Clare learned that Evelyn's father had actually died in jail where he'd been sent for performing illegal abortions, she'd thought what an odd picture to have on an abortionist's desk. But at the time, it had just seemed marvelous. She used to unfocus her eyes and tilt her head so that it flipped back and forth. Skull, ladies. Skull, ladies. Skull.

Dottie's new hairdo, a wide corolla of pale blond curls, makes her look even more like a sunflower—spindly, graceful, rather precariously balanced. At one, when Dottie comes to pick up Miranda, Claire decides not to tell her about the shampoo bottle.

Lately, Dottie's had her mind on higher things. For the past few months, she's been driving down to the New Consciousness Academy in Bennington where she takes courses with titles like "Listening to the Inner Silence" and "Weeds for Your Needs." Claire blames this on one of Dottie's friends, an electrician named Jeanette. Once at a party, Claire overheard Jeanette telling someone how she and her boyfriend practice birth control based on lunar astrology and massive doses of wintergreen tea.

"Coffee?" says Claire tentatively. It's hard to keep track of what substances Dottie's given up. Sometimes, most often in winter when Joey and Raymond are working and the girls are at school, Dottie and Claire get together for lunch. Walking into Dottie's house and smelling woodsmoke and wine and fresh-baked bread, seeing the table set with blue bowls and hothouse anemones and a soup thick with sausage, potatoes, tomatoes put up from the fall, Claire used to feel that she must be living her whole life right. All summer, she's been praying that Dottie won't give up meat.

Now Dottie says, "Have you got any herbal tea?" and Claire

says, "Are you kidding?" "All right, coffee," says Dottie. "Just this once."

As Claire pours the coffee, Dottie fishes around in her enormous parachute-silk purse. Recently, Dottie's been bringing Claire reading material. She'd started off with Krishnamurti, Rajneesh, the songs of Milarepa; Claire tried but she just couldn't, she'd returned them unread. A few weeks back, she'd brought something by Dashiell Hammett about a man named Flitcraft who's walking to lunch one day and a beam falls down from a construction site and just misses him, and he just keeps walking and never goes to his job or back to his wife and family again.

When Claire read that, she wanted to call Dottie up and make her promise not to do something similar. But she didn't. The last time she and Dottie discussed the Academy, Dottie described a technique she'd learned for closing her eyes and pressing on her eyelids just hard enough to see thousands of pinpricks of light. Each one of those dots represents a past life, and if you know how to look, you can see it. In this way, Dottie learned that she'd spent a former life as a footsoldier in Napoleon's army on the killing march to Moscow. That's why she so hates the cold. Somehow Claire hadn't known that Dottie hated the winter, but really, it follows: a half-starved, half-frozen soldier cooking inspired sausage soup three lives later.

"I meant to bring you a book," says Dottie. Then she says, "A crazy thing happened this morning. I was working in front of the house, digging up those irises by the side of the road so I could divide them. I didn't hear anything but I must have had a sense because I turned around and there was this old lady—coiffed, polyestered, dressed for church, it looked like. She told me she'd come over from Montpelier with some friends for a picnic and got separated. Now she was lost and *so* upset.

"I said, Well, okay, I'll drive you back to Montpelier. We got as far as Barre when suddenly her whole story started coming apart and I realized: She hadn't been in Montpelier for twenty years. She was from the Good Shepherd House, that old folks' home up the road from us. I drove her back to the Good Shepherd, what else could I do? The manager thanked me, he was very embarrassed she'd escaped. Then just as I was pulling out, the old lady pointed up at the sky and gave me the most hateful triumphant smile, and I looked up through the windshield and there was this flock of geese heading south." Dottie catches her breath, then says, "You know what? It's August. I'd forgotten."

What Claire can't quite forget is that years ago, the first time she and Joey met Dottie and Raymond, afterwards Joey said, "They don't call her dotty for nothing." It took them both a while to see that what looked at first like dottiness was really an overflow of the same generosity which makes Dottie cook elegant warming meals and drive senile old ladies fifty miles out of her way to Montpelier. On Tuesdays and Thursdays, when Dottie goes down to the Academy, she's a volunteer chauffeur service, picking up class-mates—including Jeanette the electrician—from all over central Vermont. Even Joey's come around to liking her, though Claire's noticed that he's usually someplace else when Dottie's around.

Now he's in the garden, tying up some tomatoes which fell last night in the wind. Finding them this morning—perfect red toma-toes smashed on top of each other—had sent her straight to the bathroom with her handful of star decals. That's the difference between me and Joey, Claire thinks. Thank God there's someone to save what's left of the vines.

Joey doesn't see Claire watching him but Dottie does and starts to flutter, as if she's overstayed. She calls up to Miranda, and just when it begins to seem as if they might not have heard, the girls drag themselves downstairs.

"Why does Miranda have to go?" says Poppy.

"Because it's fifteen miles and Miranda's mom isn't driving fifteen miles back and forth all day," says Claire.

"But I don't want to go," says Miranda.

They stand there, deadlocked, until Poppy says, "I've got an idea. I'll go home with Miranda and tonight her mom and dad can come to dinner and bring us both back and then Miranda can sleep over."

"That's fine with me," says Claire.

"Are you sure?" says Dottie.

Claire's sure. As Dottie leans down to kiss her good-bye, Claire thinks once more of sunflowers, specifically of the ones she and Joey and Poppy plant every summer on a steep slope so you can stand underneath and look up and the sunflowers look forty feet tall.

Washing his hands at the sink, Joey says, "One day she's going to show up in saffron robes with a begging bowl and her hair shaved down to one skanky topknot and then what?"

Claire thinks: Well, then we'll cook up some gluey brown rice and put a big glob in Dottie's bowl. But this sounds like something they'd say at the New Consciousness Academy, some dreadful homily about adaptation and making do. All she can think of is, "I cried because I had no shoes until I met a man who had no feet," and that's not it.

One night, not long after Dottie started attending the Academy, they were all sitting outside and Dottie looked up and said, "Sometimes I feel as if my whole life is that last minute of the planetarium show when they start showing off—that is, showing off what their projector can do—and the moon and planets and stars and even those distant galaxies begin spinning like crazy while they tell you the coming attractions and what time the next show begins. I just want to find someplace where it's not rushing past me so fast. Or where, if it is, I don't care."

"I hope you find it," Joey said. "I really do." Later that night, he told Claire that he knew what Dottie meant. "Still," he said, "it was creepy. The whole conversation was like talking to someone who still thinks *El Topo* is the greatest movie ever made."

Joey had gone through his own spiritual phase: acid, Castenada, long Sunday afternoons in front of the tonkas in the Staten Island Tibetan museum. All this was before he met Claire. He feels that his having grown out of it fifteen years ago gives him the right to criticize. Though actually, he's not mocking Dottie so much as protecting her husband Raymond, his best friend. Remote as the possibility seems, no one wants Dottie to follow in Flitcraft's footsteps.

Now Claire says, "I don't think she'd get her hair permed if she was planning to shave it." Then she steels herself, and in the tone of someone expecting bad news asks if any tomatoes are left. Joey says, "We'll be up to our *ears* in tomatoes," and Claire thinks: He'd say that no matter what.

One thing she loves about Joey is his optimism. If he's ever discontent, she doesn't know it. Once he'd wanted to be on stage, then he'd worked for a while as a landscaper, now he's a junior-high science teacher—a job which he says requires the combined talents of an actor and a gardener. His real passion is for the names of things: trees, animals, stars. But he's not one of those people who use such knowledge to make you feel small. It's why he's a popular teacher and why Poppy so loves to take walks with him, naming the wildflowers in the fields. Claire knows how rare it is for children to want to learn anything from their parents.

When Claire met Joey, she'd just moved up to Vermont with a semi-alcoholic independently wealthy photographer named Dell. Dell hired Joey to clear a half-acre around their cabin so they could have a garden and lawn. Upstairs there's a photo Dell took of them at the time and later sent as a wedding present to prove there were no hard feelings. It shows Claire and Joey leaning against Joey's rented backhoe; an up-rooted acacia tree is spilling out of the bucket. Joey and Claire look cocky and hard in the face, like teen-age killers, Charlie Starkweather and his girl. Claire can hardly remember Dell's face. He always had something in front of it—a can of beer, a camera. If he had only put it down and looked, he'd have seen what was going on. Anyone would have. In the photo, it's early spring, the woods are full of musical names: trillium, marsh marigold, jack in the pulpit.

On the day they learned Claire was pregnant and went straight from the doctor's to the marriage license bureau in Burlington, Joey pulled off the road on the way home and took Claire's face in his hands and told her which animals mated for life. Whooping cranes, snow geese, macaws, she's forgotten the rest. Now they no longer talk this way, or maybe it goes without saying. Claire's stopped imagining other lives; if she could, she'd live this one forever. Though she knows it's supposed to be dangerous to get too comfortable, she feels it would take a catastrophe to tear the weave of their daily routine. They've weathered arguments, and those treacherous, tense, dull periods when they sneak past each other as if they're in constant danger of sneezing in each other's faces. Claire knows to hold on and wait for the day when what interests her most is what Joey will have to say about it.

Some things get better. Claire used to hate thinking about the lovers they'd had before; now all that seems as indistinct as Dell's face. Though they've had eight years to get used to the fact of Poppy's existence, they're still susceptible to attacks of amazement that they've created a new human being. And often when they're doing something together—cooking, gardening, making love—

132

Claire comes as close as she ever has to those moments of pure alchemy, that communion Poppy and Miranda must share if they're storing their pee in bottles.

Soon they'll get up and mix some marinade for the chickens they'll grill outside later for Dottie and Raymond. But now Joey pours himself some coffee and they sit at the table, not talking. It is precisely the silence they used to dream of when Poppy was little and just having her around was like always having the bath water running or something about to boil over on the stove.

First the back doors fly open and the girls jump out of the car and run up to Poppy's room. Then Dottie gets out, then Raymond. From the beginning, Raymond's reminded Claire of the tin woodsman in *The Wizard of Oz*, and often he'll stop in the middle of things as if waiting for someone to come along with the oil can. He goes around to the trunk and takes out a tripod and something wrapped in a blanket which looks at first like a rifle and turns out to be a telescope.

"Guess what!" When Raymond shouts like that, you can see how snaggletoothed he is. "There's a meteor shower tonight. The largest concentration of shooting stars all year."

The telescope is one of the toys Raymond's bought since his paintings started selling. Raymond's success surprises them all, including Raymond. His last two shows were large paintings of ordinary garden vegetables with skinny legs and big feet in rather stereotypical dance situations. It still surprises Claire that the New York art world would open its heart—would have a heart to open— to work bordering on the cartoonish and sentimental. But there's something undeniably mysterious and moving about those black daikon radishes doing the tango, those little cauliflowers in pink tutus on points before an audience of sleek and rather parental-looking green peppers. And there's no arguing with Raymond's draftmanship or the luminosity of his color; it's as if Memling lived through the sixties and took too many drugs. What's less surprising is that there are so many rich people who for one reason or another want to eat breakfast beneath a painting of the dancing vegetables.

Claire has a crush on Raymond; at least that's what she thinks it is. It's not especially intense or very troublesome; it's been going on a long time and she doesn't expect it to change. If anything did change, it would probably disappear. She doesn't want to live with

133

Raymond and now, as always when he hugs her hello, their bones grate; it's not particularly sexual.

She just likes him, that's all. When it's Raymond coming to dinner, she cooks and dresses with a little more care than she otherwise might, and spends the day remembering things to tell him which she promptly forgets. Of course, she's excited when Dottie or anyone is coming over. The difference is: With Dottie, Claire enjoys her food. With Raymond, she often forgets to eat.

Barbecued chicken, tomatoes with basil and mozzarella, pasta with chanterelles Joey's found in the woods—it all goes right by her. Luckily, everyone else is eating, the girls trekking back and forth from the table to the TV. The television noise makes it hard to talk. It's like family dinner, they can just eat. Anyway, conversation's been strained since Dottie started at the Academy. Claire fears that Joey might make some semi-sarcastic remark which will hurt Raymond more than Dottie. Raymond's protective of her; they seem mated for life. It's occurred to them all that Dottie is the original dancing vegetable.

What does get said is that the meteor shower isn't supposed to pick up till around midnight. But they'll set up the telescope earlier so the girls can have a look before they're too tired to see.

Joey and Raymond and the girls go outside while Dottie and Claire put the dishes in the sink. Claire asks if Poppy was any trouble that afternoon and Dottie says, "Oh, no. They played in the bathroom so quiet, I had to keep yelling up to make sure they were breathing. Later they told me they'd been making vanishing cream from that liquidy soap at the bottom of the soap dish. I said, You're eight years old, what do you need with vanishing cream? They said, to vanish. I told them they'd better not use it till they had something to bring them back from wherever they vanished to, and they said, yeah, they'd already thought of that."

"Where did they *hear* about vanishing cream?" says Claire. She feels she ought to tell Dottie—feels disloyal for not telling her—to watch for suspicious-looking shampoo bottles on the upper shelves. But she doesn't. It's almost as if she's saving it for something.

"Speaking of vanishing," says Dottie. She hands Claire the book she'd forgotten that afternoon. It's Calvino's *The Baron in the Trees*. Claire's read it before, and it seems like the right moment to ask, so she says, "Does this mean that you're going to get up from

134

the table one night and climb up in the trees and never come down again?"

Dottie just looks at her. "Me in the trees?" she says. "With *my* allergies?"

They're amazed by how dark it is when they go outside. "I told you," says Dottie. "It's August."

The grass is damp and cool against their ankles as they walk across the lawn to where Miranda and Poppy are taking turns at the telescope. "Daddy," Claire hears Poppy say. "What's that?"

Joey crouches down and looks over her shoulder. Claire wonders what they see. Scorpio? Andromeda? Orion? Joey's told her a thousand times but she can never remember what's in the sky when.

Before Joey can answer, Raymond pulls Poppy away from the telescope and kneels and puts one arm around her and the other around Miranda. "That one?" he says, pointing. "That one's the Bad Baby. And it's lying in the Big Bassinet."

"Where?" cry the girls, and then they say, "Yes, I see!"

"And that one there's the Celestial Dog Dish. And that"—he traces his finger in a wavy circle—"is the Silver Dollar Pancake."

"What's that one?" says Miranda.

"Remember *Superman II*?" Raymond's the one who takes the girls to movies no one else wants to see. "That's what's left of the villains after they get turned to glass and smashed to smithereens."

"Oh, no," say the girls, and hide their faces against Raymond's long legs.

Claire's tensed, as if Raymond's infringed on Joey's right to name things, or worse, is making fun of him. But Joey's laughing, he likes Raymond's names as much as the real ones. Claire steps up to the telescope and aims it at the thin crescent moon, at that landscape of chalk mountains and craters like just-burst bubbles. But all she sees is the same flat white she can see with her naked eye. Something's wrong with the telescope, or with her. The feeling she gets reminds her of waking up knowing the day's already gone wrong but not yet why, of mornings when Poppy's been sick in the night, or last summer when Joey's father was dying.

By now the others have all lain down on the hillside to look for shooting stars. There aren't any, not yet. Claire wonders if Dottie is listening to the inner silence or thinking of past lives, if Raymond

135

is inventing more constellations. She can't imagine what Joey's thinking. She herself can't get her mind off Jeanette the electrician and her boyfriend, drinking penny-royal tea and checking that sliver of moon to see if this is a safe night for love.

On the way in, Joey says, "Lying out there, I remembered this magazine article I haven't thought of in years, about Jean Genet at the '68 Democratic convention in Chicago. The whole time, he kept staring at the dashboard of the car they were driving him around in. And afterwards, when they asked him what he thought of it—the riots, the beatings and so forth—he just shrugged and said, 'What can you expect from a country that would make a car named Galaxy?' "

Over coffee, the conversation degenerates into stories they've told before, tales of how the children tyrannize and abuse them, have kept them prisoner in their own homes for years at a time. The reason they can talk like this is that they all know: The children are the light of their lives. A good part of why they stay here is that Vermont seems like an easy place to raise kids. Even their children have visionary names: Poppy, Miranda. O brave new world!

When Claire first moved here with Dell, she commuted to New York, where she was working as a free-lance costume designer. She likes to tell people that the high point of her career was making a holster and fringed vest and chaps for a chicken to wear on "Hee Haw." Later she got to see it on TV, the chicken panicky and humiliated in its cowboy suit, flapping in circles while Grandpa Jones fired blanks at its feet and yelled, "Dance!" Soon it will be Halloween and Claire will sew Poppy a costume. So far she's been a jar of peanut butter, an anteater with pockets full of velveteen ants, Rapunzel. Last fall Claire made her a caterpillar suit with a back which unzipped and reversed out into butterfly wings. Poppy's already told her that this year she wants to be a New Wave, so all Claire will have to do is rip up a T-shirt and buy tights and wraparound shades and blue spray-on washable hair dye.

Dottie is telling about the girls making vanishing cream when Joey pretends to hear something in the garden and excuses himself and goes out. Dottie says she wants to stay up for the meteor shower but is feeling tired so she'll lie down awhile on the living-room couch.

Claire and Raymond are left alone at the table. It takes them so

136

long to start talking, Claire's glad her crush on Raymond will never be anything more; if they had to spend a day in each other's company, they'd run out of things to say. Still it's exciting. Raymond seems nervous, too.

Finally he asks how her day was, and Claire's surprised to hear herself say, "Pretty awful." She hadn't meant to complain, nor had she thought her day was so awful. Now she thinks maybe it was. "Nothing really," she says. "One little thing after another. Have you ever had days when you pick up a pen and the phone rings and when you get off, you can't find the pen?"

"Me?" says Raymond. "I've had decades like that."

Claire says, "I woke up thinking I'd be nice and cook Poppy some French toast. So I open the egg carton and poke my finger through one of those stuck-on leaky eggs. When I got through cleaning the egg off the refrigerator, the milk turned out to be sour. I figured, Well, I'll make her scrambled eggs with coriander, she likes that. I went out to the garden for coriander and all the tomatoes were lying on the ground. The awful part was that most of them looked fine from on top, you had to turn them over to see they were smashed. You know: first you think it's all right and then it isn't all right."

"I almost never think it's all right," says Raymond. "That's how I take care of that."

"Know how *I* took care of it?" says Claire. "I went crying to Joey. Then I went upstairs and got out these star decals I'd been saving, I thought it would make me feel better. I'd been planning to paste them on the ceiling over the tub so I could take a shower with all the lights out and the stars glowing up above and even in winter it would be like taking a shower outside." Suddenly Claire is embarrassed by this vision of herself naked in the warm steamy blackness under the faint stars. She wonders if Dottie is listening from the other room and is almost glad the next part is about finding the shampoo bottle.

"That's life," says Raymond. "Reach for the stars and wind up with a bottle of piss."

"That's what I thought," says Claire. "But listen." She tells him about calling the girls in and when she says, "Like newborn giraffes," she really does feel awful, as if she's serving her daughter up so Raymond will see her as a complicated person with a daily life rich in similes and astonishing spiritual reverses. Now she understands why she hadn't mentioned the incident to Dottie or Joey. She was saving it for Raymond so it wouldn't be just a story she'd told before. But Raymond's already saying, "I know. Sometimes one second can turn the whole thing around.

"One winter," he says, "Miranda was around two, we were living in Roxbury, freezing to death. We decided it was all or nothing. We sold everything, got rid of the apartment, bought tickets to some dinky Caribbean island where somebody told us you could live on fish and mangoes and coconuts off the trees. I thought, I'll paint shells, sell them to the tourists. But when we got there, it wasn't mango season, the fish weren't running, and the capital city was one giant cinderblock motel. There was a housing shortage, food shortage, an everything shortage.

"So we took a bus across the island, thinking we'd get off at the first tropical paradise, but no place seemed very friendly and by then Miranda was running another fever. We wound up in the second-biggest city, which looked pretty much like a bad neighborhood in L.A. We were supposed to be glad that our hotel room had a balcony facing main street. Dottie put Miranda to bed, then crawled in and pulled the covers over her head and said she wasn't coming out except to fly back to Boston.

"At that moment, we heard a brass band, some drums. By the time I wrestled the balcony shutters open, a parade was coming by. It was the tail end of carnival, I think. The whole island was there, painted and feathered and glittered to the teeth, marching formations of guys in ruffly Carmen Miranda shirts with marimbas, little girls done up like bumblebees with antennae bobbing on their heads. Fever or no fever, we lifted Miranda up to see. And maybe it was what she'd needed all along. Because by the time the last marcher went by, her fever was gone.

"Miranda fell asleep, then Dottie. I went for a walk. On the corner, a guy was selling telescopes. Japanese-made, not like that one out there, but good. They must have been stolen off some boat, they were selling for practically nothing. So I bought one and went down to the beach. The beach was deserted. I stayed there I don't know how long. It was the first time I ever looked through a telescope. It was something."

For the second time that day, Claire's struck speechless. Only this time, what's astonishing is, she's in pain. She feels she's led her whole life wrong. What did she think she was doing? If only

138

she could have been on that beach with Raymond looking through a telescope for the first time, or even at the hotel when he came back. Suddenly her own memories seem two-dimensional, like photographs, like worn-out duplicate baseball cards she'd trade all at once for that one of Raymond's. She tells herself that if she'd married Raymond, she might be like Dottie now, confused and restless and wanting only to believe that somewhere there is a weed for her need. She remembers the end of the Hammett story: After Flitcraft's brush with death, he goes to Seattle and marries a woman exactly like the wife he left on the other side of that beam. There's no guarantee that another life will be better or even different from your own, and Claire knows that. But it doesn't help at all.

There's a silence. Claire can't look at Raymond. At last he says, "If I could paint what I saw through that telescope that night, do you think I'd ever paint another dancing vegetable in my whole fucking life?"

For all Raymond's intensity, it's kind of a funny question, and Claire laughs, mostly from relief that the moment is over. Then she notices that Dottie has come in. Dottie looks a little travel-worn, as if she might actually have crossed the steppes from Moscow to Paris. She seems happy to be back. As it turns out, she's been closer than that. Because what she says is, "Suppose I'd believed that old lady and dropped her off in the middle of Montpelier? What would have happened then?"

Claire wants to say something fast before Raymond starts inventing adventures for a crazy old lady alone in Montpelier. Just then, Joey reappears. Apparently, he's come back in and gone upstairs without their hearing; he's got the girls ready for bed, scrubbed and shiny, dressed in long white cotton nightgowns like slender Edwardian angels. Claire looks at the children and the two sets of parents and thinks a stranger walking in would have trouble telling: Which one paints dancing vegetables? Which one's lived before as a Napoleonic soldier? Which ones have mated for life? She thinks they are like constellations, or like that engraving on Evelyn's father's desk, or like sunflowers seen from below. Depending on how you look, they could be anything.

Then Raymond says, "It's almost midnight," and they all troop outside. On the way out, Raymond hangs back and when Claire catches up with him, he leans down so his lips are grazing her ear

139

and says, "I hope this doesn't turn out to be another Comet Kohoutek."

Outside, Claire loses sight of them, except for the girls, whose white nightgowns glow in the dark like phosphorescent stars. She lays down on the grass. She's thinking about Kohoutek and about that first winter she and Joey lived together. How excited he was at the prospect of seeing a comet, and later, how disappointed! She remembers that the Museum of Natural History set up a dial-in Comet News Hot-line which was supposed to announce new sightings and wound up just giving data about Kohoutek's history and origins. Still Joey kept calling long distance and letting the message run through several times. Mostly he did it when Claire was out of the house, but not always. Now, as Claire tries not to blink, to stretch her field of vision wide enough for even the most peripheral shooting star, she keeps seeing how Joey looked in those days when she'd come home and stamp the snow off her boots and see him—his back to her, his ear to the phone, listening. And now, as always, it's just when she's thinking of something else that she spots it—that ribbon of light streaking by her so fast she can never be sure if she's really seen it or not.

HOUSEWORK

by KRISTINA McGRATH

THE WORLD would come to an end, she thought, and she'd be here handwashing his linen handkerchiefs. She loved the dangerous rush of water, the small white sink near brimful. There were at least ten things left to do before he got home but she stood at the sink and listened, scrubbing the linen thin, taking pleasure in the way light fell through the cloth when she held each handkerchief to the fluorescent. She loved fluorescent light. Fluorescent never lies, she thought, and scrubbed the linen thin.

She loved to feed him. She honestly loved to clean his clothes. And when she picked up what he let fall to the floor, mended his underwear or just plain splurged and bought him new ones, she felt that she healed him, partook in him, and life also. What she touched, he ate, he wore, and was where he sat or crossed space. The peeled peach (he insisted) was so ripe, so intimate, had been touched nearly everywhere, had changed shape even, that it almost embarrassed her to see him eating it with absolute faith. She pictured him, and he sat there, spotless, eating a peach. It was 1948. She was the secret of his magnificence, and the handkerchiefs rose higher with the water.

Not that she ever thought of it that way. It just made her feel good to have everything done for him. He was somebody. And, he could be so appreciative. Not that that was everything, or anything really. The doing was everything and the thanks was just a little something extra. Well, yes, she decided almost guiltily, she like to be thanked, it made it nice. She loved it when he knew exactly who he had married. Three years ago, come June.

141

You're so good for me, we'll give it a whirl, he said, get married and she nearly keeled right over. As if God himself had come down from heaven just to tell her: What you are doing for me is fine. She had said no to marriage more than once or twice. His was her fifth proposal. It seemed that every man and his brother from the North Side of Pittsburgh, who was just a little too nice or too shy or too something, had wanted to marry her; but he was somebody. He did drink just a little too much. But she would make him a life so good, there would be no reason for running from things as they are. The regatta of his handkerchiefs floated in the sink.

Life is either pleasant or my responsibility to make it so, she thought. Another clean Monday. She shut the taps and slapped the sink. 100% linen, she said. He would be home soon.

With the car door slam, the songs began. He loved to make up little stories about his day at The Radiant Oven Company by stringing together various song titles and phrases. After roaring up to the curb, skidding on the cobblestone of Franklin Way, shutting off the motor and the radio songs, he boomed. Right then and there in front of the neighbors. Waving from their porches, they seemed to appreciate it, so she didn't mind enjoying it herself. He climbed the twenty stairs of the rented house at 432 Franklin Way, a narrow alleyway cut from the backs of East End streets near Trenton Avenue and the trolley line. The high house suited him. He waved back at the neighbors from the landing, and the door swung open.

Finding her there with everything dropped perfectly into place, including herself at the door, he'd widen his eyes and grin but keep on singing, and without the loss of one beat, hurl himself onto the sofa in time to The Gal (he sat) From Kalamazoo (he crossed his legs with a flourish). She knew that that was Miss Glenny Hayes, Shoo Shoo Baby, who had been fired, My Darlin, My Darlin, In Tulip Time (it was spring). Then suddenly remembering her, he'd say, Whoops well so how are you? and then they'd laugh. He was the first person in the world who had ever really spoken to her in full sentences.

And so, with an old bent butter knife, she crawled to some far off corner (he would be home soon) and began scraping the floorboards, unimportant, invisible really because of the monstrous furniture, except to her, she knew it was there. Dirt should be taken care of like the first small sign of sadness or flu. Otherwise, catching his eye, it would spread under the feet of their company, gad about

142

like sugar, unfurl into the yards of lazy neighbors, the whole city a shambles before you knew it, if each one in it did not take it on under their own roof. Besides, he noticed everything.

It made him happy to see her doing things and she was happy to be of use while listening to the radio news. The world interested her, but there was that problem with the newspaper a year or yes it was two ago (it was his, he said, snatching it back), so she never touched it again. She's Funny That Way, he sang.

Things made such an impression, she thought, as she scraped behind the china closet, remembering that time as a schoolgirl in that convent she loved so much in the best of times. She had accidentally stepped on a white chrysanthemum in the convent yard. It had fallen from some poor excuse for a bush which Sister What-was-her-name-anyway cared for, every day of her life it seemed she was out there, digging. She like talking to nuns. Well not really talking, just listening to them pass in the halls, mouse mouse mouse and holy holy holy (she counted them), was enough. She was one of the chosen, sent regularly on errands, who got to see nuns actually do things like stir soup or crouch digging by a bush. She felt it under her foot. The old nun scowled and lifted, with thumb and forefinger, as if it were a repulsive thing, the farthest tip of her old brown shoe that was always dancing in a place beyond itself. That, child, the old nun snarled, could have been the heart of Jesus. Even now, eleven years later, she felt mortified. It could have been the old nun's heart itself, with all it had to live for other than that old bush. It could have been her own, or his. She promised to be more careful.

On those quick bird feet on her small feet she tiptoed on a Wednesday through the house when no one was there but her and her girl. She knew she was tiptoeing when the girl started it too. She stopped on the cellar stairs, on her way to the kitchen, and set down her heels. Perhaps she had made a mistake, she thought, he was not the marrying kind. There was one child already; he loved her like the dickens, capable of it. But what were these sudden outbursts, what had she done? Perhaps it was the eggs this morning that made him a stranger. She went to an empty room, shut the door, and gave him time. She had broken the yolks. She had done something. She would sit there at the edge of the bed and find it out.

143

With a confident dash of salt, she seasoned a pot of water. She had the cookbooks memorized like a Shakespeare play. It was a common form of magic, pulling suppers from midair and boiling water on a low budget. Rattling something silver, at her business of which she was fond, of feeding who was hers and scooting them into a design around the table, she built with pots and pans the idyll of her mind and this was daily life: around it with a rag, picking up after it, rowing with the oar of it to the Mother of God, placing it next to itself where it huddled warm and clean in a bunch.

So this was life and this was life. The days were like rows of her bargain shoes that shone in the closet next to his. And here was the sound of the 19th century in a long dress brushing against the cold plaster as she pushed through the closet. And there was the cat on the stairs, climbing toward some higher realm where things would work out. Things would work out because she was in love with the everlasting furniture, with the restfulness of plates stacked in painted cupboards, with the raising of husbands and children all the way down the alley, because she knew she was a part: of something that keeps so many alive. She can please you, knowing the pleasure of safe mason jars and the calm of wooden spoons, the thud of good wood (her mother would have made that sound had she lived). Something sure as a cake could be done, and all of this was great and kind, small hellos to God. She would take care of hers, her corner of it would be a place to live. Cut carrots ran through the water rolling in the pot. The silverware lay ordered in blue shoeboxes with cardboard partitions in the deep drawers with which they were blessed. He had painted flowers and she had painted leaves on the face of the drawers and the cupboards, the two of them conspiring in some small but complicated plot against the larger tides of tornados and gunshots, of derelicts, senators and failed lovers, to be here, to be counted, she said, in this strange world.

Good people, she reminded herself, are recorded in books. Everyone had at least one thing to be recorded. Any sadness you might have is often recorded as a good work. This is the way it is, she said to herself, in love with the beautiful ordeal of packing in the sheets in the small upstairs cupboard, and with the arabesques he sawed into tables and shelves. A good house, she thought, and slapped the sheets. Love, she said, this would sustain, and the feeling went with her into the supermarkets, into the streets, God bless us all. The feeling could go as far as The Radiant Oven Company, into the

144

world, he would carry it there to Penn Avenue. And so she went on with it, this knowledge of where everything absolutely is, all the designs of which she was capable, as she built, to the last detail, the house from the inside.

And he had helped. His heart was to the wheel. He had given her a floor to match her Sunday dress. He painted it yellow with black polka dots, each dot a monument to something they could not understand. He loved doing and doing, yet how he sweat when he did it, sprawled there like a little boy or folded all upon himself, bug-eyed in the corner, goggling his own perfection for days afterward, visiting it like a relative, and they said it couldn't be done. But everything was possible, she thought, what a talent. And told him so. You are a talented man. Everything he did, floor arabesque or drawer, he ran to have her see, and she would say, how lovely, you are a talented man. Tasks like this made him kind, and when he wasn't, well she had enough love to change ten people let alone just one. He showed promise, able to love like that a floor. She had the power. She was in the house.

She had joined history. She was in the house. I love how you touch things, he told her, I know where to find them afterward. He took it personally when she reordered the drawers or dusted the wooden hands of the sofa where he burrowed or sprawled, depending on his mood. It seemed to calm him. But everything needed so much like the banisters. He slid down them just to rile her. Sometimes it seemed he was beyond her like the congressmen and the senators, only a little nearer, when he screamed like that, questioning where she'd been, who had she been with. Everything was converging in their own bedroom, as if they were in an auto accident with history. My husband, right or wrong, she said, wishing there was someone to talk to about birth, about Hollywood and the Attorney General, about Hoover, about hiccups. The child still preferred crying over any other form of human expression. She was expecting again and the house seemed to run under her feet. Mouse mouse mouse, she sang to the child. She would take care of everything. She knew how.

Housework made her dizzy sometimes the way the seasons did when she thought of them too much, how they kept reoccurring like stacks of dirty dishes. She stood at the sink, washing the dishes, feeling at peace with the whiteness of the appliances. Eventually it was her youngest daughter, their last and not yet born, who would replace the seasons and the dishes as an image of time where she saw herself lost, important, found, small, and going on from there in a spin, but now it was the dishes that made her feel eager, indebted, and a part of some great wheel.

Why some of the best things in the world, she thought, happen like housework in circles. Birth and death, for example, not that you could call that best. Funny, but it wasn't anything really, just everything, whole kit and caboodle, one of the few facts (people get born and they die) that was neither good nor bad, though secretly she was convinced: birth was good, death was bad; and she was here and so she swept, on the fifth day, the floor for the fifth time that week. (They hated sugar under their shoes and he was always leaving it there.) And so she swept (the broom was new and bristly) as she said her secret prayer for her father never to die.

Her actions, she felt for a moment, were like those of God. He repeated himself too, heaping snow and flowers, tornados and children down onto earth, taking them away, then heaping it all back down again. God was like one huge housewife, she thought, then blessed herself for the blasphemy. And please, she whispered into the towels, let it be a son.

Anyways, she thought, God was one huge housewife and everything big was patterned after something small, even though they told her it was the other way around. She stuffed the towels into the washer, considering the idea. Neighborhood pride, for example. Why all he had to do was put in one new step, let alone the whole set that he did, and there were new steps all the way down the block, a whole way of life born from a single pair of steps. Enough good alleys like this and you'd have a city. I bring you, she said, this handkerchief, this man; this birdsong, symphony; this washed down wall, this whole shebang. She was brimful with the idea of babies. This woman, she thought, and stopped.

This was silliness and, Skittery, she said, liking the word better than what it meant. The insides of the washing machine twisted back and forth like the shoulders of someone at the scene of an accident. Her daughter made a sound, and suddenly she remembered the head of that lovely African insect she saw in *Life* last night. It resembled the monkey, and the monkey, man; though little girls, she thought, wiping her daughter's chin, resembled nothing and nobody but maybe other women. Your Mummy's a real rum-dum, a real odd bird, she said to her girl, making her laugh.

She was afraid to be such an odd brown bird. This was how she thought of herself when she thought too much. When she was in company, some party he was always dragging her to and then he never wanted to leave, she sat in a corner, seeking out other people (usually other women, and only with her eyes, she didn't want to start up anything like a conversation) who could possibly be odd brown birds. Actually, it wasn't odd at all. Brown birds are very common, she thought, except when you felt like one.

Just last night her husband screamed that there was something wrong with her. She felt (whenever he swore like that) picked up and thrown into herself. It just took a while to get back out again, that's all. Anyways, Tip tip, she said to her girl, taking her hand and climbing from the bottoms of the house and thinking (that's what her daughter called it, the bottoms) there was probably some truth to what he said because she did think too much.

She knew she thought too much when she found herself disagreeing with the Bible. Suddenly she believed in evolution and hoped no one would ever find out. Who was she to disagree? Well, she must be somebody (she laughed and snapped the cellar light) because she did disagree, even with Darwin just a little, even if it was as a little joke. Man, she agreed, descended from the monkey—already her son, not yet born or of any shape much beyond light inside her, scrambled like one and tasted sweet as mud, while her daughter, born, sat there like an unborn, like a piece of silk—and women (she went on) descended from space itself (outer space), resembling more a swirl of air than anything with a nose on it.

She meant no disrespect. Women were strangers, unfamiliar in their babushkas, their get-ups, odd and poking in their heads with apology, waiting on their pins and needles to say hello. They apologized for a lack of salt in things they brought, for unrisen cakes, the rain, a husband's lack of social grace. They apologized for being happy (they were never happy, just a little flushed), sad (they were never sad, only slightly under the weather or a little lightheaded), or there at all. Chafing at the bit, skirting the furniture, or wringing their hands in front of movie houses they waited to be invited in and seated. Even in their own houses they were visitors, choosing wooden chairs. And when something buzzed, thudded, was still, they sprang into place which was nowhere. Wherever they were, it was only temporary (they sat on window ledges, they stood on ladders). And finally, they weren't even sure about being a pedestrian in a public space. She watched from the window their feet brimming over curbs or onto them (they raced on their toes), letting automobiles or businessmen pass. They looked funny through the glass, distorted somehow (and pity-full, she said) like large girls.

Men were such a relief. And she was here, surefooted, taking care of one. She enjoyed it. Being inside the house was a comfort. She felt sorry he couldn't get to be a woman too sometimes. Large spaces made her anxious lately, especially when she thought of how she used to cross them, on horseback no less, at a gallop. Even now it made her giddy. Silenced at the moment of the jump, she soared (or rather the old moment did) inside her body, and from this great height she looked down on it (her body), a stranger with whom she no longer liked to dance. Lately she never got far into conversation or Lake Erie, except a toe. The shell was water enough for her and she'd let him do the talking. She rocked her girl.

He was on this talking jag. All a lot of me me me or about people's rumps, everything flowered with parts of the body. You may as well listen to nothing as to that. He was drinking too much, flirting with anything in a skirt, and what was worse, he spit on people's porches. (Like some large space that would outlive her, he was getting out of hand; then he bought her flowers.) It was just another of his many jokes as they stood there marooned on the porch. Thank God, the nice people (relatives) hadn't answered the door yet. Giving him one of her famous looks (at his feet), she bent down and with her new white handkerchief (the one with her initial stitched on it, she loved her own name) wiped at the bleached porch boards, and with the opening door, rose up and smiled.

Housework, she thought, was an act of forgiveness for what you read in the newspapers. (He no longer minded that she read it; he was always off somewhere she didn't name.) By having supper always on time, whether he showed up or not, she felt she forgave some great evil, or death itself, by the fact she went on with it.

The girl in her lap was laughing now and talking of ponies, ready to play alone again. She always invited her everywhere through the house if she cared to come though lately she did not. The child shook her head to the outstretched hand, preferred not to go into the kitchen (she dropped greens into water, flooded a pot in a rush of metal at the sink), into the cellar (she swept with a sawed off broom the last of black water into the bubbling holes of the floor drain), into the upstairs room (she set out his evening clothes, he appreciated it). The girl was forever plopping herself down and having to jump back up again this time of day, late late afternoon (her mother tempted her along with songs) until she gave it up and sat. Little white ponies, baby ones, she said to her girl, and racing by, tickled her on the stomach with her mouth, then was off again on her toes in the staccato of last minute tasks.

What was mean or ugly was not going to stop her, she swore it, from finding something to look forward to. Her son was born. She could hardly bear to look at him she loved him so much. Real corn, she thought, but that's the way I am. She felt accomplished as she climbed down the cellar stairs with her son in a basket. It was 1949.

She felt so clear and sad about the world when she did laundry. She liked this feeling of melancholy. It made her feel like she was telling the truth. It made her feel large, and above her head (she saw it), her soul seemed to drift like a paper boat out the cellar window into the gray sea of all Pittsburgh.

Cellar light was like a trapped thing and the same in every house. She studied it on walks. Windows half above, half below ground interested her, and the tops of ladies' heads bobbing in an element like water at twilight. It was always twilight in cellars, even in summer, even at noon. Down there the day was always ending like someone good who was dying. It made her want to stop and talk on her walks to the store. She imagined herself kneeling at cellar windows, Hey, and tapping on the glass, Hello, all the way down the block. The ladies would be shocked. What a novelty. Seeing someone there full in the face. Not the usual detachments: sawed off ankles and shoes, the eerie crawl of living hoses and grass overhead, all things plain misunderstood into wonderment or fear, or found there as they truly were, a wonderment, a fear: the earth was there, it was watered, it was soft, though sliced, suspended over your head, a lid; the living ones walked there in their shoes, their feet ran to meet each other. But here, a sudden human face, flesh, eyes. From sheer surprise, the ladies' heads would rise like balloons into daylight, followed shortly after by their bodies, one by one, ascending into Wilkensburg (their skin and dresses would be damp, smelling of soap, storage and earth, the twilight smell of warm leftover water, of green things kept out of light, also the sweetness of their tied back hair) and, bursting into view, bumping into one another, all twenty-three of them at once, they would chat, the women of Franklin Way, East End of Pittsburgh.

149

Dazzling, she thought. And in a rare backward look: I would have been a poet were it not for Sister What-was-her-name. She kissed six of her son's ten perfect fingers in time to the beat of Sister What-was-her-name, six kisses springing from the invisible rhythms of her invisible thought. She should have been a poet, she thought, because she felt aware of things that other people forgot. Not many took pride in what they did. But what she did made her sing, high and slow, this melancholy (as long as it didn't go on about itself more than it had to, she hated anybody brooding) made her feel like she loved her own heart. Always she had this slightest inkling she was somebody.

She held his head for hours and listened. He was so easily upset. Last night President Truman had finally told her that the Russians had set off an atomic explosion and she wished he wouldn't find out. And not about this morning sickness either. He was still upset about that Alger Hiss and his communist spy ring, so they said. Gospel truth, sons a bitches, he said, we'll be on their plates in the end. He sat on the sofa, his legs crossed, flipping his ankle.

Helen Keller was on the radio last night, she said, ironing. He burrowed down into the sofa as if into her voice where he could disappear. Helen Keller listens to the radio, donya know. So how does she do it? Well, it seems she can just feel it. Sound has vibrations, you know, and all she has to do is touch the radio and there it is, the song.

It would be such a joy, she thought, gliding the iron across the deep green of his workshirt, to see Helen Keller actually listening to music. A true and happy Christian, Helen sways lightly by the radio. It was an act of grace to find something lovely. Helen waves a hand to the rhythms of Tuxedo Junction, and with the other listens. In Helen's house, everything has to be just so they said, otherwise, walking across the room would be a terrible danger, from the stairs to her study, a terrible risk. It's like you're in the right church, but which pew do you go into? Was it like stepping through her own mind? she wondered. "Miss Keller rises early and answers all of her own letters." The announcer's voice sounded almost merry.

No one was ungrateful for Helen's sorrow. Everyone seemed to believe in it so, as if Jesus himself lay across her eyes and ears. After all, exactly who would Helen be without her sorrow? To what do you attribute the reasons for your success? asked no one. Our little agonies, your gifts, she answered the same no one and stared at his body, slumped and snoring.

Any day now she would have to tell him about the morning sickness. She was pregnant with their third child. The doctor told her she was in no condition to have two children in two years, what with the miscarriages she had had so far. Her head reeled but the child pulled her to earth with its own slight gravity. She had told her sister months ago. You're thin as a rail, sick as a dog, her sister said, and hit the roof. We will all come out of this better people, she thought, it was a sin to be unhappy.

It was that old public high school feeling. It was a standing joke there, Doncha get it she's Catholic, and the iron shimmied in small tight strokes on the collar of his Richmond Brothers shirt. She stood off in the distance again, it was 1941 in the public schoolyard by a wire fence. She shuffled her feet, burrowing into the dirt her own slight place. She watched the others run shouting across the yard, their sound lost now, but their bodies still twisting with laughter nine years later as if poked with invisible sticks. She stared at the crowd of young men and women. They could all be sent off to war or marriage, packed into houses or trenches, with bad grammar and (she gave them the benefit of the doubt) the tenderness of their pin-cushion hearts. She wished they would all stop having such a good time. It was 1941 by a wire fence in America and she wanted a cookie and rubbed her eye. You're nothing, she thought, without your sorrow. But still it was a sin to be unhappy. For lack of money she had to be sent here and there went peace and quiet, the convent, the singing lessons. (Not that she ever wanted to be a nun, she didn't, she loved horses, children, tennis, men.) That was the only thing she ever pleaded for, those singing lessons, and now, without them, she saw all the little O mouths of the people, empty and soundless, and his, opening and closing. Without your little sorrows, she knew it, you saw nothing beyond your own nose. She made an O in the dirt with the tip of her black shoe. She looked at it and it made her like everyone a little more.

Housework had a rhythm like prayer. During a Hail Mary, God help him, the iron wobbled over the difficult cloth in his work pants, burnishing and polishing at the slightest touch. He hated that. God help him to be happy and nice. Her stomach felt wooden but it made her real. Her legs felt flimsy, as if they were scribbled there in chalk beneath her, somewhere over the flowered carpet. Imag-

151

ine, she thought, something nice. Imagine a tree in full blossom, she thought, a sunrise, a saint at your front door, the begonias on the sill outside your window and you refused to look. You missed out on something brief that would boost you and your husband and your children up forever. The sunrise, to her way of thinking, was a saint. She would have made a good pagan. There would be so many things to adore. I should have been a pagan, she said to herself, a few years later, and began a rosary then for Senator McCarthy to remain silent, to please shut his trap, as she caught her hand in the wringer and screamed.

TELL ME EVERYTHING

by LEONARD MICHAELS

CLAUDE RUE had a wide face with yellow-green eyes and a long aristocratic nose. The mouth was a line, pointed in the center, lifted slightly at the ends, curving in a faint smile, almost cruelly sensual. He dragged his right foot like a stone, and used a cane, digging it into the floor as he walked. His dark blue suit, cut in the French style, arm holes up near the neck, made him look small in the shoulder, and made his head look too big. I liked nothing about the man that I could see.

"What a face," I whispered to Margaret, "Who would take anything he says seriously?"

She said, "Who wouldn't? Gorgeous. Just gorgeous. And the way he dresses. Such style."

After that, I didn't say much. I hadn't really wanted to go to the lecture in the first place.

Every seat in the auditorium was taken long before Rue appeared on stage. People must have come in from San Francisco, Oakland, Marin, and beyond. There were even sad creatures from the Berkeley streets, some loonies among them, in filthy clothes, open sores on their faces like badges. I supposed few in the audience knew that Claude Rue was a professor of Chinese history who taught at the Sorbonne, but everyone knew he'd written *The Mists of Shanghai*, a thousand-page, best-selling novel.

On stage, Rue looked lonely and baffled. Did all these people actually care to hear his lecture on the loss of classical Chinese?

153

He glanced about, as if there had been a mistake and he was searching for his replacement, the star of the show, the real Claude Rue. I approved of his modesty, and I might have enjoyed listening to him. But then, as if seized by an irrational impulse, Rue lifted the pages of his lectures for all to witness, and ripped them in half. "I will speak from my heart," he said.

The crowd gasped. I groaned. Margaret leaned toward him, straining, as if to pick up his odor. She squeezed my hand and checked my eyes to see whether I understood her feelings. She needed a reference point, a consciousness aside from her own to slow the rush of her being toward Rue.

"You're terrible," I said.

"Don't spoil my fantasy. Be quiet, O.K.?"

She then flattened her thigh against mine, holding me there while she joined him in her feelings, on stage, fifty feet away. Rue began his speech without pages or notes. The crowd grew still. Many who couldn't find seats stood in the aisles, some with bowed heads, staring at the floor as if they'd been beaten on the shoulders into penitential silence. For me it was also penitential. I work nights. I didn't like wasting a free evening in a crowded lecture hall when I could have been alone with Margaret.

I showed up at her loft an hour before the lecture. She said to her face in the bathroom mirror, "I can hardly wait to see the man. How do I look?"

"Chinese." I put the lid down on the toilet seat, sat on it.

"Answer me. Do I look all right, Herman?"

"You know what the ancient Greeks said about perfume?"

"I'm about to find out."

"To smell sweet is to stink."

"I use very little perfume. There's a reception afterwards, a party. It's in honor of the novel. A thousand pages and I could have kept reading it for another week. I didn't want it to end. I'll tell you the story later."

"Maybe I'll read it, too," I said, trying not to sound the way I felt. "But why must you see what the man looks like? I couldn't care less."

"You won't go with me?" She turned from the mirror, as if, at last, I'd provoked her into full attention.

"I'm not saying I won't."

"What are you saying?"

"Nothing. I asked a question, that's all. It isn't important. Forget it."

"Don't slither. You have another plan for the evening? You'd rather be somewhere else?"

"I have no other plan. I'm asking why should anyone care what an author looks like."

"I'm interested. I have been for months."

"Why?"

"Why not? He made me feel something. His book was an experience. Everybody wants to see him. Besides, my sister met him in Beijing. She knows him. Didn't I read you her letter?"

"I still don't see why. . ."

"Herman, what do you want me to say? I'm interested, I'm curious. I'm going to his lecture. If you don't want to go, don't go."

That is, leave the bathroom. Shut the door. Get out of sight.

Margaret can be too abrupt, too decisive. It's her business style carried into personal life. She buys buildings, has them fixed up, then rents or sells, and buys again. She has supported herself this way since her divorce from Sloan Pierson, professor of linguistics. He told her about Claude Rue's lecture, invited her to the reception afterwards, and put my name on the guest list. Their divorce, compared to some, wasn't bad. No lingering bitterness. They have remained connected—not quite friends—through small courtesies, like the invitation; also, of course, through their daughter, Gracie, ten years old. She lives with Sloan except when Margaret wants her, which is often. Margaret's business won't allow a strict schedule of visits. She has sometimes appeared without notice. "I need her," she says. Gracie scampers to her room, collects school books for the next day, and packs a duffle bag with clothes and woolly animals.

Sloan sighs, shakes his head. "Really, Margaret. Gracie has needs, too. She needs a predictable, daily life." Margaret says, "I'll phone you later. We'll discuss our needs."

She comes out of the house with Gracie. Sloan shouts, "Wait. Gracie's pills."

There's always one more word, one more thing to collect. "Goodbye. Wait." I wait. We all wait. Margaret and Gracie go back inside. I wait just outside. I am uncomfortable inside the house, around Sloan. He's friendly, but I know too much about him. I can't help thinking things, making judgments, and then I feel guilty. He's a fussy type, does everything right. If he'd only fight Margaret, not be so good, so right. Sloan could make trouble about Margaret's unscheduled appearances, even go to court, but he thinks, if Margaret doesn't have her way, Gracie will have no mother. Above all things, Sloan fears chaos. Gracie senses her daddy's fear, shares it. Margaret would die for Gracie, but it's a difficult love, measured by intensities. Would Margaret remember, in such love, about the pills?

Sloan finds the pills, brings them to the foyer, hands them to Margaret. There. He did another right thing. She and Gracie leave the house. We start down the path to the sidewalk. Gracie hands me her books and duffle bag, gives me a kiss, and says, "Hi, Herman German. I have an ear infection. I have to take pills four times a day." She's instructing Margaret, indirectly.

Margaret glares at me to show that she's angry. Her ten-year-old giving her instructions. I pretend not to understand. Gracie is a little version of Margaret, not much like Sloan. Chinese chemistry is dominant. Sloan thinks Gracie is lucky. "That's what I call a face," he says. He thinks he looks like his name—much too white.

I say, "Hi, Gracie Spacey." We get into my Volvo. I drive us away.

Gracie sits in back. Margaret, sitting beside me, stares straight ahead, silent, still pissed, but after awhile she turns, looks at Gracie. Gracie reads her mind, gives her a hug. Margaret feels better, everyone feels better.

While Margaret's houses are being fixed up, she lives in one, part of which becomes her studio where she does her painting. Years ago, at the university, studying with the wonderful painters Joan Brown and Elmer Bischoff, Margaret never discovered a serious commitment in herself. Later, when she married and had Gracie, and her time was limited, seriousness arrived. Then came the divorce, the real estate business, and she had even less time. She paints whenever she can, and she reads fifty or sixty novels a year; also what she calls "philosophy," which is religious literature. Her imagery in paintings comes from mythic, visionary works. From the *Kumulipo*, the Hawaiian cosmological chant, she took visions of land and sea, where creatures of the different realms are mysteriously related. Margaret doesn't own a television set or go to movies. She denies herself common entertainment for the same reason that Rilke refused to be analyzed by Freud. "I don't want my soul diluted," she says.

Sometimes, I sit with her in her loft in Emeryville—in a four-story brick building, her latest purchase—while she paints. "Are you bored?" she asks.

I'm never bored. I like being with her. I like the painting odors, the drag and scratch of brush against canvas. She applies color, I feel it in my eyes. Tingling starts along my forearms, hairs lift and stiffen. We don't talk. Sometimes not a word for hours, yet the time lacks nothing.

I say, "Let's get married."

She says, "We are married."

Another hour goes by.

She asks, "Is that a painting?"

I make a sound to suggest it is.

"Is it good?"

She knows.

When one of her paintings, hanging in a corner of a New York gallery owned by a friend, sold—without a formal show, and without reviews—I became upset. She'll soon be famous, I thought.

"I'll lose you," I said.

She gave me nine paintings, all she had in the loft. "Take this one, this one, this one. . ."

"Why?"

"Take them, take them."

She wanted to prove, maybe, that our friendship is inviolable; she had no ambition to succeed, only to be good. I took the paintings grudgingly, as if I were doing her a favor. In fact, that's how I felt. I was doing her a favor. But I wanted the paintings. They were compensations for her future disappearance from my life. We're best friends, very close. I have no vocation. She owed me the paintings.

I quit graduate school twenty years ago, and began waiting table at Gemma's, a San Francisco restaurant. From year to year, I

157

expected to find other work or to write professionally. My one book, *Local Greens,* which is about salads, was published by a small press in San Francisco. Not a best seller, but it made money. Margaret told me to invest in a condominium and she found one for me, the top floor of a brown shingle house, architect unknown, in the Berkeley hills. I'd been living in Oakland, in a one-room apartment on Harrison Street, near the freeway. I have a sedentary nature. I'd never have moved out. Never really have known, if not for Margaret, that I could have a nicer place, be happier. "I'm happy," I said. "This place is fine." She said my room was squalid. She said the street was noisy and dangerous. She insisted that I talk to a realtor or check the newspapers for another place, exert myself, do something. Suddenly, it seemed, I had two bedrooms, living room, new kitchen, hardwood floors, a deck, a bay view, monthly payments—property.

It didn't seem. I actually lived in a new place, nicer than anything I'd ever known.

My partner, so to speak, lives downstairs. Eighty-year-old Belinda Forster. She gardens once a week by instructing Pilar, a silent Mexican woman who lives with Belinda, where to put the different new plants, where to prune the apple trees. Belinda also lunches with a church group, reviews her will, smokes cigarettes. She told me, if I find her unconscious in the garden, or in the driveway, or wherever, to do nothing to revive her. She looks not very shrunken, not extremely frail. Her eyes are beautifully clear. Her skin is without the soft, puffy surface you often see in old people.

Belinda's husband, a professor of plant pathology, died about fifteen years ago, shortly after his retirement. Belinda talks about his work, their travels in Asia, and his mother. Not a word about herself. She might consider that impolite, or boastful, claiming she too had a life, or a self. She has qualities of reserve, much out of style these days, which I admire greatly, but I become awkward talking to her. I don't quite feel that I say what I mean. Does she intend this effect? Is she protecting herself against the assertions, the assault, of younger energies?

Upstairs, from the deck of my apartment, I see sailboats tilted in the wind. Oil tankers go sliding slowly by Alcatraz Island.

Hovering in the fuchsias, I see hummingbirds. Squirrels fly through the black, light-streaked canopies of Monterey pines. If my temperament were religious, I'd believe there had to be a cause, a divinity in the fantastic theater of clouds above San Francisco Bay.

Rue spoke with urgency, his head and upper body lifting and settling to the rhythm of his sentences. His straight, blond hair, combed straight back, fell toward his eyes. He swept it aside. It fell. He swept it aside, a bravely feminine gesture, vain, distracting. I sighed.

Margaret pinched my elbow. "I want to hear him, not your opinions."

"I only sighed."

"That's an opinion."

I sat quietly. Rue carried on. His subject was the loss to the Chinese people, and to the world, of the classical Chinese language. "I am saying that, after the revolution, the ancients, the great Chinese dead, were torn from their graves. I am saying they have been murdered word by word. And this in the name of nationhood, and a social justice which annihilates language, as well as justice, and anything the world has known as social."

End.

The image of ancient corpses, torn from their graves and murdered, aroused loonies in the audience. They whistled and cried out. Others applauded for a whole minute. Rue had said nothing subversive of America. Even so, Berkeley adored him. Really because of the novel, not the lecture. On the way to the lecture, Margaret talked about the novel, giving me the whole story, not merely the gist, as if to defend it against my negative opinion. She was also apologizing, I think, by talking so much, for having been angry and abrupt earlier. Couldn't just say "I'm sorry." Not Margaret. I drove and said nothing, still slightly injured, but soothed by her voice, giving me the story; giving a good deal, really, more than the story.

She said *The Mists of Shanghai* takes place in nineteenth-century China during the opium wars, when high-quality opium, harvested from British poppy fields in India, was thrust upon the Chinese people. "Isn't that interesting?" she said. "A novel should teach you something. I learned that the production, transportation, and distribution of opium, just as today, was controlled by western military and intelligence agencies, there were black slaves in Macao, and eunuchs were very powerful figures in government."

The central story of the novel, said Margaret, which is told by an evil eunuch named Jujuzi, who is an addict and a dealer, is about two lovers—a woman named Neiping and a man named Goo. First we hear about Neiping's childhood. She is the youngest in a large, very poor family. Her parents sell her to an elegant brothel in Shanghai, where the madam buys little girls, selected for brains and beauty. She tells Neiping that she will be taught to read, and, eventually, she will participate in conversation with patrons. Though only eight years old, Neiping has strong character, learns quickly and becomes psychologically mature. One day a new girl arrives and refuses to talk to anyone. She cries quietly to herself at night. Neiping listens to her crying and she begins to feel sorry for herself. But she refuses to cry. She leaves her bed and crawls into bed with the crying girl who then grows quiet. Neiping hugs her and says, "I am Neiping. What's your name?"

She says, "Dulu."

They talk for hours until they both fall asleep. She and Neiping become dear friends.

It happens that a man named Kang, a longtime patron of the brothel, arrives one evening. He is a Shanghai businessman, dealing in Mexican silver. He also owns an ironworks, and has initiated a lucrative trade in persons, sending laborers to a hellish life in the cane fields of Pacific islands and Cuba. Kang confesses to the madam that he is very unhappy. He can't find anyone to replace his recently deceased wife as his opponent in the ancient game of wei-ch'i. The madam tells Kang not to be unhappy. She has purchased a clever girl who will make a good replacement. Kang can come to the brothel and play wei-ch'i. She brings little Neiping into the room, sits her at a table with Kang, a playing board between them. Kang has a blind eye that looks smokey and gray. He is unashamedly flatulent, and he is garishly tattooed. All in all, rather a monster. Pretty little Neiping is terrified. She nods yes, yes, yes as he tells her the rules of the game, and he explains how one surrounds the opponent's pieces and holds territory on the board. When he asks if she has understood everything, she nods yes again. He says to Neiping, "If you lose, I will eat you the way a snake eats a monkey."

Margaret said, "This is supposed to be a little joke, see? But, since Kang looks sort of like a snake, it's frightening."

Kang takes the black stones and makes the first move. Neiping, in a trance of fear, recalls his explanation of the rules, then places a white stone on the board far from his black stone. They play until Kang becomes sleepy. He goes home. The game resumes the next night and the next. In the end, Kang counts the captured stones, white and black. It appears that Neiping has captured more than he. The madam says, "Let me count them." It also appears Neiping controls more territory than Kang. The madam counts, then looks almost frightened. She twitters apologies, and she coos, begging Kang to forgive Neiping for taking advantage of his kindness, his willingness to let Neiping seem to have done well in the first game. Kang says, "This is how it was with my wife. Sometimes she seemed to win. I will buy this girl."

The madam had been saving Neiping for a courtier, highly placed, close to the emperor, but Kang is a powerful man. She doesn't dare reject the sale. "The potential value of Neiping is immeasurable," she says. Kang says Neiping will cost a great deal before she returns a profit. "The price I am willing to pay is exceptionally good."

The madam says, "In silver?"

Kang says, "Mexican coins."

She bows to Kang, then tells Neiping to say goodbye to the other girls.

Margaret said, "I'll never forget how the madam bows to Kang."

Neiping and Dulu embrace. Dulu cries. Neiping says they will meet again someday. Neiping returns to Kang. He takes her hand. The monster and Neiping walk through the nighttime streets of Shanghai to Kang's house.

For the next seven years, Neiping plays wei-ch'i with Kang. He has her educated by monks, and she is taught to play musical instruments by the evil eunuch, Jujuzi, the one who is telling the story. Kang gives Neiping privileges of a daughter. She learns how he runs his businesses. He discusses problems with her. "If somebody were in my position how might such a person reflect on the matters I have described?" While they talk, Kang asks Neiping to comb his hair. He never touches her. His manner is formal and gentle. He gives everything. Neiping asks for nothing. Kang is a happy monster, but then Neiping falls in love with Goo, the son of a business associate of Kang. Kang discovers this love and he threatens to undo Neiping, sell her back to the brothel, or send her to work in the cane fields at the end of the world. Neiping flees Kang's house that night with Goo. Kang then wanders the streets of Shanghai in a stupor of misery, looking for Neiping.

Years pass. Unable to find a way to live, Goo and Neiping fall in with a guerilla triad. Neiping becomes its leader. Inspired by Neiping, who'd become expert in metals while living with Kang, the triad undertakes to study British war technology. Neiping says they can produce cannons, which could be used against opium merchants. The emperor will be pleased. In fact, he will someday have tons of opium seized and destroyed. But there is no way to approach the emperor until Neiping learns that Dulu, her dear friend in the brothel, is now the emperor's consort. Neiping goes to Dulu.

"The recognition scene," said Margaret, "is heartbreaking. Dulu has become an icy woman who moves slowly beneath layers of silk. But she remembers herself as the little girl who once cried in the arms of Neiping. She and Neiping are now about twenty-three."

Through Dulu's help, Neiping gains the emperor's support. This enrages Jujuzi, the evil eunuch. Opium trade is in his interest, since he is an addict and a dealer. Everything is threatened by Neiping's cannons which are superior to the originals, but the triad's military strategy is betrayed by Jujuzi. Neiping and Goo are captured by British sailors and jailed.

Margaret said, "Guess what happens next. Kang appears. He has vanished for three hundred pages, but he's back in the action."

The British allow Kang to speak to Neiping. He offers to buy her freedom. Neiping says he must also buy Goo's freedom. Kang says she has no right to ask him to buy her lover's freedom. Neiping accepts Kang's offer, and she is freed from jail. She then goes to Dulu and appeals for the emperor's help in freeing Goo. Jujuzi, frustrated by Neiping's escape, demands justice for Goo. The British, who are in debt to Jujuzi, look the other way while he tortures Goo to death.

The emperor, who has heard Neiping's appeal through Dulu, asks to see Neiping. The emperor knows Goo is dead. He was told by Jujuzi. But the emperor is moved by Neiping's beauty and her poignant concern to save the already dead Goo. The emperor tells her that he will save him, but she must forget Goo. Then he says that Neiping, like Dulu, will be his consort. In the final chapter, Neiping is heavy with the emperor's child. She and Dulu wander in the palace gardens. Jujuzi watches the lovely consorts passing amid flowers, and he remembers in slow, microscopic detail the execution of Neiping's lover.

"What a story."

"I left most of it out."

"Is that so?"

"You think it's boring."

"No."

"You do."

"Don't tell me what I think. That's annoying."

"Do you think it's boring?"

"Yes, but how can I know unless I read the book?"

"Well, I liked it a lot. The last chapter is horribly dazzling and so beautiful. Jujuzi watches Neiping and Dulu stroll in the garden, and he remembers Goo in chains, bleeding from the hundred knives Jujuzi stuck in him. To Jujuzi, everything is aesthetic, knives, consorts, even feelings. He has no balls so he collects feelings. You see? Like jewels in a box."

Lights went up in the midst of the applause. Margaret said, "Aren't you glad you came?" Claude Rue bowed. Waves of praise poured onto his head. I applauded, too, a concession to the community. Besides, Margaret loved the lecture. She watched me from the corners of her eyes, suspicious of my enthusiasm. I nodded, as if to say yes, yes. Mainly, I needed to go to the toilet, but I didn't want to do anything that might look like a negative comment on the lecture. I'd go when we arrived at the reception for Rue. This decision was fateful. At the reception, in the Faculty Club, I carried a glass of white wine from the bar to Margaret, then went to the men's room. I stood beside a man who had leaned his cane against the urinal. He patted his straight blond hair with one hand, holding his cock with the other, shaking it. The man was, I suddenly realized, himself, Claude Rue. Surprised into speech, I said I loved his lecture. He said, "You work here?"

Things now seemed to be happening quickly, making thought impossible. I was unable to answer. Exactly what was Rue asking—was I a professor? a men's room attendant? a toilet cruiser? Not waiting for my answer, he said he'd been promised a certain figure for the lecture. A check, made out to him from the regents of the university had been delivered to his hotel room. The check shocked him. He'd almost cancelled the lecture. He was still distressed, unable to contain himself. He'd hurried to the men's room, after the lecture, to look at his check again. The figure was less than promised. I was the first to hear about it. Me. A stranger. He was hysterical, maybe, but I felt very privileged. Money talk is personal, especially in a toilet. "You follow me?" he said.

"Yes. You were promised a certain figure. They gave you a check. It was delivered to your hotel room."

"Precisely. But the figure inscribed on the check is less than promised."

"Somebody made a mistake."

"No mistake. Taxes have been deducted. But I came from Paris with a certain understanding. I was to be paid a certain figure. I have the letter of agreement, and the contract." His green stare, fraught with helpless reproach, held me as he zipped up. He felt that he'd been cheated. He dragged to a sink. His cane, lacquered mahogany, with a black, iron ferrule, clacked the tile floor. He washed his hands. Water raged in the sink.

"It's a mistake, and it can be easily corrected," I said, speaking to his face in the mirror above the sink. "Don't worry, Mr. Rue. You'll get every penny they promised."

"Will you speak to somebody?" he said, taking his cane. "I'm very upset."

"Count on it, Mr. Rue."

"But will you speak to somebody about this matter?"

"Before the evening is over, I'll have their attention."

"But will you speak to a person?"

164

"Definitely."

I could see, standing close to him, that his teeth were heavily stained by cigarette smoke. They looked rotten. I asked if I might introduce him to a friend of mine. Margaret would get a kick out of meeting Claude Rue, I figured, but I mainly wanted her to see his teeth. He seemed thrown off balance, reluctant to meet someone described as a friend. "My time is heavily scheduled," he muttered; but, since he'd just asked me for a favor, he shrugged, shouldering obligation. I led him to Margaret. Rue's green eyes gained brightness. Margaret quickened within, but offered a mere "Hello," no more, not even the wisp of a smile. She didn't say she loved his lecture. Was she overwhelmed, having Claude Rue thrust at her like this? The silence was difficult for me, if not for them. Lacking anything else to say, I started to tell Margaret about Rue's problem with the university check. "It wasn't the promised amount." Rue cut me off:

"Money is offal. Not to be discussed."

His voice was unnaturally high, operatic and crowing at once. He told Margaret, speaking to her eyes—as if I'd ceased to exist—that he would spend the next three days in Berkeley. He was expected at lunches, cocktail parties, and dinner parties. He'd been invited to conduct a seminar, and to address a small gathering at the Asian Art museum.

"But my lecture is over. I have fulfilled my contract. I owe nothing to anybody."

Margaret said, "No point, then, cheapening yourself, is there?"

"I will cancel every engagement."

"How convenient," she said, hesitated, then gambled, adding, "for us."

Her voice was flat and black as an ice slick on asphalt, but I could hear, beneath the surface, a faint trembling. I prayed that she would look at Rue's teeth, which were practically biting her face. She seemed not to notice.

"Do you drive a car?"

She said, "Yes," holding her hand out to the side, toward me, blindly. I slipped the keys to my Volvo into her palm. Tomorrow, I'd ride to her place on my bike and retrieve the car. Margaret wouldn't remember that she'd taken it. She and Rue walked away, but I felt it was I who grew smaller in the gathering dis-

165

tance. Margaret glanced back at me to say goodbye. Rue, staring at Margaret, lost peripheral vision, thus annihilating me. I might have felt insulted, but he'd been seized by hormonal ferocity, and was focused on a woman. I'd have treated him similarly.

Months earlier, I'd heard about Rue from Margaret. She'd heard about him from her sister May who had a PhD in library science from Berkeley, and worked at the university library in Beijing. In a letter to Margaret, May said she'd met Professor Claude Rue, the linguistic historian. He was known in academic circles, but not yet an international celebrity. Rue was in Beijing completing his research for *The Mists of Shanghai*. May said, in her letter, that Rue was a "womanizer." He had bastard children in France and Tahiti. She didn't find him attractive, but other women might. "If you said Claude Rue is charming or has pretty green eyes, I wouldn't disagree, but, as I write to you, I have trouble remembering what he looks like."

Margaret said the word "womanizer" tells more about May than Rue. "She's jealous. She thinks Rue is fucking every woman except her."

"She says she doesn't find him attractive, and she knows what he looks like, what he sounds like, smells like, feels like. May has no respect for personal space. She touches people when she talks to them. She's a shark, with taste sensors in her skin. When May takes your hand, or brushes up against you, she's tasting you. Nobody but sharks and cannibals can do that. She shakes somebody's hand, then tells me, 'Needs salt and a little curry.' "

"All right. Maybe 'womanizer' says something about May, but the word has a meaning. Regardless of May, 'womanizer' means something."

"What?"

"You kidding?"

"Tell me. What does it mean?"

"What do you think? It means a man who sits on the side of the bed at two in the morning, putting on his shoes."

"What do you call women who do that? Don't patronize me, Herman. Don't you tell me what 'womanizer' means."

"Why did you ask?"

"To see if you'd tell me. So patronizing. I know exactly what the word means. 'Womanizer' means my sister May wants Claude Rue to fuck her."

"Get a dictionary. I want to see where it mentions your sister and Claude Rue."

"The dictionary is a cemetery of dead words. All words are dead until somebody uses them. 'Womanizer' is dead. If you use it, it lives, uses you."

"Nonsense."

"People once talked about nymphomaniacs, right? Remember that word? Would you ever use it without feeling it said something embarrassing about you? Get real, Herman. Everyone is constantly on the make—even May. Even you."

"Not me."

"Maybe that's because you're old-fashioned, which is to say narrow-minded. Self-righteous. Incapable of seeing yourself. You disappoint me, Herman. You really do. What about famous men who had bastards? Rousseau, Byron, Shelley, Wordsworth, the Earl of Gloucester, Edward VII."

"I don't care who had bastards. That isn't pertinent. You're trying to make a case for bad behavior."

"Rodin, Hegel, Marx, Castro—they all had bastards. If they are all bad, that's pertinent. My uncle Chan wasn't famous, but he had two families. God knows what else he had. Neither family knew of the other until he died. Then it became pertinent, everyone squabbling over property."

"What's your point, if you have one, which I seriously doubt?"

"And what about Kafka, Camus, Sartre, Picasso, Charlie Chaplin, Charlie Parker, JFK, MLK? What about Chinese emperors and warlords, Arab sheiks, movie actors, thousands of Mormons? Everybody collects women. That's why there are prostitutes, whores, courtesans, consorts, concubines, bimbos, mistresses, wives, flirts, hussies, sluts, etc., etc. How many words are there for man? Not one equivalent for 'cunt,' which can mean a woman. 'Prick' means some kind of jerk. Look at magazine covers, month after month. They're selling clothes and cosmetics? They sell women, stupid. You know you're stupid. Stupid Herman, that's you."

"They're selling happiness, not women."

"It's the same thing. Lions, monkeys, horses, goats, people . . . Many, many, many animals collect women animals. When they stop, they become unhappy and they die. Married men live longer than single men. This has long been true. The truth is the truth. What am I talking about? Hug me, please."

"The truth is you're madly in love with Claude Rue."

"I've never met the man. Don't depress me."

"Your sister mentions him in a letter, you imagine she wants him. She wants him, you want him. You're in love, you're jealous."

"You're more jealous."

"You admit it? You never before conceded anything in an argument. I feel like running in the streets, shrieking the news."

"I admit nothing. After reading my sister May's gossipy, puritanical letter, I find that I dislike Claude Rue intensely."

"You never met the man."

"How can that have any bearing on the matter?"

As for the people in the large reception room at the Faculty Club—deans, department heads, assistant professors, students, wives, husbands—gathered to honor Claude Rue—he'd flicked us off like a light. I admired Rue for that, and I wished his plane back to Paris would crash. Behind me, a woman whispered in the exact tone Margaret had used, "I dislike him intensely."

A second woman said, "You know him?"

"Of course not. I've heard things, and this novel is very sexist."

"You read the novel. Good for you."

"I haven't read it. I saw a review in a magazine at my hairdresser's. I have the magazine. I'll look for it tonight when I get home."

"Sexist?" said the first woman. "Odd. I heard he's gay."

"Gay?" said a man. "How interesting. I suppose one can be gay and sexist, but I'd never have guessed he was gay. He looks straight to me. Who told you he's gay? Someone who knows him?"

"Well, not with a capital K, if that's what you mean by 'knows,' but he was told by a friend of Rue's, that he agreed to fly here and give his lecture only because of the Sanfran bath houses. That's what he was told. Gossip in this town spreads quick as genital warts."

168

"Ho, ho, ho. People are so dreadfully bored. Can you blame them? They have no lives, just careers and Volvos."

"That's good. I intend to use it. Do look for conversational citations in the near future. But who is the Chinese thing? I'll die if I don't find out. She's somebody, isn't she? Ask him."

"Who?"

"Him, him. That man. He was standing with her." Someone plucked my jacket sleeve. I turned. A face desiccated by propriety, leaned close, old eyes, shimmering liquid gray, bulging, rims hanging open with thin crimson labia. It spoke:

"Pardon me, sir. Could you please tell us the name of the Chinese woman who, it now seems, is leaving the reception with Professor Rue?"

"Go fuck yourself."

Margaret said the success of his lecture left Rue giddily deranged, expecting something more palpable from the night. He said, she said, that he couldn't have returned to his hotel room, watched TV, and gone to sleep. " 'Why is it like this for me, do you think?' " he said, she said. " 'It would have no style. You were loved,' " she said, she said, sensing his need to be reminded of the blatant sycophancy of his herdlike audience. " 'Then you appeared,' " he said, she said. " 'You were magnificently cold.' "

Voila! Margaret. She is cold. She is attentive. She is determined to fuck him. He likes her quickness, and her legs. He says that to her. He also likes the way she drives, and her hair—the familiar black Asian kind, but which, because of its dim coppery strain, is rather unusual. He likes her eyes, too. I said: "Margaret, let me. Your gray-tinted glasses give a sensuous glow to your sharply tipped Chinese eyes, which are like precious black glittering pebbles washed by the Yangtze. Also the Yalu."

Margaret said, "Please shut up, dog-eyed white devil. I'm in no mood for jokes."

Her eyes want never to leave Rue's face, she said, but she must concentrate on the road as she drives. The thing is underway for them. I could feel it as she talked, how she was thrilled by the momentum, the invincible rush, the necessity. Resentment built in my sad heart. I thought, 'Margaret is over thirty years old. She has been around the block. But it's never enough. Once more around the block, up the stairs, into the room, and there lies happiness.'

169

" 'Why shouldn't I have abandoned the party for you?' " he said, she said, imitating his tone, plaintive and arrogant. " 'I wrote a novel.' " He laughs at himself. Margaret laughs, imitating him, an ironic self-deprecatory laugh. The moment seemed to her phony and real at once, said Margaret. He was nervous, as he'd been on stage, unsure of his stardom, unconvinced even by the flood of abject adoration. " 'Would a man write a novel except for love?' " he said, she said, as if he didn't really know. He was sincerely diffident, she said, an amazing quality considering that he'd slept with every woman in the world. But what the hell, he was human. With Margaret, sex will be more meaningful. " 'Except for love?' " she said, she said, gayly, wondering if he slept with her sister. " 'How about your check from the university?' "

" 'You think I'm inconsistent?' " He'd laughed. Spittle shot from his lips and rotten teeth. She saw everything except the trouble, what lay deep in the psychic plasma that rushed between them.

She drove him to her loft, in the warehouse and small factory district of Emeryville, near the bay, where she lived and worked, and bought and sold. Canvases, drawings, clothes—everything was flung about. She apologized.

He said, " 'A great disorder is an order.' ' "

"Did you make that up?"

He kissed her. She kissed him.

" 'Yes,' " he said. Margaret stared at me, begging for pity. He didn't make that up. A bit of an ass, then, but really, who isn't? She expected Rue to get right down to love. He wanted a drink first. He wanted to look at her paintings, wanted to use the bathroom and stayed inside a long time, wanted something to eat, then wanted to read poetry. It was close to midnight. He was reading poems aloud, ravished by beauties of phrasing, shaken by their music. He'd done graduate work at Oxford. Hours passed. Margaret sat on the couch, her legs folded under her. She thought it wasn't going to happen, after all. Ten feet away, he watched her from a low slung, leather chair. The frame was a steel tube bent to form legs, arms, and back-rest. A book of modern poetry lay open in his lap. He was about to read another poem when Margaret said, in the flat black voice. " 'Do you want me to drive you to your hotel?' "

170

He let the book slide to the floor. Stood up slowly, struggling with leather-wheezing-ass-adhesive chair seat, then came toward her, pulling stone foot. Leaning down to where she sat on the couch, he kissed her. Her hand went up, lightly, slowly, between his legs.

"He wasn't a very great lover," she said.

She had to make him stop, give her time to regather powers of feeling and smoke a joint before trying again. Then, him inside, "working on me," she said, she fingered her clitoris to make herself come. "There would have been no payoff otherwise," she said. "He'd talked too much, maybe. Then he was a tourist looking for sensations in the landscape. He couldn't give. It was like he had a camera. Collecting memories. Savoring the sex, you know what I mean? I could have been in another city." Finally, Margaret said, she screamed, " 'What keeps you from loving me?' " He fell away, damaged.

" 'You didn't enjoy it'?" he said, she said.

She turned on the lamp to roll another joint, and told him to lie still while she studied his cock, which was oddly discolored and twisted left. In the next three days, the sex got better, not great. She'd say, " 'You're losing me.' " He'd moan.

When she left him at the airport, she felt relieved, but, driving back to town, she began to miss him. She thought to phone her psychotherapist, but this wasn't a medical problem. The pain surprised her and it wouldn't quit. She couldn't work, couldn't think. Despite strong reservations—he hadn't been very nice to her—she was in love, had been since she saw him on stage. Yes; definitely love. Now he was gone. She was alone. In the supermarket, she wandered the aisles, unable to remember what she needed. She was disoriented—her books, her plants, her clothes, her hands—nothing seemed really hers. At night, the loneliness was very bad. Sexual. Hurt terribly. She cried herself to sleep.

"Why didn't you phone me?"

"I knew you weren't too sympathetic. I couldn't talk to you. I took Gracie out of school. She'd been here for the last couple of days."

"She likes school."

"That's just what you'd say, isn't it? You know, Herman, you are a kind of person who makes me feel like shit. If Gracie misses a couple of days it is no big deal. She's got a lot of high Q's. I

171

found out she also has head lice. Her father doesn't notice anything. Gracie would have to have convulsions before he'd notice. Too busy advancing himself, writing another ten books that nobody will read, except his pathetic graduate students."

"That isn't fair."

"Yes, it is. It's fair."

"No, it isn't."

"You defending Sloan? Whose friend are you?"

"Talking to you is like cracking nuts with my teeth."

She told me Rue had asked if she knew Chinese. She said she didn't. He proposed to teach her, and said, " 'The emperor forbid foreigners to learn Chinese, except imperfectly, only for purposes of trade. Did you know that?' "

" 'No. Let's begin.' "

Minutes into the lesson, he said, " 'You're pretending not to know Chinese. I am a serious person. Deceive your American lovers. Not me.' "

She said, "Nobody ever talked to me like that. He was furious."

"Didn't you tell him to go to hell?"

"I felt sorry for him."

She told him that she really didn't know a word of Chinese. Her family had lived in America for over a hundred years. She was raised in Sacramento. Her parents spoke only English. All her friends had been white. Her father was a partner in a construction firm. His associates were white. When the Asian population of the Bay Area greatly increased, she saw herself, for the first time, as distinctly Chinese. She thought of joining Chinese cultural organizations, but was too busy. She sent money.

" 'You don't know who you are,' " said Rue.

" 'But that's who I am. What do you mean?' "

" 'Where are my cigarettes?' "

"Arrogant bastard. Did you?"

"What I did is irrelevant. He felt ridiculed. He thought I was being contemptuous. I was in love. I could have learned anything. Chinese is only a language. It didn't occur to me to act stupid."

"What you did is relevant. Did you get his cigarettes?"

"He has a bald spot in the middle of his head."

"Is there anything really interesting about Rue?"

"There's a small blue tattoo on his right shoulder. I liked it. Black moles are scattered on his back like buckshot. The tattoo is an ideograph. I saw him minutely, you know what I mean? I was on the verge of hatred, really in love. But you wouldn't understand. I won't tell you anymore."

"Answer my question."

She didn't.

"You felt sorry for him. I feel sorry for you. Is it over now?"

"Did it begin? I don't really know. Anyhow, so what?"

"Don't you want to tell me? I want to know. Tell me everything."

"I must keep a little for myself. Do you mind? It's my life. I want to keep my feelings. You can be slightly insensitive, Herman."

"I never dumped YOU at a party in front of the whole town. You want to keep your feelings? Good. If you talk, you'll remember feelings you don't know you had. It's the way to keep them."

"No, it isn't. They go out of you. Then they're not even feelings anymore. They're chit-chat commodities. Some asshole like Claude will stick them in a novel."

"Why don't you just fly to Paris? Live with him."

"He's married. I liked him for not saying that he doesn't get along with his wife, or they're separated. I asked if he had an open marriage."

"What did he say?"

"He said, 'Of course not.' "

Margaret spoke more ill than good of Rue. Nevertheless, she was in love. Felt it every minute, she said, and wanted to phone him, but his wife might answer. He'd promised to write a letter, telling her where they would meet. There were going to be publication parties for his book in Rome and Madrid. He said that his letter would contain airline tickets and notification about her hotel.

"Then you pack a bag? You run out the door?"

"And up into the sky. To Rome. To Madrid."

"Just like that? What about your work? What about Gracie?"

"Just like that."

I bought a copy of The Mists of Shanghai, and began reading with primitive, fiendish curiosity. Who the hell was Claude Rue? The morning passed, then the afternoon. I quit reading at twilight, when I had to leave for work. I'd reached the point where Dulu comes to the brothel. It was an old-fashioned novel, something like Dickens, lots of characters and sentimental situations, but carefully written to seem mindless, and so clear that you hardly feel you're reading. Jujuzi's voice gives a weird edge to the story. Neiping suffers terribly, he says, but she imagines life in the brothel is not real, and that someday she will go home and her mother will be happy to see her. Just as I began to think Rue was a nitwit, Jujuzi reflects on Neiping's pain. He says she will never go home, and a child's pain is more terrible than an adult's, but it is the nourishment of sublime dreaming. When Dulu arrives, Neiping wishes the new girl would stop crying. It makes Neiping sad. She can't sleep. She stands beside the new girl, staring down through the dark, listening to her sob, wanting to smack her, make her be quiet. But then Neiping slides under the blanket and hugs the new girl. They tell each other their names. They talk. Dulu begins slowly to turn. She hugs Neiping. The little bodies lie in each other's arms, face to face. They talk until they fall asleep.

Did Claude Rue imagine himself as Neiping? Considering Rue's limp, he'd known pain. But maybe pain made him cold, like Jujuzi, master of sentimental feelings, master of cruelty. Was Claude Rue like Jujuzi?

A week passed. Margaret called, told me to come to her loft. She sounded low. I didn't ask why. When I arrived, she gave me a brutal greeting. "How come you and me never happened?"

"What do you mean?"

"How come we never fucked?"

She had a torn-looking smile.

"We're best friends, aren't we?"

I sat on the couch. She followed, plopped beside me. We sat beside each other, beside ourselves. Dumb. She leaned against me, put her head on my shoulder. I loved her so much it hurt my teeth. Light went down in the tall, steel-mullioned, factory windows. The air of the loft grew chilly.

"Why did you phone?" I asked.

"I needed you to be here."

"Do you want to talk?"

"No."

The perfume of her dark hair came to me. I saw dents on the side of her nose, left by her eyeglasses. They made her eyes look naked, vulnerable. She'd removed her glasses to see less clearly. Twisted the ends of her hair. Chewed her lip. I stood up, unable to continue doing nothing, crossed to a lamp, then didn't turn it on. Electric light was violent. Besides, it wasn't very dark in the loft, and the shadows were pleasant. I looked back. Her eyes had followed me. She asked what I'd like to drink.

"What do you have?"

"Black tea?"

"All right."

She put on her glasses and walked to the kitchen area. The cup and saucer rattled as she set them on the low table. I took her hands. "Sit," I said. "Talk."

She sat, but said nothing.

"Do you want to go out somewhere? Take a walk, maybe."

"We were together for three days," she said.

"Did he write to you?"

"We were together for hours and hours. There was so much feeling. Then I get this letter."

"What does he say? Rome? Barcelona?"

"He says I stole his watch. He says I behaved like a whore, going through his pockets when he was asleep."

"Literally, he says that?"

"Read it yourself."

"It's in French." I handed it back to her.

"An heirloom, he says. His most precious material possession, he says. He understands my motive, and finds it contemptible. He wants his watch back. He'll pay. How much am I asking?"

"You have his heirloom?"

"I never saw it."

"Let's look."

"Please, Herman, don't be tedious. There is no watch."

With the chaos of art materials scattered on the vast floor, and on table tops, dressers, chairs, and couch, it took twenty minutes before she found Claude Rue's watch jammed between a bedpost and the wall.

I laughed. She didn't laugh. I wished I could redeem the moment. Her fist closed around the watch, then opened slowly. She said, "Why did he write that letter?"

"Send him the watch and forget it."

"He'll believe he was right about me."

"Who cares what he believes?"

"He hurt me."

"Oh, just send him the watch."

"He hurt me, really hurt me. Three days of feeling, then that letter."

"Send it to him," I said.

But there was a set look in Margaret's eyes. She seemed to hear nothing.

YUKON

by CAROL EMSHWILLER

H<small>E'S A DRAGON</small>. He's a wolf. He's caribou. She tries to please him. She tries to keep out of his way and, at the same time, tries to get him to notice her by doing little things for him when he's gone or asleep. She needs him for warmth so they can cuddle up and he can warm her. She's afraid to leave because that's all the warmth she has. But she's afraid to stay. Is it possible to rush away when you live this far north? These high valleys never get warm. Mountain water coming down from glaciers is bright turquoise.

He's always looking at the sky or the ground or the horizon, not at her. But bits of red wool are all she has to look good in and then she never was a popular girl. If had big fur boots and hat, then maybe make a move. Make a run for it.

As valley to mountaintop . . . might as well be ship-to-shore, sending signals. How live that way? How love?

He's a rattlesnake, but no immediate threat (that she can tell). Comes home when he feels like it, bringing dead things to eat. Holds conventional views. Passes judgment on. Everything that needs to be said, he says, already said, and she thinks he's probably right, or almost. Make him chopped liver. Make him hasenpfeffer. Make him big mugs of glogg, but might not be home till three a.m. anyway. Wait up. And always those Englemann spruce. A couple of hundred years old—even more—but still skinny. Nothing to them. She loves them, though what else is there to love? It's the only tree around.

He's a giant. He's a dwarf. She has to help him climb up onto his throne. For the love of the spruce trees, she nuzzles into his furry chest, thinking that to love him you have to love horses, spiders and raw oysters, thinking how now she's going to have a baby. Should she tell him? She's already fairly big-with-child, but he hasn't noticed. She decides not to tell him. She decides, boy or girl, she will name it Englemann as though they were Mr. and Mrs. Spruce.

Their mansion is unfinished still. Only the vestibule built (but it's a big one, even as mansion vestibules go) and one tower (small) from which to view the mountains above the tops of trees. Both vestibule and tower are made out of the local rocks, so on the walls are the faint etchings of trilobites and prints of the leaves of ancient, ginko-like trees. In the fireplace they stand out clear, outlined by the smoke. Once upon a time it was warm here, and covered with water. The land has shifted, quake by quake, away from some southern latitude and it's still going. North by northwest. Also rising straight up. On land such as this, it's easy to go astray.

And now she's going just a little bit crazy. She wants and wants. Stands at window as if caged. Plastic that's in front of the glass to keep the heat in, makes things fuzzy. Snow outside begins to look soft and warm. Just right. So she leaves. She's not so crazy she doesn't take cheese sandwiches, peanuts, raisins, carrots. . . . Also takes his big fur boots and hat and now she's out in those nice adolescent-looking spruce trees that are older . . . much, much older than they look. She hugs some (though not much to hug). Touches them as she goes by. Wants to soak up the stolid way they are and also wants them to know how she feels: that even though they're stunted because of their hardships, she loves them all the more for it. She stops to drink glacier milk along the way. She's following, at first, browse trails that go no special place. It's cold. She just goes on. Easy to go astray. Thinks: years of going astray . . . was always astray, so if now astray, it's no different from before.

Meanwhile he's home, just woke up and sitting by the fire she'd laid before she left, asking himself ultimate questions, or, rather, penultimate questions as, What about the influence of theory on action? What about negative ends vs. positive means and vice versa? He doesn't notice she's gone, slipping around out there in his too-big-for-her boots. She had not meant to be going in a northerly direction. She had not meant to be climbing on up higher into the cold. She thought for a while she'd maybe creep

178

back after he'd gone to sleep with no supper, but she's too far now for that. (He'll miss his boots before he'll miss her.) She was thinking: South and warm and down, down, into the lower valleys, but she's been going up because it's the hardest and she's always done whatever was the hardest. The spruce get older and smaller the higher she goes until there're, all at once, no more of them. Meanwhile he keeps putting on another log until the whole vestibule dances with the fire and he pulls off sweater after sweater, watches his giant shadow writhe along the walls, falls asleep in his chair.

If there had been flowers blooming up there on the mountains, she would have known the names of every single one. If birds had called out, she'd have known which birds and would have whistled back.

Since she'd started in the morning after a sleepless night (though all her nights have been sleepless for a long time, she can hardly remember the times when she used to sleep well). . . . Since she'd started early she gets almost all the way to the top before it's too dark to go on. She finds a kind of cairn built by summer climbers. There's a slit at the bottom big enough to slither into. She does. Sleeps, not well, but better than she's slept in a long time, dreaming: Loves me? Loves me not? and: Who (or what!) is number one in his heart? It's his boots and his hat keeps her warm enough, or almost warm enough all night, so in the morning she's, as usual, full of grateful love for him and wondering: Why hasn't he followed no matter how hard? Why hasn't he come for her by now with something nice and warm to drink? He's never done anything remotely like that, but still she wonders why he's not already there, maybe having climbed all night just for her.

She squirms out and up and, first thing, she sees she's almost to the top, so goes on up. What she thought was five minutes worth of climbing turns out to take a half an hour. At top she sits on fossils and looks out—little shivers of pleasure or of cold—eating raisins and soaking up comfort and courage from the view, this side, too, Englemann, Englemann, everywhere Englemann below her, first in the sheltered hollows and then, lower down, nothing but. Thinks: Nothing like them, and nothing like being up this high, and nothing like what it took to get this far, nothing like the cold, clear air. She even forgets she's pregnant.

Now, down in that big, stone vestibule, he is shouting, "Bacon,

bacon!" Searches what few crooks and crannies there are to search, groans and spits, hisses into the corner under the king-sized bed, makes his own black coffee, spends the morning writing out new rules while she walks the col, too exhilarated to feel fear of heights. One last bit of glacier still sits in the steep pocket below her. She can tell by the old blue ice showing where the pure white snow's been blown off. She follows the ridge above and then past and then starts down, but she's being too courageous . . . too sure of herself now, falls, slides the whole bare slope till stopped . . . saved by one thin old Englemann, her knee twisted back behind. Hurts. Probably nothing broken though she's not sure. Waits, lying there clutching tree because of pain. She's looking straight up through the narrow, scraggly circle of branches to the sky that's clouding over, thinking: Tree, tree, *this* tree and sky. Ties her scarf tight around her leg. That helps. It's getting windier. Big black clouds off over next mountain. She must get lower and to some sheltered spot. Can't stop now. Gets up. Goes from tree to tree to tree (she's *depending* on them) steeply down. Thinks: If not for Englemann spruce to hang onto! . . .

By late afternoon finds bear's cave still warm from that big body. She knows it's a bear's cave. She can smell it. She can see the footprints in the snow, people-like prints but wider, leading out. She needs the shelter now and the warmth of it. Can't go on. And she's more cold than scared. Also it's beginning to snow. She creeps in. Wedges herself among the tree roots along the left-hand side, away from the more open part of the cave. She knows the bear will come back, but she thinks she already knows how to keep away from something big (or small) and dangerous. She falls asleep, a seemingly dreamless sleep and not so full of unanswered questions about love or the lack of it.

The bear comes back at three a.m. She hears him sniffing around outside and giving little warning growls. Also he's got the hiccups. Nothing here she hasn't heard already, and many times. She's only half-awake. Before she realizes it she's told him she loves him. She's talking soft and low. He grunts, then hunkers on in, rolls to far side, back turned. (She thinks: As usual.) He lets her be. Snores. Storm goes on outside. Later (as usual) she moves close, snug against his back.

They sleep two days and nights, or so she guesses. When she

wakes up later, as he's leaving, she finds he's eaten all her cheese sandwiches, carrots, peanuts and raisins, and she thinks: As usual.

She hurries to the entrance of the cave and calls out to him before he goes. Her knee hurts and maybe she's a little feverish. She speaks without thinking. That's not her usual way, but he seems a little bit safer than her own male even though he's the biggest and most masculine thing she's ever been this close to; dangerous, too. No doubt about it. She does like his looks, though: his hump, his shoulders, his yellow-brown fur. . . . Now he hangs his head low, almost to the snow, and looks back at her suspiciously, and it isn't as if she hasn't seen that same look a thousand times before. But what is there to lose? She talks to him of things she'd never dared to talk about before. "How can love last," she says, "if this goes on? How can love even begin? How can it go on and on, and we all," she says, "want undying love. Even you, though you may not think so. It's normal. And, by the way," she says, "food is love, you know. Love is food. It's how we live. It's what we live by, and you've eaten it all up."

Needless to say she'd never said any such thing to her own overbearing, legal, lord and master, though she'd wanted to for a long time.

The bear watches her as she speaks as though too polite to interrupt or move, even. His little beady black eyes take everything in, that's clear. There's a dull, sleepy, intelligent look about him. He waits patiently until she's finished, then humps off in the powdery snow.

She sucks ice from the cave entrance. Finds a piece of root to make a splint for her knee. After that makes a broom from root ends and tidies up, all the while chewing root hairs from the cave ceiling. When everything is spic-and-span she sleeps again. At three a.m. or thereabouts he comes back with a small black bass for her. It seems as if he's taken what she said to heart. She lets him have half though she knows he's already eaten (not only all her food, but lots more, too). He licks up the fish scales she leaves. He eats the head (she gets the cheeks and also swallows down the eyes, though that's not easy to do). While they eat she talks and talks like she never talked before. She tells him all she knows about bears and that she hopes to learn lots more. Later she rubs the back of his neck and behind his ears. Top of his head. She likes the feel of him, and he's so warm. It's like the fireplace is lit when he comes in. She sings and he hums back a tune of his own she learns by heart. (She loves the sound of his voice.) They sleep again, she can't tell how long. Next time he leaves, they kiss, and not just cheeks. When he comes back, he brings another fish. And it goes on like this except they're kissing more and sleeping longer and longer periods, breathing slowly into each other's faces and not even getting up to pee, he not turning his back to her except now and then and, when he does, giving her a bear hug first. It's a whole other rhythm she'd never known about before. And not bad, she thinks, to let the storms go on by themselves and forget about everything and just be warm and cuddled and cuddling all the time. It's what she's always wanted: arms around her that hardly ever let go. It's what she didn't get when she was little.

They don't even feel the earthquake, though it shakes a little dirt and pebbles down on them. She dreams it, though, and in the dreams the quake is her husband's big feet shaking the mountain as he comes to get her to tear her away from her embrace. Before that she's sometimes dreamt that the storms are him, too, tearing at the cave to pull her out. When those dreams come, she hugs tighter to her bear and he embraces her yet more snugly. Then she knows she's safe and thinks she finally has all one needs of real love and that it will last forever though maybe that's too much to hope for.

Meanwhile, back at the vestibule, the earthquake has caused quite a bit of damage. Some walls have crumbled and part of the roof has come down. The fireplace is still O.K., though. He can squat in front of it mooing for his woman, and he still has most of his tower from which to growl out at the moon or stars or sun. Now he'll have to clean up the debris by himself as well as cook, cut his own firewood, skin his own marmots. If she knew this she could feel some sweet revenge, or maybe I-told-you-so, except she never did.

One starry winter night when her knee is better, though not completely, she limps out with her bear and it's so nice the bear stands up and does a little soft-shoe while she throws snowballs at the sky. She limps, but she can shuffle and wobble from tree to tree, kissing them and him. They're singing all the songs they know, but by now she's forgotten most of the words. Knows only rhyme and alliteration though she remembers the oxymorons, especially since "the brightness of midnight" is all around them right now. It's sharply cold, but even so they both know spring is in the air. After this night, they begin to sleep less and then she has the baby. He's so small and thin she hardly knows she's birthed him except she hears the peeping. The bear helps by licking it clean and then eats the placenta, not letting her have even a taste. By then it's not a question of naming it. She can't even remember what names are for.

It gets warmer and the bear's gone more and more and brings back less and less. The baby might as well be a little bird. Besides her own milk, she feeds it worms and grubs. She tweets at it and it tweets back. When the bear stays out six days in a row, she suspects she's made the same old mistake . . . same kind of destructive relationship she's always had before. He'll go for good. He'll forget about her. Or, if he comes back, turn savage on her. Maybe push her out along with her robin, sparrow, little tufted titmouse.

Then, when he doesn't come back at all anymore, thinks: Yes, yes, she knew it would happen and now she'll have to go, too. Be out on her own. Find the next meal herself. It's a bright spring day, wild flowers coming out, but she no sooner starts down, baby perched on her shoulder, pecking at her ear, than it flies away and she has no name to call it back by. She tries to caw him down. She whistles all the birdcalls she knows, but none work. He circles for a few minutes while she finds the words to tell him he can't fly, or, anyway, not yet. It only wobbles him a little. He utters one harsh quack she's never heard him make before, then soars away, out over the valley. She thinks she hears soft coos and cuckoos even after he disappears into the trees below.

Well, she'll just go down by herself. And south. But this other valley, not towards home. This time maybe not take the hard way, and maybe she's had enough hugging to last a while, though she's wondering, as usual, Where is the creature with which she can live happily ever after?

Then she sees a figure climbing up. First it's just a greenish-brown slowly moving spot, but then it becomes green and brown . . . tweeds and corduroys. Thin, small, wiry. Has a greenish-gray beard. Alpine hat with little red feathers in it. Black-button bearish eyes. She sees them as he comes closer. Though she's never seen him before, she knows who it is. Knickers, hiking boots—the old fashioned kind. "Englemann," she says, "Englemann, Englemann." It's one of the few words she's not forgotten . . . never would forget though she is, by then, almost free of words. She would have to start over now from the beginning with wah, bah and boo.

He comes up the last switch back. They look at each other and smile. He has a little tuft of fragrant mountain misery in his buttonhole. He takes it out, sniffs it once, then gives it to her.

"Oh, Englemann," she says, and, "wah" and "bah" and "boo."

THE MIDDLE OF NOWHERE

by KENT NELSON

T HIS HAPPENED JUST after I'd dropped out of high school, when I was seventeen and living with my father. We had this trailer southwest of Tucson about twenty-three miles, right at the edge of the Papago Reservation at the end of a dirt road which petered out into the Baboquivari Mountains. Across to the east you could see the Sierritas, which were a low rim of ragged hills, and to the south where there was not much of anything except saguaros and greasewood and mesquite and the highway that ran from Robles Junction to Sasabe on the Mexican border.

Our trailer sat on a hill above two sand gullies. The previous occupants had seen fit to throw their trash into the steeper ravine, but the other one was a nice broad wash, rocky in places, with good cover for deer in the thickets of paloverde and ironwood. There were a couple of other trailers back down toward the highway, their TV antennas and satellite dishes the main evidence that someone else lived out there. Now and then you could hear a dog barking at the coyotes at night.

By this time in my life I'd pretty much seen everything. I don't mean I had anything figured cold or that I possessed some ultimate knowledge. Pretty much the opposite was true. I mean, nothing surprised me anymore. When I was nine and ten I lived with my mother in Phoenix, and she had done about everything I could imagine. She drank and went on benders, leaving me in

185

the apartment for two or three days at a time. Once she said she was going down to the Red Onion for some cigarettes and didn't come back for a week. I knew enough to go to a neighbor's place. People got beaten up there, and one man got killed. I remember watching him being carried out on a stretcher.

My mother had boyfriends. When a man stayed over, I slept on the sofa instead of in the one bed we shared, and I could hear through the thin wall my mother's calling out a stranger's name. When the man liked me, it was all right, but when he didn't, which was more usual, I got shipped down on the Greyhound to my father.

I didn't mind it in Tucson. My father had a house in the barrio then, and there were lots of people moving around the streets at all hours. I liked to watch them doing their deals and loving up and just walking around. I liked the sirens and shouts in Spanish and the music.

Sometimes I stayed a few days, sometimes a few weeks. But always a time came to go back.

"You sure you want to go?" my father used to ask.

"Why wouldn't I?"

"Your mother's not very well," he said. "She's fragile."

"I can take care of her."

The truth was I didn't know whether I wanted to go back. I didn't much like the apartment on the eighth floor or my mother's boyfriends. My father's girlfriends were much nicer. But I kept thinking of my mother's sad face and how much she wanted to be happy.

So it went that way for a long time, back and forth between Phoenix and Tucson. I tried to get my mother to take better care of herself—to go to sleep earlier so she could get to her job, which was in a plant nursery over in Mesa, to eat better, and not to drink so much. She did all right, too, for a while, until she met this man named Ray, who started her on some pills. He moved in, and I went off to Tucson, thinking I'd stay for good.

My father and I got along. He was a spindly man, wiry, very good-looking in a rough way. He had good hands and a sleek brown mustache, and he was a smooth talker. Over against him, I was softer like my mother, with a disposition more inclined to observation. We weren't close in the sense of camaraderie or

186

talking things out. Maybe he felt guilty about leaving. Anyway, we didn't discuss things much, so there were spaces around us unfilled, like something way late at night left unsaid.

I spent a whole school year when I was sixteen with my father, and only saw my mother once. In the fall she got sick and went to the hospital, and she called for me. I stayed up in Phoenix for three months until she died.

I guess I knew she was dying because I asked her questions I never had thought of before—what she used to be like when she was a girl in California, about her parents I'd never met (they owned a small artichoke farm), what she had hoped for in her life. She couldn't speak very well. By then she was sleeping most of the time, and she'd wake up only for brief glimpses of me. She'd start to talk and in the middle of a sentence, when she was describing a place she remembered or a special day, she'd drift off into a terrible stillness.

When she died, I was left hanging.

After that I decided not to go back to school. I wasn't a bad student or a troublemaker. I just didn't do anything. I wrote my homework but couldn't turn it in, and even when I knew the answer in class, I'd sit with my head down on the desk. The teachers didn't know what to do. They talked to me; they sent me to counselors. Why wouldn't I try? Why not cooperate? They even got my one friend, George White Foot, a half-breed Apache, to speak to me. But finally they gave up and let me seep down into groundwater.

About this time was when my father got hold of the trailer. He had been evicted from his house to make way for some renewal project, but I suspected he had other reasons for wanting to be out of town. He liked women. He had a way with them, too, but unlike my mother, he wanted the relationship to be simple. My mother was in love with every man she met, and she'd say "Stevie, he's so wonderful. He *feels* so good. What do you think?"

I thought she wanted love more than anything, but my father didn't. He liked things uncomplicated, and one way to keep them that way was to live out so far no one could drop by.

So pretty much I stayed out at the trailer for the next year. My father might have made me get a job, but in a way I had the upper hand there. My mother had left me a few thousand dollars, and I was able to pay my share of rent and food. Now and then I'd go into Tucson to the library or to a movie, but mostly I stayed home, as if I were waiting for something to happen. I didn't know what. It wasn't waiting, exactly, either. It was passing time. It was as if everything up to then had been a test of endurance, and I had to recover from it. I needed to rest.

I spent some time watching the cars float along the highway in the distance, imagining who was in them and what future they were headed toward. I could see pickup trucks coming from Mexico, red sedans, half-tons, vans. At night the headlights skimmed through the darkness like comets.

For a month I exhumed the trash in the ravine and tried to piece together the lives of the people who'd lived there before. I couldn't come up with much except they were poor and someone had done a good trade with whoever sold Jim Beam.

But mostly I took target practice with the .22 and I read. I read everything I could get my hands on. My father brought me books and magazines whenever he happened to think of me— from the 7-Eleven, from someone's house where he was repairing an air conditioner or a washing machine, from a friend's apartment, sometimes even from the bookmobile parked in the mall where his appliance repair company had its dispatch office. He never asked me what I liked, though. It was his idea that in the general variety he'd hit on something that would move me off high-center. He gave me manuals about engines, a history of Vietnam, a book on oil painting, porno magazines, English novels. I imagined him standing in front of a library shelf or a magazine rack wondering what to choose. What should he take home to a boy about whom he had not the slightest notion?

But I knew him. His whole life was women. He met women in bars or on the job or at diners, supermarkets, offices, even at the bookmobile. He had a gift for it, a genius. Educated or uneducated, black, white, Hispanic; tall or short; he could have charmed the underwear off a nun. But there weren't many nuns that made the long drive to the trailer.

He had a system worked out. He'd bring a woman for a night and take her back to Tucson in the morning. It'd be dark when they'd get there—a turn at Robles Junction, head west on gravel, keep left when the road forked, and so on. The woman would be riding blindfolded, so to speak. There was no telephone, so she couldn't ever call.

Sometimes he'd bring someone home on a Friday night, and she'd stay until Monday. I dreaded these times because my father worked Saturdays half-days, and often overtime, and he'd leave the woman, whoever she was, with me. On such occasions the woman usually slept late. One slept all day without stirring, and I was certain she was dead; and another one, when she woke up late and looked out the window, thought she'd been sent to hell.

But the worst thing was there were no introductions. Sometimes my father hadn't even told the woman I was there, and more than once a woman I'd never seen before came naked from my father's bedroom and, when she saw me, started screaming. After a few times, I made it a habit on Saturday mornings to take target practice with the .22 from the kitchen window.

Even that wasn't enough every time. Once, despite a half-hour's fusillade from the porch on a dead washing machine, a blonde came out half-naked. She was twenty-four or so, hung over, but still pretty, even with her make-up smudged. All she had on were a pair of green panties and a blouse with one button fastened.

"Who is the enemy?" she asked, shielding her eyes from the sun and peering off into the gully.

"Indians."

She moved to the rail of the landing. "Where?"

"You'd better go back inside," I told her. "We're the only wagon train in this circle."

She nodded, "You come with me," she said, as she walked by and dragged her fingers across my shoulder. "I'd feel safer."

But I didn't go. I spent the rest of the morning at the edge of the yard shooting the arms off saguaro Indians.

That wasn't the only incident like that either. I had the suspicion my father may have asked some of his lesser friends to flirt with me, but it was a suspicion I never proved.

One rainy afternoon when he was late, for example, I was reading in the living room, listening occasionally to the barrage on the tin roof. Out the window, little water-falls collected from nowhere and rushed into the gullies. The sandwash was a torrent. Then this woman, whose name was Jake, came to the window. Maybe she was watching for my father; maybe she thought

189

he'd never get there in the storm. Maybe she was bored. Anyway, she turned to me and said, "Steve, do you want to make love?"

"Who-what?"

"Don't you think I'm pretty?"

Jake was pretty. She had a smooth oval face and dark eyes, and nice high breasts which stood out under my father's shirt she had on. "I think you're very pretty."

"Well, then?"

"You're my father's girl."

She made a face that was supposed to show hurt or maybe defiance, but which made her look spoiled. "I'm not anybody's girl," she said.

I won't say I wasn't tempted. Under ordinary circumstances I wouldn't have cared whose girl she was, but these were not ordinary circumstances. I wanted to kiss her and slap her both. I wanted to shake her. What did she mean offering herself like that? But I didn't say anything.

She came over and put her hand on my arm, and I felt a terrible dark chill run through me like a sliver of cold steel. In that instant I knew what torture my mother must have suffered to be so helpless in desire. But the rain stopped abruptly. The drumming on the roof ebbed to a hum, and not far down the gravel road, the headlights of my father's truck delved through the steam rising from the hot earth.

There was one woman who stayed nearly a month. Her name was Esther, and she'd just been divorced from a doctor in Tucson and was waiting to hear about a nursing job in Los Angeles. She didn't have a place to stay, so my father said what-the-hell, and she came to the trailer.

She was not so pretty as most of the women my father had. She had curly hair and a broad face and rather sad blue eyes which looked right at you, which I liked. We used to drink beer together in the afternoons and play gin rummy at the kitchen table. She never asked about my father like some women did. Instead she asked about my mother: what was she like, what did she do, where was she? Why did she and my father get divorced?

I was usually a little drunk, and trying to answer was like exploring a region of myself I'd never encountered. I went down

190

one wrong path after another, found dead ends, labyrinths. If I forced words too quickly, I missed details; if I labored too long, I became lost in a confusion of images. At the same time as it was hopeless to answer, I understood it was important to try. No matter what fleeting impression I gave, no matter how mystified I felt, I needed to know who my mother was to know who I was.

Esther didn't hurry me. She'd listen one day and the next. She'd fetch new beers. She was as solid as I was shaky. Her own divorce, she said, made her tougher, and she knew what she wanted. I admired her patience, and I remember it seemed hopeful to me at the time that someone could choose to change her life, get on a bus one day, and do it.

After Esther left for L.A., there was a month or so when my father didn't bring anyone home. During this stretch, George White Foot showed up one day with a bottle of tequila, which we took down into the sandwash, along with the .22. George said he'd run into my father in a bar, and my father said I was anxious for company.

George had quit school, too. He was bagging groceries temporarily at the Safeway and thinking of going over to Safford to work in the copper mine. "You want to go?" he asked. "I got Apaches who can get you in." He gulped the tequila.

"I'm not done here yet," I said.

George nodded. "What are you doing out here?"

"Taking notes."

He laughed and drank some more. "Taking notes on what?"

I didn't have an answer. I thought I was taking notes. I sighted the rifle and picked off a cholla blossom. "I bet I can out-shoot you," I said. "I'll stand and you can shoot prone. A dollar a target."

"You have to drink some tequila," he said.

I drank some tequila, and George picked the targets, and I beat him five times in a row.

"Where'd you get the name White Foot?" I asked.

"Where'd you get the name Steve?"

He sat down in the sand and skewered the bottle down and took off his tennis shoes and socks. One of his feet was brown like his arms, but the other was albinistic—almost totally white up to the ankle.

I took off my boots and socks. "I got two of them."

We laughed and drank more tequila, and he called me Steve White Feet. "I'll bet the five dollars I owe you you can't give me the right question to the answer 'sis-boom-bah.'"

I pretended to think for a minute, but nothing came to mind. "I don't know."

"Guess."

I didn't want to guess. I was getting drunk and it struck me that George couldn't go to work in the copper mine in Safford, even though that was where the Apaches had their land. "Don't go, George," I said.

He stared at me. He was drunker than I was. "Don't you want to know the question?" he asked.

"I want to know every question."

"An exploding sheep."

He laughed, but it wasn't funny.

We finished the bottle of tequila, and after that we staggered up the sandwash to hunt rabbits. But by then the rabbits were safe.

It was late fall when something changed. The long-day heat was out of the rocks, and I had found a ledge behind an outcropping where I could sit and read and see nothing at all except the blue Sierritas and farther away the Las Guijas Hills and the Santa Ritas. Now and then through my binoculars I'd watch a hawk drifting on the updrafts which poured from the ravines.

Then one evening my father came home early with a stack of books from the bookmobile and some groceries. He actually sat down in the living room.

"I'm going to stay in town for a couple of days," he said.

"Oh, yeah? What's her name?"

"Don't be that way."

"What way? I just asked what her name was."

"Goldie."

I didn't think much of it at the time. My father didn't often stay in town, but that was his business, and it didn't matter to me one way or the other. He didn't give me the details, and I didn't ask.

"You be okay?"

"Sure," I said. "Thanks for the books."

A couple of days later I heard the horn of his truck. I was on the ledge, and I scrambled up to the ridge where I could see down to the trailer. In the circle of my glasses, I made out my father standing on the porch beside a short-haired, dark-haired woman. He was waving to me to come down.

I figured this was Goldie, though I'd imagined her as a blonde. She looked tall from a distance, as tall as my father anyway, who was six feet. She wore fancy sandals, and he had on cowboy boots. She looked like some kind of real-estate person, dressed in a gray business suit, or maybe a social worker, and for a moment I wondered whether my father had some deal going, some scam. Then a piece of sunlight flashed from one of her earrings.

When I had climbed down into the sandwash and half-way up the hill, they appeared at the lip of the trail above me. I paused amidst the tangle of cholla and ocotillo and looked up. The woman's hair, which I'd thought was short, was pushed up on top of her head in a twist. The gray business suit was a sweater and slacks. I guessed she was about thirty, maybe a little older.

What impressed me most, though, was not the way she looked; it was the way my father looked. He kept motioning for me to hurry, and he had a grin on his face that seemed to say he had this secret he couldn't wait to tell me. He must have won the lottery, I thought, the way he was grinning.

"Steve," he said. "Come on up here. This is Goldie. Goldie, this is my boy, Steve."

I climbed the last few yards, and Goldie took a step forward and put out her hand.

I took her hand, felt her smooth palm. "You don't look like a Goldie," I said.

She squeezed my hand and smiled. "You don't look like a boy."

When I heard her voice, I knew she was not the lottery representative or a real-estate lady or like any of the other women who'd ever been to the trailer before. Her voice slid over words with a lilting inflection like water over slick rock, or maybe like the chinooks blow under the eaves of the tin roof.

"She's Irish," my father said. "I met her on a job at her uncle's place out Gates Pass. We've been up at the Grand Canyon for a couple of days."

"Your father rescued me," Goldie said. She gave a small, sweet laugh.

"I thought, if she wants, she might as well stay out here a while," my father said. "What do you think, Steve?"

He'd never asked me before what I thought. "Sounds all right to me," I said. "If she wants."

Right away it was strained. Goldie liked privacy, and in a trailer privacy's as scarce a commodity as snow in hell. From back to front there was a bedroom, a hall-way up one wall which joined the bathroom and a second small bedroom where I slept. The kitchen opened into the living room. Whenever Goldie wanted to use the bathroom, she knocked to make certain it was empty. And when she walked around the house, she had on at least a robe. In some ways it would have been easier having around a woman who didn't mind being seen half-undressed, even a flaunter, than one who was so prissy about things.

She also changed the hours of our days. My father didn't go drink in bars anymore, which was his usual habit. Even when Esther was here for that month, he might as well have been in a bar because as soon as he got home he took her to bed. But with Goldie it was more civilized. When my father got home and tried to talk her into going to bed, she'd laugh and say in a voice both teasing and gentle, "You're nothing but a rotten Englishman."

Goldie wanted to learn to cook—not necessarily fancy things, but something more substantial than hamburgers. She was anxious to try rabbit and venison and rattlesnake, and she liked Mexican food—burritos, jalapeño omelettes, enchiladas—which my father and I were pretty good at. So the three of us ate dinners at a normal hour. She called me Stephen, and I called her Blackie, and we talked about whatever happened to strike Goldie's fancy.

I could take the knocking on the bathroom door and the robe and the family dinners, but I chafed under Goldie's idea that the day started at five A.M. I liked to stay up late and read and then sleep in the next morning. So to hear Goldie making coffee in the dark drove me crazy. The kettle whistled, and she clanked silverware and unscrewed the jar of instant and got out the milk. Then the front door opened and closed. I'd lie there as the gray light seeped through the window, angry, unable to sleep. What was she doing outside? And how long was my father going to let this last?

Once I got up to see why she went outside at that hour. I expected to see her doing calisthenics or praying or something, but when I opened the door, she was sitting on the porch steps

194

bundled up in a wool coat against the chill of the desert. Her coffee was steaming into the air.

"What the hell are you doing?" I asked.

"Sometimes I miss Ireland," was all she said.

For those first several weeks, she went into town with my father in the mornings. She borrowed his truck and toured the countryside—the Desert Museum, the mission of San Xavier, the university, the Pima Air Museum. She ranged as far as Phoenix and Nogales, even drove by herself through the Papago Reservation to Puerto Peñasco on the Gulf of California.

She asked me to go with her once. It was on one of those stormy days when low-flying clouds banked into the Baboquivaris and slipped over into the basin. I couldn't go up to my ledge, so I said all right, I'd go. She wanted to go into the Catalinas—to the top of Mount Lemmon. So that's what we did. The road started in ocotillo and saguaro along Tanque Verde Drive and wound up into oaks and sycamores. A warm misty rain was falling. But when we got higher into the pines it was snowing. I'd seen snow before, but I'd only been in it once up in Flagstaff when I was about nine. My mother had gone up to surprise a man—just the scene my father hated. This man said he owned a sporting goods store, and we went to every store in Flagstaff before we found him. It turned out he was a salesman, and he obviously wasn't expecting to see my mother. She sent me outside to play, and it was snowing on the streets. I remember how dirty the snow seemed, mashed down by tires and turning the buildings gray.

But at the top of Mount Lemmon the snow was clean. The pale trees were ghostly as the air, and even the road was white and unmarked.

"You should see the snow fall into the sea," Goldie said.

"I've never seen the sea."

"Oh, you must, Stephen. I live in Donaghadee, which is a fishing village near Belfast, and to watch the snow settle over the boats in the harbor and sweep across the gray water . . . it's lovely, really."

The snow was beautiful then, too, coming down through the huge ponderosas. We came out of the trees into a clearing where the whole world looked white.

"Stop." Goldie said.

I pulled over, though there were no other cars. Goldie got out and ran into the meadow full of snow. It was so white you couldn't tell where the hills were or how far the meadow extended into the whiteness. I didn't know what she was doing. She looked so frail, running like that into the wide expanse of nothing. It was eerie to see her fading behind the white sheen, as if the air were a deep hole and would swallow her.

I rolled down the window and called to her, but she didn't stop running.

Two months went by, right into December, and Goldie was still there. She had stopped going into town with my father. I guess she'd seen as many museums and churches as anyone could stand.

So she stayed at the trailer with me. Not that I found that a problem: by then I was used to the way she did things. When she was getting dressed, I stayed out of her way, and I developed a grudging respect for her five A.M. coffee. Sometimes I got up and watched the sunrise with her, and we all had breakfast together like ordinary people.

After my father went off to work, Goldie and I sorted out the day. Sometimes we hunted the wash. We'd go after rabbits or quail, and Goldie got so she could shoot a bird in the head from twenty-five yards. I showed her how to hold the dead birds tightly and break their skin at the breastbone so the skin and feathers peeled back like a jacket. We cleaned the quail and soaked them in salt water and made stuffing with bread and spices.

More often we just scouted the terrain. Goldie liked the desert because Ireland was cool and wet, the antithesis of the Southwest. She was fascinated how the ocotillo rolled its leaves in the dryness and the saguaros stored tons of water. We looked for animals—coatis, javelinas, snakes. She seemed to see things more quickly than I, maybe because the land was new to her. She picked out a stockstill deer on the hillside, an eagle sitting on rocks with a rock background.

"Do you think we could see a mountain lion?" she asked.

"Not in daytime."

"I'd like awfully to see one."

"They're here," I said, "but they hunt at night."

196

That night she begged my father to take her to look for a mountain lion.

"A puma? Hah! We wouldn't have the chance of a pimp at St. Peter's to see a mountain lion."

"Stephen says they're around."

"Oh, they're around. But they don't want to see you."

"We could drive the back roads," Goldie said. "Don't they hunt at night?"

"No way," my father said. He smiled patiently and pinched her arm, and every night for two weeks after that, they drove the back roads over in the Papago Reservation.

Something happened on these excursions. When they returned late at night my father looked haggard and drawn, and he'd sit down and have a stiff shot of rye whiskey. He wasn't angry or short with me or with Goldie. He'd talk normally, but I could tell the trip had exhausted him in a way that was beyond just the driving. At first I thought it was burning the candle late and early. My father wasn't used to staying up late and getting up at five. But it was more than that.

The next night, just as they were about to leave, I asked whether I could go along. "Do you mind?" I asked Goldie.

"You don't want to go," my father said.

"Why don't I?"

"You don't."

But he wouldn't give me a reason, and Goldie didn't mind. She sat between us in the front seat, her hands braced on the dashboard, her face pressed close to the windshield. We proceeded slowly, thirty miles an hour or so, the speed at which Goldie said she could see best. The headlights jerked over mesquite and saguaro and cholla, and sometimes we ran without a bend in the track for ten miles or more toward some village whose name was no name—Vamori, Idak, Gu Oidak.

All the while Goldie talked. The silhouette of her glassy forehead and her arced nose and her mouth blurred against the splayed light that moved in front of the truck, but she spoke without a pause, in that lilting voice. She recounted incidents from her childhood in Donaghadee. Her father was a fisherman, her mother a baker. They had a small house, old it was, she said, down at the rocks. She had got a scholarship to school, the first of

197

her family to go away. They had all been fishermen laboring over nets and boats . . .

And I gradually began to feel the cloudy days over the sea, and to see the long sloping green farms bordered by gray stone walls. And I felt my father sink down gently behind the wheel.

We saw kangaroo rats, badgers, snakes, deer. Once a coyote crossed the tracks in front of the lights. But there were no mountain lions.

Not long after that my father stopped taking Goldie on those late rides. He said it was the expense of the gas; and finding a mountain lion was against all odds. But I understood it was something else that troubled him. He had come up against something he'd never faced before, which was what to do next. He liked Goldie. She was the first woman he'd cared about since my mother, or maybe ever, but she was a strain on him, too. Normally he was the one in control, the person to say yes or no to things, but with Goldie he found himself the one holding on. At dinner he'd stare at her, not listening to her talk, but looking at her as if he were trying to figure out something. From what I could tell, Goldie was satisfied with her life. She had no plans to leave. But the idea of her leaving was always there in the air like a hawk circling, throwing its shadow across the ground.

It was about this time, too, that I went to see George White Foot. He was on the last half-hour of his shift at the Safeway over on Speedway, and when I first got a glimpse of him—black hair in a pony tail, tall, slouched over the end of one of the check-out stands—he looked as though he were moving in slow motion.

"Hey, George," I said.

"If it isn't Steve White Feet," he said. "What you got, man?"

His eyes were glazed, and I could tell he was operating on batteries. "I was going to buy a six-pack," I said. "What kind do you like?"

"Anything."

I bought a double-pack of Miller and waited in the truck. When George finished, we drove out Tanque Verde. All along the highway huge divots had been scoured in the saguaro and greasewood for new houses. While one crew scraped the hillside, another was erecting frames for the families that would settle there.

198

"It makes you wonder, doesn't it?" I said.

"Wonder what?" George stared straight ahead.

"Look at the houses. Where's the water coming from?"

George wasn't paying attention to the houses. He was swilling beer and staring through the neon lights. "I'm going to Safford next week," he said. "Are you done out there yet with your old man?"

"Not yet."

"Shit," George said in a disgusted voice. Then he softened. "It's not bad pay. The union takes an interest."

"I'm not a copper miner," I said.

"Neither am I."

I imagined the daylight breaking across the huge orange copper pit, and men filing one at a time through a metal gate. All day they would chew the earth with huge machines, then go home and come back the next day. At the end of the week, they'd have money.

"You got to do something, Steve," George said.

He looked at me, but his eyes were blank. "Give yourself a break," I told him. "You don't have to go."

"A break? Like you? Give myself a break like you? At least I see my chances when they come at me. I got to jump."

"Jump where?"

"Fuck you," George said. He turned away and swigged the beer. He was afraid, that was all. But he wasn't afraid of Safford. He was afraid of the same thing I was: that dark land up ahead beyond the headlights where the highway went on into nothing.

In January my father became more distant, as if he were edging away from us. I didn't notice it at first because it was a gradual shift and day-to-day things didn't change much. He was often late for dinner—that's what I remember—and I began to wonder whether he was working late or going drinking or what.

One night Goldie and I had prepared a rabbit with gravy and rice and a nice salad. She'd dressed up for the occasion in a Mexican skirt and blouse she'd bought in Nogales as a souvenir, and she'd fixed her hair with turquoise pins. She'd put on perfume, too, which she seldom wore.

We were drinking Coors to tide us over, watching out the kitchen window at the gray dusk sliding down from the mountains. I was conscious how soft her skin looked above the scalloped neckline of her blouse, how her bare neck curved so delicately from her rounded shoulders. Her cheeks were flushed from the beer and from the heat of the rabbit's cooking.

"Where is he, do you think?" she asked.

"Looking for mountain lions."

She smiled but did not look at me. "They must be in caves all through these hills."

I nodded. The land out the window had faded. The Sierritas were lavender and blue, ebbing toward black, and in the yard the arc light had come on.

"You'd look for a mountain lion for me, wouldn't you, Stephen?"

"I would," I said.

She laughed and stood up and twirled around in the small space of the kitchen. Then she stopped and looked back out the window. "Do you know what he's really doing?"

"No."

"You do."

"He's looking for a place in town," I said.

Goldie seemed surprised. "What place?"

"Somewhere better than the trailer. He wants it for you."

We were silent for a long time, and the small space tightened up. Goldie didn't move from the window.

"Are you going to stay with him?" I asked.

That was the only time Goldie didn't say anything. She looked around at me with an expression so pained I couldn't move.

"Let's drink," she said finally. "The Irish are famous for drinking."

She got out the whiskey bottle from under the sink and poured two glasses and gave me one. Then she went into the living room.

A moment later, I heard the door open and close, and the trailer was silent.

That was when I knew how my mother had lived through all those years. I felt at that moment the weight of that emptiness of love, that terrible absence which wanted filling. Momentum was like wind seeking and seeking: even when it was invisible it was there, driving forward, unable to be calm. I held my breath for a minute, and then I followed Goldie.

200

I stood on the landing. Goldie was in the yard, illuminated by the arc light, holding her glass of whiskey above her head. She swirled through the light, lifting her skirt with one hand, twirling like a dancer across the gravel. She paused and drank and continued toward the rim of the trail into the sandwash.

"Stephen," she said. "Come on."

But she didn't wait for me. Her voice carried through the stillness and then she was gone over the edge and into the ravine.

I glanced down the dirt road toward the highway hoping to see the headlights of my father's truck sweeping up among the saguaros. But there was nothing there but the vacant dark highway and the barely perceptible ridge of the hills.

I went after Goldie, not knowing what else to do. By the time I reached the sandy wash, she had started upstream. Her dark tracks curved through the sand and around the first bend, and I called to her and heard my own voice echo against the rocks.

I knew she was waiting for me. I walked slowly, feeling my steps yield to the soft sand.

She was there, around that first outcropping of rocks. Her white blouse was vivid in the air. She had taken the turquoise pins from her hair, and it fell across her shoulder like black feathers.

I stopped and waited.

"Come here, Stephen," she said.

I went closer.

"Smell my hair." She bent her head back so that her black hair cascaded into her hand, and she held it up to me.

I breathed in. She pushed her hair into my face, across my cheek. Her hair smelled of apricot.

"Smell here," she said. "What does my skin smell like?" She pulled her blouse down over one shoulder.

"Cholla blossoms."

"Close your eyes."

I closed my eyes.

"Tight," she said.

I kept my eyes tightly closed, feeling my heart beat different colors behind the lids. The breeze smoothed across my damp forehead. In the thicket not far away, thrashers and quail were settling in. I heard the swishing of Goldie's skirt, the movement of cloth, the sigh she made when the cool air touched her skin.

201

*　*　*

In the early morning, while my father and Goldie were still sleeping, I packed the few things I had and coasted the truck out of the yard. About a mile down, I abandoned the truck where the sand gully intersected the gravel. It would take my father a while to understand, then at least an hour to reach the truck. I walked from there to Sasabe road, and sometime toward dawn got a ride north from a Mexican businessman. A Papago took me west on the main road to Sells, and by evening I was in Blythe, California.

I was going somewhere where it snowed into the sea— Northern California or maybe Oregon. I wasn't certain of anything. It was the beginning for me of a sadness which, I suppose, had to come to me sometime, an aching that lasted for years.

WAITING FOR MR. KIM

by CAROL ROH-SPAULDING

W<small>HEN</small> G<small>RACIE</small> K<small>ANG'S</small> elder twin sisters reached the age of eighteen, they went down to the Alameda County Shipyards and got jobs piecing battleships together for the U.S. Navy. This was the place to find a husband in 1945, if a girl was doing her own looking. They were Americans, after all, and they were of age. Her sisters caught the bus down to the waterfront every day and brought home their paychecks every two weeks. At night, they went out with their girlfriends, meeting boys at the cinema or the drugstore, as long as it was outside of Chinatown.

Gracie's parents would never have thought it was husbands they were after. Girls didn't choose what they were given. But the end of the war distracted everybody. While Mr. Kang tried to keep up with the papers and Mrs. Kang tried to keep up with the laundry, Sung-Sook slipped away one day with a black welder enrolled in the police academy and Sung-Ohk took off with a Chinatown nightclub singer from L.A. with a sister in the movies.

Escaped. Gracie had watched from the doorway that morning as Sung-Sook pulled on her good slip in front of the vanity, lifted her hair, breathed in long and slow. Her eyes came open, she saw Gracie's reflection. "Comeer," she said. "You never say goodbye." She kissed Gracie between the eyes. Gracie had only shrugged: "See you." Then Sung-Ohk from the bathroom: "This family runs a laundry, so where's all the goddamn towels?"

When the girls didn't come home, the lipstick and rouge wiped off their faces, to fold the four o'clock sheets, she understood what was what. On the vanity in the girls' room she found a white paper bell with sugar sprinkles. In silver letters, it read:

CALL TODAY!
Marry Today!
Your Wedding! Your Way!
Eighteen or Over?
We Won't Say Nay!
(May Borrow Veil and Bouquet)

As simple as having your hair done. Gracie sat at the vanity, thinking of the thousand spirits of the household her mother was always ticking off like a grocery list—spirit of the lamp, the clock, the ashtray. Spirit in the seat of your chair. Spirit of the stove, the closet, the broom, the shoes. Spirit of the breeze in the room, the Frigidaire. Gracie had always been willing to believe in them; she only needed something substantial to go on. Now, in her sisters' room, she felt that the spirits had been there, had moved on, to other inhabited rooms.

Those girls had escaped Thursday evenings with the old *chong-gaks*, who waited effortlessly for her father to give the girls away. No more sitting, knees together, in white blouses and circle skirts, with gritted smiles. Now Gracie would sit, the only girl, while her father made chitchat with Mr. Han and Mr. Kim. Number three daughter, much younger, the dutiful one, wouldn't run away. If her mother had had the say, the girls would have given their parents grandchildren by now. But she didn't have the say, and her father smiled his pleasant, slightly anxious smile at the *chong-gaks* and never ever brought up payment.

He was the one paying now. No one got dinner that night. Pots flew, plates rattled in the cabinets, the stove rumbled in the corner, pictures slid, clanked, tinkled. "Now we'll have a nigger for a grandson and a chink for a son-in-law, Mr. Kang!" her mother shouted. She cursed Korean, but had a gift for American slurs, translating the letter found taped to the laundry boiler into the horrors of marrying for love.

Gracie and Little Gene pressed themselves against the wall, squeezed around the Frigidaire, sidled to the staircase. They sat and backed up one step at a time, away from the stabs and swishes of the broom. "Or didn't you want Korean grandchildren,

Mr. Kang? You're the one who let them fall into American love. Could I help it there aren't any good *chong-gaks* around? Thought we'd pack the girls off to Hawaii where the young ones are? Ha. I'd like to see the missionaries pay for that!"

Their father came into view below. Hurried, but with his usual dignity, he ducked and swerved as necessary. Silently, solemnly, he made for the closet, opened the door, and stepped in among the coats. The blows from first the bristled then the butted end of the broom came down upon the door.

Little Gene whispered, "I'm going outside."

"Fine," Gracie told him. "If you can make it to the door."

"Think I can't manage the window? I land in the trash bin, pretty soft!"

Gracie told him, "Bring me back a cigarette, then," and he left her there. A year younger than she and not very big for thirteen, he was still number one son. Gracie stuck her fingers in her mouth all the way to the knuckle, clamped down hard.

She chopped cabbage, scrubbed the bathhouses, washed and pressed and folded linen and laundry, dreaming up lives for her sisters. From their talk and their magazines, she knew how it should go. Sung-Sook stretched out by the pool in a leopard-print bathing suit with pointy bra cups and sipped colored drinks from thin glasses, leaving a pink surprise of lips at the rim. Somebody else served them, fetched them, cleaned them. Her husband shot cardboard men through the heart and came home to barbecue T-bones. Every night they held hands at the double feature. Sung-Ohk slipped into a tight Chinese-doll dress and jeweled cat-eyes, sang to smoky crowds of white people from out of town. Her lips grazed the mike as she whispered, "Thank you, kind people, thank you." In the second act, her husband, in a tux, dipped her, spun her, with slant-eyed-Gene-Kelly-opium flair. All the white people craned their necks and saw that Oriental women could have good legs.

They left Gracie and her mother with all the work. At first, her father tried to help out. He locked up the barbershop at lunch, crossed the street, passed through the kitchen, and stepped into Hell, as they called it. But her mother snapped down the pants press when she saw him and from a blur of steam shouted, "Fool for love! I'm warning you to get out of here, Mr. Kang!"

She bowed her head at the market now. She had stopped going to church. Lost face, it was called. And there was the worry of it. No one knew these men who took the girls away. Maybe one was an opium dealer and the other was a pimp. Maybe those girls were in for big disappointment, even danger. Her father twisted his hands, helpless and silent in the evenings. Her mother clanked the dishes into the sink, banged the washers shut, punched the buttons with her fists, helpless, too.

It was true he was a fool for love, as far as Gracie could tell. Her mother slapped at his hands when he came up behind her at the chopping board to kiss her hair—pretty brave, considering that knife. When her mother tried to walk behind him in the street, he stopped and tried to take her hand. Gracie and her mother were always nearly missing buses because she'd say, "Go on, Mr. Kang. We're coming," and they'd stay behind as she cleaned out her purse or took forever with her coat, just to have it the way she had learned it, her husband a few paces ahead, women behind. Maybe the girls would never have gotten away if he'd been firm about marriage, strict about love.

Where her parents were from, shamans could chase out the demon spirits from dogs, cows, rooms, people. Maybe her father had had the fool chased out of him, because when Thursday came around, he sat in the good chair with the Bible open on his knees, and Gracie sat beside him, waiting. Life was going to go on without her sisters. Her life. Gracie watched her father for lingering signs of foolishness. Above the donated piano, the cuckoo in the clock popped out seven times. As always, her father looked up with a satisfied air. He loved that bird. Her mother believed there was a spirit in the wooden box. The spirit was saying it was time.

Little Gene was free in the streets with that gang of Chinese boys. She waited for her cigarette and his stories—right now, he might be breaking into the high school, popping open the Coca-Cola machine, busting up some lockers. There weren't any Jap boys left to beat up on, and they stayed away from the mostly black neighborhoods or they'd get beat up themselves. Gracie sat with her hands clasped at her knees, worrying about him, admiring him a little.

First came the tap-tap of the missionary ladies from the United Methodist Church. Their hats looked like squat birds' nests through the crushed ice window. Every Thursday, they seemed to have taken such pains with their dresses and hats and shoes, Gracie couldn't think how they had lasted in the mountain villages of Pyongyang province. She had never been there herself, or been to mountains at all, but she knew there were tigers in Pyongyang.

Her father rose and assumed his visitors smile. "Everyone will be too polite to mention the girls, Gracie," he told her. That was the only thing at all he said about them to her.

The ladies stepped in, chins pecking. One bore a frosted cake, the other thrust forward a box of canned goods. American apologies. As though the girls had died, Gracie thought. Her father stiffened, but kept his smile.

"We think it's wonderful about the war," the cake lady began.

"Praise be to God that we've stopped the Japanese," the Spam lady went on. They looked at one another.

"The *Japanese* Japanese," said the second. She paused. "And we are so sorry about your country, Mr. Kang."

"But this is your country now," said the first.

Her father eased them onto more conversational subjects. They smiled, heads tilted, as Gracie pressed out "Greensleeves," "Colonial Days," "Jesus, We Greet Thee," on the piano. And at half past the hour, they were up and on their way out, accepting jars of *kimch'i* from her mother with wrinkle-nosed smiles.

The barbershop customers did not come by. Mr. Woo from the bakery and Mr. and Mrs. Lim from the Hunan restaurant stayed away. All the Chinese and Koreans knew about saving face. Except the *chong-gaks,* who knew better, surely, but arrived like clockwork anyway, a black blur and a white blur at the window. They always shuffled their feet elaborately on the doorstep before knocking, and her father used to say, "That's very Korean," to Sung-Sook and Sung-Ohk, who didn't bother to fluff their hair or straighten their blouses for the visitors. They used to moan, "Here come the old goats. Failure One and Failure Two." Her father only shushed them, saying, "Respect, daughters, respect." Gracie saw that he could have done better than that if he really expected the girls to marry these men, but after all, the girls were right. Probably her father could see that. They were failures. No families, even at their age. Little money, odd jobs, wasted lives. A week before, they had been only a couple of nuisances who brought her sticks of Beechnut gum and seemed never to fathom her sisters' hostility. They were that stupid, and now they were back. One Korean girl was as good as any other.

Gracie could actually tolerate Mr. Han. He had been clean and trim in his black suit, pressed shirt, and straight tie every Thursday evening since her sisters had turned sixteen. He was a tall, hesitant man with most of his hair, surprisingly good teeth, and little wire glasses so tight over his nose that the lenses steamed up when he was nervous. Everyone knew he had preferred Sung-Ohk, whose kindest remark to him ever was that he looked exactly like the Chinese servant in a Hollywood movie. He always perched on the piano bench as though he didn't mean to stay long, and he mopped his brow when Sung-Ohk glared at him. But he never pulled Gracie onto his lap to kiss her and pat her, and he never, as the girls called it, licked with his eyes.

He left that to Mr. Kim. Mr. Kim in the same white suit, white shirt, white tie, and white shoes which had never really been white, but always the color of pale urine. His teeth were brown from too much tea and sugar and opium. This wasn't her hateful imagination. She had washed his shirts ever since she'd started working. She knew the armpit stains that spread like an infection when she tried to soak them. The hairs and smudges of ash and something like pus in his sheets. She could smell his laundry even before she saw the ticket. His breath stank, too, like herring.

Mr. Kim found everything amusing. "It's been too warm, hasn't it, Mr. Kang?" he said by way of greeting. Then he chuckled, "I'm afraid our friend Mr. Han is almost done in by it."

"Yes, let me get you some iced tea," her father announced. "Mrs. Kang!"

Mr. Kim chuckled again at his companion. "Maybe his heart is suffering. Nearly sixty, you know. Poor soul. He's got a few years on me, anyway, haven't you, old man?"

Mr. Han lowered himself on the piano bench. "Yes, it's been too warm, too much for me."

His companion laughed like one above that kind of weakness. Then he said, "And how is Miss Kang? She's looking very well. She seems to be growing."

Gracie hunched her shoulders, looked anywhere but at him.

"Yes, she's growing," her father answered carefully. "She's still a child." The men smiled at each other with a lot of teeth showing, but their eyes were watchful. "Of course, she's a little lonesome nowadays," her father continued. Mr. Kim eyed him, then he seemed to catch on and slapped his knee—good joke. Mr. Han squinted in some sort of pain.

If Mr. Kim hadn't been in America even longer than her father had, with nothing to show for it but a rented room above the barbershop, then he might have been able to say, "What about this one, Mr. Kang? Are you planning to let her get away, too?" But if he'd had something to show for his twenty or so years in America, he wouldn't be sitting in her father's house and she wouldn't be waiting to be his bride.

Then from the piano bench: "Lonesome, Miss Kang?" Everybody looked. Mr. Han blinked, startled at the attention. He quietly repeated, "Have you, too, been lonesome?" Gracie looked down at her hands. Her father was supposed to answer, let him answer. At that moment, her mother entered, head bowed over the tea tray. Gracie could hear the spirit working in the cuckoo clock.

Her father had told her once that he'd picked cotton and grapes with the Mexicans in the Salinas Valley, and it got so hot you could fry meat on the railroad ties. But that was nothing compared to the sticky summers in Pyongyang, where the stench of human manure brought the bile to your throat. That was why he loved Oakland, he said, where the ocean breeze cleaned you out. It reminded him of his childhood visits to Pusan Harbor, when he'd traveled to visit his father who had been forced into the service of the Japanese. And it reminded him of the day he sailed back from America for his bride.

Bright days, fresh wind. Gracie imagined the women who had waited for the husbands who had never returned. Those women lived in fear, her mother had said. They were no good to marry if the men didn't come back, or if they did return but had no property, they had no legal status in America and no prospects in Korea. Plenty of the women did away with themselves, or their families sold them as concubines. "You think I'm lying?" she told Gracie. "I waited ten years for him. People didn't believe the letters he sent after a while. My family started talking about what to do with me, because I had other sisters waiting to marry, only I was the oldest and they had to get rid of me first!"

Gracie imagined those women, their hands tucked neatly in their bright sleeves, their smooth hair and ancient faces looking out over the water from high rooms. And she thought of Mr. Han

209

gazing from his window out over the alley and between skyscrapers and telephone poles to his glimpse of the San Francisco Bay. Where he was, the sky was black, starless in the city. Where she was, the sun rose, a brisk, hopeful morning.

On a morning like that, Gracie took the sheets and laundry across the street and up to the rented rooms. Usually the *chonggaks* had coffee and a bun at the bakery and then strolled around the lake, but Gracie always knocked and set the boxes down.

Mr. Han's door inched open under her knuckles. The breeze in the bright room, the sterile light of morning in there, the cord rattling at the blinds. Something invisible crept out from the slit in the door and was with her in the hall.

"Mr. Han? Just your laundry, Mr. Han." Spirits of memory— she and Little Gene climbing onto his knees, reaching into his pockets for malted milk balls or sticks of gum. "Where are *your* children?" they'd ask. "Where is your stove? Where is your sink? Where is your mirror?" Mr. Han had always smiled, as though he were only hiding the things they named, could make them appear whenever he wanted.

She pushed the door open, and the spirits of memory mingled with the spirits of longing and desire. The bulb of the bare night light buzzed, like a recollection in a head full of ideas. Mr. Han lay half-on, half-off the bed. One shoe pressed firmly on the floor, as though half of him had had somewhere to go. The glasses dangled from the metal bed frame. That was where his head was, pressed against the bars. His eyes were rolled back, huge and amazed, toward the window. And at his throat, a stripe of beaded red, the thin lips of flesh puckering slightly, like the edges of a rose.

Spirits scuttered along the walls, swirled upwards, twisting in their airy, familiar paths. They pressed against the ceiling. They watched her in the corner. His spirit was near, she felt, in the white field of his pillow. Or in the curtains that puffed and lifted at the sill like a girl's skirt in the wind.

Gracie squatted and peered under the bed. The gleam there was a thing she had known all of her life, a razor from the barbershop. Clean, almost no blood, like his throat. She knew it was loss of air, not loss of blood, that did it. She knew because she'd heard about it before. Two or three of the neighborhood Japs had done the same, when they found that everything they thought

210

they owned they no longer had a right to. They'd had three days to sell what they could and go. She didn't know where. She only knew that her father had been able to buy the barbershop and the bathhouse because of it.

Wind swelled in the hall, with the spirits of car horns, telephone wires, shop signs, traffic lights, and a siren, not for him. They were present at the new death—curious, laughing, implacable. They sucked the door shut. Gracie started. "Leaving now," she announced. "Mr. Han," she whispered to the *chong-gak*. Then she remembered he'd become part of something else, something weightless, invisible, near. She said it louder. "Mr. Han. I'm sorry for you, Mr. Han."

Mr. Kim ate with the Kangs that afternoon, after the ambulances had gone, and again in the evening. His fingers trembled. He lowered his head to the rice, unable to lift it to his mouth, scraping feebly with his chopsticks. Of the death he had one thing to say, which he couldn't stop saying: "I walked alone this morning. Why did I decide to walk alone, of all mornings?"

Mrs. Kang muttered guesses about what to do next, not about the body itself or the police inquiry or who was responsible for his room and his things, but about how best to give peace to the spirit of the *chong-gak*, who might otherwise torment the rest of their days. He didn't have a family of his own to torment. She'd prepared a plate of meat and rice and *kimch'i,* saying, "Where do I *put* this?"

Little Gene, jealous that Gracie had found the body and he hadn't, offered, "How 'bout on the sill? Then he can float by whenever. Or in his room? I'll stay in there all night and watch for him." Then he patted his stomach. "Or how 'bout right here?"

"Damn," her mother went on. "I wish now I'd paid more attention to the shamans. But we stayed away from those women unless we needed them. My family was afraid I'd get the callbecause I was sickly and talked in my sleep, and we have particularly restless ancestors. But I didn't have it in me. Was it food every day for a month or every month for a year? What a mystery. Now we'll have spirits till we all die."

"Girls shouldn't be shamans, anyway," Little Gene announced. "Imagine Gracie chasing spirits away."

211

Asshole, Gracie mouthed. Little Gene flipped her off. None of the adults understood the sign.

"You don't chase them, honey," Gracie's mother said to her. "You feed them and pay them and talk to them."

"Tell *him*," Gracie answered. "He's the one who brought it up."

"Feed everyone who's here first," Little Gene suggested. Gracie flipped him off in return.

"What's that you're doing with your fingers, Gracie?" he shot back. She put her finger to her lips and pointed at her father. His eyes were closed. He kept them that way, head bowed, lips moving.

"Fine," her mother announced. "Let's do Christian, Mr. Kang. It's simpler, as far as I'm concerned."

Mr. Kim lifted his head from his rice bowl, looking very old.

Her mother eyed him sternly. "Cheaper, too."

That night Gracie lay in her bed by the open window. Where was his spirit now? In heaven, at God's side? Or restlessly feeding on *bulgogi* and turnips in his room? Or somewhere else entirely, or nowhere at all? Please God or Thousand Spirits, she prayed. Let me marry for love. Please say I'm not waiting for Mr. Kim. It's fine with me if I'm a *chun-yo* forever.

They held a small service at the Korean United Methodist Church. Her father stood up and said a little about the hard life of a *chong-gak* in America, the loneliness of these men, the difficulties for Oriental immigrants. Gracie felt proud of him, though he was less convincing about heaven. No one even knew for certain if Mr. Han had converted.

Mr. Kim sat in white beside Gracie. "Thy kingdom come," he murmured, "thy will be done." And he reached out and took her hand, looking straight ahead to her father. His hand was moist. She could smell him.

"And forgive us our trespasses," she prayed.

"As we forgive those who trespass against us," he continued, and he squeezed her hand with the surety of possession, though her fingers slipped in his palm.

Gracie never got to the "amen." Instead, she leaned into his side, tilted her face to his cheek, and brought her lips to his ear. "You dirty old bastard," she whispered. Then she snatched her hand back and kept her head bowed, trembling. She wished she could pray that he would die, too, if it was the only way. From the corner of her eye, she could see Mr. Kim's offended hand held open on his knee. Sweat glistened in the creases of his palm. She would never be able to look into his eyes again. For a moment, pity and disgust swept through her. Then, as the congregation stood, she said her own prayer. It went, Please oh please oh please.

Little Gene stuck his head in the laundry room. "Hey, you! Mrs. Kim!"

Gracie flung a folded pillowcase at him.

"Whew. Step out of that hellhole for a minute. I've got something to show you."

He slid a cigarette from behind his ear and they went out the alley-side steps and shared it by the trash bin. "The day they give you away, I'll have this right under your window, see? I'll even stuff it with newspapers so you'll land easy."

"Nowhere to run," Gracie told him. It was the name of a movie they'd seen.

"Isn't Hollywood someplace? Isn't Mexico someplace?"

Gracie laughed out loud. "You coming?"

"'Course I am. Mama's spirit crap is getting on my nerves."

Gracie shrugged. "You're too little to run away. Why should I need help from someone as little as you?"

Little Gene stood on tiptoe and sneered into her face. "Because I'm a boy." Then he grinned and exhaled smoke through his nose and the sides of his mouth.

"Dragon-breath," she called him.

"Come on, Mrs. Kim. This way." They scrambled up the steps, took the staircase to the hall, then stepped through the door that led down again to the ground floor through an unlit passage to the old opium den. It was nothing but a storage room for old washers now, a hot box with a ceiling two stories above them. It baked, winter or summer, because it shared a wall with the boiler.

They'd hid there when they were little, playing hide-and-seek or creating stories about the opium dealers and the man who was supposed to have hung himself in there. They could never figure out where he might have hung himself from since the ceiling was so high and the walls so bare. They looked up in awe. Once, Little Gene thought he'd be clever, and he shut himself in the dryer. Gracie couldn't find him for the longest time, but when she came back for a second look, the round window was steamed up and he wasn't making any noise. She pulled him out. He was grinning, eyes vacant. "You stupid dumb stupid stupid kid."

Little Gene felt for the bulb on the wall, pulled the chain. Now the old dryer was somehow on its side. There were two busted washers and a cane chair. The air was secret, heavy with dust and heat. Gracie felt along the walls for loose bricks, pulled one out, felt around inside like they used to do, looking for stray nuggets or anything else that might have been hidden and forgotten by the Chinese who had lived there before.

Little Gene got on his hands and knees. "Lookit." He eased out a brick flush with the floor. "Lookit," he said again.

Gracie crouched. He crawled back to make way for her, then pushed her head down. "Down there, in the basement."

She saw dim, natural light, blackened redwood, steam-stained. The bathhouse. "So what? I clean 'em every day of my life."

"Just wait," he said.

Then the white blade of a man's back rose into view. Little Gene's hand was a spider up and down her side. "See him, Mrs. Kim? Bet you can't wait."

The back lowered, rose, lowered again, unevenly, painfully. She saw hair slicked back in seaweed streaks, tea-colored splotches on his back, the skin damp and speckled like the belly of a fish. Little Gene's hand was a spider again at her neck. Gracie slapped at him, crouched, looked again. "What the hell's he doing? Rocking himself?"

Little Gene only giggled nervously.

The eyes of Mr. Kim stared toward the thousand spirits, his mouth hung open. Then those eyes rolled back in his head, pupil-less, white, and still. "God, is he dying?" Gracie asked. If she moved a muscle, she would burst. "Is he dying?" she asked again. "Don't touch me," she told her brother, who was impatient with spidery hands.

Little Gene rolled his eyes. "That's all we need. He's not dying stupid. Unless he dies every day." Life in a dim bathhouse, Gracie thought. Deaths in bright rooms.

A door slammed hard on the other side of the wall. Her mother cursed, called her name. Little Gene giggled and did the stroking motion at his crotch, then Gracie scrambled to her knees

214

and pulled him up with her. He grabbed for the chain on the bulb. Dark. "Don't scream," he giggled.

"Gracie! Damn you!" her mother called.

Then his hands flew to her, one at her shoulder, the other, oily and sweet, cupping her open mouth.

A letter arrived the next Thursday. Sung-Sook had used her head and addressed it to the barbershop. Her father brought it up to her in the evening. Gracie was at her window, leaning out, watching the sky begin to gather color. "For 'Miss Gracie Kang,' " he read. " 'Care of Mr. Park A. Kang.' " There was no return address. The paper smelled faintly like roses.

With his eyes, her father pleaded for news of them. He said, "You look like you're waiting for someone."

She shrugged. "It's Thursday." She wanted him to leave her alone until it was time to go downstairs and sit with Mr. Kim. Instead, he came to the window and looked out with her. "Where's your brother?"

"Wherever he feels like being."

He only smiled. Then he told her, "Mr. Kim has given me money. A lot of money."

She drew herself up. She couldn't look at him. "What money?"

"It's for a ticket, Gracie. He wants me to purchase him a ticket to Pusan and arrange some papers for him."

"Alone?" she asked.

"Alone."

She smiled out at the street, but asked again, "What money?"

Her father answered, "He will be happy to have a chance to tell you goodbye." And he left her at the window.

His money, she knew. Her father's. She kept still at the window. With her eyes closed, she saw farther than she had ever seen. "Did you hear that?" she said out loud, in case any spirits, celestial or domestic, were listening.

Then she carefully opened her letter. There was a piece of pale, gauzy paper, and a couple of photographs—a good thing, since the girls had stolen a bunch of family snapshots when they left.

Dear Gracie,
    I hope they let you see this. You're going to be an auntie now. Sung-Ohk's the lucky one, but me and El

are really trying. For a baby, you know. That's El in his rookie uniform and I'm in my wedding dress. We're at the Forbidden City, the club in San Francisco. Louie, that's Sung-Ohk's husband, got us in free on our wedding night. The other picture is of Louie and Sung-Ohk at Newport Beach. Isn't he handsome? Like El. We all live near the beach, ten minutes by freeway.

You'd love it here, but I guess you'd love it anywhere but Oakland. How are the old creeps, anyway? Maybe they'll die before Mom and Dad give you away, ha-ha.

Be good. Don't worry. We're going to figure something out. El says you can stay with us. Sung-Ohk sends her love. I do, too.

The letter fluttered in her hand in the window. She pulled open the drawer at her bedside table, folded the paper neatly back in its creases, and set it inside. Then she took out the only thing her sisters had left behind, the sugar-sprinkled, silver-lettered, instant-ceremony marriage advertisement. Gracie breathed in deeply, as her sister had done with the hope of her new life—as, perhaps, Mr. Han had done, with the hope of his release. Somewhere near, Little Gene laughed out loud in the street. Her mother banged dinner into the oven. Her father waited below, his Bible open on his knees, to greet the missionary ladies, to say goodbye to Mr. Kim. Below, a white, slow figure stepped from a door and headed across the street. Again, she breathed in. And what she took in was her own. Not everything had a name.

JACK OF DIAMONDS
by ELIZABETH SPENCER

ONE APRIL AFTERNOON, Central Park, right across the street, turned green all at once. It was a green toned with gold and seemed less a color of leaves than a stained cloud settled down to stay. Rosalind brought her bird book out on the terrace and turned her face up to seek out something besides pigeons. She arched, to hang her long hair backwards over the terrace railing, soaking in sunlight while the starlings whirled by.

The phone rang, and she went inside.

"I just knew you'd be there, Rosie," her father said. "What a gorgeous day. Going to get hotter. You know what I'm thinking about? Lake George."

"Let's go right now," Rosalind said.

The cottage was at Bolton Landing. Its balconies were built out over the water. You walked down steps and right off into the lake, or into the boat. In a lofty beamed living room, shadows of water played against the walls and ceiling. There was fine lake air, and chill pure evenings. . . .

The intercom sounded. "Gristede's, Daddy. They're buzzing."

Was it being in the theater that made her father, whenever another call came, exert himself to get more into the first? "Let's think about getting up there, Rosie. Summer's too short as it is. You ask Eva when she comes in. Warm her up to it. We'll make our pitch this evening. She's never even seen it . . . can you beat that?"

"I'm not sure she'll even like it," Rosalind said.

"Won't like it? It's hardly camping out. Of course, she'll love it. Get it going, Rosie baby. I'm aiming for home by seven."

The grocer's son who brought the order up wore jeans just like Rosalind's. "It's getting hot," he remarked. "It's about melted my ass off."

"Let's see if you brought everything." She had tried to give up presiding over the food after her father remarried, but when her stepmother turned out not to care much about what happened in the kitchen, she had cautiously gone back to seeing about things.

"If I forgot, I'll get it. But if you think of something—"

"I know, I'll come myself. You think you got news?"

They were old friends. They sassed each other. His name was Luis—Puerto Rican.

It was after the door to the service entrance closed with its hollow echo, and was bolted, and the service elevator had risen, opened, and closed on Luis, that Rosalind felt the changed quality in things, a new direction, like the tilt of an airliner's wing. She went to the terrace, and found the park's greenness surer of itself than ever. She picked up her book and went inside. A boy at school, seeing her draw birds, had given it to her. She stored it with her special treasures.

Closing the drawer, she jerked her head straight, encountering her own wide blue gaze in her bedroom mirror. From the entrance hall, a door was closing. She gathered up a pack of cards spread out for solitaire and slid them into a gilded box. She whacked at her long brown hair with a brush; then she went out. It was Eva.

Rosalind Jennings's stepmother had short, raven black glossy hair, a full red mouth, jetty brows and lashes. Shortsighted, she handled the problem in the most open way, by wearing great round glasses trimmed in tortoise shell. All through the winter—a winter Rosalind would always remember as The Stepmother: Year I—Eva had gone around the apartment in gold wedge-heeled slippers, pink slacks, and a black chiffon blouse. Noiseless on the wall-to-wall carpets, the slippers slapped faintly against stockings or flesh when she walked—spaced, intimate ticks of sound. "Let's face it, Rosie," her father said, when Eva went off to the kitchen for a fresh drink as he tossed in his blackjack hand. "She's a sexy dame."

Sexy or not, she was kind to Rosalind. "I wouldn't have married anybody you didn't like," her father told her. "That child's got *the* most heavenly eyes," she'd overheard Eva say.

Arriving now, having triple-locked the apartment door, Eva set the inevitable Saks parcels down on the foyer table, and dumped her jersey jacket off her arm onto the chair with a gasp of relief. "It's turned so hot!" Rosalind followed her to the kitchen where she poured orange juice and soda over ice. Her nails were firm, hard, perfectly painted. They resembled, to Rosalind, ten small creatures who had ranked themselves on this stage of fingertips. Often they ticked off a pile of poker chips from top to bottom, red and white, as Eva pondered. "Stay . . ." or "Call . . ." or "I'm out . . ." then, "Oh, damn, you, Nat . . . that's twice in a row."

"I've just been talking on the phone to Daddy," Rosalind said. "I've got to warn you. He's thinking of the cottage."

"Up there in Vermont?"

"It's in New York, on Lake George. Mother got it from her folks. You know, they lived in Albany. The thing is, Daddy's always loved it. He's hoping you will too, I think."

Eva finished her orange juice. Turning to rinse the glass in the sink, she wafted out perfume and perspiration. "It's a little far for a summer place. . . . But if it's what you and Nat like, why then—" She affectionately pushed a dark strand of Rosalind's hair back behind her ear. Her fingers were chilly from the glass. "I'm yours to command." Her smile, intimate and confident, seemed to repeat its red picture on every kitchen object.

Daughter and stepmother had got a lot chummier in the six months since her father had married. At first, Rosalind was always wondering what they thought of her. For here was a new "they," like a whole new being. She had heard, for instance, right after the return from the Nassau honeymoon:

Eva: "I want to be sure and leave her room just the way it is."

Nat: "I think that's right. Change is up to her."

But Rosalind could not stop her angry thought: *You'd just better try touching my room!* Her mother had always chosen the decor, always the rose motif, roses in the wallpaper and deeper rose valances and matching draperies. This was a romantic theme with her parents, accounting for her name. Her father would warble "Sweet Rosie O'Grady," while downing his whiskey. He would waltz his little girl around the room. She'd learned to dance before she could walk, she thought.

"Daddy sets the music together with what's happening on the stage. He gets the dancers and actors to carry out the music. That's different from composing or writing lyrics." So Rosalind would

219

explain to new friends at school, every year. Now she'd go off to some other school next fall, still ready with her lifelong lines. "You must have heard of some of his shows. Remember So-and-So, and then there was. . . ." Watching their impressionable faces form their cries. "We've got the records of that!" "Was your mother an actress?" "My stepmother used to be an actress—nobody you'd know about. My mother died. She wasn't ever in the theater. She studied art history at Vassar." Yes, and married the assistant manager of his family firm: Jennings's Finest Woolen Imports; he did not do well. Back to his first love, theater. From college on they thought they'd never get him out of it, and they were right. Some purchase he had chosen in West Germany turned out to be polyester, sixty percent. "I had a will to fail," Nat Jennings would shrug, when he thought about it. "If your heart's not in something, you can't succeed," was her mother's reasoning, clinging to her own sort of knowing which had to do with the things you picked, felt about, what went where. Now here was another woman with other thoughts about the same thing. She'd better not touch my room, thought Rosalind, or I'll . . . what? Trip her in the hallway, hide her glasses, throw the keys out the window?

"What are you giggling at, Rosie?"

Well might they ask, just back from Nassau at a time of falling leaves. "I'm wondering what to do with this leg of lamb. It's too long and skinny."

"Broil it like a great big chop." Still honeymooning, they'd be holding hands, she bet, on the living room sofa.

"Just you leave my room alone," she sang out to this new Them. "Or I won't cook for you!"

"Atta girl, Rosie!"

Now, six months later in the balmy early evening with windows wide open, they were saying it again. Daddy had come in, hardly even an hour later than he said, and there was the big conversation, starting with cocktails, lasting through dinner, all about Lake George and how to get there, where to start, but all totally impossible until day after tomorrow at the soonest.

"One of the few unpolluted lakes left!" Daddy enthused to Eva. It was true. If you dropped anything from the boat into the water, your mother would call from the balcony, "It's right down there, darling," and you'd see it as plainly as if it lay in sunlight at your feet and you could reach down for it instead of diving. The caretaker they'd had for years, Mr. Thibodeau, reported to them from time to time. Everything was all right, said Mr. Thibodeau. He had about fifteen houses on his list, for watching over, especially during the long winters. He was good. They'd left the cottage empty for two summers, and it was still all right. She remembered the last time they were there, June three years back. She and Daddy were staying while Mother drove back to New York, planning to see Aunt Mildred from Denver before she put out for the West again. "What a nuisance she can't come here!" Mother had said. "It's going to be sticky as anything in town, and when I think of that thruway!"

"Say you've got food poisoning," said Daddy. "Make something up."

"But Nat! Can't you understand? I really *do* want to see Mildred!" It was Mother's little cry that still sounded in Rosalind's head. "Whatever you do, please don't go to the apartment," Daddy said. He hadn't washed dishes for a week; he'd be ashamed for an in-law to have an even lower opinion of him, though he thought it wasn't possible. "It's a long drive," her mother pondered. "Take the Taconic, it's cooler." "Should I spend one night or two?"

Her mother was killed on the Taconic Parkway the next day by a man coming out of a crossover. There must have been a moment of terrible disbelief when she saw that he was actually going to cross in front of her. Wasn't he looking, didn't he see? They would never know. He died in the ambulance. She was killed at once.

Rosalind and her father, before they left, had packed up all her mother's clothing and personal things, but that was all they'd had the heart for. The rest they walked off and left, just so. "Next summer," they had said, as the weeks wore on and still they'd made no move. The next summer came, and still they did not stir. One day they said, "Next summer." Mr. Thibodeau said not to worry, everything was fine. So the Navaho rugs were safe and all the pottery, the copper and brass, the racked pewter. The books would all be lined in place on the shelves, the music in the Victorian music rack just as it had been left, Schumann's "Carnaval" (she could see it still) on top. And if everything was really fine, the canoe would be dry, though dusty and full of spiderwebs, suspended out in the boat house, and the roof must be holding firm and dry, as Mr. Thibodeau would have reported any

221

leak immediately. All that had happened, he said, was that the steps into the water had to have new uprights, the bottom two replaced, and that the eaves on the northeast corner had broken from a falling limb and been repaired.

Mention of the fallen limb recalled the storms. Rosalind remembered them blamming away while she and her mother huddled back of the stairway, feeling aimed at by the thunderbolts; or if Daddy was there, they'd sing by candlelight while he played the piano. He dared the thunder by imitating it in the lower base. . . .

"Atta girl, Rosie."

She had just said she wasn't afraid to go up there alone tomorrow, take the bus or train, and consult with Mr. Thibodeau. The Thibodeaus had long ago taken a fancy to Rosalind; a French Canadian, Mrs. Thibodeau had taught her some French songs, and fed her on tourtière and beans.

"That would be wonderful," said Eva.

"I just can't let her do it," Nat said.

"I can stay at Howard Johnson's. After all, I'm seventeen."

While she begged, her father looked at her steadily from the end of the table, finishing coffee. "I'll telephone the Thibodeaus," he finally said. "One thing you aren't to do is stay in the house alone. Howard Johnson's is okay. We'll get you a room there." Then, because he knew what the house had meant and wanted to let her know it, he took her shoulder (Eva not being present) and squeezed it, his eyes looking deep into hers, and Irish tears rising moistly. "Life goes on, Rosie," he whispered. "It has to."

She remembered all that, riding the bus. But it was for some unspoken reason that he had wanted her to go. And she knew that it was right for her to do it, not only to see about things. It was an important journey. For both of them? Yes, for them both.

Mr. Thibodeau himself met her bus, driving up to Lake George Village.

"Not many people yet," he said. "We had a good many on the weekend, out to enjoy the sun. Starting a baseball team up here. The piers took a beating back in the winter. Not enough ice and too much wind. How's your daddy?"

"He's fine. He wants to come back here now."

"You like your new mother? Shouldn't ask. Just curious."

"She's nice," said Rosalind.

"Hard to be a match for the first one."

Rosalind did not answer. She had a quietly aware way of closing her mouth when she did not care to reply.

"Pretty?" pursued Mr. Thibodeau. Not only the caretaker, Mr. Thibodeau was also a neighbor. He lived between the property and the road. You had to be nice to the Thibodeaus; so much depended on them.

"Yes, she's awfully pretty. She was an actress. She had just a little part in the cast of the show he worked with last year."

"That's how they met, was it?"

To Rosalind, it seemed that Eva had just showed up one evening in her father's conversation at dinner. "There's somebody I want you to meet, Rosie. She's—well, she's a she. I've seen her once or twice. I think you'll like her. But if you don't, we'll scratch her, Rosie. That's a promise."

"Here's a list, Mr. Thibodeau," she said. "All the things Daddy wants done are on it. Telephone, plumbing, electricity . . . maybe Mrs. Thibodeau can come in and clean. I've got to check the linens for mildew. Then go through the canned stuff and make a grocery list."

"We got a new supermarket since you stopped coming, know that?"

"I bet."

"We'll go tomorrow. I'll take you."

The wood-lined road had been broken into over and over on the lake side, the other side, too, by new motels. Signs about pools, TV, vacancy, came rudely up and at them, until, swinging left, they entered woods again and drew near the cutoff to the narrow winding drive among the pines. "Thibodeau" the mail box read in strong, irregular letters, and by its side a piece of weathered plywood nailed to the fence post said "Jennings," painted freshly over the ghost of old lettering beneath.

She bounced along with Mr. Thibodeau, who, his black hair grayed over, still had his same beaked nose, which in her mind gave him his Frenchness and his foreignness. Branches slapped the car windows. The tires squished through ruts felted with fallout from the woods. They reached the final bend. "Stop," said Rosalind, for something white had passed beneath the wheels which gave out a sound like dry bones breaking. She jumped out. It was only birch branches, half rotted. "I'll go on alone." She ran ahead of his station wagon, over pine needles and through the fallen leaves of two autumns, which slowed her motion until she felt the way she did in dreams.

The cottage was made of natural wood, no shiny lacquer covering it; boughs around it, pine and oak, pressed down like protective arms. The reach of the walls was laced over with undergrowth, so that the house at first glance looked small as a hut, not much wider than the door. Running there, Rosalind tried the knob with the confidence of a child running to her mother, only to find it locked, naturally; then with a child's abandon, she flung out her arms against the paneling, hearing her heart thump on the wood until Mr. Thibodeau gently detached her little by little as though she had got stuck there.

"Now there . . . there now . . . just let me get hold of this key." He had a huge wire ring for his keys, labels attached to each. His clientele. "Des clients, vous en avez beaucoup," Rosalind had once said to him as she was starting French in school. But Mr. Thibodeau was unregretfully far from his Quebec origins. His family had come there from northern Vermont to get a milder climate. Lake George was a sun trap, a village sliding off the Adirondacks toward the lake, facing a day-long southeast exposure.

The key ground in the lock. Mr. Thibodeau kicked the base of the door, and the hinges whined. He let her enter alone, going tactfully back to his station wagon for nothing at all. He gave her time to wander before he followed her.

She would have had to come someday, Rosalind thought, one foot following the other, moving forward: the someday was this one. It wasn't as if anything had actually "happened" there. The door frame which opened from the entrance hall into the living room did not face the front door but was about ten feet from it to the left. Thus the full scope of the high shadowy room, which was the real heart of the cottage, opened all at once to the person entering. Suddenly, there was an interior world. The broad windows opposite, peaked in an irregular triangle at the top, like something in a modernistic church, opened onto the lake, and from the water a rippling light, muted by shade, played constantly on the high-beamed ceiling. Two large handwoven Indian rugs covered the central area of floor; on a table before the windows, a huge pot of brown and beige pottery was displayed, filled with money plant which had grown dusty and ragged. There were coarse-fibered curtains in off-white monk's cloth, now dragging askew, chair coverings in heavy fabric, orange and white cushions, and the piano, probably so out of tune now with the damp it would never sound right, which sat closed and silent in the corner. An open stairway more like a ladder than a stair, rose to the upper floor balcony, with bedrooms in the wing. "We're going to fall and break our silly necks someday," she could hear her mother saying. "It is pretty, though." The Indian weaving of the hawk at sunrise, all black and red, hung on the far left wall.

She thought of her mother, a small quick woman with bronze close-curling hair cut short, eager to have what she thought of as "just the right thing," wandering distant markets, seeking out things for the cottage. It seemed to Rosalind that when she opened the door past the stairwell into the bedroom which her parents had used, that surely she would find that choosing, active ghost in motion over a chest or moving a curtain at the window, and that surely, ascending the dangerous stair to look into the two bed-rooms above, she would hear the quick voice say, "Oh, it's you, Rosalind, now you just tell me. . . ." But everything was silent.

Rosalind came downstairs. She returned to the front door and saw that Mr. Thibodeau had driven away. Had he said something about going back for something? She closed the door quietly, reentered the big natural room and let the things there speak.

For it was all self-contained, knowing and infinitely quiet. The lake gave its perpetual lapping sound, like nibbling fish in shallow water, now and then splashing up, as though a big one had flourished. Lap, lap against the wooden piles which supported the balcony. Lap against the steps, with a swishing motion on the lowest one, a passing-over instead of an against sound. The first steps were replaced, new, the color fresh blonde instead of worn brown. The room heard the lapping, the occasional splash, the swish of water.

Rosalind herself was being got through to by something even less predictable than water. What she heard was memory: voices quarreling. From three years ago they woke to life. A slant of light—that had brought them back. Just at this time of day, she had been coming in from swimming. The voices had climbed the large clear windows, clawing for exit, finding none, had fled like people getting out of a burning theater, through the door to the far right that opened out on the balcony. She had been coming up the steps from the water, when the voices stampeded over her, frightening, intense, racing outward from the panic within. "You know you do and you know you will . . . there's no use to lie, I've been through all that. Helpless is all I can feel, all I can be. That's the awful part . . . !" "I didn't drive all this way just to get back into that. Go on, get away to New York with dear Aunt Mildred. Who's to know, for that matter, if it's Mildred at all?" "You hide your life like a card in the deck and then have the nerve—! Oh, you're a great magician, aren't you?" "Hush, she's out there . . . hush, now . . . you must realize. . . ." "I do nothing but realize. . . ." "Hush . . . just . . . no. . . ." And their known selves returned to them as she came in, dripping, pretending nothing had happened, gradually believing her own pretense.

The way she'd learned to do, all the other times. Sitting forgotten, for the moment, in an armchair too big back in New York, listening while her heart hurt until her mother said, "Darling, go to your room, I'll be there in a minute." Even on vacation, it was sometimes the same thing. And Mother coming in later, as she half-slept, half-waited, to hold her hand and say, "Just forget it now, tomorrow it won't seem real. We all love each other. Tomorrow you won't even remember." Kissed and tucked in, she trusted. It didn't happen all the time. And the tomorrows were clear and bright. The only trouble was, this time there hadn't been any tomorrow, only the tomorrow of her mother's driving away. Could anybody who sounded like that, saying those things, have a wreck the very next morning and those things have nothing to do with it?

Maybe I got the times mixed up.

("She had a little part in the cast of the show he did last year. . . ." "So that's how they met, was it?") ("Your mother got the vapors sometimes. The theater scared her." She'd heard her father say that.)

I dreamed it all, she thought, and couldn't be sure this wasn't true, though wondered if she could dream so vividly that she could see the exact print of her wet foot just through the doorway there, beside it the drying splash from the water's runnel down her leg. But it could have been another day.

Why not just ask Daddy?

At the arrival of this simple solution, she let out a long sigh, flung her hands back of her head and stretched out on the beautiful rug which her mother had placed there. Her eyes dimmed; she felt the lashes flutter downward. . . .

A footstep and a voice awakened her from how short a sleep she did not know. Rolling over and sitting up, she saw a strange woman—short, heavyset, with faded skin, gray hair chopped off around her face, plain run-down shoes. She was wearing slacks. Then she smiled and things about her changed.

"You don't remember me, do you? I'm Marie Thibodeau. I remember you and your mom and your dad. That was all bad. *Gros dommage*. But you're back now. You'll have a good time again, eh? We thought maybe you didn't have nothing you could eat yet. You come back with me. I going make you some nice lunch. My husband said to come find you."

She rose slowly, walked through shadows toward the woman, who still had something of the quality of an apparition. Did she think that because of her mother, others must have died too? She followed. The lunch was the same as years before: the meat pie, the beans, the catsup and relish and the white bread taken sliced from its paper. And the talk, too, was nearly the same: kind things said before, repeated now: chewed, swallowed.

"You don't remember me, but I remember you. You're *the* Nat Jenning's daughter, used to come here with your folks." This was what the boy said, in Howard Johnson's.

"We're the tennis ones . . . Dunbar," said the girl, who was his sister, not his date; for saying "tennis" had made Rosalind remember the big house their family owned—"the villa," her father called it—important grounds around it, and a long frontage on the lake. She remembered them as strutting around, smaller then, holding rackets which looked too large for their bodies. They had been allowed on the court only at certain hours, along with their friends, but even then they had wished to be observed. Now here they were before her, grown up and into denim, like anybody else. Paul and Elaine. They had showed up at the entrance to the motel restaurant, tan and healthy. Paul had acquired a big smile; Elaine a breathless hesitating voice, the kind Daddy didn't like, it was so intended to tease.

"Let's all find a booth together," Paul Dunbar said.

Rosalind said, "I spent half the afternoon with the telephone man, the other half at the grocery. Getting the cottage opened."

"You can come up to our house after we eat. Not much open here yet. We're on spring holidays."

"They extended it. Outbreak of measles."

"She made that up," said the Dunbar boy who was speaking straight and honestly to Rosalind. "We told them we had got sick and would be back next week."

"It's because we are so in-tell-i-gent. . . . Making our grades is not a problem," Elaine said in her trick voice.

"We've got the whole house to ourselves. Our folks won't be coming till June. Hey, why don't you move down with us?"

"I can't," said Rosalind. "Daddy's coming up tomorrow. And my stepmother. He got married again."

"Your parents split?"

"No . . . I mean, not how you think. My mother was killed three years ago, driving to New York. She had a wreck."

"Jesus, what a break. I'm sorry, Rosalind."

"You heard about it, Paul. We both did."

"It's still a tough break."

"Mr. Thibodeau's been helping me. Mrs. Thibodeau's cleaning up. They're coming tomorrow." If this day is ever over.

She went with them after dinner. . . .

The Dunbar house could be seen from the road, a large two-story brick house on the lake, with white wood trim. There were two one-story wings, like smaller copies of the central house, their entrances opening at either side, the right one on a flagstone walk, winding through a sloping lawn, the left on a porte cochère, where the Dunbars parked. Within, the large rooms were shuttered, the furniture dust covered. The three of them went to the glassed-in room on the opposite wing and put some records on. They danced on the tiled floor among the white wicker furniture.

Had they heard a knocking, or hadn't they? A strange boy was standing in the doorway, materialized. Elaine had cried, "Oh, goodness, Fenwick, you scared me!" She moved back from Paul's controlling rhythm. They were all facing the stranger. He was heavier than Paul; he was tall and grown to the measure of his big hands and feet. He looked serious and easily detachable from the surroundings; it wasn't possible to guess by looking at him where he lived or what he was doing there.

"Fenwick . . ." Paul was saying to him. What sort of name was that? He strode over to the largest chaise longue, and fitted himself into it. Paul introduced Rosalind to Fenwick.

"I have a mile-long problem to solve before Thursday," Fenwick said. "I'm getting cross-eyed. You got a beer?"

"Fenwick is a math-uh-mat-i-cul gene-iyus," Elaine told Rosalind. The record finished and she switched off the machine.

"Fenwick wishes he was," said Fenwick.

It seemed that they were all at some school together, called Wakeley, over in Vermont. They knew people to talk about together. "I've been up about umpteen hours," Rosalind said. "I came all the way from New York this morning."

"Just let me finish this beer, and I'll take you home," said Fenwick.

"It's just Howard Johnson's," she said.

"There are those that call it home," said Fenwick, downing beer.

They walked together to the highway where Fenwick had left his little old rickety car. The trees were bursting from the bud, you could practically smell them grow, but the branches were still dark, and cold looking and wet, because it had rained while they were inside. The damp road seamed beneath the tires. There were not many people around. She hugged herself into her raincoat.

"The minute I saw you I remembered you," Fenwick said. "I just felt like we were friends. You used to go to that little park with all the other kids. Your daddy would put you on the seesaw. He pushed it up and down for you. But I don't guess you'd remember me."

"I guess I ought to," Rosalind said. "Maybe you grew a lot."

"You can sure say that. They thought I wasn't going to stop." The sign ahead said Howard Johnson's. "I'd do my problem better if we had some coffee."

"Tomorrow maybe," she said. "I'm dead tired." But what she thought was, He likes me.

At the desk she found three messages, all from Daddy and Eva. "Call when you come in. . . ." "Call as soon as you can. . . ." "Call even if late. . . ." She called.

"So it'll be late tomorrow, maybe around dinner. What happened was—" He went on and on. With Nat Jennings, you got used to postponements, so her mother always said. "How's it going, Rosie? I've thought about you every minute."

229

"Everything's ready for you, or it will be when you come."

"Don't cook up a special dinner. We might be late. It's a long road."

In a dream her mother was walking with her. They were in the library at Lake George. In the past her mother had often gone there to check out books. She was waiting for a certain book she wanted, but it hadn't come back yet. "But you did promise me last week," she was saying to somebody at the desk; then she was walking up the street with Rosalind, and Rosalind saw the book in her shopping bag. "You got it after all," she said to her mother. "I just found it lying there on the walk," her mother said, then Rosalind remembered how she had leaned down to pick up something. "That's nice," said Rosalind, satisfied that things could happen this way. "I think it's nice, too," said her mother, and they went along together.

By noon the next day her work was done, but she felt bad because she had found something—a scarf in one of the dresser drawers. It was a sumptuous French satin scarf in a jagged play of colors, mainly red, a shade her mother with her coppery hair had never worn. It smelled of Eva's perfume. So they had been up here before, she thought, but why—this far from New York? And why not say so? Helpless was what her mother said she felt. Can I, thought Rosalind, ask Daddy about this, too?

In the afternoon she drove up into the Adirondacks with Elaine and Paul Dunbar. They took back roads, a minor highway that crossed from the lakeshore road to the thruway; another beyond that threaded along the bulging sides of the mountains. They passed one lake after another: some small and limpid, others half-choked with water lilies and thickly shaded where frogs by the hundreds were chorusing, invisible among the fresh lime green; and some larger still, marked with stumps of trees mysteriously broken off. From one of these, strange bird calls sounded. Then the road ran upward. Paul pulled up under some tall pines and stopped.

"We're going to climb," he announced.

It suited Rosalind because Elaine had just asked her to tell her "all about the theater, every single thing you know." She wouldn't have to do that, at least. Free of the car, they stood still in deserted air. There was no feel of houses near. The brother and sister started along a path they apparently knew. It led higher, winding through trees, with occasional glimpses of a rotting lake below, and promise of some triumphant view above. Rosalind followed next to Paul, with Elaine trailing behind. Under a big oak they stopped to rest.

Through the leaves a small view opened up; there was a little valley below with a stream running through it. The three of them sat hugging their knees and talking, once their breath came back. "Very big deal," Paul was saying. "Five people sent home, weeping parents outside offices, and everybody tiptoeing past. About what? The whole school smokes pot, everybody knows it. Half the profs were on it. Remember old Borden?"

Elaine's high-pitched laugh. "He said, 'Just going for a joint,' when he pushed into the john one day. Talking back over his shoulder."

"What really rocked the boat was when everybody started cheating. Plain and fancy."

"What made them start?" Rosalind asked. Pot was passed around at her school, too, in the upper eighties, but you could get into trouble about it.

"You know Miss Hollander was heard to say out loud one day, 'The dean's a shit.' "

"That's the source of the whole fucking mess," said Paul. "The stoopid dean's a shit."

"Is he a fag?" asked Rosalind, not too sure of language like this.

"Not even that," said Paul, and picked up a rock to throw. He put down his hand to Rosalind. "Come on, we got a little further to climb."

The path snaked sharply upward. She followed his long legs and brown loafers, one with the stitching breaking at the top, and stopping for breath, she looked back and discovered they were alone. "Where's Elaine?"

"She's lazy." He stopped high above to wait for her. She looked up to him and saw him turn to face her, jeans tight over her narrow thighs and flat waist. He put a large hand down to pull her up, and grinned as she came unexpectedly too fast; being thin and light, she sailed up so close they bumped together. His face skin was glossy with sweat. "Just a little farther," he encouraged her. His front teeth were not quite even. Light exploded from the tips of his

231

ears. Grappling at roots, avoiding sheer surfaces of rock, gaining footholds on patches of earth, they burst finally out on a ledge of rough but fairly flat stone, chiseled away as though in a quarry, overlooking a dizzying sweep of New York countryside. "Oh," Rosalind caught her breath. "How gorgeous! We live high up with a terrace over Central Park," she confided excitedly. "But that's nothing like this!"

Paul put his arm around her. "Don't get too close. You know some people just love heights. They love 'em to death. Just show them one and off they go."

"Not me."

"Come here." He led her a little to the side, placing her—"Not there, here"—at a spot where two carved lines crossed, as though Indians had marked it for something. Then, his arm close round her, he pressed his mouth down on hers. Her long brown hair fell backward over his shoulder. If she struggled, she might pull them both over the edge. "Don't." She broke her mouth away. His free hand was kneading her.

"Why? Why not?" The words burrowed into her ear like objects.

"I hadn't thought of you ... not for myself."

"Think of me now. Let's just stay here a minute."

But she slipped away and went sliding back down. Arriving in the level space with a torn jacket and a skinned elbow, she found Elaine lying back against a rock, apparently sleeping. A camera with a telescope lens was resting on the canvas shoulder bag she had carried up the hill.

Elaine sat up, opening her eyes. Rosalind stopped, and Paul's heavy stride, overtaking, halted close behind her. She did not want to look at him, and was rubbing at the blood speckled out on her scratched arm where she'd fallen against a limb.

"Paul thinks he's ir-ree-sisty-bul," Elaine said. "Now we know it isn't so."

Looking up, Rosalind could see the lofty ledge where she and Paul had been. Elaine picked up the camera, detached the lens, and fitted both into the canvas bag. "Once I took a whole home movie. That was the time he was screwing the waitress from the pizza place."

"Oh, sure, get funny," said Paul. He had turned an angry red.

In the car, Elaine leaned back to speak to Rosalind. "We're known to be a little bit crazy. Don't you worry, Ros-ul-lind."

Paul said nothing. He drove hunched forward over the wheel.

"Last summer was strictly crazy, start to finish," said Elaine. "Wasn't that true, Paul?"

"It was pretty crazy," said Paul. "Rosalind would have loved it," he added. He was getting mad with her now, she thought.

She asked to hop out at the road to the cottage, instead of going to the motel. She said she wanted to see Mr. Thibodeau.

"Sorry you didn't like the view," said Paul from the wheel. He was laughing now; his mood had changed.

Once they'd vanished, she walked down the main road to the Fenwick mailbox.

From the moment she left the road behind she had to climb again, not as strenuously as up to the mountain ledge, but a slow winding climb up an ill-tended road. The house that finally broke into view after a sharp turn was bare of paint and run-down. There was a junk car in the wide yard, the parts just about picked off it, one side sitting on planks, and a litter of household odds and ends nearby. A front porch, sagging, was covered with a tangle of what looked to be hunting and camping things. From behind, a dog barked, a warning sound to let her know who was in charge. There was mud in the path to the door.

Through the window of a tacked-on wing to the right, there was Fenwick, sure enough, at a table with peeling paint, in a plain kitchen chair, bending over a large notebook. Textbooks and graph papers were scattered around him. She rapped on the pane and summoned his attention, as though from another planet. He came to the door.

"Oh, it's you, Rose."

"Rosalind."

"I'm working on my problem." He came out and joined her. Maybe he was a genius, Rosalind thought, to have a fellowship to that school, making better grades than the Dunbars.

"I've been out with Paul and Elaine."

"Don't tell me Paul took you up to that lookout."

She nodded. They sat down on a bench that seemed about to fall in.

"Dunbar's got a collection of pictures—girls he's got to go up there. It's just a dumb gimmick."

"He thinks it's funny," she said, and added, "I left."

233

"Good. They're on probation, you know. All that about school's being suspended's not true. I'm out for another reason, studying for honors. But—"

A window ran up. A woman's voice came around the side of the house. "Henry, I told you—"

"But I need a break, Mother," he said, without turning his head.

"Is your name Henry?" Rosalind asked.

"So they tell me. Come on, I'll take you back where you're staying."

"I just wanted to see where you lived." He didn't answer. Probably it wasn't the right thing. He walked her down the hill, talking all the way, and put her into his old Volkswagen.

"The Dunbars stick too close together. You'd think they weren't kin. They're like a couple dating. They make up these jokes on people. I was there the other night to help them through some math they failed. But it didn't turn out that way. Know why? They've got no mind for work. They think something will happen, so they won't have to." He hesitated, silent, as the little car swung in and out of the wooded curves. "I think they make love," he said, very low. It was a kind of gossip. "There's talk at school. Now don't go and tell about it."

"You're warning me," she said.

"That's it. There's people living back in the woods, no different from them. Mr. Thibodeau and Papa—they hunt bear together, way off from here, high up. Last winter I went, too, and there was a blizzard. We shot a bear but it looked too deep a snow to get the carcass out, but we did. We stayed with these folks, brother and sister. Some odd little kids running around.

"If they get thrown out of Wakeley, they can go somewhere else. Their folks have a lot of money. So no problem."

"But I guess anywhere you have to study," said Rosalind.

He had brought her to the motel, and now they got out and walked to a plot where shrubs were budding on the slant of hill above the road. Fenwick had speculative eyes that kept to themselves, and a frown from worry or too many figures, just a small thread between his light eyebrows.

"When I finish my problem, any minute now, I'll go back to school."

"My mother died three years ago, in June," said Rosalind. "She was killed in a wreck."

"I knew that. It's too bad, Rosalind. I'm sorry."

"Did you know her?" Rosalind experienced an eagerness, expectation, as if she doubted her mother's ever having been known.

"I used to see her with you," said Fenwick. "So I guess I'd know her if I saw her." His hand had appeared on her shoulder. She was at about the right height for that.

"Nobody will ever see her again," she said. He pulled her closer.

"If I come back in the summer, I'd like to see you, Rosalind."

"Me too," she said.

"I've got some stuff you can read." He was squinting. The sun had come through some pale clouds.

"Things you wrote?" She wondered at him.

"I do a lot of things. I'll have the car." He glanced toward it doubtfully. "It's not much of a car, though."

"It's a fine car," she said, so he could walk off to it, feeling all right, and wave to her.

Rosalind was surprised and obscurely hurt by the message she received at the motel: namely, that her father and stepmother had already arrived and had called by for her. She had some money left over from what her father had given her, and not wanting to call, she took a taxi down to the cottage.

Her hurt sprang from thwarted plans. She had meant to prepare for them, greet them, have dinner half done, develop a festive air. Now they would be greeting her.

In the taxi past Mr. Thibodeau's house, she saw a strange car coming toward them which made them draw far to one side, sink treacherously among loose fallen leaves. A Chevrolet sedan went past; the man within, a stranger, was well dressed and wore a hat. He looked up to nod at the driver and glance keenly within at his passenger.

"Who was that?" Rosalind asked.

"Griffin, I think his name is," the driver said. "Real estate," he added.

There had been a card stuck in the door when she had come, Rosalind recalled, and a printed message: "Thinking of selling . . .? Griffin's the Guy."

Then she was alighting, crying, "Daddy! Eva! It's me!" And they were running out, crying, "There she is! You got the call?" Daddy was tossing her, forgetting she'd grown; he almost banged her head

235

against a beam. "You nearly knocked my three brains out," she laughed. "It's beautiful!" Eva cried, about the cottage. She spread her arms wide as wings and swirled across the rugs in a solo dance. "It's simply charming!"

Daddy opened the piano with a flourish. He began thumping the old keys, some of which had gone dead from the damp. But "Sweet Rosie O'Grady" was unmistakably coming out. They were hugging and making drinks and going out to look at the boat, kneeling down to test the still stone-chill water.

"What good taste your mother had!" Eva told her, smiling. "The apartment . . . now this!" She was kind.

In the late afternoon Rosalind and her father lowered and launched the canoe and, finding that it floated without a leak and sat well in the water, they decided to test it. Daddy had changed his gray slacks and blazer for gabardine trousers and a leather jacket. He wore a denim shirt. Daddy glistened with life, and what he wore was more important than what other people wore. He thought of clothes, evidently, but he never, that she could remember, discussed them. They simply appeared on him, like various furs or fleece that he could shed suddenly and grow just as suddenly new. Above button-down collars or open-throated knit pullovers or turtlenecks or black bow ties, his face, with its slightly ruddy look, even in winter, its cleft chin and radiating crinkles, was like a law of attraction, drawing whatever interested, whatever lived. In worry or grief, he hid it, that face. Then the clothes no longer mattered. Rosalind had sometimes found him in a room alone near a window, still, his face bent down behind one shoulder covered with some old faded shirt, only the top of his head showing and that revealed as startlingly gray, the hair growing thin. But when the face came up, it would seem to resume its livingness as naturally as breath, his hair being the same as ever, barely sprinkled with gray. It was the face for her, his gift.

"Did you see the real estate man?" Rosalind asked, over her shoulder, paddling with an out-of-practice wobble.

"Griffin? Oh yes, he was here. Right on the job, those guys."

They paddled along a stone's throw from the shore. To their right the lake stretched out wide and sunlit. One or two distant fishing boats dawdled near a small island. The lake, a creamy blue, flashed now and again in air that was still sharp.

"Daddy, did you know Eva a long time?"

There was a silence from behind her. "Not too long." Then he said what he'd said before. "She was a member of the cast. Rosie, we shouldn't have let you go off by yourself. I realized that this morning. I woke up early thinking it, and jumped straight out of bed. By six I'd packed. Who've you been seeing?"

"I ran into the Dunbars, Paul and Elaine, down in the big white house, you know. They're here from school. I have to run from Mrs. Thibodeau. She wants to catch and feed me. And then there's Fenwick."

"Some old guy up the hill who sells junk . . . is that the one?"

"No, his son. He's a mathematical genius, Daddy."

"Beware of mathematical geniuses," her father said, "especially if their fathers sell junk."

"You always told me that," said Rosalind. "I just forgot."

When they came in they were laughing. She and Eva cooked the meal. Daddy played old records, forgoing gin rummy for once. That was the first day.

"Wait! Look now! Look!"

It was Eva speaking while Daddy blindfolded Rosalind. They had built a fire. Somebody had found in a shop uptown the sort of stuff you threw on it to make it sparkle. The room on a gloomy afternoon, though shut up tight against a heavy drizzle, was full of warmth and light. Elaine and Paul Dunbar were there, sitting on the couch. Fenwick was there, choosing to crouch down on a hassock in the corner like an Indian, no matter how many times he was offered a chair. He had been followed in by one of the Fenwick dogs, a huge German shepherd with a bushy, perfectly curling tail lined with white, which he waved at times from side to side like a plume, and when seated furled about his paws. He smelled like a wet dog owned by a junk dealer.

At the shout of "Look now!" Daddy whipped off the blindfold. The cake had been lighted—eighteen candles—a shining delight. They had cheated a little to have a party for Rosalind; her birthday wasn't till the next week. But the idea was fun. Eva had thought of it because she had found a box full of party things in the unused bedroom: tinsel, sparklers, masks, and a crepe paper tablecloth with napkins. She had poured rum into some cherry Koolaid and floated orange slices across the top. She wore a printed off-the-shoulder blouse with a denim skirt and espadrilles. Her big glasses glanced back fire and candlelight. The young people watched her lighting candles for the table with a long, fancy match held in brightly tipped fingers. Daddy took the blue bandana blindfold and wound it pirate-fashion around his forehead. He had contrived an eye patch for one eye. "Back in the fifties these things were a status symbol," he said, "but I forget what status they symbolized."

"Two-car garage but no Cadillac," Paul said.

Daddy winked at Elaine. "My daughter's friends get prettier every day."

"So does your daughter," Paul said.

Eva passed them paper plates of birthday cake.

"*She's* getting to the dangerous age, not me. Hell, I was there all the time."

Everyone laughed but Fenwick. He fed small bites of cake to the dog and large ones to himself, while Rosalind refilled his glass.

The friends had brought her presents. A teddy bear dressed in blue jeans from Elaine. A gift shop canoe in birchbark from Paul. The figure of an old man carved in wood from Fenwick. His father had done it, he said. Rosalind held it up. She set it down. He watched her. He was redeeming his father, whom nobody thought much of. "It's grand," she said, "I love it." Fenwick sat with his hand buried in the dog's thick ruff. His nails, cleaned up for coming there, would get grimy in the dog's coat.

Rosalind's father so far had ignored Fenwick. He was sitting on a stool near Elaine and Paul, talking about theater on campuses, how most campus musicals went dead on Broadway, the rare one might survive, but usually—Eva approached the dog, who growled at her. "He won't bite," said Fenwick.

"Is a mathematician liable to know whether or not a dog will bite?" Eva asked.

"Why not?" asked Fenwick.

"You've got quite a reputation to live up to," Eva pursued. She was kneeling near him, close enough to touch, holding her gaze, like her voice, very steady. "I hear you called a genius more often than not."

"You can have a genius rating in something without setting the world on fire," said Fenwick. "A lot of people who've got them are just walking around doing dumb things, the same as anybody."

"I'll have to think that over," Eva said.

There came a heavy pounding at the door, and before anybody could go to it, a man with a grizzled beard, weathered skin, battered clothes and a rambling walk, entered the room. He looked all around until he found Fenwick. "There you are," he said.

Rosalind's father had risen. Nobody said anything. "I'm Nat Jennings." Daddy put out his hand. "This is my wife. What can we do for you?"

"It's my boy," said Fenwick's father, shaking hands. "His mother was looking for him, something she's wanting him for. I thought if he wasn't doing nothing . . ."

"Have a drink," said Nat.

"Just pour it straight out of the bottle," said Fenwick's father, who had taken the measure of the punch.

Fenwick got up. "That's OK, Mr. Jennings. I'll just go on with Papa."

The dog had moved to acknowledge Mr. Fenwick, who had downed his drink already. Now the boy came to them both, the dog being no longer his. He turned to the rest of the room, which seemed suddenly to be of a different race. "We'll go," he said. He turned again at the living room entrance. "Thanks."

Rosalind ran after them. She stood in the front door, hidden by the wall of the entrance from those in the room, and leaned out into the rain. "Oh Mr. Fenwick, I love the carving you did!"

He glanced back. "Off on a bear hunt, deep in the snow. Had to do something."

"Goodbye, Fenwick. Thanks for coming!"

He stopped to answer, but said nothing. For a moment his look was like a voice, crying out to her from across something. For the first time in her life, Rosalind felt the force that pulls stronger than any other. Just to go with him, to be, even invisibly, near. Then the three of them—tall boy, man and dog, stairstepped together—were walking away on the rainy path.

When she went inside, she heard Paul Dunbar recalling how Nat Jennings used to organize a fishing derby back in one of the little lakes each summer. He would get the lake stocked, and everybody turned out with casting rods and poles to fish it out.

(Rosalind remembered: she had ridden on his shoulder everywhere, till suddenly, one summer, she had got too big for that, and once it had rained.) "And then there were those funny races down in the park—you folks put them on. One year I won a prize!" (Oh, that too, she remembered, her mother running with two giant orange bows like chrysanthemums, held in either hand, orange streamers flying, her coppery hair in the sun.) "You ought to get all that started again."

"It sounds grand, but I guess you'd better learn how yourselves," Eva was saying. "We'll probably not be up here at all."

"Not be here!" Rosalind's cry as she returned from the door was like an alarm. "Not be here!" A silence was suddenly on them.

Her father glanced up, but straightened out smoothly. "Of course, we'll be here. We'll all have to work on it together."

It had started raining harder. Paul and Elaine, though implored to stay, left soon.

When the rain chilled the air, Eva had got out a fringed Spanish shawl, embroidered in bright flowers on a metallic gold background. Her glasses above this, plus one of the silly hats she'd found, made her seem a many-tiered fantasy of a woman, concocted by Picasso, or made to be carried through the streets for some Latin holiday parade.

Light of movement, wearing a knit tie, cuff links on his striped shirt ("In your honor," he said to Rosalind), impeccable blue blazer above gray slacks, Nat Jennings played the country gentleman with pleasure to himself and everyone. His pretty daughter at her birthday party was his delight. This was what his every move had been saying. And now she had gone to her room. He was knocking on its door. "Rosie?"

"I'm drunk," said Rosalind.

He laughed. "We're going to talk at dinner, Rosie. When you sober up, come down. Did you enjoy your birthday party, Baby?"

"Sure I did."

"I like your friends."

"Thank you."

"Too bad about Fenwick's father. That boy deserves better."

"I guess so."

She was holding an envelope Paul had slipped into her hand when he left. It had a photo and its negative enclosed, the one on the high point, the two of them kissing. The note said, "We're leaving tomorrow, sorry if I acted stupid. When we come back, maybe we can try some real ones. Paul."

There won't be any coming back for me, she lay dazed, thinking, but this was your place, Mother. Mother, what do I do now?

He was waiting for her at the bottom of the stairs and treating her with delightful solemnity, as though she was the visiting daughter of an old friend. He showed her to her place and held the chair for her. Eva, now changed into slacks, a silk shirt, and nubby sweater, came in with a steaming casserole. The candles were lighted again.

"I'm not a grand cook, as Rose knows," she smiled. "But you couldn't be allowed, on your birthday . . ."

"She's read a hole in the best cookbook," said Daddy.

"I'm sure it's great," Rosalind said in a little voice, and felt tension pass from one of them to the other.

"I'm in love with Fenwick," Eva announced, and dished out coq au vin.

"Won't get you anywhere," Daddy said. "I see the whole thing: he's gone on Rosie, but she's playing it cool."

"They're all going back tomorrow," Rosalind said. "Elaine and Paul were just on suspension, and Fenwick's finished his problem."

They were silent, passing dishes. Daddy and Eva exchanged glances.

"Rosie," said Daddy, filling everyone's wine glass, "we've been saving our good news till after your party. Now we want you to know. You remember the little off-Broadway musical I worked with last fall? Well, Hollywood is picking it up at quite a hefty sum. It's been in negotiation for two months. Now, all's clear, and they're wanting to hire me along with the purchase. Best break I ever had."

"I'm so happy I could walk on air," said Eva.

"Are we going to *move* there?" Rosalind felt numb.

"Of course not, Baby. There'll be trips, some periods out there, nothing permanent."

Before Rosalind suddenly, as she glanced from one of them to the other, they grew glossy in an extra charge of flesh and beauty. A log even broke in the fireplace, and a flame reached to some of the sparkler powder which was unignited, so that it flared up as

241

though to hail them. They grew great as faces on a drive-in movie screen, seen floating up out of nowhere along a highway; they might mount skyward any minute and turn to constellations. He had wanted something big to happen, she knew, for a long time. "They never give me any credit," was a phrase she knew by heart. Staying her own human size, Rosalind knew that all they were saying was probably true. They had shoved her birthday up by a week to tidy her away, but they didn't look at it that way, she had to guess.

"Let's drink a toast to Daddy!" she cried, and drained her wine glass.

"Rosalind!" her father scolded happily. "What does anyone do with an alcoholic child?"

"Straight to AA," Eva filled in, "the minute we return."

"Maybe there's a branch in Lake George," Daddy worried.

"I'll cause spectacles at the Plaza," Rosalind giggled through the dizziness of wine. "I'll dance on the bar and jump in the fountain. You'll be so famous it'll make the *Daily News*."

"I've even got some dessert," said Eva, who, now the news was out, had the air of someone who intends to wait on people as seldom as possible. The cottage looked plainer and humbler all the time. How could they stand it for a single other night? Rosalind wondered. They would probably just explode out of there by some chemical process of rejection, which not even Fenwick could explain.

"If things work out," Daddy was saying, "we may get to make Palm Beach winters yet. No use to plan ahead."

"Would you like that?" Rosalind asked Eva, as if she didn't know.

"Why, I just tag along with the family," Eva said. "Your rules are mine."

That night Rosalind slipped out of her upstairs room. In order to avoid the Thibodeaus, whose house had eyes and ears, she skirted through the woods and ran into part of the lake, which appeared unexpectedly before her, like a person. She bogged in spongy loam and slipped on mossy rocks, and shivered, drenched to the knees, in the chill night shade of early foliage. At last she came out of shadow onto a road, but not before some large shape, high up, had startled her, blundering among the branches. A car went past and in the glancing headlights she saw the mailbox and its lettering and turned to climb the steep road up to the Fenwicks. What did she expect to happen there? Just who did she expect to find? Fenwick himself, of course, but in what way? To lead her out of here, take her somewhere, take her off forever? Say she could stay on with him, and they'd get the cottage someday and share it forever? That would be her dream, even if Fenwick's daddy camped on them and smelled the place up with whiskey.

She climbed with a sense of the enveloping stillness of the woods, the breath of the lake, the distant appeal of the mountains. The road made its final turn to the right, just before the yard. But at that point she was surprised to hear, as if growing out of the wood itself, murmurous voices, not one or two, but apparently by the dozen, and the sound of a throbbing guitar string, interposing from one pause to the next. She inched a little closer and stopped in the last of the black shade. A fire was burning in a wire grating near the steps. Tatters of flame leaped up, making the shadows blacker. High overhead, the moon shone. Fenwick, too, was entitled to a last night at home, having finished some work nobody else could have understood. He would return that summer. He was sitting on the edge of the porch, near a post. Some others were on the steps, or on chairs outside or even on the ground.

They were humming some tune she didn't know and she heard a voice rise, Mrs. Thibodeau's, beyond a doubt! "Now I never said I knew that from a firsthand look, but I'd have to suppose as much." Then Mr. Thibodeau was joining in: "Seen her myself . . . more than a time or two." The Thibodeaus were everywhere, with opinions to express, but about what and who? All went foundering in an indistinct mumble of phrases until a laugh rose and then another stroke across the strings asked them to sing together, a song she'd never heard. "Now that's enough," a woman's voice said, "I ain't pitching no more tunes." "I've sung all night, many's the time." "Just you and your jug."

From near the steps a shape rose suddenly; it was one of the dogs, barking on the instant of rising—there had been a shift of wind. He trotted toward her. She stood still. Now the snuffling muzzle ranged over her. The great tail moved its slow white fan. It was the one she knew. She patted the intelligent head. Someone whistled. It was Fenwick, who, she could see, had risen from his seat.

Something fell past him, out of the thick-bunched human shapes

243

on the porch. It had been pushed or shoved and was yelling, a child. "Stealing cake again," some voice said, and the body hit the ground with a thump. The mother in the chair, not so much as turning, said, "Going to break ever' bone in her one o' these days." "Serve her right," came from the background—Mr. Fenwick. It was young Fenwick himself who finally went down to pick her up (by the back of her shirt, like a puppy), Mrs. Thibodeau who came to dust her off. The yelling stopped. "Hush now," said Mrs. Thibodeau. Rosalind turned and went away.

"Who's there?" Fenwick was calling toward the road. "Nobody," a man's voice, older, said. "Wants his girl friend," said the father. "Go and git her, fella."

The mountain went on talking. Words faded to murmurs, losing outline; as she stumbled down turns of road, they lost even echoes. She was alone where she had not meant to be, but for all that, strangely detached, elated.

Back on the paved road, she padded along in sneakers. Moonlight lay bright in patterns through the trees. Finally the Dunbar house rose up, moonlight brightening one white portico, while the other stood almost eclipsed in darkness. In a lighted interior, through a downstairs window, she could see them, one standing, the other looking up, graceful hands making gestures, mouths moving—together and alone. Great white moths circling one another, planning, loving maybe. She thought they were like the photographs they took. The negative is me, she thought.

Far up the road, so far it tired her almost as much to think of it as to walk it, the old resort hotel looked out on Lake George with hundreds of empty windows, eyes with vision gone, the porticos reaching wide their outspread arms. Water lapped with none to hear. "No Trespassing," said the sign, and other signs said "For Sale," like children calling to one another.

Rosalind looked up. Between her and the road, across the lawn, a brown bear was just standing up. He was turning his head this way and that. The head was small, wedge-shaped. The bear's pelt moved when he did, like grass in a breeze. Pointing her way, the head stopped still. She felt the gaze thrill through her with long foreverness, then drop away. On all fours, he looked small, and moved toward the lake with feet shuffling close together, rather like a rolling ball, loose and tumbling toward the water. The moon sent a shimmering, golden path across the lake. She was just remembering that her mother, up here alone with her, claimed to have seen a bear late at night, looking through the window. Daddy didn't doubt she'd dreamed it. He didn't think they came so close. Rosalind knew herself as twice seen and twice known now, by dog and bear. She walked the road home.

Voices sounding in her head, Rosalind twisted and turned that night, sleepless. She got up once and taking the red scarf she had found from the drawer, she put it down on the living room table near the large vase of money plant. Then she went back up and slept, what night was left for it.

Daddy came in for Eva's coffee and then they both appeared, he freshly shaved and she perfect in her smooth makeup, a smartly striped cassock flowing to her ankles. Rosalind had crept down in wrinkled pajamas, her bare feet warping back from the chill floor.
"Today's for leaving," her father said. When Rosalind dropped her gaze, he observed her. They were standing in the kitchen before the stove. They were alone. He was neat, fit, in slacks, a beige shirt checked in brown and blue, and a foulard—affected for anyone but him. His amber eyes fixed on her blue ones, offered pools of sincerity for her to plunge into.
"What's this?" Eva asked. She came in with the scarf.
"I found it," said Rosalind. "Isn't it yours?"
Eva looked over her head at Nat. "It must have been your mother's."
"No," said Rosalind. "It wasn't."

After breakfast, by common consent, Rosalind and her father rose from the table and went down to the boat. Together they paddled out to the island. They had done this often in the past. The island was inviting, slanted like a turtle's back, rich with clumps of birch and bushes, trimmed with gray rock. Out there today, their words came out suddenly, like thoughts being printed on the air.
"We aren't coming back," said Rosalind. "This is all."
"I saw you come in last night."
A bird flew up out of the trees.
"Did you tell Eva?"
"She was asleep. Why?"
"She'll think I just sneaked off to see Fenwick. But I didn't. I went off myself . . . by myself."

245

He played with rocks, seated, forearms resting on his knees, looking at the lake. "I won't tell."

"I wanted to find Mother."

"Did you?"

"In a way . . . I know she's here, all around here. Don't you?"

"I think she might be most everywhere."

Maybe what he was saying was something about himself. The ground was being shifted; they were debating without saying so, and he was changing things around without saying so.

"I let you come up here alone," he went on, "because I thought you needed it—your time alone. Maybe I was wrong."

"If you'd just say you see it too."

"See what?"

"What I was saying. That she's here. No other places. Here."

The way he didn't answer her was so much a silence she could hear the leaves stir. "You didn't love her." The words fell from her, by themselves, you'd have to think, because she hadn't willed them to. They came out because they were there.

"Fool! Of course, I did!"

Long after, she realized he had shouted, screamed, almost. She didn't know it at the moment because her eyes had blurred with what she'd accused him of, and her hearing too had gone with her sight. She was barely clinging to the world.

When her vision cleared, she looked for him and saw that he was lying down on gray rock with his eyes closed, facing upward, exactly as though exhausted from a task. Like the reverse picture on a face card, he looked to be duplicating an opposite image of his straight-up self; only the marked cleft in his chin was more visible at that angle, and she recalled her mother holding up a card when they were playing double solitaire once while waiting for him for dinner: "Looks like Daddy . . ." "Let me see . . . sure does . . ." She had seen the florid printed face often enough, the smile affable, the chin cleft. "Jack of Diamonds," her mother said. For hadn't the two of them also seen the father's face turn fixed and mysterious as the painted image, unchanging from whatever it had changed to? The same twice over: she hadn't thought that till now. He reached up and took her hand. The gesture seemed to say they had blundered into the fire once, but maybe never again.

The scent of pine, the essence of oak scent, too, came warm to her senses, assertive as animals. She rubbed with her free hand at the small debris that hugged the rock. In former times she had

246

peeled away hunks of moss for bringing back. The rock was old enough to be dead, but in school they said that rocks lived.

"You're going to sell it, aren't you? The cottage, I mean."

"I have to. I need the money."

"I thought you were getting money, lots."

"I'm getting some. But not enough."

So he had laid an ace out before her. There was nothing to say. The returned silence, known to trees, rocks and water, went agelessly on.

Nat Jennings sat up lightly, in one motion. "What mysteries attend my Rosalind, wandering through her forest of Arden?"

"I was chased by a bear," said Rosalind, attempting to joke with him, but remembering she had almost cried just now, she blew her nose on a torn Kleenex.

"Sleeping in his bed, were you? Serves you right."

He scratched his back where something bit. "I damned near fell asleep." He got to his feet. "It's time." It's what he'd said when they left that other time, three years ago. He put out his hand.

Pulling her up, he slipped on a mossy patch of rock and nearly fell. But dancing was in his bones; if he hadn't been good at it, they would have fallen. As it was they teetered, clung and held upright.

Rosalind and her father got into the boat and paddled toward the cottage, keeping perfect time. Eva, not visible, was busy inside. They found her in the living room.

She had the red scarf wound about her head gypsy-fashion. Above her large glasses, it looked comical, but right; sexy and friendly, the way she was always being. She had cleared up everything from breakfast and was packing.

"You two looked like a picture coming in. I should have had a camera."

"Oh, we're a photogenic pair," Nat said.

"Were you ever tempted to study theater?" Eva asked her.

"I was, but—Not now. Oh, no, not now!" She stood apart, single, separate, ready to leave.

Startled by her tone, Nat Jennings turned. "I think it was her mother," he quickly said. "She didn't like the idea."

HUSH HUSH

by STEVEN BARTHELME

W HEN PAULIE ON her way to her interview with the arts people had stopped by his office at the bank, she laughed and said,
"Tilden, when're you going to move in?" He had ignored it, but
now he agreed.

His office was dull, as dull as people had always said it was
the first time they saw it. The first six months he had left it as he
had found it, the shelves empty, the walls bare. Wooden coatrack
in front of the windows. But it drew so many comments and
strange looks that he had taken a weekend and moved all the
furniture around; everybody else was always doing that. Then he
bought Mexican rugs for the walls and, for the table, marketing
and shelter magazines which, when they were superseded each
month, moved to tidy stacks on the shelves. Got rid of the damn
coatrack.

Still they told him it was dull, and although he thought their
offices no more interesting than his—Loeffler's Pirrelli calendars
and butterfly chairs—he now agreed with them about his own.
Dull. Maybe a two-headed secretary out front. But where would
Kelli sit? Where would she put her cat snapshots and dead sea-
shells? Maybe some posters, for some television religion or a
fifth-rate rock group, one he had never heard of, which wouldn't
be hard to find, as he never listened to the radio anymore, or
watched the music channels, or turned on the stereo, for that
matter. Silence, Tilden thought, was sweet, as Saturday mornings
had been.

The Saturday that Paulie had first arrived at his door, he had ignored her knock, sat beside the plants sipping coffee in the slanting light from the miniblinds over the windows, but she would not go away, so he finally got up and went to the door and opened it, then stood there denying he was her father, she, who should have been more embarrassed than he was, because she was outside and he was inside, just as adamantly, one foot up on a suitcase, asserting it.

He had shut the door on her, at least twice, then looked out through the blinds in the vain hope that she'd go away. She was tall, nearly six feet, muscular, dark-haired. Italian. Jeans and khaki shirt. She had settled on the top step and lit a cigarette, coughed, then, after five minutes or so, knocked again.

"Tilden," she said, through the door. "This is silly. You think you can ignore me and I'll go away? I've got no place to go." More knocking. "Nineteen sixty-six. Boston. My mother's name was Tina. You were drunk. You made a big thing about never drinking anything but vodka. Stupid, right? But what can you expect from a twenty year old? You had a show on the college radio station; you played Doors records, over and over. You have a big scar across the back of your neck. They took off a birthmark or something. Let me in."

It had ruined his morning, and all the mornings since, because now she was up before seven every day, with the blinds open and coffee brewing, like one of those women in the ads on the Weather Channel, leaping out of bed, where she had somehow mysteriously washed her face—there was never any oil on it—and her nightgown unwrinkled, so that he wondered if she had slept in it at all. He had been married twice, and women just didn't look like this in the morning, and their voices weren't light and had no lilt, and their eyes were bleary. Like his own. But Paulie came out of the back bedroom of the small apartment new-born, every morning. It was misery.

One Friday, before leaving for work, she said, "Still don't like me, do you?" and he had said, "You get in my way," and then he had thought about it all day at the office.

When he got home, she wasn't there yet, so he went to the market around the corner and bought a loaf of bread, and a jar of his brand of peanut butter, and two rib-eyes, meat, and a case of

249

Schaefer, which he counted on to have all the additives and unnatural junk that she claimed gave her headaches. He was arranging it all on the kitchen counter when she got back.

"Where've you been?"

"What's all this stuff?" she said, throwing her hair back with
her hand. "Steaks, no less. You're showing the flag, right? That's
so cute!"

"Where have you been?"

"Had to work late. Some very important cultural stuff happening next week, some kind of meeting. I met this very sexy British
guy. His name is Ryan. Only he's short. Comes to here," she
said, drawing a hand across her breasts. "If you didn't want me to
work late, you shouldn't have gotten me a job."

"Does this little guy have a little apartment?"

"You mean," she said, "a little apartment I could move into?
Let's not rush things. I only just met him. When do we eat?"

They ate the steaks—he cooked—and then drank the entire
case of beer, save one, until to her, the headache she planned
became somehow uproariously funny, and to him, she began to
look more like a woman, and less like a problem, or at least like a
different kind of problem, until he was shaking his head, mostly
to stop looking at her, stop noticing how pretty and how perfect
she was, like the pretty, perfect vegetables she brought home
from the natural store, or her sweet breath, which he knew came
from some kind of natural toothpaste she got at the same place.

He got up and walked from the front room into the kitchen,
and opened the refrigerator. "You want this?" he said, holding
the last can of Schaefer up in the triangle of light from the refrigerator, above the door.

She shook her head. "You're jealous, aren't you?" she said. "Of
Ryan? You don't want your daughter going—"

"Oh no," he said. "I've gotten rid of two wives. I'm not going
to have a daughter. The price is too high." And that ended the
party.

She stopped, blinked, looked at him, then started to cry,
quietly.

"I'm going to sleep," he said. "I'm sorry. You forced your way
in here. I got you a job. I had a nice, quiet, sensible life, before.
Peaceful, goddamn it. I pay the rent. I like you, but . . . "

"But?"

"I'm going to sleep," he said. "There's one more can of beer. On the top shelf. And some bourbon in the cabinet. And I sleep all day Saturday, so if you get up at the crack of dawn, don't start playing the radio and singing, for God's sake." He looked at her. "Tiptoe, for God's sake. Understand?" He looked away, and walked back to his bedroom and took his clothes off and got into bed, and fell asleep before he could get angry. She was right; he was jealous, but only a little. It would pass.

The next morning, he woke up at eleven, with a headache. When he got to the front of the apartment the glare from the windows hurt. He closed the blinds, twisting one of the plastic wands until he felt it break up at the top behind the sheet metal where you couldn't see what was going on. He thought, briefly, of going to the other windows and breaking the other two, on purpose, but let it go, settled down into the couch.

"Aspirin?" she said, from the kitchen.

He nodded.

When she brought him the pills and a glass of water, she was decked out in high heels and a long rayon dress, black, all open lace over a black slip, or a bodystocking, or something. "Anything else you want?"

He squinted and blinked. "What is this?" he said, waving his hand at her clothes.

"This is the Forties' look. You like it?"

"On Saturday?" he said. "Anyway, I thought high heels were unnatural. A chauvinist conspiracy or something."

She gave him a blank look, and then said, "I need the car. Okay? I'm not walking nineteen blocks looking like this. I have to go in today. Big project." When she saw his squinting, smug expression, she said, "I'm going to work because Ryan will be there and I put on some stuff because Ryan will be there, fancy stuff, this dress, the stockings. I feel stupid enough without you staring at me." She stood looking at him. "Why're you shaking your head?"

He smiled. "I'm remembering the years I spent worrying about whether women cared about me, noticed me. The work they must have been doing that I never saw." He shut his eyes.

"If it's non-effective, I'll put my Soviet outfit back on. If it's—"

251

"It's effective," he said. "Maybe too effective. Just make sure old Ryan's got a nice apartment."

"I told you last night. He lives in a hotel."

He nodded. "I figure about twenty minutes for the aspirin to work. Ten more minutes."

"Tilden? Tell me something." She picked her purse out of the seat of the armchair at the end of the couch, stood pushing things around in the purse until she came up with a tiny maroon brush. She drew it slowly through her long dark hair. "Why do you live this way?"

There was a time when a woman brushing her hair was the most beautiful thing in the world to him. "This way?"

"In the dark," she said.

"I'm a mole," he said, and pointed to his eyes.

"Don't you ever want to dance? Or go to a movie or— Or a woman? People die, you know? Then it's over. I mean, you bought a brown car, for God's sake. Mamma— She told me you used to be brash. What happened?" She dropped the hairbrush back into the purse and zipped it up, put her hands on her hips. "All you do is work and eat. And sleep."

"I drink."

"Not very much," she said. "Never enough."

"If you drink too much, you have to think about it." He looked up, but the light still hurt. "The car keys are on the hook, by the door." Squinting.

"Yeah, I got them." She shook her head, opened her purse again. "I've gotta go." She leaned over and gently kissed his hair. "I could stay home. We could drink up the bourbon. Go to bed."

"Get out!"

"Just kidding, Tilden. Jesus. Calm down. You're acting like my father or something."

He lifted his feet up on the couch and turned to face the back, heard the purse zip closed again, and then her heels on the hard-wood floor, finally the spring slip the bolt into the latch of the door.

Paulie was gone all day, and all day Sunday. Some time during the night she had returned the car, because when he looked out the blinds on Sunday morning, there it sat in front of the building. Brown.

He tried not to wait for her, even tried *60 Minutes* after the football games were over, but got distracted trying to tell whether the newsmen's suits were expensive, and their watches and their haircuts. He even thought of trying to call the hotel—but then remembered that he didn't know the kid's last name. He used to read, but that was no good either; he couldn't concentrate, so finally he got out the vacuum cleaner.

He straightened the rugs, pushed the chairs and the couch around, and ran the old vacuum back and forth, sweating, until the plug jerked out of the wall and he moved it to a new outlet. He left her room until last, stood before the door for a minute, and finally pushed open the door. The floor was littered with coathangers and panties, khaki shirts, sections of newspapers and crisp department store bags, leg weights, running clothes, and small balls of black hair. Tilden let the hose drop, walked over and sat on her unmade bed. He could smell Shalimar, or Emeraude, one of those.

There had been a girl, before he left school the first time, in Boston, a pretty quiet Italian so shy she could barely speak. He remembered riding her bicycle into an old church, sitting up by the altar. "I'm the bishop. You're the bishop's whore." He put his hand to the back of his neck, touched the scar. Vodka, that was right. The time he had gotten beat up on Marlborough Street, for taking somebody's liquor, she took care of him, covered his face with hot wet towels, touched his forehead, and brought him aspirin for three days. "I don't believe it," he said, out loud, and looked at the floor, settling for a moment on her discarded underwear, then quickly looking at the vacuum in the doorway.

Tilden stood up, and then sat back down, looking at a Vogue on top of a stack of magazines. He thought the telephone was ringing, in the front of the apartment, but listening harder, heard nothing. Jesus, he thought, no thank you.

The girl on the magazine cover, blond, in a three-quarter pose, her perfect face disappearing under the logo and her soft breasts nearly bare above a pale blue evening dress, holding his eyes, spaghetti straps, that's what they used to call them, ten years since he'd done this, looked at the goddamn pictures so hard it was as if you were trying to make the photograph start breathing, and he remembered knowing their names. Rene Russo, and Lois

253

what's her name, and Kim Alexis, and Lauren Hutton, of course. Verushka, way back, and Karen Graham.

"Fuck this," he said, shoving the magazines off onto the floor so that they slid over the clothes and hangers all the way to the wall. Tilden lay back on the bed, but when he felt his shoulders touch the sheet, jerked back up onto his elbows, then sat straight up and grabbed the clock from the table and threw it against the wall, and then, for good measure, finding nothing else, threw the table the clock had been on and picked up magazines from the floor and threw them too, tearing the covers, listening to the pages slap against each other until they hit the walls.

I am enjoying this, he thought, and looked at the radio, on the carpet. I am enjoying this very much. He brought his shoe down on the imitation wood grain plastic, in which there was a little too much black, and it only sort of squeaked, so he stepped back to kick it into the wall, getting a little lift so that it hit about two feet up from the floor molding, leaving a black dent in the paint and loose plastic below. "Up, and . . . good!" He was almost shouting, twisting around, turning back, looking, and he tried the bed, with both hands managing to throw the mattress against the other wall, a spinning throw which let him fall, like a dancer, on top of the box spring where he lay looking up, gasping for breath. This is it, he thought. This is the way I used to be. He laughed and looked around. Standing in the doorway, her feet in carefully chosen spots in the pretzel formed by the hose of the vacuum cleaner, Paulie was looking back at him, smiling. "You taking a break or what?" she said.

He started giggling, watching her, staring at her, the black dress, which was all holes, black faded to a sort of charcoal color, her hip cocked, her pelvis pushed front and center by the high heels like the models in the magazines, staring, and he could feel the look on his face, just past a smile, enjoying it, drunk with love, or something like love, thinking, I'm giggling, for God's sake, like everybody else.

"Tilden? Are you okay? Should I call somebody?"

He blinked. "You hurt," he said, "you know, just standing there in that goddamn dress. But . . . don't move. Are you tired?"

She stood, motionless, like a woman on display with her perfect brown eyes, perfect black hair, and glowering dark skin

wrapped around the muscles of her neck. "Now?" she said, reading his eyes. "Now you want to fuck?"

"No . . . " Tilden shut his eyes. "Yes. I wish you hadn't said
it that way. We could break some more stuff instead," he said.
"Let's do that." He got up, reached down for one of the pastel
blue leg weights, hesitated, and picked up the radio, the cord
wrapping itself around his leg until he kicked loose and reached
out with it, saying, "Yeah. Here. You go first. I'm buying." He
handed her the radio, which, missing only a couple of clear plastic lenses from the front, felt like a brick.

She kicked her shoes into the room and stood weighing the
radio in her hand, taking practice throws, sidearm.

"Hard," Tilden said. "Throw it hard. It's a tough little bastard."
He leaned over, kissing her neck just as she threw. The radio hit
the opposite wall and fell apart.

"Good," Tilden said. "That was good. Great. Sorry about . . . "

"It's okay," she said. "It felt . . . nice. How much shit can we
break?"

"A prudent amount."

She rolled her eyes. "You're buying?"

He nodded. "Get the bourbon," he said, and then followed her
as she walked down the hall, her long arms stretched out so that
her hands slid along the walls tearing the Jazz Festival posters in
half, leaving meandering white edges which looked like the stock
charts the newspapers published. She rose up on her toes to slap
the sickly beige cover off the smoke alarm, which immediately
began howling. In the living room she pushed over a lamp, and
Tilden stepped on the shade until the bulb shattered inside. She
cleared a bookshelf, hooked her stockinged foot under the table
in front of the couch, lifted it a quarter-inch, and yelped. Turned
around, picked up books from the carpet. "Here," she shouted,
handing him one, pointing at the three plants under the window,
and then they threw books, one by one, until the plants were
down. She turned and put her arms around his neck, sagging
against him, pulling him down. "Tilden," she said, her lips to his
ear to be heard above the screaming smoke alarm, wrapping herself around him, "let's break a rule." He reached down, put his
hands on her, feeling her through the dress, and felt as if he were
all hands.

"Tilden?" she said, in the morning, leaning over him, in the nightgown although she had slept without it, standing now with a cup of coffee in her hand, finger marks up and down her bare arms, her eyes clear, her hair shining, brushed to within an inch of its life. "You've gotta get up."

Sitting up in the bed, he set the coffee aside, and drew his fingers along her forearm. "Me?"

She nodded, sat beside him. "I bruise easily," she said, and grinned. "I was always very proud of that. If you say you're sorry, I'll break your face." She looked at her arms, and the grin turned to a broad smile. "I mean, I'd rather you didn't."

"I'm sorry."

She looked at him.

"How bad is it out there?" he said, pointing out the bedroom door. "The furniture. It's all coming back to me."

She shook her head. "Minor league," she said. "I've already put most of it back. I put that ugly plant in some water, in a mayonnaise jar. You're going to need a new lamp, though. You can probably replace that one for a buck and half."

"The lady has never bought a lamp."

"The gentleman has never been to the Salvation Army store."

"Right," he said. He put his hands on her breasts, felt her nipples through the thin nylon.

"Work," she said.

"Screw work."

"Tilden, you devil. You're going to break another rule?"

"Hey," he said. "There's only one rule. Jesus said. And then there're a lot of second-rate types making up a lot of extras. Middle management types. And Jesuits." He drew his hands away. "You in love with this Ryan person?"

"You mean, did I sleep with him?"

He laughed. "No, I meant what I said." He kissed her through the nightgown, pulled away, smiled at her. "I assumed you screwed the child's brains out. Isn't that what you young people do?"

"That's it," she said. "I mean when we aren't snorting, shooting, smoking, dropping, popping, or tearing the wings off angels. Or stealing stuff or—"

"Hush," he said. "Hush hush."

She looked at him.

256

"It's a song. Was a song. When were you born, what year?" He shook his head. "Nevermind. In olden times this blues guy, Jimmy Reed, I think he was from Dallas— He played harmonica and guitar and he had this trashy blues voice, we played him on the radio. A song called 'Hush Hush.' It was about noise. Sort of wonderful."

"I don't know whether I'm in love with him or not. Too soon to tell. He wants me to move in."

"A girl's got to find out, I guess." Tilden lay back in the bed, watching her.

"It was nice, last night, I mean throwing things and the rest of it, mostly the rest of it. I mean, I loved it. I mean, you. But look—" She was drawing circles in the sheet with her finger. "Look. When I was about six, Mamma gave me a picture, this glossy picture of you, of my father." She smiled, shook her head. "That picture was my favorite thing for about six years. You signed it. When I was about twelve, a girl told me it was Jim Morrison. The singer." She shrugged. "So I need another picture, see? Girl needs a picture."

"Let me get this straight," Tilden said. "Somehow you knew my—"

"Mamma gave it to me. Your name? I got it from Mamma."

"Okay. Anyway—"

"And Boston is right, and Baltimore, you living in Baltimore. There is a scar on the back of your neck. I've seen it. You want blood tests and shit? Paternity?"

"I want you not to be my kid. I like looking at you. Only not like you look at a daughter."

"There's lots of people to look at." She stood up, reached her hand up and split her hair between her fingers. "I've gotta go to to work. You know, Tilden, you're really fucked up," she said, and walked out of the room.

He looked toward the empty doorway. "Now!" he shouted. "I am now!"

But she didn't answer. He thought of getting up, of following her into the room and talking some sense into her, but when he imagined her shoulder in his hand, his face red and words spewing out in the southern accent that he fell into when he got angry, cared too much, the image reminded him of the bruises all over her arms, made him recall that he really didn't know what

257

to say, that two women he had married and loved and looked at ended up, after a while, looking at him, just as he ended up looking at them, sometimes fondly, each to the other a special piece of furniture. He let himself settle back into the bed, feeling comfortable and familiar, and he thought, Nestling, I'm nestling down here—just like everybody else, just before he fell asleep.

Sometime after noon, he went into work. Kelli said Loeffler had called him three times. He was supposed to be working on an incentive plan, but he spent most of the afternoon staring down out his office window at a bench and a pathetic tree set in the sidewalk, wine bottles around the tree reflecting the dirty sunlight. The bench, like all the other damn benches, had "William Donald Schaefer and the Citizens of Baltimore" painted on in script. Blue and white. He thought about calling Paulie at work but didn't, it became a test of his character, one he passed. When you make love to a woman, he thought, if you accidentally make something, you're supposed to make a son. If you accidentally make a daughter, that's all right, but you're not supposed . . . It thins out the blood or something. They make this stuff up. He put his feet on the desk and looked around. Dull, he thought, but not loud, ugly, pathetic, cruel. Decorating an office was like decorating a Buick. He closed his eyes, looking for her, and waited for five o'clock.

When he got to the apartment, she hadn't come home. Tilden fell asleep.

An hour and a half later, he woke up on the couch in the living room, in the dark, and reached up where the lamp had been, but then he remembered. So he sat in the dark. He had been having a particularly gaudy dream, he was sweating, but he couldn't remember anything except that it had something to do with work. He never remembered dreams. When he tried, all he could ever bring to mind was the dance dream, which he had had fifteen or more years earlier, a dream about his first wife. Floating around the kitchen of his parents' house in Richmond, she was dancing in the air, in a short, flimsy dress, a '60's dress from Paraphernalia, green with big yellow flowers, and he finally caught her and tied her up with white rope.

Guilt, Tilden thought. People are always talking about guilt, and this is what they mean. I'm feeling guilty, like everybody

258

else. He got up, made his way to the wall switch and stood, thinking about turning it on, decided not to.

On the steps outside the front door, he looked up and his car seemed far away, reflecting a dozen colors from the lights up and down the street. He made himself walk the fifteen feet, took a businesslike look at the traffic on the gray street, circled the brown Toyota, got in. I remember this, Tilden thought, pulling into the traffic. This is high school. He laughed.

When he got to the hotel, he left the car on the street, and was inside before he realized he still didn't know the kid's last name; Tilden stood looking. In the center of the huge, dim lobby, under a high ceiling decorated with lost chandeliers, was a flat fountain where people were pitching pennies into the water. Others sat on gray couches scattered to one side. Tourists were taking photographs of each other around the fountain, using flashes. On the far side of the fountain a recessed bar faced fat green couches set beside stingy glass tables on a gaudy carpet in a slightly darker green. The bar was railed off in brass, and packed. Another recess farther down, and corridors leading off at each corner. The elevator doors, opposite the fountain, were the same smoky marbled glass mirror as the wall. Tilden retreated to the gray couches, sat down, glanced around for short-looking men. Boys. Paulie.

Christ, he thought, it's some kind of designer whorehouse. Haven't been in a hotel for ten years. On the other couches, over-dressed women, with children standing beside them like miniatures, in crooked coats and ties. He looked around for telephones, but remembered he had no one to call. Hi, thought I'd call to say . . . well, I'm in love with my daughter . . . well, I didn't know either . . . well, she's sort of . . . tall . . . no, I'm at her boyfriend's hotel . . . well, I'm sort of spying on them . . . only I'm not spying very well . . . well . . .

He was cold, and thought of his coat, back at the apartment. He let his head sink into his hands, felt his elbows pressing into his knees, listening to high heels slap across the marble floor. His hair felt greasy. He thought of calling his wife, the second one. Beth. Her name was Beth, and she said she was going to look for somebody who'd let her have a dog. When he tried to picture her, what she looked like, he started to shake. He couldn't hear anything. Then he saw her all in white walking toward him across

259

the lobby, from around the elevators, and, a little behind, a short guy with shaggy hair, black suit, purple shirt, cowboy boots. Paulie, he thought. Paulie, I want to talk to you.

"You don't look well, Tilden," she said, waiting for the boy to arrive beside her. "Ryan, this is my father. Tilden, Ryan."

The boy held out his hand, but then, seeing Tilden's face, withdrew it. "Hello," he said. "Paulinda has told me a great deal about you."

Tilden looked at her. She was shaking her head. This is strange, Tilden thought, he's got to think it strange. Some quaint American custom, maybe. Perhaps. They say 'perhaps.'

"I hope you're not angry," Ryan said. "I told Paulie she should call." He looked at her, for an acknowledgment, then at Tilden, and getting nothing, no smile, shook his head. "You are angry. I'm sorry. But this is a little much, you know."

Tilden nodded. "A little much," he said. "Maybe."

Paulie was smiling, carefully. She had the boy's arm, slowly pressing him backward, but he was still talking.

"I am sorry," he said. "And I am pleased to finally meet you." He turned, drew his sleeve from her. "Paulie, I'll see you up—"

Tilden grabbed Ryan's coat, pulled him up onto the balls of his feet. "Little scumbag . . ." he said. But that was all he could think of. He stared at the kid's face.

He was looking at Tilden as if the older man were a child, a particularly wearisome child, who only had to be outwaited, who couldn't win, but had nonetheless to be allowed some time before the weight of decorum hit him. Tilden let go. "Get rid of him," he said. "He says your name again, I'll kill him."

"You actually do this over here," Ryan said. He was straightening his coat. "I thought it was only in films."

Paulie had stopped smiling. "Tilden, Jesus." She and Ryan exchanged looks, she taking him by the arm and leading him the first few steps back toward the elevators.

When she walked back, she was angry. "Real shabby, daddy. What were you thinking?" She looked around, took Tilden's arm, tightly, and led him toward the marble steps down to the street door. "What the hell are you doing here, anyway? You locate some paternal instinct?" She stopped on the steps, cocked her hip, released him, and stared. "Or do you just like making scenes in hotels? You're acting like fifteen."

260

"I know." Tilden stood three steps down, looking back at her. "But you don't understand."

She laughed, shook her head.

She was wearing some kind of white, long, T-shirt dress, stretched over her hip in a kind of perfection that only women seemed able to achieve, and it seemed to him that because she fit so perfectly in this hotel lobby, with the Givenchy whorehouse bar, and the orgy of glass and chrome and brass, green and gray and marble and the idiot chandeliers so high no one would call them to come back, and the other people with their impossibly brisk strides and Sunday clothes—what they used to call Sunday clothes—because she fit, so did he. That's how it seemed, but he knew he didn't.

"Call me tomorrow," he said. "Tell him I haven't been well or something. Call me at work."

He smiled and turned his face away, didn't look back until he was through the glass doors and out on the sidewalk. She was posed on the broad marble steps. He stood on the sidewalk, staring back over something written in gold on the glass, her clear eyes, the black hair, soft breasts with the big nipples, her hip high, and he felt his eyes smile and felt them blink once, twice, three, four times, and he thought, You can't look at anyone this way unless you've slept with her, and she, smiling, stepped back up a step. He jerked forward, a fraction of an inch, looked down, then back up at her for another second's worth of it, then raised his hand and waved. Someone was standing behind him, a copy of the Sun under her arm, looking at him like he was some sort of space creature. Tilden smiled. He wanted to look back through the glass doors. The woman circled around him and into the hotel.

The next day, a Tuesday, she never called, but around three-thirty Tilden was looking out his window when they came up the street and stopped at the corner. A short boy and a tall girl, arguing. They worked their way toward the building and then worked their way away. She was coming; he was going. When the boy began winning the argument, they would fade toward the sad little tree and the bench for the bus. When she got the upper hand, toward the building they came. Her dress was light, nylon or polyester, and swung as the boy grabbed her arm and released it, grabbed again. She threw her hands up, threw her head back, sat down on the bench. Tilden's telephone buzzed.

"Yes," he said, and then. "Okay," and then, "Oh, Kelli, when Paulie . . . If Paulie comes, just send her in," and then Tiny Loeffler came on the line.

"Let me guess," Loeffler said. "You've been busy—that teenager you had up here last month? You recall we talked about an incentive plan? We're tired of hiring new tellers every week. So think of something. You know, nifty prizes."

"We could pay them a living wage," Tilden said. He was straightening out the telephone cord. "Microwaves again?"

"That's a breakthrough," Loeffler said.

Tilden snorted. "If they aren't going to okay cash, the whole thing is a waste anyway. I can do you up a microwave plan by five this afternoon, no problem." The telephone cord was stretched out flat. They were still on the bench. Her arms were down, one hand caressing the hem of her dress, her black hair sparkling in the sunlight.

"Okay, but hurry the hell up."

His left hand, with the receiver, fell to his side; he could hear Loeffler talking distantly. "Put your arms around her," Tilden said, "you sleazy little creep." He laughed and pulled the phone back up.

"You there? Tilden? Hey, what's that little girl's name? She's in the book?"

Tilden was silent, turned away from the window. He felt blank, holding the telephone, waiting.

"Okay," Loeffler said, "but I think she needs a younger man. You're a little long in the tooth here. Aren't you? Has her daddy seen you yet? Hey?"

Tilden began to smile. "I'm her daddy," he said. "Her name is Paulinda. She's my daughter. You ought to get married, Tiny."

He heard part of a laugh, then silence, then a click, and the dial tone. Tilden, listening, stepped back to the window. She was straightening herself, patting her hair, setting seams, shifting her shoulders. Cotton. The dress was cotton. He set the telephone receiver down. I'm not a bad guy, Tilden thought, for wanting this woman to be wearing a nylon dress, for wanting to look at her, for wanting her to hush and put her hands on me, for any of

262

it. She'll be quiet now, and go away. She's already gone. Maybe sometime she'll need money and she'll call. He looked around the room. Place's okay, he thought. Peaceful. You ought to have a kid.

He stood at the tall blue windows, which stretched to the floor—it made you sick when you stood too close—and looked to his right then back to his left, but the street was empty. In his mind he saw them again, moving, talking, a mimed argument on the blue and white bench. Stand up, sit down. Stand up, sit down. I remember that, he thought. He reached out, his hand moving as if by itself, and touched the thick glass.

"BY LOVE POSSESSED"

by LORNA GOODISON

SOMETIMES, SHE USED to wake up and just look at him lying asleep beside her; she would prop herself up on one elbow and study his face. He slept like a child, knees drawn up to his stomach, both hands tucked between his thighs. His mouth was always slightly open when he slept, and his mouth water always left a damp patch on the pillowcase; no matter how many days after, it seems the patch would always be damp and every time she washed it, she would run her finger over the stain and her mind would pick up the signal and move back to the image of him lying asleep. When the radio next door began to play the first of the morning church services, she would know that it was time to begin to get ready to go to work. From Monday to Saturday, every day, her days began like this. She would go to the kitchen to prepare his breakfast, then she would leave it covered up on top of the stove over a bowl of hot water. Then she would go to the bathroom, bathe in the cold early morning water and then get dressed. Just before she left, she always placed some money on the top of the bureau for his rum and cigarettes, then she would say to his sleeping form, "Frenchie, ah gone, take care till I come back." Dottie sometimes wondered how she was so lucky to be actually living with Frenchie. He was easily the best looking man in Jones Town, maybe in the whole of Jamaica and she, ten years older than him, tall and skinny and 'dry up'. She had never had luck with men and she had resigned herself to being an old maid a long time ago. She was childless, 'a mule' as really unkind people would say. She worked hard and saved her money, and she kept a good house. Her two rooms in the big yard were spotless. She had a big trunk bed, that was always made up with pretty chenille spreads, a lovely mahogany bureau, a big wardrobe with good quality glass (mirrors) and in the front room, in pride of place, her China Cabinet. Nobody in the yard, maybe in Jones Town, maybe in the whole of Jamaica, had a China Cabinet so full of beautiful things. Dottie had carefully collected them over the years and she never used them. Once a year when she was fixing up her house at Christmas, she would carefully take them out, the ware plates, cups and saucers, tureens, glasses, lemonade sets, serving dishes and teapots, and she would carefully wash them. This took her nearly a whole morning. She washed them in a pan of soapy warm water, rinsed them in cold water, then dried them with a clean towel. Then she would rearrange them artistically in the Cabinet. On that night, she would sometimes treat herself to a little drink of Porto Pruno wine, sitting by herself in her little living room and would gaze on her China Cabinet enjoying the richness within, the pretty colours and the lights bouncing off the glasses. Her sister always said that she worshipped her possessions; maybe she did, but what else did she have? Till she met Frenchie.

There was one other thing that Dottie really liked, she liked the movies and that is how she met Frenchie. She was in the line outside the Ambassador theatre one Saturday night, waiting to get into a hot triple bill when she struck up a conversation with him. He was standing in the line behind her and she remembered feeling so pleased that a man as good looking as this was talking to her. They moved up in the line till they got to the cashier, and she being ahead of him, took out ten shillings to pay for herself. It was the easiest most natural thing in the world for her to offer to pay for him when he suddenly raised an alarm that his pocket had been picked. If she had been seeing straight, she would have noticed that some people were laughing when he raised the alarm. But she didn't see anything but the handsome brown skin man with 'good hair', straight nose and a mouth like a woman's. It was the best triple bill Dottie ever watched. He had walked her home. All the way home they talked about the movie . . . His favourite actor was Ricardo Montalban, she liked Dolores Del Rio, for that is how she would like to have looked, sultry and Spanish, for then she and Frenchie would make a striking couple, just like two movie stars. As it was she looked something like Popeye's girlfriend Olive Oyl and he was probably better looking than Ricardo Montalban.

Frenchie did not work. He explained that he used to have a job at the wharf but he got laid-off when his back was damaged unloading some cargo. She sympathized with him and some nights she would rub the smooth expanse of his back with wintergreen oil. He said he liked how her hands felt strong. Frenchie moved in with Dottie about two weeks after they met. At first, she was a little shy about having a man living in her room, then she began to be very proud of it. At least she was just like any other woman in the yard. As a matter of fact, she was luckier than all of them, for Frenchie was so good looking. "She mind him. Dottie buy down to the very drawers that Frenchie wear," said her sister, "not even a kerchief the man buy for himself". The people in the yard would laugh at her behind her back, they wondered if Frenchie kept women with her. Winston her nephew said, "Cho, Rum a Frenchie woman, man, you ever see that man hug up a rum bottle?"

Now that was true. Frenchie loved rum and rum loved him, for he never seemed to get drunk. As a matter of fact, every day he spent a good eight hours like a man going to work, in Mr. Percy's bar at the corner. After Dottie had gone to work at the St. Andrew House where she did domestic work for some brown people, Frenchie would wake up. He would bathe, eat the breakfast that Dottie had left for him and get dressed, just like any man going to work. He always wore white short sleeved shirts which Dottie washed whiter than 'Pelican shit'; he favored khaki pants, so she ironed both shirt and pants very carefully.

He would get dressed very, very carefully; put some green brilliantine in his hair and brush it till it had the texture of a zinc fence, or as one of the men in the yard said, "Everytime I see you hair Frenchie, I feel sea-sick". Frenchie would laugh showing his gold crown on his front teeth, run his hand over his hair and say, "Waves that behaves, bwoy, waves that behaves." When his toilette was over, he would walk leisurely up the road to the bar. The one thing which made you realize that he could not have been going to work like any other decent man was his shoes: he always wore backless brown slippers. Frenchie would sit in the bar and make pronouncements on matters ranging from the private life of the Royal Family (Princess Margaret was a favourite topic), to West Indian Cricket (he always had inside knowledge on these matters), general world affairs and most of all the movies.

Everybody was in awe of Frenchie, he was just so tough, handsome and in control of life. His day at the bar usually ended around 5:00 p.m., just like any other working man. Then he would walk home and join the Domino game which went on constantly in the yard. Usually Dottie would find him at the Domino table, when she burst in through the gate, always in a hurry, anxious to come home and fix his dinner. She always said the same thing when she came through the gate, "Papa, ah come" and he looking cool and aloof, eyes narrowed through the cigarette smoke, would say, "O, yu come." Dottie always experienced a thrill when he said that, it was a signal of ownership, the slight menace in his voice was exciting, you knew it gave the right to say, "Frenchie vex when I come home late . . ."

She would hurry to fix his dinner and set it on the table before him. She hardly ever ate with him, but sat at the table watching him eat. "Everyday Frenchie eat a Sunday dinner," Winston would say. It was true, Dottie cooked only the best for Frenchie, he ate rice and peas at least three times per week unlike everybody else who only ate it on Sunday . . . Dottie would leave the peas soaking overnight and half boil them in the morning, so that they could finish cooking quickly, when she hurried home in the evenings. He also had beef steak at least twice a week and 'quality fish' and chicken, the rest of the week.

Dottie lived to please Frenchie. She was a character in a film, 'By Love Possessed.' Then one day in Mr. Myers' bar, the movies turned into real life . . . Frenchie was sitting with his usual group of drunkalready friends talking about a movie he had seen, when a stranger stepped into the saloon, actually he was an ordinary man. He had a mean and menacing countenance, because he was out of work and things were bad at home. He walked into the bar and ordered a white rum and sat on a barstool scowling, screwing up his face everytime he took a sip of the pure 100% proof cane spirit, and suddenly Frenchie's incessant talking began to bother the stranger. The more Frenchie talked, the more it bothered him. He looked at Frenchie's pretty boy face and his soft looking hands and he hated him.

Then Frenchie reached a high point of the story he was telling. He was painting a vivid picture of the hero, wronged by a man who doubted his integrity and Frenchie was really into it . . . he became the wronged hero before everyone's eyes, his voice trembled, his eyes widened in disbelief as the audience gazed spell-bound at him . . . "Then the star boy say," said Frenchie, him say, "What kind of man do you think I am?" The stranger at the bar never missed a beat . . . he replied, "A batty Man." And the bar erupted. The laughter could be heard streets away, the barmaid laughed till they had to throw water on her to stop her from becoming hysterical, all the people who had ever wanted to laugh at Frenchie, laughed at him, all the people who envied him, his sweet boy life, laughed at him, everybody was laughing at him. The uproar didn't die down for almost half an hour and people who heard came running in off the streets to find out what had happened. One man took it upon himself to tell all the newcomers the story, over and over again. Frenchie was sitting stunned, he tried to regain face by muttering that the man was a blasted fool . . . but nobody listened.

Finally, the self-appointed raconteur went over to him and said, "Cho Frenchie, you can't take a joke?" Then he lowered his voice, taking advantage of the fallen hero and said, "All the same yu know everybody must wonder bout you, how a good looking man like you, live with a mawgre dry up ooman like Dottie, she fava man, she so flat and crawny . . ." Upon hearing this, Frenchie got angrier and funnily enough, he wasn't angry at the man, he was angry at Dottie. It was true, she didn't deserve him, she was mawgre and crawny and dry up and really was not a woman that a handsome sexy man like him should be with . . . No wonder the blasted ugly bwoy coulda facety with him. He understood what the hero meant in the movies when he said he saw red . . . Frenchie felt like he was drowning in a sea of blood . . . he wanted to kill Dottie! He got up and walked out of the bar to go home. When Dottie hurried in through the door that evening, saying breathlessly, "Papa ah come," she was met with the following sight. Frenchie was standing at the door of her front room with her best soup tureen in one hand and four of her best gold rimmed tumblers stacked inside each other in the other hand, and as soon as he saw her he flung them into the street. He went back inside and emerged with more of the precious things from her China Cabinet and he flung them into the street where they broke with a rich full sound on the asphalt. After a while, he developed a steady rhythm, he began to take what looked like the same amount of steps each time he went into the house, then he'd

emerge with some crockery or glass, walk to the edge of the veran-
dah taking the same amount of steps and with an underarm bowling
action, fling the things into the street. Dottie screamed, she ran up
the steps and clutched at him, he gave her a box which sent her
flying down the steps. Everybody screamed, the men kept saying
that he had gone rass mad . . . nobody tried to restrain him for he
had murder in his eyes . . . and he never stopped till he had broken
all of Dottie's things and then he walked out of the yard.

"Frenchie bad no rass bwoy . . . You see when him just fling the
things, chuh." Frenchie's name became a great legend in the neighborhood, nobody ever seen anybody 'mash it up' like that, so nobody had ever seen anybody in such a glorious temper, "mash up
the place to blow wow" . . . Nobody remembered him for "What
kind of man do you think I am?" Even poor broken Dottie remembered him for his glorious temper . . . She would have forgiven him
for breaking her precious things, she would have liked to have told
the story of how bad her man was and the day he broke everything
in her China Closet and boxed her down the steps . . . But he
didn't give her a chance. She kept going to the Sunday night triple
bills at the Ambassador, but she never saw him again and after that,
she took a live-in job and gave up her rooms in the Yard.

ASTRONAUTS

by WALLY LAMB

"NEXT SLIDE," THE astronaut says. For a second, the auditorium is as void and dark as space itself. Then a curve of the earth's ulcerated surface flashes on the screen and the students' silhouettes return, bathed in tones of green. This is the third hour in a row Duncan Foley has seen this picture and heard the smiling public relations astronaut, sent, in the wake of the Challenger disaster, to the high school where Duncan teaches. It's September; attendance at the assembly is mandatory.

A hand goes up.

"Yes?" the astronaut says.

"What did it feel like out there from so far away?"

"Well, it was exhilarating. A whole different perspective. I felt privileged to be a part of a great program."

"But was it scary?"

"I'm not sure I know what you mean?"

"Could you sleep?"

The astronaut's smile, which has lasted for three periods, slackens. He squints outward; his hands are visors over his yes. "Truthfully?" he says. "No one's ever asked me that one. I didn't sleep very well, no."

"What were you afraid of?" another voice asks. "Crashing?"

"No," the astronaut says. He has walked in front of the screen so that the earth's crust is his skin, his slacks and shirt. "It's hard to explain. Let's call it indifference. The absolute blackness of it. Life looks pretty far away from out there."

270

For five seconds longer than is comfortable, no one moves. Then ten seconds. "So, no," the astronaut repeats. "I didn't sleep well."

A student stands, his auditorium seat flapping up behind him, raising a welcome clatter. "How do you go to the bathroom in a space suit?"

There is laughter and applause. Relief. The astronaut grins, returning to his mission. He's had the same question in the first two sessions. "I knew *some*body was going to ask me that," he says.

Scanning his juniors in the middle rows, Duncan spots James Bocheko, his worst student. Jimmy's boots are wedged up against the back of the seat in front of him, his knees gaping out of twin rips in his jeans. There's a magazine in his lap, a wire to his ear. He's shut out the school and the astronaut's message from space. Duncan leans past two girls and taps Jimmy's shoulder.

"Let's have it," he says.

The boy looks up—a confused child being called out of a nap rather than a troublemaker. His red bangs are an awning over large, dark eyes. He remembers to scowl.

"What?"

"The Walkman. You know they're not allowed. Let's have it."

Jimmy shakes his head. Students around them are losing interest in the astronaut. Duncan snatches up the recorder.

"Hey!" Jimmy says out loud. Other teachers are watching.

"Get out," Duncan whispers.

"Get laid," the boy says. Then he unfolds himself, standing and stretching. His boots clomp a racket up the aisle. He's swaggering, smiling. "Later, Space Cadets!" he shouts to all of them just before he gives the door a slam.

On stage, the astronaut has stopped to listen. Duncan feels the blood in his face. His hand is clamped around the Walkman, the thin wire rocking back and forth in front of him.

Stacie Vars can't stand this bus driver. She liked the one they had last year—that real skinny woman with braids who let them smoke. Linda something—she used to play all those Willie Nelson songs on her boombox. Stacie saw Willie Nelson in a cowboy movie on Cinemax last night. It was boring. He wears braids, too, come to think of it. This new bus driver thinks her shit don't flush.

271

Nobody at school knows Stacie is pregnant yet, not even the kids in Fire Queens. She's not sure if they'll let her stay in the drum corps or not. She doesn't really care about marching; maybe she could hold kids' jackets and purses or something. Ever since she got pregnant, she has to go the bathroom all the time. Which is a pain, because whenever you ask those teachers for the lav pass, it's like a personal insult or something. She couldn't believe that geeky kid who asked the astronaut today about taking a crap. God. That whole assembly was boring. Except when Jimmy got kicked out by her homeroom teacher. She's not sure if Jimmy saw her or not when he passed her. He gets mad if she speaks to him at school. He's so moody. She doesn't want to take any chances.

The bus jerks and slows. Up ahead Stacie can see the blue winking lights of an accident. The kids all run over to that side of the bus, gawking. Not her; she doesn't like to look at that kind of thing. Jimmy says there's this movie at the video store where they show you actual deaths from real life. Firing squads and people getting knifed, shit like that. He hasn't seen it yet; it's always out. "Maybe it's fake," she told him. He laughed at her and said she was a retard—that if it was fake, then you could rent it whenever you wanted to. She hates when he calls her that. She's got feelings, too. Last week Mrs. Roberge called Stacie's whole science class "brain dead." Stacie doesn't think that's right. Somebody ought to report that bitch. Those police car lights are the same color of the shaving lotion her father used to keep on top of the toilet. Ice Blue Aqua Velva. She wonders if he still uses that stuff. Not that it's important. It's just something she'd like to know.

Duncan is eating a cheese omelet from the frying pan, not really tasting it. He's worried what to do about Jimmy Bocheko's hatred; he wishes he didn't have all those essays to grade. Duncan replays the scene from two days ago when he'd had the class write on their strengths and weaknesses. Bocheko had done his best to disrupt the class. "Is this going to count? . . . What do we have to write on something so stupid for? . . . "

"Just do it!" Duncan shouted.

The boy reddened, balled up the paper he'd just barely started, and threw it on the floor. Then he walked out.

The other students, boisterous and itchy, were suddenly still, awaiting Duncan's move.

"Okay, now," he said in a shaky voice. "Let's get back to work." For the rest of the period, Duncan's eyes kept bouncing back to the paper ball on the floor. The astronaut's assembly today was *supposed* to have given them distance from that confrontation.

At the sink of his efficiency apartment, Duncan scrapes dried egg off the frying pan with his fingernails. This past week when he did the grocery shopping (he uses one of those plastic baskets now, instead of a wheel-around cart), he forgot the S.O.S. Yesterday he forgot to go to a faculty meeting. He was halfway home before he remembered Mrs. Shefflot, his carpooler, whose husband was already there picking her up by the time Duncan got back to school. He knows three people his age whose parents have Alzheimer's. He wonders if it ever skips a generation—plays a double dirty trick on aging parents.

When the phone rings, Duncan tucks the receiver under his chin and continues his chores. The cord is ridiculously long; he can navigate his entire residence while tethered to the phone.

The caller is Rona, a hostess at the racquetball club Duncan joined as part of his divorce therapy. Rona is divorced, too, but twenty-three, eleven years younger than Duncan—young enough to have been his student, though she wasn't. She grew up near Chicago.

"What's worse than getting AIDS on a blind date?" Rona asks in her cheerful rasp. At the club, she is known as a hot shit. Kevin, Duncan's racquetball partner, thinks she's desperate, would screw anything.

Duncan doesn't know.

She is giggling; he has missed the punchline. This is the second AIDS joke he's heard this week. Duncan waters his plant and puts a bag of garbage on the back porch while Rona complains about her boss.

" . . . to get you and me over the mid-week slump," she is saying. She may have just asked him out for a drink. There is a pause. Then she adds, "My treat."

Duncan has had one date with Rona. More or less at her insistence, he cooked dinner at his apartment. She arrived with two gifts: a bottle of Peachtree schnapps and a copy of *People* magazine. All evening she made jokes about his kitchen curtains being too short. Fingering through his record collection, she told him it was "real vintage." (Her favorite group is Whitesnake, plus she likes jazz.) After dinner they smoked dope, hers, and settled for James Taylor's Greatest Hits. She didn't leave until twelve thirty, two hours after the sex. This struck Duncan as inconsiderate; it was a school night.

"I think I'd better beg off," Duncan says. "I've got essays to correct tonight." He holds them to the phone as if to prove it's the truth. Kevin is probably right about her. He's glad he used that rubber she had in her purse, embarrassing as that was.

"Oh wow," she says. "I'm being shot down for 'What I Did Over Summer Vacation.' " Duncan tells her he'll see her at the club.

Duncan's ex-wife used to love to read his students' work. She always argued there was a certain nobility amidst all the grammatical errors and inarticulateness. Kids being confessional, kids struggling for truth. After they separated, Duncan kept dropping by unannounced with half-gallons of ice cream and papers he thought might interest her. Then, when she had her brother change all the locks, Duncan would sit on the front porch step like Lassie, waiting for her to relent. Once she stood at the picture window with a sheet of notebook paper pressed against the glass. *Cut this shit out*, it said in Magic Marker capitals. *Grow up!* Duncan assumes he will love her forever.

Wearing underpants, sweatshirt, and gym socks, Duncan crawls between his chilly sheets. He snaps on his clock radio and fans out the essays before him. He'll do the worst ones first. The disc jockey has free movie tickets for the first person who can tell him who sang "If You're Going to San Francisco, Be Sure To Wear Some Flowers in Your Hair."

"Scott MacKenzie," Duncan says out loud. He owns the album.

Halfway through his third paper, he looks up at the radio. The announcer has just mentioned James Bocheko.

"Bocheko, a local youth, was dead on arrival at Twin Districts Hospital after the car he was driving . . . "

When the music starts again, Duncan turns off the radio and lies perfectly still, confused by his own giddy feeling. He leans over and picks up James Bocheko's paper which he took from the floor that afternoon and flattened with the palm of his hand. The

274

wrinkled yellow paper is smudgy with fingerprints, the penman-ship as large and deliberate as a young child's.

Strength's: I am HONEST. Not a wimp.

Weakness's: Not enouf upper body strength.

Duncan drinks bourbon from a jelly jar until the shivering stops. Then he dials his old telephone number. "Listen," he says to his ex-wife. "Can I talk to you for a minute? Something awful happened. One of my kids got killed."

At two, he awakens totally cold, knowing that's it for the night's sleep. When he rolls over, his students' papers crinkle in the folds of the quilt.

Stacie sits with her hands on the table, waiting for her mother to go to work.

"You ought to eat something besides this crap," her moth-er tells her, picking up the large box of Little Debbie cakes. She blows a cone of cigarette smoke at Stacie. "A fried egg or something."

It's the second morning since Stacie's felt like eating, but the thought of an egg puckering in a frying pan gives her a queasy feeling. She's eaten three of the cakes and torn the cellophane packaging into strips.

"Mrs. Faola's knitting a sweater and booties for the baby," she says, trying to change the subject. "Pale pink."

"Well, that'll look pretty g.d. foolish if you end up with a boy, won't it?"

"Mrs. Faola says if I wear something pink every day for a month, it will be a girl."

Her mother takes a deep drag on her cigarette and exhales. "If that wasn't so pathetic, it'd be hilarious, Stacie. Real scientific. I don't suppose you told the mystery man the good news yet."

Stacie picks at a ball of lint on the sleeve of her pink sweater. "You better get going," she says. "You'll be late for work."

"Have you?"

"What?"

"Told him yet?"

Stacie's cuticles go white against the table top. "I *told* you I was telling him when the time is right, Mommy. Get off my fuck-ing case."

275

Linda snatches up her car keys and gives her daughter a long, hard stare. "Nice way for a new mother to talk," she says. Stacie stares back for as long as she can, then looks away. A ripple of nausea passes through her.

Her mother leaves without another word. Stacie watches the door's Venetian blind swing back and forth. God, she hates her mother. That woman is so intense.

If it's a girl, Stacie's decided to name her Desiree. Desiree Dawne Bocheko. Stacie's going to decorate her little room with Rainbow Brite stuff. Mrs. Faola says they sell scented wallpaper now. Scratch'n'sniff—she seen it in a magazine. Stacie might get that, too. She's not sure yet.

Everything is finally falling into place, in a way. At least she can eat again. This weekend, Stacie's going to tell him. "Jimmy," she'll say, "Guess what? I'm having your baby." She hopes they're both buzzed. She could very well be a married woman by Halloween; it could happen. God. She already feels older than the kids in Fire Queens. Maybe they'll give her a surprise baby shower. She imagines herself walking into a room filled with balloons, her hands over her face.

When the phone rings, it embarrasses her. "Oh, hi, Mrs. Faola. No, she left about ten minutes ago. Yeah, my pink sweater and pink underpants. No, I'm going to school today."

Mrs. Faola lives in Building J. She watches for Stacie's mother's car to leave, then calls and bribes Stacie to skip school and visit. Today she has cheese popcorn. Oprah Winfrey's guests are soap stars.

"Nah, I really think I should go today," Stacie repeats. She loves to see Jimmy in the hall, even though she can't talk to him. No one's supposed to know they're semi-going out. "When *can* I tell people," she asked him once. "When you lose about half a ton," he said. She's *going* to lose weight, right after the baby. Mrs. Faola says Stacie better get used to having her feelings hurt—that that's just the way men are. Stacie would die for Jimmy. Mrs. Faola had an unmarried sister that died having a baby. Stacie's seen her picture.

"Tomorrow I'm staying home," she promises Mrs. Faola. "Gym on Friday."

She guesses most people would find it weird, her friendship with Mrs. Faola, but she don't care. Last week they played slapjack and Mrs. Faola gave her a crocheting lesson. She's going to give her a home perm when Stacie gets a little farther along, too. In her mind, Stacie's got this picture of herself sitting up in a hospital bed wearing a French braid like Kayla Brady on *Days of Our Lives*. Desiree is holding on to her little finger. They're waiting for Jimmy to visit the hospital. He's bringing a teddy bear and roses for Stacie. The baby has made him wicked happy.

Mrs. Faola is right about abortion being a fancy name for murder. Stacie won't even say the word out loud. At least her mother's off her case about that.

She stands up quick and gets that queasy feeling again, but it passes. She coats her mouth with cherry lip gloss and picks up her notebook. On the cover she's drawn a marijuana leaf and surrounded it with the names of rock groups in fancy letters. She keeps forgetting to erase BonJovi. Jimmy says they're a real suck group, and now that she thinks about it, they aren't that good.

On her way out, she looks at the cowgirl on the Little Debbie box. She's so cute. Maybe Desiree will look something like her.

Unable to sleep, Duncan has dressed and walked, ending not by design at an early morning mass at the church of his childhood. In the unlit back pew he sits like a one-man audience, watching uniformed workers and old people—variations on his parents—huddled together, making their peace. They seem further away than the length of the church. In his coat pocket Duncan fingers James Bocheko's list of strengths and weaknesses. The priest is no one he knows. His hair is an elaborate silver pompadour. From the lectern he smiles like a game show host, coaxing parishioners to be ready for their moment of grace when it comes hurling toward them. Duncan thinks of spiraling missiles, whizzing meteors. He imagines the priest naked with a blow-dryer, vainly arranging that hair. He leaves before communion.

This early, the teachers' room is more quiet than Duncan is used to. He listens to the sputter of a fluorescent light, the gurgle of the coffee maker. Jimmy Bocheko stares back at him indifferently, his eyes blank and wide-set. A grammar school picture. Duncan draws the newspaper close to his face and listens to his own breathing against the paper. The boy dissolves into a series of black dots.

At 8:15, Duncan is seated at his desk, eavesdropping. His home-room students are wide-eyed, animated.

"My brother-in-law's on the rescue squad. The dude's head was ripped right off."

" . . . No, that red-haired kid in our health class last year, the one with the earring."

"Head-on collision, man. He bought it."

A girl in the front row asks Duncan if he knew a boy named Jim Bocheko.

"Yes," Duncan says. "Awful." The girl seems disappointed not to be the one breaking the news. Then she is looking at his reaction. He thinks foolishly of handing her Jimmy's list.

The restless liquor night has already settled in Duncan's stomach, behind the lids of his eyes. The P.A. hums on. "All right, quiet now," Duncan says, pointing half-heartedly toward the box on the wall.

" . . . a boy whose tragic death robs us just as his life enriched us." The principal's mouth is too close to the microphone; his words explode at them. "Would you all please rise and observe a moment of silence in memory of your fellow student and friend, James Bocheko?"

Chairs scrape along the floor. The students' heads are bowed uneasily. They wait out the P.A.'s blank hum.

Duncan notices the fat girl, Stacie, the chronic absentee, still in her seat. Those around her give her quick, disapproving glances. Should he say something? Make her stand?

The girl's head begins to bob up and down, puppet-like; she is grunting rhythmically. "Gag reflex," Duncan thinks objectively.

Yellow liquid spills out of her mouth and onto the shiny desk-top. "Oh Christ, get the wastebasket!" someone calls. "Je-sus!" The vomit splatters onto the floor. Those nearby force themselves to look, then jerk their heads away. Two boys begin to laugh uncontrollably.

A gangly boy volunteers to run for the janitor and Duncan assigns the front row girl to walk Stacie to the nurse's office. "Come on," the girl says to her, pinching a little corner of the pink sweater, unwilling to get closer. Stacie obeys her, bland and sheep-dazed, her chin still dribbling.

Jimmy Bocheko's moment of silence has ended but nobody notices. The vomit's sweet vinegar has pervaded the classroom.

278

Windows are thrown open to the cold. Everyone is giggling or complaining.

" . . . And to the republic for which it stands, one nation under God, indivisible . . . " the P.A. announcer chants.

The first period bell rings and they shove out loudly into the hall. Duncan listens to the random hoots and obscenities and details of the accident. "If he gives us a quiz today, I'll kill myself," a girl says.

Duncan turns a piece of chalk end over end. He wonders if the decapitation is fact or some ghoulish embellishment.

A freshman thumps into the room, skids his gym bag across the floor toward his seat. "Hey, Mr. Foley, did you know that kid that got wasted yesterday? He lives next door to my cousin," he says proudly. "Whoa, what stinks in here?"

Stacie keeps pushing the remote control but everything on is boring. That Willie Nelson movie is on Cinemax for the one zillionth time. She wishes she could just talk to someone like that last year's bus driver—someone who could make it clear. Only what's she supposed to do—call up every Linda in the stupid phone book? It's *weird;* he never even knew. Unless he's somewhere watching her. Like a spirit or something. Like one of those shoplifting cameras at Cumberland Farms. She lies down on the rug and covers herself with the afghan. Her stone-washed jeans are only three months old and they're already too tight. She undoes the top button and her fat flops out. She can feel it there, soft and dead against the scratchy carpet and she lets herself admit something: she didn't tell him because she was afraid to. Afraid to wreck that hospital picture she wanted. Her whole life sucks. She could care less about this stupid baby . . .

She wakes with the sound of footsteps on the porch, then the abrupt light. She clamps her eyes shut again. Her mother's shadow is by the light switch. The rug has made marks in her cheek.

"What time is it?"

"Five after seven. Get up. I'll make supper. You should eat."

Stacie begins quietly when the macaroni and cheese is on the table. "I got something to tell you," she says. "Don't get mad."

Her mother looks disgustedly at something—a gummy strand

of hair hanging down in Stacie's plate. Stacie wipes her hair with a napkin.

"There's this kid I know, Jimmy Bocheko. He got killed yesterday. In an accident."

"I know. I saw it in the paper."

"He's the one."

"The one what?"

"The father."

Stacie's mother is chewing a forkful of food and thinking hard. "Are you telling me the truth?" she says.

Stacie nods and looks away. She hates it that she's crying.

"Well, Stacie, you sure know how to pick them, don't you?" her mother says. "Jesus Christ, you're just a regular genius."

Stacie slams both fists on the table, surprising herself and her mother, who jumps. "You could at least be a little nice to me," she shouts. "I puked at school today when I found out. It's practically like I'm a widow."

This makes her mother hitting mad. She is on her feet, shoving her, slapping. Stacie covers her face. "Stop it. Mommy! Stop it!"

"Widow? I'll tell you what you are. You're just a stupid girl living in a big fat dream world. And now you've played with fire and got yourself good and burnt, didn't you?"

"Stop it!"

"Didn't you? Answer me! Didn't you?"

"The jade plant looks nice over there," Duncan says. His ex-wife has rearranged the living room. It looks more angular, less comfortable without his clutter.

"It's got aphids," she says.

He remembers the presents out on his back seat. "Be right back," he says. When he returns, he hands her a small bag of the raw cashews she loves, and a jazz album. His ex-wife looks at the album cover, her face forming a question. "I've been getting into jazz a little," he explains, shrugging.

Although he would have preferred the kitchen, she has set the dining room table. The meal is neutral; chicken, baked potatoes, salad.

After dinner, he wipes the dishes while she washes. She's bought a wok and hung it on the kitchen wall. Duncan's eyes keep landing on it. "What's the difference between oral sex and oral hygiene?" he asks abruptly after an uncomfortable silence. It's one Rona has told him.

"Oh, Duncan, how am I supposed to know? How's your family?"

"Okay, I guess. My sister is pregnant again."

"I know," she says. "I saw your father at Stop and Shop. Did he mention it?" She hands him the gleaming broiler pan. "He was wearing a jogging suit. Gee, he looked old. He was mad at your mother. She sent him to the store for yeast and birthday candles and he couldn't find the yeast. Then there I am, the ex-daughter-in-law. He was having trouble handling eye contact."

"Did you tell him where the yeast was?"

"Yeah, then he thanked a pile of apples over my left shoulder and walked up the aisle." She turns to Duncan with a worried look. "How come he's limping?"

"Arthritis. It's weird, Ruthie. He and my mother are turning into little cartoon senior citizens. They go out to lunch every day and find fault. Last week I got stuck in a line of traffic; there's some slowpoke holding everybody up. It turns out to be my father. They're, I don't know, shrinking or something. She has a jogging suit, too. They wear them because they're warm. I can't help seeing them from a distance. It's bizarre."

Two years ago, when the specialist confirmed that his wife had indeed finally conceived, Duncan drove to his parents' house to break the news. His mother was out, his father in the back yard pruning a bush. "See what a little prayer can get you, Mr. Big Deal Atheist?" his father said, jabbing Duncan in the stomach with the butt of the clippers, harping all the way back to an argument they'd had when Duncan was still in college. When he went to hug him, Duncan drew back, resentful of his father's claiming credit for himself and his god. They'd been putting up with those fertility treatments for two years.

Duncan's ex-wife begins to munch on the cashews. "These are stale," she says. "Good. Now I won't pig out."

"I'm going out with somebody. She's divorced. Somebody from racquetball."

There is a pause. She pops more nuts into her mouth and chews. "Well," she says, "that's allowed."

"So when did you take up Chinese cooking?" he asks, pointing to the wok. He means to be nonchalant but is sounding like Perry Mason grilling a guilty woman. The wok is a damning piece of evidence.

"I'm taking one of those night courses at the community college. With a friend of mine from work."

"Male or female?"

She clangs the broiler pan back into the bottom drawer of the stove. "An androgyn, okay? A hermaphrodite. I thought you wanted to talk about this kid who got killed."

He takes Bocheko's paper out of his wallet and unfolds it for her. "Oh, Duncan," his ex-wife sighs. "Oh, shit."

"The kids were high on the death thing all day, exchanging gruesome rumors. Nobody wanted to talk about anything else. Do you think I should write them a letter or something?

"Who?"

"His parents."

"I don't know," she says. "Do what you need to do."

On TV, James Taylor is singing "Don't Let Me Be Lonely Tonight." On their honeymoon, Duncan and his ex-wife sat near James Taylor at a Chinese restaurant in Soho. Duncan and he ordered the exact same meal. Duncan is dismayed to see James Taylor so bald.

"You know my record collection?" Duncan says to his ex-wife. "Do you think it's real 'vintage'?"

"Real what?" she asks in a nasal voice. He realizes suddenly that she's been crying. But when he presses her, she refuses to say why.

Yellow leaves are smashed against the sidewalk. Duncan collapses his black umbrella and feels the cold drizzle on the back of his neck. An undertaker holds open the door. Duncan nods a thank you and sees that the man is in his twenties. This has been happening more and more: people his father's age have retired, leaving in charge people younger than Duncan.

He signs a book on a lighted podium and takes a holy picture, a souvenir. On the front is a sad-eyed Jesus, his sacred heart exposed. On the back, James Bocheko's name is printed in elegant script. Duncan thinks of the boy's signature, those fat, loopy letters.

In the main room, it's that pompadour priest before the casket, leading a rosary. Duncan slips quietly past and sits in a cushioned folding chair, breathing in the aroma of carnations. Someone taps his arm and Duncan sees he has sat next to one of his students, a loud-mouthed boy in James' class.

"Hi, Mr. Foley," the boy whispers hoarsely. Duncan is surprised to see him fingering rosary beads.

James Bocheko's family is in a row of high-backed chairs at a right angle to the closed casket. They look ill at ease in their roles as the designated royalty of this occasion. A younger brother pumps his leg up and down and wanders the room. An older sister rhythmically squeezes a Kleenex. Their father, a scruffy man with a bristly crewcut and a loud plaid sports jacket, looks sadly out at nothing.

Only James Bocheko's mother seems to be concentrating on the rosary. Her prayer carries over the hushed responses of the others. "Blessed art thou who art in heaven and blessed is the fruit of thy womb."

When the prayers are finished, the priest takes Mrs. Bocheko's wrists, whispers something to her. Others shuffle to the front, forming an obedient line. Duncan heads for the foyer. They will see his signature in the book. Mrs. Bocheko will remember him from the conference. "I know he's no angel," she said specifically to Duncan that afternoon, locking her face into a defense against the teachers and counselors around the table. Only now does he have the full impact of how alone she must have felt.

He sees that girl, Stacie, at the rear of the room. She is wearing a low-cut blouse and corduroy pants; her feet are hooked around the legs of the chair in front of her.

"How are you feeling?" Duncan whispers to her.

"Okay." she says, looking away.

"Were you a friend of his?"

"Kind of." She says it to her lap.

In the vestibule, the undertaker is helping the priest into his raincoat. "So who's your money on for the Series this year, Father?" he asks him over his shoulder.

Stacie walks past two other girls, representatives from the student council who stare after her and smirk.

The door is opened again for Duncan. The drizzle has turned to slanted rain.

Stacie is lying on her bed, wondering what happened to her notebook. She hasn't been back to school in over a month, since the day she found out about Jimmy—that day she threw up. She's not going back, either, especially now that she's showing. Let the school send all the letters they want. She'll just burn them all up and flush the ashes down the toilet. She's quitting as soon as she turns sixteen anyways. What does she care?

That Mr. Foley probably has her notebook. She's pretty sure she left it in his room that morning. Of all his teachers, Jimmy hated Mr. Foley's guts the most. He was always trying to get them to write stuff, Jimmy said, stuff that wasn't any of his fucking business. What she can't figure out is why he was at Jimmy's wake—unless he was just snooping around. By now, he's probably looked through her notebook, seen the pages where she's written "Mrs. Stacie Bocheko" and "Property of Jimmy B." and the other private stuff.

Being pregnant is boring. There's nothing good on TV and nothing around to eat. She wishes she and Mrs. Faola didn't have that fight. She still wants to get that perm.

She reaches back for her pillow. Drawing it close to her face, she pokes her tongue out and gives it a shy lick. She remembers the feel of Jimmy's tongue flicking nervously all over the insides of her mouth. She remembers the part just before he finished—when he'd reach out for her like some little boy. She gives the pillow several more little cat licks. She likes doing it. It feels funny.

Then she's aware of something else funny, down there. It feels like a little butterfly bumping up against her stomach, trying to get out. It makes her laugh. She kisses the pillow and feels it again. She begins either to giggle or to cry. She can't tell which. She can't stop.

"Why don't you ever make us write *good* stuff?" they wanted to know.

Duncan turned from the chalkboard and faced them. "Like what?" he asked.

"Like stories and stuff. You know."

So he gave them what they wanted and on Friday every student had a story to hand in. He has read them over and over again, all weekend, but has not been able to grade them. Each of

284

the stories ends in death; sentimentally tragic death, the death of a thousand bad television plots. Not knowing where to put the anxiety with which James Bocheko's death has left them, they have put it down on paper, locked it into decorous penmanship, self-conscious sentences they feel are works of art. How can he affix a grade?

The newspapers are full of fatal accidents. A bride has shot her husband. A girl choked to death in a restaurant. On the hour, Duncan's clock radio warns parents against maniacs, purveyors of tainted Halloween candy.

His wife is not safe. She could die in a hundred random ways: a skidding truck, faulty wiring, some guy with AIDS.

It was in a Howard Johnson's ladies' room that she first noticed she was spotting. "It's as if her body's played a joke on itself," the gynecologist explained to Duncan the next afternoon while his wife stared angrily into her hospital sheets, tapping her fist against her lip. "The amniotic sac had begun to form itself, just *as if* fertilization had occurred. But there was no evidence of an egg inside." Duncan recalls how she spent the next several weeks slamming things, how he rushed up to the attic to cry. There was no death to mourn—only the absence of life, the joke.

When he hears the knocking, he is sure it's his ex-wife, wearing her jeans and her maroon sweater, answering his need for her. But it is Rona, shivering in a belly dancer's costume. "Trick or treat," she says, holding out a tiny vial of coke. "We deliver." Inside, she lifts her coat off her shoulders and her costume jangles. She runs her chilled fingers over the stubble of Duncan's jaw.

* * *

The janitors have taken over the school, rigging the country western station through the PA system and shouting back and forth from opposite ends of the corridor as they repair the year's damages. It's the beginning of summer vacation. Duncan sits in his classroom, surrounded by the open drawers of his desk. He's in a throwing away mood.

What he should do is make plans—get to the beach more, visit someone far away. He should spend more time with his father, who is hurting so badly. Sick with grief: that phrase taking on new meaning. "You're not alone, I know what it's like," Duncan

285

told him last week. The two of them were fumbling with supper preparations in Duncan's mother's kitchen, self-consciously intent on doing things the way she'd always done them. "When Ruthie got remarried this spring, it was like she died to me, too."

"Bullshit!" his father snapped. His grip tightened around a fistful of silverware. "That divorce was *your* doing, the two of you. Don't you *dare* compare your mother's death to that. Don't you *dare* say you know what it's like for me." That was six days ago. Duncan hasn't called since.

He's saved the bottom right desk drawer for last, avoiding it as if there's something in there—a homemade bomb or a snake. But it's the confiscated Walkman, buried under piles of notices and tests. Duncan sees again James Bocheko, crouched in the dark auditorium.

Tentatively, Duncan fixes the headphones to his ears and finds the button. He's expecting screaming guitars, a taunting vocal, but it's electronic music—waves of blips and notes that may or may not mean anything. After awhile the music lulls him, makes him feel removed and afloat. He closes his eyes and sees black.

The janitor makes him jump.

"What?" Duncan says. He yanks off the earphones to hear the sound that goes with the moving lips.

"I said, we're going now. We're locking up."

He drives to the mall for no good reason. It's becoming a pattern: tiptoeing in and out of the bright stores, making small purchases because he feels watched. At the K-Mart register, he places his lightbulbs and sale shampoo before the clerk like an offering.

Exiting, he passes the revolving pretzels, the rolling hot dogs, a snack bar customer and a baby amidst the empty orange tables.

"Hey!" she says. "Wait."

He moves toward them, questioning. Then he knows her.

"You're a teacher, ain't you?" She's flustered for having spoken. "I had you for homeroom this year. For a while."

Bocheko's wake. The one who vomited—Stacie something. It's her hair that's different—shorter, close cropped.

"Hello," he says. It scares her when he sits down.

The baby has glossy cheeks and fuzzy red hair that makes Duncan smile. He pushes the infant seat away from the edge of the table.

"Did you find a notebook in your class? It's green and it's got writing on the front."

The baby's arms are flailing like a conductor's. "What did you say?"

"My notebook. I lost it in your room and I kind of still want it."

There's a large soda on the table and a cardboard french fry container brimming with cigarette butts. Behind her, the unoccupied arcade games are registering small explosions. "I don't remember it. But I'll look."

"I thought maybe you were saving it or something."

Duncan shrugs. "Cute baby," he smiles. "Boy or girl?"

"Boy." She blushes, picks him up so abruptly that he begins to cry.

"How old?"

"Stop it," she tells the baby. She hooks a strand of hair behind her ear with her free hand.

"*How* old is he?"

"Almost three months. Shut up, will you? God," Her clutch is too tight. The crying has turned him red. "Could you hold him for a second?" she says.

Duncan receives the baby—tense and bucking—with a nervous laugh. "Like this?" he asks.

Stacie dunks her finger into her soda and sticks it, dripping, into his mouth. "This sometimes works," she says. The crying subsides. The baby begins to suck.

"Uh, what is it?" Duncan asks.

"Diet Pepsi, It's okay. He ain't really getting any. It's just to soothe him down." The baby's shoulders against Duncan's chest relax. "You have to trick them," she says. Then she smiles at the baby. "Don't you?" she asks him.

"What's his name?"

"Jesse," she says. "Jesse James Bocheko."

Her eyes are gray and marbled, non-committal. He looks away from them, down. "I'm sorry," he says.

It's she who breaks the silence. "Could you do me a favor? Could you just watch him for a couple of seconds so's I can go to the ladies' room?"

He nods eagerly. "Yes," he says. "You go."

287

The soft spot on the baby's head indents with each breath. Duncan *sees* his own thighs against the plastic chair, his shoes on the floor, but can't *feel* them. He's weightless, connected only to this warm, small body.

"Baby . . . " he whispers. He closes his eyes and puts two fingertips to the spot, feeling both the strength and the frailty, the gap and pulse together.

GREEN GROW THE GRASSES O

by D. R. MACDONALD

A SUSPICION HAD come down that Kenneth Munro was using dope in the house he rented above the road. "Harboring drugs" was the way Millie Patterson put it.

"I don't think he's that kind," Fiona Cameron said, in whose parlor Mr. Munro was being discussed. She had seen him coming and going, a thirtyish man with dark gray hair nearly to his shoulders. It was the only extravagant thing about him, how the wind would gust it across his eyes. He had left St. Aubin as a tot and returned suddenly now for reasons unclear.

"Drinking's one thing," Millie said. "But *this*."

"This what?" Fiona said. She was curious about him too, but in a different way. And Kenneth Munro, after all, was not just any outsider. His family was long gone but still remembered.

After some coaxing, Lloyd David, Millie's son, described how Munro's kitchen had been full of the smell the day he'd dropped by to cut the high wild grass out front. "There's no other smell like it," he said.

This expertise got him a hot glance from his mother. Millie missed no opportunity to point up the evils of drugs.

"But Millie," Fiona said, "a smell in his kitchen is hardly criminal."

"Fiona dear, you have no idea." Millie, a nurse for twenty-six years, recalled with horror a young man the Mounties brought

289

into the emergency ward last winter: "In that weather, crawling down the highway in his undershorts, barking like a dog." Lloyd David chuckled, then caught himself. "He was that cold," Millie went on, "he was blue." She paused. "Marijuana." But the word came out of her mouth erotically rounded somehow, lush and foreign.

"But we hardly know Kenneth Munro," Fiona said. She knew he often stood shirtless on his little front porch late in the morning, stretching his limbs. He'd just got up, it was plain to see. He was brown from the sun, though he'd brought the brown with him. Fiona could not imagine him crawling along a highway or barking either. What she could imagine she was not likely to admit. She was from the Isle of Harris in the Outer Hebrides but had lived in Cape Breton all her married life, nearly twenty years. Her eyes were an unusual pale green, peppered with colors you couldn't pin down, and they looked merry even when she was not. No, Millie would not easily let go of this matter. Kenneth Munro. And drugs. They had come to Cape Breton like everywhere else, and of course people saw on TV what drugs out there in the world could do. Marijuana? Just a hair's breadth from heroin, in Millie's eyes, whereas alcohol was as familiar as the weather. Hadn't there been a nasty murder over in Sydney where two kids on drugs stabbed an old man for his money? That shook everyone, murder being rare among Cape Bretoners, despite a reputation for lesser violence. Fiona glanced out the front window; she hadn't seen Munro all day. His bedroom window was flung high and the curtains, green as June grass, whipped in the wind.

"He's got a telescope in the backyard," Lloyd David said.

"What's he up to?" Millie said.

"Well, that's the point." Fiona took a sip of tea. It was cool. "We can't say."

"He seems like a nice fella." Harald, Fiona's husband, had come in from haying and stood stout and perspiring in his overalls. "Fiona's right," he said from the doorway. "Yesterday he was asking me about the bobolinks."

"About the *what*?"

"Birds, Ma. Tweet, tweet?"

She glared at her son; she hated his Oakland Raiders T-shirt with the insolent pirate face on the front.

"Well," Fiona said. "He's just over the road. We'll have to find out about him. Harald, won't we?"

At a table by the west window of the Sealladh Na Mara Restaurant Kenneth Munro took in the postcard view. Whatever he saw he measured against the descriptions his father had given him years ago. He could see a portion of Goose Cove and the mountain behind it whose profile darkened the water this time of the afternoon, calming the bay. Terns squabbled on a sandy bar. The waitress, whom he fancied and who, he felt, was ready for a move, came up behind him, her slender figure reflected in the glass. In her unflattering uniform—a bland aqua, the hem too long—she seemed all the more pretty. She'd worn her fine brown hair unfashionably long down her back when he had seen her walking along the road, but now it was clasped in a bun.

"Ginny, suppose I was to take you to dinner some night soon? In Sydney?"

"Oh, I don't know. You're older than I am, by more than a bit." Ginny had graduated from McGill this summer and was back home, pondering her future. She loved the country she'd grown up in but knew she would work in a big city before long.

"I can't deny it," Munro said. "I'm up in years. I expect your parents wouldn't approve."

"No, No, they wouldn't much. And they've always known just about everything I've done around here." She looked over at two elderly women picking daintily at their lobster salads. "There's no need they should keep on knowing."

"I'll get you home early," he said. "Early as you like."

"I suppose we could. I'm thinking we might." She went off to another table and stood with her back to him. Munro drank from his water glass, running the ice around his tongue, and smiled comfortably at the immobile brilliance of the bay, its surface inked in shadow.

That was the kind of light he imagined in his special afternoon, an ambience like that.

They ate in a steakhouse too open and noisy, but after a bottle of wine they talked freely in raised voices, discovering that they might be distantly related through a great-grandmother, and that brought them a few inches closer. Munro told her about his carpentry work in San Francisco, cabinetmaking and remodeling, and how he liked working for gays because they paid him well and were particular. Ginny told him about Montreal and how she always tried to speak French there because she got to know the people. She asked him why he was living alone over there in St. Aubin with hay and woods all around him.

"Only for a while," Munro said. He took a photograph out of his coat and laid it on the white tablecloth, moving his face closer to hers. "That man there is my father, Ginny. The women I don't know."

"I'd say they like him, eh?"

"Something more than that going on. Look at his face."

"Is he your age there, your dad?"

"About."

"I like your gray hair. It's a bit long. His looks black."

"And very proud of it he was. Vain, even."

"He's dead?"

"He is." Munro tapped the photo. "But not here. Here, he is very much alive." He touched her hand. "Would you come with me to a field like that? Would you be one of those women, for an afternoon?"

Ginny laughed. He looked so serious in the smoldering light of the candle jar. But the people in the photograph, the man and the two women, seemed happy, and she felt quite good herself after three glasses of wine.

"You mean like a picnic?" she said.

On the way back to Rooster Hill Munro pulled off the highway near South Gut so they could take in the bay. Along the mountain ridge the lost sun threw long red embers. In the evening water below them, still as a pond, lay the blackened timbers of an old wharf.

"My father had a picture of that," Munro said. "From back in the twenties when he was a kid. There was a schooner tied up to it. Looked like another century. Here, you want a hit of this?"

He profferred what she thought was a cigarette. She stared at it.

"Am I shocking you?" Munro said.

"I've run across it, and I don't shock easy as all that."

292

He was afraid he had blown it with her, but he was in a hurry, and for him puffs of grass were part of almost any pleasure.

"You *are* a woman," he said.

"At home here, I am still a girl."

"Well, then." He made to stub out the joint but she grabbed his wrist and took it from him, drawing a long hit.

"God help us if the Mounties come by," she said through the smoke. "And you with relatives here."

"Never met any. One afternoon of my own is all I want. With the sun out, and a warm wind coming up from the field. And women like those in the photo, at their ease. That's what I came for—to take that back with me."

"I don't want to be a woman in a picture."

"Ah, Ginny, you'll be more than that."

They kissed in the car as it idled by her mailbox, once quickly like friends, then again with a long deep taste of something further. After Ginny got out, she kissed the window on the passenger side. The fierce twilight made her reckless. Through the rosy smudge on the glass, Munro watched her walk up the hill to her house, twirling her bag.

Fiona parted the parlor curtains: Kenneth Munro's car was turning slowly up his driveway, its broad taillights reminding her, in the foggy dark, of a spaceship. Wee men would be coming out of it, heading for the scattered houses of St. Aubin. *Feasgar math*, she'd say, I've been waiting. *Fuirich beagan*. Certain feelings had no shape in English, and sometimes she whispered them to herself. Harald was not a speaker above the odd phrase, but Gaelic came to her now and then like old voices. *Air á ghainmhich*. The sands of Harris, the long shell-sand beaches that even on a dour day opened up white like a stroke of sun, still warm to your bare feet after the wind went cold and the clouds glowered over the gusting sea. Those strange and lovely summers, so distant now—brief, with emotions as wild as the weather, days whose light stretched long into evening and you went to bed in a blue dusk.

"Harald," she said, "is it time for a call on Mr. Munro?" But Harald, pink from haying, had dozed off in his chair. A rerun of *Love Boat* undulated across the television, the signals bouncing

293

badly off the mountain tonight. Fiona loathed the program. When she turned off the set Harald woke. He kissed her on the cheek, then wandered upstairs seeking his bed.

So why not go up to Munro's? Yet when she thought of him opening the door, her breath caught. Of course she could phone him first, but that was not the same thing, was it?

Fiona had shared a life with Harald for a long time, here in the country. She'd left Harris for a small farm in Nova Scotia because she loved the man who asked her away, the seaman she'd met in Stornoway where she worked in a woolen shop. Love. *An gaol.* Yes, she had no reservations about that word, and all it carried, never had. She loved his company, even when he was dull (and wasn't she the dull one too sometimes, shut into herself, beaten down by a mood?). The two of them together had always seemed enough, and although they liked other people, they never longed for them. Small delights could suffice, if you were close in that way you couldn't explain to anyone else: it was the robin who nested every summer in the lilac bush at the front door, huddled in the delicate branches as they came and went, always aware of her, pleased that she didn't flee, and the families of deer they watched from the big window at the foot of their bed, grazing elegantly one moment and exploding into motion the next, and every day the Great Bras D'Eau, the different suns on its surface, the water shaded and etched by tides, stilled by winter, the crush of drift ice, and the long mountain in autumn, swept with the brilliance of leaves. And just the day-by-day work of living seemed to have a reason that lay in their being together, but they could never have said what it was. A meal, a task, a domestic calamity—who could say what made them glad for having it? They talked about some things, but left most unsaid. She loved . . . what? Harald's presence? Was that the word, *làthair*? In some way that no one else could embrace? It was like a bit of music that was always there, behind everything, often too faint to be noticed, but there, and sometimes powerful. He knew her, and he loved her, without question. She had not yearned for any different thing between them.

Yet something shocked her out of sleep now and then, her heart galloping hard until the dream yielded to the bedroom, to the familiar window, and she knew again where she was. An impossible longing came on as she lay there in the dark, whether there was a bright moon out, or snow raging or flickering down, or a deep rain drumming on her nerves as she waited for thunder. Harald would mutter on in his own dreams. She wondered if they were anything like her own. He never said. And why anyway? They were his, he needed them. But in some dreams, she made another man care about her: his attentions were utterly new and like that first keen love when everything is on the tips of your fingers. Each time, in whatever dream place, the feeling was the same: rich in sensation, strange, like none she knew in her waking life, and there were no words for it in Gaelic or English either.

Munro's front light burned in the fog, a gathering coolness on her skin. In Harris as a girl, mists had sometimes frightened her because of the tales she'd heard and because sights would suddenly appear in her path, ambiguous shapes in a gray sea, and as she approached Munro's house, she thought maybe that was why he looked out his window a moment before disappearing from it fast. She rapped on his door. What had she seemed like to him? A specter? *Tannasg?* He was slow to answer. She stamped her feet lightly though the wind was not cold.

"Did I scare you?" she said, pleased to have that edge.

"I don't get many callers, not at night. Mrs. Cameron is it?"

He looked tense but he ushered her inside, smiling. There was an odd smoke in the air and she blushed.

"Am I interrupting you? Harald's asleep. Tired to the bone." Was she rattling on?

"Something to drink?" he said. "Rum and ginger ale maybe?"

"Well I think I will. A wee one. Thank you."

Munro pryed an ice tray from his snowy freezer, scattering frost on the floor. He jabbered on about bobolinks in the hayfield. Wouldn't the tractor mow through their nests, the females drab but the males decked out in cream cravats? Were the fledglings gone, was that it? He held ice cubes in his hands.

"Oh, yes," she said. "They've flown by now."

He poured rum into a glass. The ice crackled.

"I've seen your husband cutting hay," he said. His face was pleasantly creased, as if he'd spent time outdoors, but comfortably, skiing or swimming perhaps. His long hair looked recently trimmed.

"He sells it. Three thousand bales." She smiled. At the tips of her cheekbones she felt spots of red. Like rouge, but hot. "I used to help him."

Munro handed her the drink, then peered out the window. "I'm glad it was you coming out of that fog," he said. "Jumped out of my skin."

"Nothing to harm you here."

"I know. Sometimes I'm sensitive to surprises." He sat down at the wooden table he used for a desk. "This little house is fine for me. The roof leaks a bit, in the kitchen."

"A family of seven lived here once. Less than fine." She had taken a good swallow and could feel the rum in her blood. She was startled to see her white knees crossed at the hem of her skirt since she'd intended to wear slacks. "I'll send Lloyd David over. He'll patch your roof."

"Lloyd David's mother showed up here this morning," Munro said as if it had just come back to him. "She asked me if I knew about the Knox Church and would I like to attend." He laughed. "She was really looking me over. I said no thanks, and she said it was only what she expected. What do I make of that?"

"Millie is just concerned about your soul, Mr. Munro. Some people here feel a kind of responsibility toward you, and they don't know what you're like."

"Because I was born here?"

"Your father grew up here, your grandpa too. He's buried over in the churchyard." She nodded toward the small white church that on a clear night could be seen from the kitchen. "That's part of why Millie came to your door."

"And you?"

"It wasn't for church, Mr. Munro. I'm not a deep kneeler myself."

"Folks don't usually care about my soul, especially strangers."

"You've got kin around here, if you want to know them."

"Really, I don't." He bent a gooseneck lamp low to the table. "That is, I have something I want to live, or relive, while I'm here. It doesn't involve cousins. Just myself, and two others."

She set the glass down on the carpet, most of it gone. The rum made her bold.

"Has it anything to do with what I smell in the air? Mind you, I'm only asking."

He went still and looked at her. There was a touch of smile in his voice. "Asking's plenty, at this point."

"I'm not snooping."

"And I'm not dangerous. Every Presbyterian is safe."

"It doesn't matter, believe me. Not in my book."

"Would you come here to the table? I'll try to show you what I'm after, something I missed a long time ago."

A photograph was arranged under the table lamp like a document. "I never saw my family except in snapshots," Munro said. "My father would lay them out and tap a face or a house or a field somewhere, places I'd never seen. Bits of a puzzle, to me. People posing in kitchen chairs out back, gray shingles behind them, in Cape Breton. St. Aubin, other places. You know what I mean . . . a guy standing by a horse with his hand on its nose, and my father would say, 'Now that's cousin Murdock John Rory, and he's nearly a hundred.' And my mother would chime in, 'And isn't that Donald's Heather when she was small, with the dog Uncle Freddie left behind?' She knew all the pictures by heart. But not this one. I found it in the lining of his suitcase, after he died. No, my mother never saw this. She would have said, even though she isn't in it."

His father, shirtless, lies on his back in an unmown field. Closed in delight, his eyes are directed toward the camera through a veil of summer grass into which he seems to be settling. His smile is one of selfconscious bliss, unfeigned. A plump woman with dark hair hugs him, her cheek pressed to his bare chest as if she is listening to his heart, while a second woman, younger, her light blond hair pulled tightly back, sits in a sidesaddle way beside his head, her hand playing in his hair. Her smile, pursed with mischief, would warm any man near it. Fiona can see that. Her shorts have cuffs and her tucked-back legs are pale but pretty. It is like the photos Fiona grew up with, in its black-and-white tones of the past. Behind the father and his two women, neglected fields recede toward gray water. Shy spruce trees stand singly in the far reaches of meadow, awash in wild blond grass. Visible at the edge of the picture is a boarded window. The old house lists like a grounded ship.

"The farm was long abandoned by this time," Munro said. "Granny was dead. The land is going back to woods, slowly, and my dad didn't care. He'd had to stay home into his thirties, being the youngest. Had to see to his mother. But you see, he was cut off, for years, there in the country. No electricity. No plumbing. Nothing to tune into. A caretaker, a nurse. And Granny was hard to live with sometimes. So when he was free of all that, he took off west. He only came back here once, and this is it, I know it. On a whim he's come out to the old place, with two women. There's something he has to taste, one more time, and it's all in the air of that afternoon."

"And who *took* the picture?" Fiona said.

Munro looked the question off, his eyes still on the photograph. "I'm trying to *see* this, you understand, to get inside it. An afternoon like this one, just once. No camera has to record, only me. And the two women."

"And what happens when that day dies down and you all have to go home?"

"I'll still have the day. And I can enter it whenever I wish." He showed her a stubby joint from his shirt pocket. "This helps me. Does that make any sense?"

"Portions of it." Fiona could see right into that old house: the lamps were dry and the cold air was damp with absence. She could smell the mildewed cushions and clothes and bedding, on the beds or in the drawers. And that man in the grass, he would never be back. The women touching him were neither his wife nor his wife-to-be. What was he like? What kind of man had he been?

"But why do you need help from that?" she said, pointing to the roach in the palm of his hand. "I'm sure I sound naive."

"It helps me see things I've missed. And it makes me high." He smiled. "Are you going to evict me?"

"You're not noisy. Your rent's paid. And it's only you up here, isn't it?"

"You do understand what I'm after here? A kind of re-enactment?"

"And where will you do all this?"

"At my grandmother's old place, of course. Nobody's there. Are they?"

"No." Fiona looked to the window that faced the strait and the mountain. "But I have to tell you that your grandmother's property is gone for a gravel pit. There's little of it now but a bare cliff. I'm sorry."

298

Kenneth Munro spread the tripod legs and focused his telescope on the bare brown scar across the water: dust blew about it like smoke, and yes, it was mostly cliff now, gravel mounded for hauling at the base of it. He could just make out the monotonous grind of a stone crusher. A dump truck rumbled off with a heaped load and disappeared into the dense green mountainside.

When Harald's tractor started up the hill from the road, Munro hailed him and waited in the row he was mowing. Harald stopped and got down, leaving the engine running.

"I wanted to ask you," Munro said, offering Harald the photo and nodding toward the mountain. "How could they do *that* to *this*? How is it legal?"

Harald doffed his cap and wiped his startlingly white scalp with a red bandana. He studied the picture. "It was fallow, you know, your grandma's place, a long while. Nothing coming out, nothing going in. Just deer and hunters. So, goes for taxes. Goes for what money might be made of it."

"Gravel?"

"Gravel. God, they took ton after ton out. All under the highway now."

"Where I live you could fight that."

"Fight what? We had nice farms all over here once. The place was full of people. Lots of trees now, as you see it, everywhere." Harald patted the hood of his tractor as if it were flesh. "You liking it up here, in the house?"

They both looked at the house. Lloyd David was kneeling on the roof wielding a thick black brush. He waved.

"It's fine. Look." Munro brandished the photo. "Is there a meadow like this anywhere over there, on the other side?"

"Look east a bit. That patch. I used to cut hay for the old widow but she's gone. It's clear yet, I think. Funny how trees don't come back into certain places, just don't. Further up lies a stone house, what's left of it. We didn't build with stone. Plowed up too damn much, I guess."

"Is it grassy there?"

"Old hay and whatever." Harald yanked a stalk from the ground. "There's no single grass called hay. It's a mixture, varies from place to place. Over at the stone house, I can't recall." He blew on the timothy in his hand. "See that powder? Pollen."

"Flower tops," Munro said. "Them I know about."

299

He glanced back at the roof. Lloyd David flashed him an ambiguous peace sign and then put his forked fingers to his lips. Munro ignored him.

"Look through your scope there and you'll see the spot I'm talking about." Harald climbed up on the tractor seat. "Or is that just for stars?"

"There's a comet due pretty soon. Next Friday, I think. Come up and have a look."

"Can't stay awake for a comet, Mr. Munro. That time of night I'm sawing heavy wood." He looked toward his house where Fiona had come out. "Now, Fiona, she'd love to. You show her the stars." Harald released the brake lever and fell instantly into the rhythm of mowing. The man would keep it up until dark, and if the weather shifted, he had other things to do. Had he noticed how lovely his wife looked?

Down by her lilac bush, Fiona was taking in the morning, her face up to the sun, or so it seemed, a mist of lavender still left in the branches behind her. When she saw him, she crossed the road and came slowly up the field, the wind in her clothes, billowing her pale green skirt. She stopped short of him and shaded her eyes. The sun warmed her honey-colored hair.

"There's a stone house over there I'd like to go to," Munro said.

"I heard it's dangerous." She was a bit out of breath and her cheeks had reddened. "It's falling in."

"I suppose there's some danger, sure," he said. He looked down at her white house and the green shutters. The barn, the big doors of its threshing floor thrown wide, was painted and trimmed the same, neatly. All of a piece. "Why did my father hate his own farm so much he let it be ground up into nothing? The fields have been hauled away in trucks."

"He wasn't happy there," Fiona said.

"He was at times. At times."

The sound of the tractor was fading out beyond the rise.

"I guess you've been to the stone house," Munro said.

"I never have. I know it's there."

"Do you like comets?"

"How couldn't I?"

At the big rock behind his house he helped her up to the telescope, his hands shaping her waist. Fiona looked into the eye-

300

piece where the stone house was supposed to be. He watched her looking, her hands on her bare prim knees. Something in the tension of the skin there made him want to touch her.

"It fair puts you right there, doesn't it?" she said. She tapped the barrel of the scope. "That could find mischief far and wide." She looked down at him. "Why the stone house?"

"My afternoon lies over there. Would you come along? We'll have a look."

Harald was returning over the hill. Lloyd David had hauled his ladder down and stood smoking a cigarette. He grinned at Munro as if they both shared some secret.

"But," Fiona said, "how would I fit into an afternoon like that?"

"Just fine." He gave her his hand and she hopped down off the rock. A strap of her blouse slipped down and Munro plucked it quickly back in place. "You see," he said, "I know the mood of that day. My father could go away again any moment he wanted to. His mother wasn't in the house anymore, cranky, dying." Munro looked at the tall, almost platinum grass beside his house, beautiful as a woman's hair. He'd told Lloyd David not to cut it, to leave it as it was. "My father had the smells of summer in that grass, that air. The women felt it too. So could we, I think."

A breeze rushed through the old maples along the hayfield, a warm sound in the leaves. The ripe hay shimmered. Crows roamed the stubble like portly deacons. Down on the road a red Lada crept past, Millie hugging the wheel.

"When?" Fiona said.

Since there was an old path, she let Munro and his excitement lead the way through the foothill woods until they stepped out into a meadow, clear except for a sprinkling of wild apple, gnarled and stunted by browsing deer.

"Up there!" Munro said. In the upper boundary of the meadow sat the ruins of the house, its stones the color of damp sand. It seemed to be merging with the ground. All these years and Fiona had never seen it: strange to look upon the open gut of it, all tumbledown, mossed, grassed in, tufted with wildflowers. But then she had had no cause to come here before. Harald came haying but how would he have known she'd take an odd pleasure in beholding a stone house half broken back to where it came

301

from? Munro pulled her away to a pair of apple trees so old they knelt, their trunks extending out like thick branches, and he sat her down in the tall, fine grass.

"My father's trees were straighter," he said. He was flushed and proprietary, as if all he saw were his. "These are hardly breathing. Leaves, but not a fruit on them."

"Och, they needed pruning and propping in their later years, and who was here to do it?" Harald tended their own small orchard, and Fiona loved the apple blossoms in June, the white perfume of a new summer. Rain scattered the petals like snow.

"This can be the place," Munro said. "I know it, I feel it."

"It is a place already. People worked here, lived here."

"I'll borrow it for a day. That's all right, isn't it?"

"If there's ghosts, I doubt they'd mind."

Munro was lighting a joint as if it were no more than a cigarette, his eyes absorbed in the flame.

"They might well mind that, though," Fiona said.

"You mean they never got high, these people. Can't believe it."

"I didn't say that. But I wouldn't think you'd need that stuff up here," she said.

"My father had a bottle up here." Munro hissed more smoke from the joint and blew it out with a long sigh. "Background music, Fiona. Here, try a little. We'll see things the same way."

"Thanks, no. I'm seeing fine."

He was on his feet and striding toward the ruined house. That smoke changed him, she could see that clear enough: he took a little turn of his own and left her a step behind. What was it like? She had to wonder. She liked his eyes, but they were too light sometimes, like water in a swimming pool, and she could imagine him leaning against a palm tree. But that was unfair. His long hair suited him somehow, carefully trimmed, and the rough clothes too, the denim shirts and jeans that made no distinction between leisure and work.

She followed him up the hill, drawn more to the house itself than to Munro's investigation. She knew stone houses, growing up in Harris they were all she knew. But here she had never seen one like this, rude as an old hearth. Two of the walls, thick with stacked stones of many sizes, were nearly intact, their outer surfaces sealed in a layer of rough mortar (some crude version of harling?), but the inner ones exposed like a tall fence of field-stones, weathered and stained from rains and the earth they'd been pulled from (but chosen with the patient eye and hand of a stone setter), smaller ones (pebbles even) wedged between larger, all to complete this solid unwavering puzzle, this wall. At the corners, broken or joined, the stones had been dressed to fit flat. The lintels of the low, cramped windows were long, chiseled blocks. Never fancy, this house, but Highland skill and labor had formed it. The roof had long ago pitched itself into the living space, atumble with split timbers, gray as driftwood, and with broken stone. Among them grass and hardy flowers sprouted from sod clumps. Rubble from the collapsed sections had spilled into the fruitcellar, a cell-like pit lined with stones dressed into neat blocks like the lintels. But all was collapse now, a giving in. It must have been dark indeed, but she could attest there was nothing like two feet of stone between you and the world, a kind of safety, coming as she did from an island of wind. Wind cowered her mother's flowers, but howl as it might, the house did not budge. Only neglect could bring it down—an open roof, and no one caring.

"Look!" Munro was running his hands over an outer wall where lichen blossomed like bits of ochre. "Feel the *mass*. It's not like a wooden house going down at all, is it. See that?" Faint marks in the mortar. "Bird tracks."

She touched the wall. Odd what things stones had in them. St. Clements. On Harris, the church in Rodel so old it was worshipped rather than worshipped in. When she and her friend Morag visited there, awed by its stone mysteries inside and out, it was two sculptures that forced their glances as they wandered the wild grass of the grounds, the tombs and graves: high above a door in the east wall were two lewd sandstone effigies, a woman squatting to display her unmistakable cunt (as plain as that) still swollen after four hundred years of blurring wind and water, and balancing her out was a male also embedded in the wall stones, gripping rigidly his huge implement as if he had hold of life itself. What was this lurid couple doing high up the wall of a church, papist though it had been, burial place of MacLeod chiefs? The devil put them there, if you ask me, Morag had said, and Fiona only laughed, knowing better.

"But what bird walks on walls?" Fiona said.

303

"There are birds you don't know about, my dear Fiona."

His eyes had taken on that abstracted, detached look she noticed the other night. The stones felt cool, like cave rock. She shivered. Munro brought his face close and when she didn't move, he kissed her mouth, her chin.

"They must've been lovely cozy in that house," he whispered.

"How lovely we'll never know," she said.

"We might, we might." He smiled and moved away into the foliage that hugged the ruins. She listened to him pushing through the branches. "They must've had a garden or something here," he called back, his voice muffled in the trees, a different voice than he'd come up the hill with. She wished she had said no, had let him come alone, even that she had come herself alone, for she liked this place, liked the day, the feel of it. She hadn't kissed him, he had kissed her. She liked his mouth and that warm moment before the kiss, his eyes soft and blind, taken up with what was coming, a look she had not seen in so long she wasn't quite sure it was there. Kenneth was younger, a desirable man, a mystery of sorts—and yet not. How could she say what she was after in him? It was something beyond him, something maybe impossible, even unwise, to reach for. She caught again that smoke: a whiff of burnt grass.

Munro called out to her, "Yes there has been a garden!" He was shaking the branches of a tall shrub. "See? Lilac!" At the tips of its bony, dead-gray stalks were dry but visible blossoms, and yes, it was in leaf. Lost in the slender fir trees they found a spindly rose bush too tall to be wild, and further away a single apple tree, hoary but filled with tiny green fruit. "They had flowers here," Munro said, "no doubt about it." Then they nearly stumbled over a low stone wall, disguised by grass, much of it, and what they could make out here and there showed it as an enclosure within which the wild trees had checked their growth, the birches almost thinly decorous, the spruce lightly branched and airy. "How strange," Fiona said. A walled garden behind a small farmhouse like this, in this country, walled not to keep anything out but just to define a place, to contain pleasure. No vegetables in this space, their potatoes and turnips would have ripened elsewhere. How strong the scent of flowers must have been in the midsummer air when the people of the house came walking here, the same people who hauled and chiseled and hoisted those great

304

stones ten feet up for windows and walls. It would have been peaceful, for the men as well as the women, with the fields cleared, the wind off the water. She sat down on a mossy patch of wall and imagined the garden without the invading trees. Daisies bloomed at her feet. What other flowers of their own had they put in the ground? Was it the women of this stone house who planted them? She wanted to think it had been a man, the kind of man who, after grappling with stones in those hard days, would have, with a splayed finger, poked tiny seeds into the dirt of a flower garden.

Munro had knelt behind her and was parting, as he might a curtain, the back of her hair. He kissed her nape, and that was all she felt, just that sensation, unexpected, its surprise moving warm like wine into her face. She closed her eyes and turned her mouth to his. They slid down into the grass outside the wall. His fingers smelled of balsam, and very faintly of the lilac that had brushed him. Yes, the garden, and a coppery evening sun, the wind down, the flowers tense, waiting for the night, birds merging into trees and leaves. She felt the warm sun on her legs, and then his fingers, almost cold so that she tensed and gave into him at the same moment, and it seemed they were sinking gently into the grass, she whispering to him but not words, his mouth hot through the cloth of her blouse as his breath moved down her waist. Then he stopped, his muscles hardening and he sat up out of her arms: "Someone's coming." Her own breath stopped, then she pulled her skirt down and smoothed it over her knees. Who was the someone coming? She didn't move. To flee would look more foolish than lying in the grass, a man on his knees next to you. In her daze she nearly laughed: oh Millie, turning her tongue on them both, fiercely, first at this suspect man who had surely tricked Fiona into the trees, and then at Fiona who would have to be some kind of a thing herself to lie down in the weeds with him in the middle of a working day. Lord, the racket in the teacups, sipping her name, and his, and Harald's. Fiona sat up but stirred no further, nor did Munro while feet tramped nearer and took the forms of Lloyd David and a pal, a taller boy Fiona didn't know, their voices preceding them, earnest but unintelligible in the noise of the leaves and snapping branches as they ducked and staggered through the trees. Lloyd David was holding in his fingers a cigarette butt like a captured bug and the boys paused long enough to share its smoke, taking it gravely to their lips in turn. They were not looking for anyone, were headed elsewhere, heads down, intent, guileless, the woods just something to be got through. They passed within a few yards of Munro and Fiona, stumbling on, oblivious, their bluejeans fading out into the thicker trees.

"He had a bottle in his back pocket, that squirt," Munro said. "God, I thought he was working with Harald."

"He was, this morning. He comes and goes."

Fiona brushed off her skirt and redid two buttons of her blouse, her fingers cool and clumsy. Over on a wall of the stone house a tree shadow swayed like a flame. She stood up: something had both happened and not happened. Munro lay back in the grass, his shirt open. There was a silver medallion in the thick hair of his chest.

"What was it my father used to say?" he said. " 'Hot as Scotch love'?"

She saw in his closed eyes, in their fluttering lids, something of the father in the photo: something that had to be satisfied, but never would be.

"You're looking pleased with yourself," she said. "Does it not bother you a wee bit?"

"Does what?" He got to his feet and climbed on the stones so he could see down the hillside.

"I'm married," Fiona said. "You do know the man. You have met him."

"I like Harald. He's a worker, he is. But what have we done, you and me?"

"Half what we would do, I suppose. Isn't that part of your 'afternoon'?"

"We don't have to make love . . . if you'd rather not."

"You're an arrogant man, you are. You know I like you, and like the feel of you. But there's an ache I'll carry home with me. I don't think you know anything about that. Do you feel it at all?"

"Feel what?"

"Guilt, they call it around here."

"Over *this*?"

"Somebody could be hurt over this."

"Nobody knows, nobody will. Lloyd David and his buddy were stoned blind." He jumped off the wall and put his face close to hers. "You have beautiful eyes, extraordinary eyes. And listen: I'll be gone in a month, less."

Munro went off down the hill to pick a spot for the next visit. The wind had turned and the weather with it, chilly out of the east, the sun gone behind the rolling gray clouds. Fiona hung back. She picked up a chip of stone. How cold and damp this house must have been at times, here where the winters were so much colder than in Harris, deep frosts and blizzards. The night Harald brought her to St. Aubin it was winter and deeply cold, colder yet to her, a stranger. Harald soon put a fire in the old coal stove and she ran outside yelling into the snow, snow so cold it had bits of blue in it, and she stood there, panicked: a fire like that in a wooden house, wood from sills to rooftree? All she could think of were flames, creeping, then roaring up the walls. She soon enough felt the freezing air, Harald at the back door calling to her, laughing. Wood and paper, she'd thought, that's all this house is. But he came out into the windy snow and put himself around her like a cape. He said you're warmer now, aren't you? Aye, she said, let's go inside.

Munro beckoned to her from a heap of fieldstones in the meadow. "We'll have a picnic down here! Look at the soft grass!" He brushed his hand through it. Fiona wandered down, the chip in her fist.

"In the photograph," she said, "weren't they lying under an apple tree?"

"We're not slaves to the photo. It's the spirit we're after, Fiona. Besides, I've got to have a hand in it. I'm scripting this play. The original afternoon was as easy as living. Anyone can live. The hard part is ours."

A sweep of wind up the hillside brought a few hard, cold drops of rain.

"There were *two* women, in that picture," Fiona said.

"I have the other one," he said. "She's perfect."

Ginny was at the roadside, waiting against a tree. In a full red skirt and white blouse, there was a touch of peasant about her that he liked, the way she hailed him as she shouldered her bag: he might've been driving a bus. Beside him on the seat she was all talk and faint perfume, happy to be released from the restaurant, the duties of food. "Do I smell like a kitchen?" she said, brushing her rich brown hair. He said no, that she smelled like something he had never tasted but had always wanted to.

"You've been smoking, haven't you?" she said.

Munro smiled. He described the stone-house meadow as he drove, how perfect it was, the very place.

"And what happened to your dad's then?"

"Dug up and dispersed. There might be some of it under us right now."

"Gravel?"

"Gravel."

"Kenneth, I'm not sure who I'm supposed to be in this," she said. "The women in the picture were older than I am."

"But not prettier. I consider it a bonus. And you don't have to *be* anyone but yourself. The day will do the rest."

"But I'd like to visit the spot first."

Munro touched a fold of her skirt. "Of course. We'll go up there today."

Ginny said nothing more until they had turned onto the main highway at South Gut, passing the big motel that looked up the bay. Its restaurant's windows were cluttered with tourists and they reminded her somehow of busy chickens, feeding away, packed into that one place and cocking their heads now and then at the country around them.

"I should've worn jeans," she said, "if we're going in grass."

Munro accelerated up the mountain highway, praying the weather would hold.

Perfect? What did he mean?

Maybe he had said it only to get a rise out of her.

Fiona had not seen Munro up at his house since yesterday. Tonight the comet was due. Was he there and she'd missed his car? She picked up the phone. No. A foolish schoolgirl, wanting to hear his voice, thick with sleep even this late in the morning. What did other women do when a certain man set them wondering? Dream it out?

She set about dusting the parlor, but suddenly she flung the feather duster to the floor. What a silly object, and how silly she felt bustling around with it. Was there really another woman in this? Did he mean beauty? Youth? Someone more inclined to be the way he wanted? When they had parted that day, Fiona said yes, maybe she would meet him again at the stone house when the weather was to his liking, and it would be another step, her life into his. But a kind of acting, for a day, part of a day. And what would she say afterward, to herself, to him? Something would be altered for good. She liked being in his arms, no lie there. He was a different man and she could not get the details of him out of her mind, those she knew and those she might. Two days since they talked and she missed him, even the complication the sight of him brought.

But this other woman? Where? Fiona could not conjure her up. Why did he insist on this fantasy when common sense would tell him that his father was not out sporting with two women that afternoon, that surely there had been another man behind the lens of that camera? He couldn't wish him away, though perhaps he could smoke him away.

Kenneth had told her what the comet might look like, but her anticipation was not celestial. They would be up there alone. She would know before long whether she would go with him down below the stone house and be arranged in the grass according to an old photo, where Kenneth would be hoping to find what he was after, old moments he knew little about.

From the kitchen window she could see Harald starting in on the lower and last field, the felled hay a wake of darker green following him toward the shore. She knew the look he would be wearing: absorbed, contented, a slight smile as he rocked along in the sun, calm as a boatman. By the time he was done for the day it would be near dark, and later she would spot him in the hayloft, the bare light bulb throwing shadows around him.

Did Kenneth mean the *two* of them, to have herself and that nameless woman, both . . . ?

Fiona went out to her flower bed and weeded furiously, panting with amazement, trying to will images out of her mind before they dizzied her daft. My lover? *Mo gràdh?*

After lunch she walked up to the mailbox. Millie pulled up slowly in her car and spoke out the window.

"They caught a bunch of smugglers last night," she said, out of breath as if she'd been running instead of driving. "Along the north shore. Drugs, bales of it."

Fiona sorted through letters. "Anyone we know, Millie?"

"They were Americans, wouldn't you know! The ones behind it. And mainlanders."

Fiona could feel what was coming. Her cheeks were already hot and she ripped open an ad for weedkiller instead of looking at Millie.

"Well, anyway," Millie said. She revved the engine a little. "What about that Munro fellow over there? What did you find?"

Fiona nearly said I found your son in the woods and he wasn't hunting rabbits. "He'll be going home soon, Millie, so don't concern yourself."

She took her anger into the house, anger with herself, with everything. Not the day to have run into Millie Patterson. She banged around upstairs, cleaning their bedroom that did not need it. This was a big house but why did it seem so small, so cramped? Soon she was standing at the picture window: its view was clean and wide and took in miles up and down the strait. The water lay out blue and sheer on a slack tide. Without meaning to, she was staring at that part of the mountain where she had been with him. She could see the patch of field, and some flicker of movement there, deer, or dogs. She reached for Harald's field glasses, the powerful ones he spotted ships with. She moved the circle of vision up and down until she found them. Kenneth, for sure. And a girl with him. Kenneth was jogging ahead, towing her along by the hand. They'd soon be breathless at that clip. But she was young. And he young enough yet to take a hill on a beautiful afternoon. She watched them tumble into the grass and lie there like children, their arms flung open to the sky. Was he handing her something, like a flower? It was not a flower. Fiona was aware of her own eyes against the glasses, of the weight of them in her hands, and she set them back on the sill. Munro and the girl were up and running now, flecks of color on the green hill, but she didn't care to look at them any closer again. They'd be heading for the stone house, for the lovely ruins of the garden. You're making a mistake, she wanted to tell this girl, you don't know that man at all. But how stupid: Fiona did not know him either, and the girl was free to be foolish if she wished. And what did that girl, so much younger than herself, see in Kenneth Munro? What made her take his hand and disappear into the trees of that mountain? When they parted, what would she take away? Humbled that she had no answers, Fiona stepped back into the shadow of the room, a vague ache in her chest. Along the shoreline, Harald's tractor was passing against the strait, rocking like a boat over the uneven ground, while, unknown to him, Lloyd David danced a distance behind, spinning in circles, flinging cut hay into the air like flowers.

"Are you coming up to Kenneth Munro's? The comet is on." Fiona stood over Harald in his easy chair. "It's a right clear evening for it." She half wanted him to say yes because that might make things easier but he said no, and her heart shifted.

"I'm whacked out, dear. Anyway, what's come of your investigation up there? Was the man inhaling terrible fumes or what was he doing?"

"There's nothing there Millie need fash herself about, or anyone else either," she said with more heat than she'd intended.

Harald smiled. "I just wondered where the comets might be coming from."

"That's more than I can say. Where do they usually?"

"Oh, I guess there's all kinds," Harald said, getting up.

Fiona glanced through the curtains. "That comet, it won't come around again for sixty years," she said.

Harald kissed her as he passed. "Then we'll both miss the next one. Eh?"

She skirted the house where he'd left the lamp on, briefly annoyed that he would carelessly burn a light all day while he was off with the girl who was perfect. It illuminated the table by the front window where he did his reading and snacking, and smoking too, no doubt. Out back on the big rock the telescope waited, a spindly silhouette in the deep blue of the night. He had aimed it where he figured the comet would appear, not in the direction of the stone house but somewhere over the westerly woods. The smell of the mown grass lifted with the wind. Frogs in the spring pond chirped like sleepy birds but they were well awake. In the humid nights of the last week she had heard them shrill at the fitful corners of her sleep. The telescope trembled on its thin legs and she steadied it, startled by the cold metal. He wasn't coming.

She tried the back door and of course it was open. Hadn't she herself told him you needn't lock up here like you would in San

311

Francisco? She moved slowly through the darkened kitchen and its spicy smell she didn't recognize, into the lighted living room where his things lay about as he'd left them, trench coat tossed across the sofa (it smelled of the rain he'd worn it in), a few empties of Old Scotia Ale on the table, reeking of stale malt, a dinner plate holding two bits of butt-ends (how could he have smoked them to nubs like that? She flicked her tongue over her lips). She thumbed through his bird book, noted the kinds he'd checked off in the index. Had he really seen a Tennessee Warbler? She had never heard of one, but then he saw things here that she did not, perhaps could not, without smoking those leaves. There was visible dust on the bureau and she ran her finger through it, tempted to write him a mischievous message but realizing she had passed that stage with him. She hefted the walking stick he had whittled from a driftwood branch. Stacked neatly were letters in a woman's hand but she did not disturb them. A magnifying glass, a book about stargazing, a jar of peanuts uncapped. Harald would distrust this sort of leisure. What Harald was not using he put away in sheds or chests or closets. He would never surround himself with things as idle as these. There were no leavings of his pleasure for others to peruse. But Kenneth's were all over this house. And there was the photograph.

Stretched out in the grass, stripped to the waist of his baggy trousers, the father looks somehow naked. The women's bare legs are sexy in a way now lost, Fiona thinks. A bottle of liquor is propped against the apple tree. The tree needs pruning badly. All those years he had been under his mother's stern and jealous eye, but today no one watches him from the house. And the land, now his, is turning wild. He is free to drink inside the house or out, to play in the unruly grass of his own fields, to ignore the decaying roof, the spoor of hunters (surely that's their work—the splintered door, the riddled pail), the stealthy trees new in the distance. He's free, as dusk comes down, to steal back toward his old bedroom where wind sighs through shot-out windows, his shoes crunching over glass, a finger to his lips, mocking his mother's prohibitions. Drink, drink, drink, he wants to shout in the dark hallway, the woman behind him hugging his back, giggling with a fear she hardly understands, there in that summer twilight that smells of damp and age. He cups his ear. He pretends, for a laugh, that his mother lies listening down the hall. And of course

312

she does, even now; years after her death she is still in this house, and even on the slashed stuffing of his old mattress, in a desolate smell of winter and wet cotton where he makes the kind of noises he never dared, like love in a storm, he feels her hard rain on his back. And this his son will never know, will never see.

Fiona turned out the light.

On the rock, she put her eye to the telescope, holding down her skirt. Kenneth said it would have no fizzing tail, it wasn't that kind of comet. Far from flashing across the sky, its motion seemed little more than a waver, like a star, just brighter, more restless and low in the sky. Wasn't just the word charged with speed and color? Was it something like that he got from his smoke, from that brittle smell? The comet flared, south of west. She let her skirt go, the gusts took it away from her legs and whipped it about. If she turned the telescope toward the stone house, she wouldn't see anything now but the cold, yawning walls, heavy as dreams.

When she got into bed, she lay looking out the big window at the end of the room. Harald stirred beside her. "Did you see it?" he said. Fiona could tell from his voice that he'd been sleeping.

"The tail was magnificent. Fiery. The way you'd think it would be."

"Streaked across the sky, did it?"

"No," she said. "No, it took longer than that."

Harald touched her face, then turned back into sleep.

She remembered waking one cold, cold February morning, unaware that Harald had wakened too. From their pillows they could see that the water of the Great Bras D'Eau had vanished, become a long white field. The men had not laid down a bushline yet but someone was crossing the new ice anyway, a woman, making her way slowly over the rough snow of the surface, her trail as fragile as a bird's. Her danger seemed to enter the room, and they watched her, she and Harald, saying nothing about her, this dark, tiny figure. They never saw where she came ashore, and they never found out what woman she was, coming so early, and finding her own way across.

WAR

by MOLLY GILES

THE FIRST THINGS I noticed when I got back were all the dead plants in the yard. It was as if he'd played God with the garden hose, because the bush beans and peas were all right, but the tomatoes and peppers and corn had dried out. I always like to follow his reasoning when I can, and this, I figured, was his passive-aggressive way of killing what he considered Latin vegetables as a way of punishing me for going to Nicaragua. If I'd gone to Belfast he'd have killed the potatoes, if I'd gone to Lebanon he'd have killed the eggplant. You have to know him to understand how his mind works, and then you have to explain it to him because he pretends not to know himself. I don't bother to do this anymore; since the divorce he's on his own. I just observe.

His truck was gone—only an oil stain to show where he'd parked on the grass—and he'd put a new latch on the gate that was so complicated I had to set my duffle bag down to figure it out. I'd just about decided I'd have to climb over when Cass came running out the front door and down the path toward me. We gripped hands through the gate like two lovers in prison, hopping up and down and trying to kiss through the grids. "Are you all right?" I kept shouting. "I'm fine," she shouted back. She laughed. "Why wouldn't I be?" She slid the gate open and held her arms up, just like she used to do when she was a baby, but her arms came up to my chin now, and she was almost too heavy to lift. "I've missed you so much," she said.

314

I'd missed her too. It had only been ten days but I felt as if I'd returned from another century. Cass felt large in my arms, and solid, and astonishingly American, with her pink cheeks and bubblegum smell and rough blonde hair and new sneakers. At least he bought her decent shoes, I thought, as I swung her around and set her down. The last time he stayed with her he bought her a leather jacket like the Nazis used to wear. We'd had such a fight about it Cass had finally taken the jacket off and thrown it at both of us. Cass—we agree on this at least—deserves better parents.

She helped me with my bag and we went into the house, talking all the way. "You were in the paper," she said. "They had a big article on the peace conference and they had your name and everything, and Mrs. Bettinger read it to my class and said you were a heroine."

"Some heroine," I said. I was pleased, but I'd seen too many real heroes and heroines in the last few days. "All I did was make lists," I told her. "I helped people off one bus and onto another. It was hard work in a way, but it wasn't very exciting." I set my bag down. "How was it for you here? Did you have fun?"

"Not really," Cass said.

I nodded, sympathetic, and glanced across the front room toward the couch. You could tell it had had quite a workout while I'd been gone. There were three big dents in the cushions. The coffee table had been pulled in close, with the remote control at arm's reach, and there was a new circle stain on the wood where his beer had been set down, night after night.

"It looks like he slept on that couch," I said.

"He did."

"Every night?" I stepped closer. I could practically see him there, one hand over his mouth as he snored, the other hand over his crotch. "Just like he used to do when we were married," I marveled. "Did he take his clothes off at least?"

"He said there wasn't any point," Cass said. "He'd just have to wear them the next day."

"What about his shoes?"

"I think he took his shoes off."

"And you?"

"Me?" Cass laughed. "You want to know what I slept in?"

315

"No. I want to know—were you lonely? With him falling asleep in front of TV every night?"

"No," Cass said. "I didn't mind it."

I looked into her face. There were no dark circles under her eyes, no pinch to her lips, no sign of neglect.

"He never talks," I reminded her.

"We had popcorn every night. Kentucky Fried twice. Pizza three times. One night we just had soda and chips."

I shuddered. All those home-cooked casseroles I had left in the freezer with instructions taped on them—ignored. The bran bread and marmalade I'd made, untouched. The sprouts shriveled up in their little glass jar; the tofu amelt in its own sour juice. I pulled off my sweater and looked around. The house felt different but in a way I couldn't define, dirtier somehow, although there were no signs of dirt or disorder. The ferns were all dry in their pots, but alive. The books I'd been studying before I left were still on the table, collecting dust and overdue fines, and the Spanish language tapes Mark had smuggled off an Army base were still threaded through the cassette deck.

"It's good to be home," I said, not too sure. "But it smells funny. Do you smell anything?"

"Like what?"

"Like socks. Old socks. And . . . machine parts? And—I don't know . . . musk?"

"No. It smells like home to me."

"I think I'm going through culture shock," I admitted. "Everything down there smelled like lime trees and sewage. And the people had so little. We have so much more. This room looks . . . jammed."

I had a great urge to start carting things out to the sidewalk— lamps we didn't need, extra chairs, the wicker chest, the TV set, the couch—things other people could use. Then I wanted to scrub and air, and wash all the windows. But I was tired; the flight back had been a long one, and the conference had drained me. I felt if I closed my eyes for a second I'd see Blanca or one of the little soldiers and they'd be more real to me than this room. "It's a strange phenomenon," I said to Cass in my best speaker's voice, "but the more you know the less you know. You know?"

"I know," said Cass.

"Brought you some presents." I crouched by my pack and started to pull out the books—as always, I'd bought too many books—"Who," he used to say, "are you going to pay to read them all for you?"—and I had a lot of newspapers too—it's endlessly amazing to me, the news we don't get in the States—and my address book was jammed with new names and there were letters I'd promised to forward and articles I'd promised to try and get published. Finally I found the bright embroidered shirt I'd bought Cass and the friendship bracelets the Mendoza children had woven for her. I also brought out the big seashell I'd found on the beach. "I did have some M-16 bullets to bring you," I confessed, "but I didn't think I could get them through airport security. So I buried them beneath a jacaranda tree just before I left. Maybe someone will find them in a hundred years and make a necklace from them."

Cass smiled, the seashell balanced perfectly in her palm. I straightened and went into the kitchen to see if he'd remembered to feed the cats or water the basil in the window sill. The basil was long gone and it looked like he'd dumped coffee grounds or something on the pots. The cats looked healthy enough but they were so glad to see me, butting their old heads against my throat when I picked them up, that I knew he'd never petted them once. I hugged them close as I went through the mail. There was a long letter from Mercedes, thanking me for my speech, and a card from the head of the Direct Aid Committee. There was nothing from Mark. Unless he took it, I thought. But why would he take a letter from Mark? He doesn't know who Mark is, and even if he did, he wouldn't care. One of your little hippie friends. That's what he called the men I started to see after we split up. One of your little peace-nik pals. If he ever met Mark, who is six years younger than I, he'd call him something like Sonny and he'd shake his hand with this grim pained look on his face as if he were saying, "You poor sucker. Wait till you find out what she's really like."

I put down the mail and glanced at the message pad on the kitchen wall. There in that stingy scrawl I knew so well were two messages—two, in the whole time I'd been gone! One said, "Call your sister Barbara," and I immediately thought, "But I don't have a sister Barbara," just as, in the old days, he would trick me into saying, "But I don't have a meeting tomorrow," and he'd say,

317

"Oh, did I say tomorrow? I must have meant yesterday, looks like you missed it." The number beneath the name was one digit short, as if he were just too weary to write the whole thing out. The other message, marked, "Important! Don't forget!" was an appointment change from my dentist.

"That jerk," I muttered.

"Don't put my father down," Cass said calmly, slipping into a chair at the kitchen table beside me. "He doesn't put you down."

"Of course he does." I showed Cass the newspaper articles he'd cut out and saved for me. One was about a woman just my age who had single-handedly stopped the destruction of 10,000 acres of rain forest. Another gave new evidence that Joan of Arc was a man. Two were about AIDS, and one was about cigarettes causing facial wrinkles. "He just does it in a way no one but I can understand," I explained. I was remembering the birthday card he'd sent last month. It showed a woman in a black cloak walking toward the edge of a cliff. Inside he'd written, in pencil, "Hope some of your dreams come true," and I'd ripped it from corner to corner, thinking, *All* my dreams are going to come true, and they're not dreams, you fool, they are real choices in a real world and they are going to happen because I'm going to make them happen, and they are going to happen *soon*.

I lit the first cigarette I'd wanted since I'd been home and exhaled, staring out the kitchen window. It was strange to see my own backyard, and again I had the feeling that I wasn't home yet, that Blanca or her mother or one of the men on the bus would be walking in any second, talking to me in a language I did not understand, asking for help I could not give. I glanced at Cass. "He didn't see that article that called me a 'heroine' did he?" Cass half-shrugged and ducked her head. "Good," I said. "Because he would have used it to line the rat's cage with."

"Mom." Cass was shocked, I knew, because the only time she calls me Mom is when I'm not acting like one. I stubbed my cigarette out; I felt ashamed. After all, peace begins at home; that's what I tell everyone I talk to, and it's true, too, in some homes at least. I turned my hand toward Cass, palm up. "I'm sorry," I said. I could see her pet rat's cage in the corner and it was lined, appropriately, with the front page of the *New York Times*. "I'm not being fair," I said. "And anyway," I remembered, "it wasn't the paper that called me a heroine, it was your teacher."

"She did?" Again I felt a rush of pleasure and shame. If I were truly living by my values, I thought, I'd be back in Nicaragua, doing something real about the real horrors I saw there.

Cass looked at me. "What was it like?" she asked.

"Just like here," I said. "Only with people trying to kill you."

Cass waited, patient, and after a second I started to talk. I talked about the young boys in uniform, so playful and shy you think they're joking, and then you notice their carbines. About the flat-bed truck full of men with their hands tied behind their backs, and about the spotted dog that chased that truck, howling, through six blocks of traffic. I talked about the soldiers I'd seen at the beach, patrolling the empty waves, and about the white pig in the Mendoza's front yard, and the bombed-out school house and the bombed-out hospital and the shops full of car parts and Barbie dolls I'd seen in the city. I talked about Blanca, a girl her age who had tuberculosis, and about Blanca's mother, who claimed to see "ghosts" when she prayed, the ghosts of all the men in her village who had disappeared or been killed.

Cass listened, intent. She is a wonderful listener, so different from her father, and she asks all the right questions—questions, that is, I can't answer. "Why can't people," she asked, "just be nicer to each other? Why can't we all get along?"

"I don't know," I told her. "You'd think it would be so simple, but it's not."

Cass nodded and yawned. It was getting dark and we were both tired. She gave me a last hug and went into her room to listen to tapes before she fell asleep, and I peeled off my filthy jeans and T-shirt and went to the bathroom to take a long shower.

The bathroom looked as unfamiliar as the rest of the house, too big by far, and faintly unclean, and cluttered with things we don't need. The shower floor had that sticky tar-like substance on it that he used to bring home on his skin from the shop, so I knew that even if he hadn't slept on a real bed, he'd at least had the sense to wash once or twice. I thought of him standing here, na-ked, in the same space where I stood, with his eyes open and the water beating down and his bare feet where my feet were, and it gave me the creeps. I saw one of his brown hairs, thin as a spider leg, stuck to the wall, and I aimed the shower at it to hose it down. I wanted every last trace of him out of my house. I turned the water off, glad to step out. As I toweled my hair I noticed a bottle of perfume on the counter, an old bottle of musk stuff I used to wear when we were first married. I sniffed it, curious. Was that what I'd smelled when I first came in the house? Did he wear my perfume when I was gone?

I frowned at the bottle, troubled. It brought back a time I don't think of often, when we were living like gypsies, he and I, traveling up and down the coast in a beat-up old van, picking apples and strawberries, sleeping on beaches, fighting even then, of course, but talking. We did a lot of talking in those years, before he decided to start his own business, before I decided to go back to school, before we had Cass. We did a lot of laughing, and I miss that sometimes, the way we used to roar at each other. Now when he laughs it's this silent wheeze, as if someone just punched him, and he only laughs at the bad news—my car being towed delighted him for days, and the power failure the time I was being interviewed on the radio.

I put the perfume down, pulled on a robe, and went back to the kitchen to see if he'd left any wine. As I passed the guest room I glanced in to see if Cass had been right, and she had been—the guest bed was untouched, the curtains were drawn, the note I'd left to thank him for staying with his own child was still tucked, unread, under the vase where the roses and poppies had dried on their stalks. He never once took what I had to offer, I thought. He never liked the food I cooked or the books I read or the friends I brought home. He wasn't interested in the classes I went to or the papers I wrote or the ideas that made me want to shout all night. "It's such an act," he'd say, when I'd come home late, flushed and hoarse from one of the meetings. "You're such a fake." And his eyes, when he looked at me then from his place on the couch, were almost wide-open, almost alive. Then they'd hood again, and he'd turn from me.

I picked up the vase, crumpled the note, and went into the kitchen. The garbage bag was full of beer bottles and pizza boxes and losing lottery tickets and TV listings. I made some instant coffee. I'd lived on nothing but coffee for weeks, it seemed, and I was used to it; it didn't even keep me awake any more. As I stirred in the honey the phone rang. It was Mark. He was three-hundred miles away, at another conference, and I could hear a woman laughing and two men arguing behind him. "Hey," he said, sounding far-off and rushed, "how was your time down there? I want to hear all about it. But maybe when I get back, okay? Right now I just wanted you to know there's something on TV tonight about the Sandinistas."

"Okay," I said. "I'll watch it. And Mark? What would you think of a man who got into a woman's perfume?"

"I'd think he wanted to be close to her in some way," Mark said. "Got to run. I'll call." He blew me a kiss and hung up.

Close to me? I carried my coffee in to the couch and sat down. The pillows reeked of that old musk stuff and I pushed them away, sickened. The way to be close to me is to talk to me, and let me talk back, and to touch me, and let me reach out. He couldn't do that; it was too hard. The only thing he could do was lie on this couch, night after night, and brush me aside when I wanted to talk. "You're in my way," he'd said once, when I was trying to tell him about an article I was trying to write. "You're blocking the light."

"That's not *light*," I pointed out. "That's the TV. Don't you know the difference?"

"No," he drawled, dumb, "I don't know the difference. I'm just the bozo who brings home the bacon. You know the difference. Right? So why don't you tell me—like you tell everyone, over and over, on and on, all the time. Why don't you educate me?" he said. "Why don't you change my life?"

His life. I remembered something the woman who saw ghosts had asked me. "Do you think," she had asked, "we make our own lives?" And I'd answered, "No, how could we?"—for I was thinking of her, and the horrible things that had happened to her, none of them her fault or her choice. But what about him? Look how he lives. He still sleeps in the shop. He started to sleep there before he moved out, and he hasn't moved since. Why don't you find an apartment, I say, or a little house, some place where Cass could visit you? We could afford it. I make money now, not a lot, not what he calls a "real" salary or a "real" job but the Peace Institute has promised to give me a raise in a month and my articles are starting to sell to the bulletins. He could easily find some place with neighbors and a garden and some sunshine, some place where Cass could have her own room on weekends. But no, he stays put.

He has a television there, of course, a huge color set, and a mattress on the floor in back. He has a refrigerator with nothing

321

in it, and a hot plate he doesn't bother to use. He has some of Cass's art work on the walls, and a photo of the three of us at Disneyland when she was six, and a calendar that still shows snow. There's his desk with tools on it and gritty rags and old invoices everywhere.

He's alone most of the day and most of the night. He meets women in bars, and there was one girl, an aerobics instructor, who lasted almost three months. "She had problems," he said— which means, of course, she had life, she had hope, she moved on. He has no men friends outside the shop. He sees Cass once a week, on Sunday afternoons, and they go to the movies; Cass says he sleeps. He's lost twenty pounds and still wears that old blue jacket with the grease stain on the cuff. He won't see a ther- apist or get involved in a support group; when I suggest these things he just stares at me, his eyes bright with thoughts he finds very funny.

I set my coffee cup down with a bang on the table and reached for the remote control, wiping it first on my robe. I clicked on the set. There was the end of some comedy show: *stupid*. Then one of those wrestling matches he used to watch all the time: *stupid stupid*. Then the news: *stupid stupid stupid*. Then the show Mark wanted me to see. Some liar from Associated Press was asking some liar from the Pentagon all the wrong questions and getting all the wrong answers and despite myself I started to drift off. My head just kept getting heavier and heavier and I could feel myself fade.

I had this image—not a dream exactly, just an image that kept getting bigger and bigger. It was something I'd seen down there, from the bus, when we were driving through cane fields. It was a turkey vulture, tall and black and ugly the way vultures are, with their bare red necks and bald heads and it was sitting on a fence post hunched over watching something in the dirt below. "Look," the man beside me had said, "he's waiting for his dinner to die," and we'd shivered and talked about other things and I hadn't thought about that bird again, but now it appeared to me, huge as a man, familiar and close, and I realized it was perched on the edge of the couch. It was peering down, patient, waiting for me to get tired and give up. I wanted to, too.

The conference—I could never tell Mark this—but the confer- ence hadn't accomplished a thing. Blanca was still dying, her mother was seeing new ghosts every day, the baby boys were still aiming their guns. What's the point? I thought. What makes me think I can make any difference? I'm as weak and shallow and false as he said I was.

The vulture bent close and I hated him so I jerked up with a start. My head was buzzing and my throat was dry and my legs were numb, but I got to my feet, and even though I knew I was being what he used to call "ridiculous," I watched the rest of that damn show with my arms crossed, standing up, and when that jerk from the Pentagon said, "This is not a war, see, what we have down here is not a war, it's what we call a 'low intensity conflict,' not a war at all," I hooted so hard that I woke Cass up and she came trailing out, still wearing the embroidered shirt I'd brought her, stumbling a little with sleep as she put her arms around me saying, "Come to bed now, Mom. You're home."

ACTS OF KINDNESS

by MARY MICHAEL WAGNER

I**T'S THE DAY** after payday, and all over the city people are over-
dosing. Our calls have all been people celebrating. After a drop
at Mount Zion, we drive up to the crest of Pacific Heights, and
pull over at Vallejo and Divisadero, to look at the small patch of
bay with its sailboats.

We're there five minutes, when we get a Code Three about a
guy down and maybe not breathing. I'm driving, so Simon picks
up the handset. As he reaches across the front seat, I notice his
bare wrist, where his shirt cuff raises up. He presses his lips
against the small holes of the microphone, scribbling information
down on the clipboard. Another heroin overdose; we both groan.
Simon drains the coffee from his Styrofoam cup, and jokes with
me. The way he makes me laugh, taking the edge off things,
makes me grateful. We've been on 24-hour shifts, Tuesdays and
Thursdays, for six months now, and we feel like next-door neighbors who talk over a backyard fence and who borrow candles
from each other when the electricity goes out.

I flip on the lights and siren, and we're driving, dipping low
and easy through intersections. Simon's feet in dark-colored
bucks are up on the dashboard. He offers me a raisin from his
bran muffin, playfully wedging it between my front teeth. There
is heat from his finger tips and the smell of rubbing alcohol.

When we arrive, I'm in charge of the call. Fire is already
there, the lights blinking on their truck, people from the project
milling around waiting to see what might be carried out. I sling

324

my bag with supplies over my shoulder, and Simon grabs the oxygen. It's a small apartment, the furniture is new-looking, grainy
imitation wood. There's a nice stereo and TV and a black snake in
a terrarium twined around a dry white branch. The firemen, all
looking big like lumberjacks to me, are circled around the guy,
who is laid out on the floor. One of them is already pumping O2
into him. I watch the guy's stomach fill with it. He's young and
his shirt is pulled up. His stomach is yellowy brown and so
smooth that for a second I want to touch it. The fireman with the
bag-valve-mask says he was barely breathing when they got
there. I feel the adrenaline in my spine and then the guy becomes a body to me, a responsibility. I kneel down and check his
pulse. It is far away, reedy. His arms are clammy. Heroin is easy
though, an injection of Narcan can bring practically anybody
back, no matter how far away they've gone. I stab the guy twice
in the upper arm with two different syringes. After a minute, he
juts up, yanks off the mask, and yells, "What the fuck are you
people doing in my house?"

After we drop him at General, we call back in and then drive
up to Bernal Heights. Simon's laugh is machine-gunny, but soft.
His Kentucky accent is all over the front of the ambulance, so
that I can barely drive. The way he talks makes him seem awkward and boyish. The way his trousers, the two pockets in back,
dip down low, as if his pants were too big. The way I've wanted to
touch him since the first day we drove together.

Things are quiet so I park. I climb into the back and lie down
on the gurney; Simon lies down on the couch that runs alongside.
The aisle between us is narrow and dark. The coiled nasal canulas
look eerie and reptilian above us. He tells me a ghost story he
heard growing up, about the woman with the golden arm. His
voice is mock-ghoulish. "Give meee back my arm. Give meee
back my arm." He claws at my forearms, raising the hair there.
Then he is quiet. He climbs off the couch, leans over me, picks
up my arm. He feels for my radial pulse. "Bounding," he reports,
"Uh oh, we've lost her pulse, cardiac arrest." He leans over to
give me mouth-to-mouth. His face hovers close to mine, hesitating. His breath smells of coffee and Certs. We've played this
game before, but always pulled back, so that now we both seem
startled when Simon puts his mouth on mine. We both forget to
breathe. I pull him down onto me. I want him to get all the way

on top of me, so I can feel his whole body against mine, but he says he needs to call in and check with Central about something. The heat of his body goes away. I hear him joking with the dispatcher as I fall asleep on the gurney. Outside the tinted windows it becomes night and the electric buses make sucking sounds like the noises old men, sitting on crates, make with their teeth when I walk by in running shorts. When we have a call, he nudges me awake, his fingers shy and tentative under my shoulder.

We get off work at four in the morning. It is still dark. Simon looks haggard, driving us in his truck. We go home to my apartment. I tell him I live on a musical street. Next door is an opera singer, a couple of houses up, a trumpeter, on the other side of the street, a piano player. I tell him I go sit on the stoop of the piano player. I imagine that it is a woman and that she never stops her music, for whenever I go at night to listen, she is always playing. I sit on her cement stoop and can hear her clearly behind draped windows on the second floor.

When we get to my apartment, the opera singer is practicing. For once, I'm grateful for her rudeness, her weird hours. I open the Venetian blinds. We lie down in the small square of moon on the carpet, pulling blankets from the bed over us. The woman's voice is solemn and full. She is singing Puccini.

Simon touches my face. I think about what I've seen him do with those hands, patting arms of people who are wide-eyed afraid, maybe even dying. How those hands have brought back to life a kid who drowned in a country club pool. I feel floating and happy and want to say all the clichés I know. I want Simon to say my name over and over, as if we were in some dark place and he could only find me by calling. But as he squeezes my body, the dreaminess goes away. His tongue makes me so I can't think or protect myself. I thrash against him like a tide.

When we are finished and have kicked the blankets away, Simon whispers that he's been lonely. He whispers it like it's something to be ashamed of, like it's something he's never told anyone but me.

I wake up on the floor with Simon's legs entangled with mine. I move away and sit on my bed. I put on silk undershorts and smooth oil onto my legs, lifting my knees up to my chest. I know that he is awake and watching me through the slit his arm makes over his face. I feel ashamed, so I want to overpower him in some way. Maybe I want him to fall in love with me. He pretends he's just waking up.

We have to be on shift again at four the next morning, so we spend the day together. We go see an old Fred Astaire and Ginger Rogers movie at the Castro. I don't pay attention. I think about going back to Kentucky with him. I imagine the South to be like his accent, which is lulling and outdoors-sounding. I think of us living out in the country. We'd have yellow farm equipment, yellow like my brother's Tonka trucks, machines that chew up the land. I would want a tire swing—a barn—a llama. Simon. I would want him to come to bed smelling of dogwood trees and soil and hay.

Blinking out of the movie, into the late afternoon, we laze along Castro Street. I ask him questions just to hear his accent. His voice makes me think of boys with hairless faces and paper routes, boys who play basketball in pocked driveways wearing ragged canvas hightops. I ask him to tell me about home.

He says, "You know more people die of lung cancer in Kentucky than any other state."

"Of course they do," I say, "It's all those coal mines." I think of men with their foreheads sooty like Ash Wednesday, unstrapping hats with small round lights on them.

He laughs, "No, it's the tobacco, it's the biggest crop. Everybody smokes."

I do not want to believe this. I think of Kentucky as hills and hills of impossible color, bluegrass, where people drink iced tea and sit on porch swings. I cannot see these people with cigarettes wedged between their innocent white teeth.

We make love again that night. Afterwards, before we fall asleep, Simon gets out of bed and puts on his boxer shorts and a sweatshirt. He says it's because he's cold, but under the covers it's warm. I think it is really because he feels afraid of something.

We go to work at four groggy. They tell us we won't have an ambulance until five, so I go to take a nap in the bunk beds upstairs. I can't sleep, so I put my shoes on and go back downstairs to get the book I left in the common room. The door is cracked. The light from the room is orange. I hear Simon's voice, its accent, like doorbell chimes across a yard. It makes me freeze, I

327

don't know why. I've already walked through the slit of doorway, the conversation has already washed over me, someone else is answering him: "Jesus, in the back of the ambulance. It's probably the one I'm taking out today. You let her snail all over my gurney."

I stand there, half in the room, looking at a cigarette burning down in the ashtray. I cross my arms over my chest. I feel like these men can see inside me. I feel that Simon's the one who should feel caught. I smile, pointing at my book. "I left my book," I say.

At five we go out on our shift. I act like nothing's happened, but all morning I make mistakes. Heartbeats sound so distant I can't count them. I forget to throw away the needle from a syringe and leave it pointing dangerously on the counter. Simon picks it up and throws it away. I need to get back my rhythm of working.

We pick up someone with AIDS over on Noe. His flannel pajamas are big on him, like he is a child wearing his father's pajamas as a joke. They smell of old fruit juice and urine. I can't start the IV, the man's arm seems pale and utterly veinless. Simon takes the needle from me and rubs the man's forearm, bringing a pale blue vein to the surface of his skin. He slides the needle in easily, the glass reservoir filling with blood. The man's rattling breath makes me shiver. I want to ask him how he got it. "Did somebody you love do this to you? Was it the first and only man you ever loved? Did he do something stupid and maybe even spiteful once, in a dark, curtained-off room in a grimy bar, before coming home to you?" Simon checks the vitals. I offer to drive. It begins to rain. In the mirror, I see Simon adjust the drip.

When things quiet down early in the afternoon, we stop at Denny's. I take a raincoat out of the cabinet before climbing out of the ambulance, but just carry it over my arm into the restaurant. We both order French dips. The rain streaks the glass windows. It is too late in the season for rain like this. I remember when my mother made me and my brother walk to school in a storm. She opened the door, held out her hand, palm up: "See, there's not even a drop. Besides, a little rain's not going to hurt you." The sky was curdled black. But I knew about rubber, how it protected you from getting struck by lightning. I walked out in a rain coat and rubber boots, holding an old inner tube over my head. In Kansas you can see lightning for miles and miles, so you can never be sure how far away it really is. In the short gaps between houses, my brother and I seemed to be the highest things around. I crouched down as I walked—crooked spears of lightning rammed into the fields around us. My mother yelled out at us, "Just stay under the rubber hood of your slicker and keep both feet on the ground and you'll be fine."

I open my eyes. Simon is saying something to me. He's swabbing French fries through a small mound of ketchup. With the other hand, one that is also sticky with ketchup, he's playing with my fingers. He's smiling at me. He asks if I'm all right. "Fine," I say, "just cold." I pick up the slicker and ease it on over my shirt, fastening all the snaps. Then I lift my sneakered feet off his side of the booth. I press both rubbery soles firmly down onto the cold tiled floor.

We sit like that eating hot fudgecake sundaes, the vanilla ice cream making my teeth hurt, not talking or looking at each other, until we get a Code Three. Then it's not like we're on a date anymore, we don't have to be mad at each other anymore, the sound of the siren outside the closed windows is familiar and gets caught in our chests.

The rain has stopped and the clouds are thinning. The house is white, but most of the parts that haven't burned are smudged black. The fire makes the air quivery. Simon and I move inside the circle of yellow police tape, our foreheads sweaty like we've been standing too long in front of a grille in an all-night diner.

The flames have just started on the second floor. I see a face appear then disappear in the unshattered panes of glass. It is ghostly. I think I hear a voice, a child's. I yell to Fire. A few of the fireman jog up to the house carrying a ladder. In their masks and helmets, they look like insects. They lean a ladder against the sill of the window. One of them climbs up, a hose strapped under his armpit. He smashes the window with a small ax, and the people in the street sigh together like a crowd at a sporting event. For a long time he stands at the window sending water into the jagged hole in the glass. My skin is itchy and uncomfortable. I tell myself there's no way I could have heard a voice, not over the crackling of the fire and the gushing water. I ask Simon if he saw anything, and he tells me not to worry, that it was probably my imagination. He says people see things in flames that

329

aren't there, like in clouds. I lean back against the ambulance, the scissors in the holster around my waist feeling comforting like a gun I could use if I had to.

The fireman comes out of the smoking window with a little girl held in his free arm. Simon and I run over with the gurney. The fireman sets her down. Her arms and face are blistered, but I know it's the smoke, not the burns, that might get her. The skin around her nostrils is raw and charred from inhaling the hot smoky air. Her heart's still going, but it's faint and drowned. Her throat is swollen and closed from the smoke. I hand Simon an airway, and he eases the tube down her throat. I start pumping O2 into her with the bag-valve-mask. I call for one of the firemen to drive us to the hospital, so we can both be in back in case we start to lose her. We push her through the open door to the ambulance and climb in. Someone shuts the door behind us. Simon takes the oxygen. I put a clean sheet over her gently, because this is all we can do for her burns in the field. I check her pulse and blood pressure. Her vitals are waning. Her throat is so swollen she's not getting enough oxygen. When I look at Simon, I see his jauntiness has evaporated. He seems pale and confused. His arms stick out in front of him like a sleepwalker's. The girl's burned face looks peaceful as if she weren't trying to stay alive anymore. In her ears are little gold dots. They are the kind of earrings you get when you've just had your ears pierced for the first time.

At the burn center orderlies in white are waiting for us. They whisk her away from us as soon as we have opened the ambulance door.

Even after we have filled out all the forms, Simon and I sit drinking coffee in the cafeteria, not wanting to leave. He looks so lost that I want to take him home and feed him warm, comforting things—sweet potatoes, corn pudding, turkey. I want to tell him he will never have to sleep alone again. But we have to take the fireman back, so we crumple our cups and throw them away and go back outside where he is hanging around the emergency room dock smoking a hand-rolled cigarette.

When we get back, the house is still smoking. Fire is carrying out a body, I cannot believe how brown it is, and how small. I hear people on the street say it is the little boy who lived in the house. His arms are spread as if he had been running to hug someone. I can tell by the way they are carrying his burnt body that there is nothing left inside him. The medical examiner puts the child in a white bag that zips. I am told by a fireman, rolling a flat hose, that the boy had squirted barbeque-lighter fluid into the gas furnace. The girl was his babysitter.

Simon and I get another call and wave to the firemen close to us, like we've just met them for drinks or something. We climb into the front seat and I nudge the ambulance through the people still hanging around in front of the house.

I let myself fall into work as if I were falling off a very high place and all that exists are what my hands grab hold of, IV bags and wrists and blood-pressure cuffs. At four in the morning Simon drives us to my house in his truck. It is not yet light, but teenage boys ride bare-waisted down Haight Street on bikes. They don't hold onto the handlebars. I want to lean out the window and touch their long smooth backs. I have not forgotten what happened this morning. I sit far away from Simon. When we get to my house, I don't want to let him inside, but I do.

I don't want to get into my bed, I want to be asleep already. I don't take off my clothes. I lie down on the bed nudging the wall, probably getting it dirty from the grit on my uniform. I tell Simon I just want to sleep. He doesn't move to touch me. We are so light on the bed, I imagine us like the skin of onions wound around air or dry leaves.

I dream that Simon and I are married and that we have two daughters, who are scarecrows. Simon chases them through fields and fields of corn, flicking lit matches at them, trying to light their straw pigtails on fire. I run after him. I try to grab him around the ankles and pull him down. The dream smells of manure and sulfur and when I wake up, I am sweating, but very cold. I get up, take off my uniform, and put on sweat pants and two sweat shirts.

I call the emergency room. The nurse tells me the girl died minutes after we brought her in. I sit on the bed and watch Simon sleeping. Then I dig my toes into his shoulders. "Hey," I say. He lifts his head quickly as if he hadn't been asleep at all. "I don't want you here anymore," I say. "I want you to leave."

331

He doesn't say anything. He gets out of bed and starts putting on his clothes. With my eyes closed, I hear his hands moving into sleeves.

I tell him to shut the front door when he leaves, that I'm going to sit and wait in the backyard until he's gone. He looks hurt, but I refuse to see it.

Outside, the night feels like summer nights in Kansas, the kind that has heat lightning. I sit on the grass and Simon comes out the back door. He looks large and intimidating. I want to shout, "I told you to get outta here," and throw rocks and sticks at him as if he were a mangy dog who might have rabies.

He sits down close enough to touch me. I draw my knees up into my sweat shirt. "That girl died," I tell him, saying it like it's his fault.

"I know, I just called the hospital."

"I wanted her to live," I say, "but I keep thinking she would have felt responsible for the boy. Still, I wanted her to live." Then I can't stop talking, even though I don't want to tell him anything else. I tell him about my dream. I tell him I don't trust him anymore, not after what he told everyone we work with.

He plucks up blades of grass, until I look at him like even that proves he's violent and dangerous. He puts his hands at his side and talks with his head tilted down: "I want to not have said those things. I want to feel like I'll never act like that again. When we were driving that girl to the hospital, I knew just by looking at your neck that you were praying. I thought I might cry. Then I hated you."

He moves towards me. I still want him to leave, but I also want him to love me. There are other things too, that I want. I want us to move to Kentucky where there aren't cities or overdoses or betrayal, where we'd fly over our farm in a biplane that droned and vibrated under our thighs and all we could see would be hills of bluegrass for miles and miles, like the sea.

Simon says in the quietest voice I've ever heard him use, "I saw her there too. I saw her in the window and I wanted to make you think it wasn't true. I just wanted to protect you. Even if only for a minute."

I want to say, who cares, it's too late for being kind. But the truth is, kindness is the only thing that matters. And the truth is that we should be curled up someplace safe, like our parents' bed during a lightning storm, like the back of the ambulance with the doors locked, me on the gurney and him on the couch, not even holding hands, just breathing the same close air that smells of astringent and gasoline.

ROSE

by ANDRE DUBUS

In memory of Barbara Loden

Sometimes, when I see people like Rose, I imagine them as babies, as young children. I suppose many of us do. We search the aging skin of the face, the unhappy eyes and mouth. Of course I can never imagine their fat little faces at the breast, or their cheeks flushed and eyes brightened from play. I do not think of them beyond the age of five or six, when they are sent to kindergartens, to school. There, beyond the shadows of their families and neighborhood friends, they enter the world a second time, their eyes blinking in the light of it. They will be loved or liked or disliked, even hated; some will be ignored, others singled out for daily abuse that, with a few adult exceptions, only children have the energy and heart to inflict. Some will be corrupted, many without knowing it, save for that cooling quiver of conscience when they cheat, when they lie to save themselves, when out of fear they side with bullies or teachers, and so forsake loyalty to a friend. Soon they are small men and women, with adult sins and virtues, and by the age of thirteen some have our vices too.

There are also those unforgiveable children who never suffer at all: from the first grade on, they are good at schoolwork, at play and sports, and always they are befriended, and are the leaders of the class. Their teachers love them, and because they are humble and warm, their classmates love them too, or at least respect them, and are not envious because they assume these children will excel at whatever they touch, and have long accepted this truth. They

334

come from all manner of families, from poor and illiterate to wealthy and what passes for literate in America, and no one knows why they are not only athletic and attractive but intelligent too. This is an injustice, and some of us pause for a few moments in our middle-aged lives to remember the pain of childhood, and then we intensely dislike these people we applauded and courted, and we hope some crack of mediocrity we could not see with our young eyes has widened and split open their lives, the homecoming queen's radiance sallowed by tranquilized bitterness, the quarter-back fat at forty wheezing up a flight of stairs, and all of them living in the same small town or city neighborhood, laboring at vacuous work that turns their memories to those halcyon days when the classrooms and halls, the playgrounds and gymnasiums and dance floors were theirs: the last places that so obediently, even lovingly, welcomed the weight of their flesh, and its displacement of air. Then, with a smile, we rid ourselves of that evil wish, let it pass from our bodies to dissipate like smoke in the air around us, and freed from the distraction of blaming some classmate's excellence for our childhood pain, we focus on the boy or girl we were, the small body we occupied, watch it growing through the summers and school years, and we see that, save for some strength gained here, some weaknesses there, we are the same person we first knew as ourselves; or the one memory allows us to see, to think we know.

People like Rose make me imagine them in those few years their memories will never disclose, except through hearsay: *I was born in Austin. We lived in a garage apartment. When I was two we moved to Tuscaloosa . . .* Sometimes, when she is drinking at the bar, and I am standing some distance from her and watch without her noticing, I see her as a baby, on the second or third floor of a tenement, in one of the Massachusetts towns along the Merrimack River. She would not notice, even if she turned and looked at my face; she would know me, she would speak to me, but she would not know I had been watching. Her face, sober or drunk or on the way to it, looks constantly watched, even spoken to, by her own soul. Or by something it has spawned, something that lives always with her, hovering near her face. I see her in a tenement because I cannot imagine her coming from any but a poor family, though I sense this notion comes from my boyhood, from something I learned about America, and that belief has hardened inside me, a

335

stone I cannot dissolve. Snobbishness is too simple a word for it. I have never had much money. Nor do I want it. No: it's an old belief, once a philosophy which I've now outgrown: no one born to a white family with adequate money could end as Rose has.

I know it's not true. I am fifty-one years old, yet I cannot feel I am growing older because I keep repeating the awakening experiences of a child: I watch and I listen, I write in my journal, and each year I discover, with the awe of my boyhood, a part of the human spirit I had perhaps imagined, but had never seen nor heard. When I was a boy, many of these discoveries thrilled me. Once in school the teacher told us of the men who volunteered to help find the cause of yellow fever. This was in the Panama Canal Zone. Some of these men lived in the room where victims of yellow fever had died; they lay on the beds, on sheets with dried black vomit, breathed and slept there. Others sat in a room with mosquitoes and gave their skin to those bites we simply curse and slap, and they waited through the itching and more bites, and then waited to die, in their agony leaving sheets like the ones that spared their comrades living in the room of the dead. This story, with its heroism, its infinite possibilities for human action, delighted me with the pure music of hope. I am afraid now to research it, for I may find that the men were convicts awaiting execution, or some other persons whose lives were so limited by stronger outside forces, that the risk of death to save others could not have, for them, the clarity of a choice made with courage, and in sacrifice, but could be only a weary nod of assent to yet another fated occurrence in their lives. But their story cheered me then, and I shall cling to that. Don't you remember? When first you saw or heard or read about men and women who, in the face of some defiant circumstance, fought against themselves and won, and so achieved love, honor, courage?

I was in the Marine Corps for three years, a lieutenant during a time in our country when there was no war but all the healthy young men had to serve in the armed forces anyway. Many of us, who went to college, sought commissions so our service would be easier, we would have more money, and we could marry our girl friends; in those days, a young man had to provide a roof and all that goes under it before he could make love with his girl; of course there was lovemaking in cars, but the ring and the roof waited somewhere beyond the windshield.

Those of us who chose the Marines went to Quantico, Virginia, for two six-week training sessions in separate summers during college; we were commissioned at graduation from college, and went back to Quantico for eight months of Officers' Basic School; only then would they set us free among the troops, and into the wise care of our platoon sergeants. During the summer training, which was called Platoon Leaders' Class, sergeants led us, harrassed us, and taught us. They also tried to make some of us quit. I'm certain that when they first lined us up and looked at us, their professional eyes saw the ones who would not complete the course: saw in a young boy's stiffened shoulders and staring and blinking eyes the flaw—too much fear, lack of confidence, who knows—that would, in a few weeks, possess him. Just as, on the first day of school, the bully sees his victim and eyes him like a cat whose prey has wandered too far from safety; it is not the boy's puny body that draws the bully, but the way the boy's spirit occupies his small chest, his thin arms.

Soon the sergeants left alone the stronger among us, and focused their energy on breaking the ones they believed would break, and ought to break now, rather than later, in that future war they probably did not want but never forgot. In another platoon, that first summer, a boy from Dartmouth completed the course, though in six weeks his crew cut black hair turned grey. The boy in our platoon was from the University of Chicago, and he should not have come to Quantico. He was physically weak. The sergeants liked the smaller among us, those with short lean bodies. They called them feather merchants, told them You little guys are always tough, and issued them the Browning Automatic Rifle for marches and field exercises, because it weighed twenty pounds and had a cumbersome bulk to it as well: there was no way you could comfortably carry it. But the boy from Chicago was short and thin and weak, and they despised him. Our platoon sergeant was a staff sergeant, his assistant a buck sergeant, and from the first day they worked on making the boy quit. We all knew he would fail the course; we waited only to see whether he would quit and go home before they sent him. He did not quit. He endured five weeks before the company commander summoned him to his office; he was not there long; he came into the squad bay where we lived and changed to civilian clothes, packed the suitcase and seabag, and was gone. In those five weeks he had dropped out of conditioning

337

marches, forcing himself up hills in the Virginia heat, carrying seventy pounds of gear—probably half his weight—until he collapsed on the trail to the sound of shouted derision from our sergeants, whom I doubt he heard.

When he came to Quantico he could not chin himself, nor do ten push-ups. By the time he left he could chin himself five quivering times, his back and shoulders jerking, and he could do twenty push-ups before his shoulders and chest rose while his small flat belly stayed on the ground. I do not remember his name, but I remember those numbers: five and twenty. The sergeants humiliated him daily, gave him long and colorful ass-chewings, but their true weapon was his own body, and they put it to use. They ran him till he fell, then ran him again: a sergeant running alongside the boy, around and around the hot blacktop parade ground. They sent him up and down the rope on the obstacle course. He never climbed it, but they sent him as far up as he could go, perhaps halfway, perhaps less, and when he froze then worked his way down, they sent him up again. That's the phrase: *as far up as he could go*.

He should not have come to Virginia. What was he thinking? Why didn't he get himself in shape during the school year, while he waited in Chicago for what he must have known would be the physical trial of his life? I understand now why the sergeants despised him, this weak college boy who wanted to be one of their officers. Most nights they went out drinking, and once or twice a week came into our squad bay, drunk at three in the morning, to turn on the lights, shout us out of our bunks, and we stood at attention and listened to their cheerful abuse. Three hours later, when we fell out for morning chow, they waited for us: lean and tanned and immaculate in their tailored and starched dungarees, and spit-shined boots. And the boy could only go so far up the rope, up the series of hills we climbed, up toward the chinning bar, up the walls and angled poles of the obstacle course, up from the grass by the strength of his arms as the rest of us reached fifty, seventy, finally a hundred push-ups.

But in truth he could, and that is the reason for this anecdote while I contemplate Rose. One night in our fifth week the boy walked in his sleep. Every night we had fire watch: one of us walked for four hours through the barracks, the three squad bays that each housed a platoon, to alert us of fire. We heard the story

338

the next day, whispered, muttered, or spoken out of the boy's hearing, in the chow hall, during the ten minute break on a march. The fire watch was a boy from the University of Alabama, a football player whose southern accent enriched his story, heightened his surprise, his awe. He came into our squad bay at three-thirty in the morning, looked up and down the rows of bunks, and was about to leave when he heard someone speak. The voice frightened him. He had never heard, except in movies, a voice so pitched by desperation, and so eerie in its insistence. He moved toward it. Behind our bunks, against both walls, were our wall lockers. The voice came from that space between the bunks and lockers, where there was room to stand and dress, and to prepare your locker for inspection. The Alabama boy stepped between the bunks and lockers and moved toward the figure he saw now: someone squatted before a locker, white shorts and white tee shirt in the darkness. Then he heard what the voice was saying: *I can't find it. I can't find it.* He closed the distance between them, squatted, touched the boy's shoulder, and whispered: *Hey, what you looking for?* Then he saw it was the boy from Chicago. He spoke his name, but the boy bent lower and looked under his wall locker. That was when the Alabama boy saw that he was not truly looking: his eyes were shut, the lids in the repose of sleep, while the boy's head shook from side to side, in a short slow arc of exasperation. *I can't find it,* he said. He was kneeling before the wall locker, bending forward to look under it for—what? any of the several small things the sergeants demanded we care for and have with our gear: extra shoelaces, a web strap from a haversack, a metal button for dungarees, any of these things that became for us as precious as talismans. Still on his knees, the boy straightened his back, gripped the bottom of the wall locker, and lifted it from the floor, six inches or more above it and held it there as he tried to lower his head to look under it. The locker was steel, perhaps six feet tall, and filled with his clothes, boots, and shoes, and on its top rested his packed haversack and helmet. No one in the platoon could have lifted it while kneeling, using only his arms. Most of us could have bear-hugged it up from the floor, even held it there. *Gawd damn,* the fire watch said, rising from his squat; *Gawd damn, lemmee help you with it,* and he held its sides; it was tottering, but still raised. Gently he lowered it against the boy's resistance, then crouched again and, whispered to him, *like to a baby*, he told us, he said: *All rot now. It'll be all rot now. We'll find that damn thing in the mawnin';* as he tried to ease the boy's fingers from the bottom edge of the locker. Finally he pried them, one or two at a time. He pulled the boy to his feet, and with an arm around his waist, led him to his bunk. It was a lower bunk. He eased the boy downward to sit on it, then lifted his legs, covered him with the sheet, and sat beside him. He rested a hand on the boy's chest, and spoke soothingly to him as he struggled, trying to rise. Finally the boy lay still, his hands holding the top of the sheet near his chest.

We never told him. He went home believing his body had failed; he was the only failure in our platoon, and the only one in the company who failed because he lacked physical strength and endurance. I've often wondered about him: did he ever learn what he could truly do? Has he ever absolved himself of his failure? His was another of the inspiring stories of my youth. Not *his* story so much as the story of his body. I had heard or read much of the human spirit, indomitable against suffering and death. But this was a story of a pair of thin arms, and narrow shoulders, and weak legs: freed from whatever consciousness did to them, they had lifted an unwieldy weight they could not have moved while the boy's mind was awake. It is a mystery I still do not understand.

Now, more often than not, my discoveries are bad ones, and if they inspire me at all, it is only to try to understand the unhappiness and often evil in the way we live. A friend of mine, a doctor, told me never again to believe that only the poor and uneducated and usually drunk beat their children; or parents who are insane, who hear voices commanding them to their cruelty. He has seen children, sons and daughters of doctors, bruised, their small bones broken, and he knows that the children are repeating their parents' lies: they fell down the stairs, they slipped and struck a table. He can do nothing for them but heal their injuries. The poor are frightened by authority, he said, and they will open their doors to a social worker. A doctor will not. And I have heard stories from young people, college students who come to the bar during the school year. They are rich, or their parents are, and they have about them those characteristics I associate with the rich: they look healthy, as though the power of money had a genetic influence on their very flesh; beneath their laughter and constant talk there lies always a certain poise, not sophistication, but confidence in life and their places in it. Perhaps it comes from the knowledge that they will never be stranded in a bus station with two dollars. But probably its source is more intangible: the ambience they grew up in: that strange paradox of being from birth removed, insulated, from most of the world, and its agony of survival that is, for most of us, a day-to-day life; while, at the same time, these young rich children are exposed through travel and—some of them—culture, to more of the world than most of us will ever see.

Years ago, when the students first found Timmy's and made it their regular drinking place, I did not like them, because their lives were so distant from those of the working men who patronize the bar. Then some of them started talking to me, in pairs, or a lone boy or girl, drinking near my spot at the bar's corner. I began enjoying their warmth, their general cheer, and often I bought them drinks, and always they bought mine in return. They called me by my first name, and each new class knows me, as they know Timmy's before they see either of us. When they were alone, or with a close friend, they talked to me about themselves, revealed beneath that underlying poise deep confusion, and abiding pain their faces belied. So I learned of the cruelties of some of the rich: of children beaten, girls fondled by fathers who were never drunk and certainly did not smoke, healthy men who were either crazy or evil beneath their suits and briefcases, and their punctuality and calm confidence that crossed the line into arrogance. I learned of neglect: children reared by live-in nurses, by housekeepers who cooked; children in summer camps and boarding schools, and I saw the selfishness that wealth allows, a selfishness beyond greed, a desire to have children yet give them nothing, or very little, of oneself. I know one boy, an only child, whose mother left home when he was ten. She no longer wanted to be a mother; she entered the world of business in a city across the country from him, and he saw her for a week-end once a year. His father worked hard at making more money, and the boy left notes on the door of his father's den, asking for a time to see him. An appointment. The father answered with notes on the boy's door, and they met. Then the boy came to college here. He is very serious, very polite, and I have never seen him with a girl, or another boy, and I have never seen him smile.

So I have no reason to imagine Rose on that old stained carpet with places of it worn thin, nearly to the floor; Rose crawling

341

among the legs of older sisters and brothers, looking up at the great and burdened height of her parents, their capacity, their will, to love long beaten or drained from them by what they had to do to keep a dwelling with food in it, and heat in it, and warm and cool clothes for their children. I have only guessed at this part of her history. There is one reason, though: Rose's face is bereft of education, of thought. It is the face of a survivor walking away from a terrible car accident: without memory or conjecture, only shock, and the surprise of knowing that she is indeed alive. I think of her body as shapeless: beneath the large and sagging curve of her breasts, she has such sparse curvature of hips and waist that she appears to be an elongated lump beneath her loose dresses in summer, her old wool overcoat in winter. At the bar she does not remove her coat; but she unbuttons it and pushes it back from her breasts, and takes the blue scarf from her head, shakes her greying brown hair, and lets the scarf hang from her neck.

She appeared in our town last summer. We saw her on the streets, or slowly walking across the bridge over the Merrimack River. Then she found Timmy's and, with money from whatever source, became a regular, along with the rest of us. Sometimes, if someone drank beside her, she spoke. If no one drank next to her, she drank alone. Always screwdrivers. Then we started talking about her and, with that ear for news that impresses me still about small communities, either towns or city neighborhoods, some of us told stories about her. Rumors: she had been in prison, or her husband, or someone else in the family had. She had children but lost them. Someone had heard of a murder: perhaps she killed her husband, or one of the children did, or he or Rose or both killed a child. There was a talk of a fire. And so we talked for months, into the fall then early winter, when our leaves are gone, the reds and golds and yellows, and the trees are bare and grey, the evergreens dark green, and beyond their conical green we have lovely early sunsets. When the sky is grey, the earth is washed with it, and the evergreens look black. Then the ponds freeze and snow comes silently one night, and we wake to a white earth. It was during an early snowstorm when one of us said that Rose worked in a leather factory in town, had been there since she appeared last summer. He knew someone who worked there and saw her. He knew nothing else.

On a night in January, while a light and pleasant snow dusted the tops of cars, and the shoulders and hats and scarves of people coming into Timmy's, Rose told me her story. I do not know whether, afterward, she was glad or relieved; neither of us has mentioned it since; nor have our eyes, as we greet each other, sometimes chat. And one night I was without money, or enough of it, and she said *I owe you*, and bought the drinks. But that night in January she was in the state when people finally must talk. She was drunk too, or close enough to it, but I know her need to talk was there before vodka released her. I won't try to record our conversation. It was interrupted by one or both of us going to the bathroom, or ordering drinks (I insisted on paying for them all, and after the third round she simply thanked me, and patted my hand); interrupted by people leaning between us for drinks to bring back to booths, by people who came to speak to me, happy people oblivious of Rose, men or women or students who stepped to my side and began talking with that alcoholic lack of manners or awareness of intruding that, in a neighborhood bar, is not impolite but a part of the fabric of conversation. Interrupted too by the radio behind the bar, the speakers at both ends of the room, the loud rock music from an FM station in Boston.

It was a Friday, so the bar closed at two instead of one; we started talking at eleven. Gradually, before that, Rose had pushed her way down the bar toward my corner. I had watched her move to the right to make room for a couple, again to allow a man to squeeze in beside her, and again for some college girls, then the two men to my left went home, and when someone else wedged his arms and shoulders between the standing drinkers at the bar, she stepped to her right again and we faced each other across the corner. We talked about the bartender (we liked him), the crowd (we liked them: loud, but generally peaceful) and she said she always felt safe at Timmy's because everybody knew everybody else, and they didn't allow trouble in here.

"I can't stand fight bars," she said. "Those young punks that have to hit somebody."

We talked about the weather, the seasons. She liked fall. The factory was too hot in summer. So was her apartment. She had bought a large fan, and it was so loud you could hear it from outside, and it blew dust from the floor, ashes from ash trays. She

343

liked winter, the snow, and the way the cold made her feel more alive; but she was afraid of it too: she was getting old, and did not want to be one of those people who slipped on ice and broke a hip.

"The old bones," she said. "They don't mend like young ones."

"You're no older than I am."

"Oh yes I am. And you'd better watch your step too. On that ice," and she nodded at the large front window behind me.

"That's snow," I said. "A light, dry snow."

She smiled at me, her face affectionate, and coquettish with some shared secret, as though we were talking in symbols. Then she finished her drink and I tried to get Steve's attention. He is a large man, and was mixing drinks at the other end of the bar. He did not look our way, so finally I called his name: my voice loud enough to be heard, but softened with courtesy to a tenor. Off and on, through the years, I have tended bar, and I am sensitive about the matter of ordering from a bartender who is making several drinks and, from the people directly in front of him, hearing requests for more. He heard me and glanced at us and I raised two fingers; he nodded. When I looked at Rose again she was gazing down into her glass, as though studying the yellow-filmed ice.

"I worry about fires in winter," she said, still looking down. "Sometimes every night."

"When you're going to sleep? You worry about a fire?"

She looked at me.

"Nearly every night."

"What kind of heat does your building have?"

"Oil furnace."

"Is something wrong with it?"

"No."

"Then—" Steve is very fast; he put my beer and her screwdriver before us, and I paid him; he spun, strode to the cash register, jabbed it, slapped in my ten, and was back with the change. I pushed a dollar toward him, he thanked me, and was gone, repeating an order from the other end of the bar, and a rock group sang above the crowd, a ceiling of sound over the shouts, the laughter, and the crescendo of juxtaposed conversations.

"Then why are you worried?" I said. "Were you in a fire? As a child?"

"I was. Not in winter. And I sure wasn't no child. But you hear them. The sirens. All the time in winter."

344

"Wood stoves," I said. "Faulty chimneys."

"They remind me. The sirens. Sometimes it isn't even the sirens. I try not to think about them. But sometimes it's like they think about me. They do. You know what I mean?"

"The sirens?"

"*No.*" She grabbed my wrist and squeezed it, hard as a man might; I had not known the strength of her hands. "The flames," she said.

"The flames?"

"I'm not doing anything. Or I'm at work, packing boxes. With leather. Or I'm going to sleep. Or right now, just then, we were talking about winter. I try not to think about them. But here they come, and I can see them. I feel them. Little flames. Big ones. Then—"

She released my wrist, swallowed from her glass, and her face changed: a quick recognition of something forgotten. She patted my hand.

"Thanks for the drink."

"I have money tonight."

"Good. Some night you won't, and I will. You'll drink on me."

"Fine."

"Unless you slip on that ice," nodding her head toward the window, the gentle snow, her eyes brightening again with that shared mystery, their luster near anger, not at me but at what we shared.

"Then what?" I said.

"What?"

"When you see them. When you feel the fire."

"My kids."

"No."

"Three kids."

"No, Rose."

"Two were upstairs. We lived on the third floor."

"Please: no stories like that tonight."

She patted my hand, as though in thanks for a drink, and said: "Did you lose a child?"

"Yes."

"In a fire?"

"A car."

"You poor man. Don't cry."

And with her tough thumbs she wiped the beginning of my tears from beneath my eyes, then standing on tiptoe she kissed my cheek, her lips dry, her cheek as it brushed mine feeling no softer than my own, save for her absence of whiskers.

"Mine got out," she said. "I got them out."

I breathed deeply and swallowed beer and wiped my eyes but she had dried them.

"And it's the only thing I ever did. In my whole fucking life. The only thing I ever did that was worth a shit."

"Come on. Nobody's like that."

"No?"

"I hope nobody is."

I looked at the clock on the opposite wall; it was near the speaker that tilted downward, like those mirrors in stores, so cashiers can watch people between shelves. From the speaker came a loud electric guitar, repeating a series of chords, then two or more frenetic saxophones blowing their hoarse tones at the heads of the drinkers, like an indoor storm without rain. On that clock the time was two minutes till midnight, so I knew it was eleven: thirty-eight; at Timmy's they keep the clock twenty minutes fast. This allows them time to give last call and still get the patrons out by closing. Rose was talking. Sometimes I watched her; sometimes I looked away, when I could do that and still hear. For when I listened while watching faces I knew, hearing some of their voices, I did not see everything she told me: I saw, but my vision was dulled, given distance, by watching bearded Steve work, or the blonde student Ande laughing over the mouth of her beer bottle, or old grey-haired Lou, retired as a factory foreman, drinking his shots and drafts, and smoking Camels; or the young owner Timmy, in his mid-thirties, wearing a leather jacket and leaning on the far corner of the bar, drinking club soda and watching the hockey game that was silent under the sounds of rock.

But most of the time, because of the noise, I had to look at her eyes or mouth to hear; and when I did that, I saw everything, without the distractions of sounds and faces and bodies, nor even the softening of distance, of time: I saw the two little girls, and the little boy, their pallid terrified faces; I saw their father's big arm and hand arching down in a slap; in a blow with his fist closed; I saw the five year old boy, the oldest, flung through the air, across the room, to strike the wall and drop screaming to the couch

346

against it. Toward the end, nearly his only sounds were screams; he virtually stopped talking, and lived as a frightened yet recalcitrant prisoner. And in Rose's eyes I saw the embers of death, as if the dying of her spirit had not come with a final yielding sigh, but in a blaze of recognition.

It was long ago, in a Massachusetts town on the Merrimack River. Her husband was a big man, with strongly muscled arms, and the solid rounded belly of a man who drinks much beer at night and works hard, with his body, five days a week. He was handsome too. His face was always reddish-brown from his out-door work, his hair was thick and black, and curls of it topped his forehead, and when he wore his cap on the back of his head, the visor rested on his curls. He had a thick but narrow moustache, and on Friday and Saturday nights, when they went out to drink and dance, he dressed in brightly colored pants and shirts that his legs and torso and arms filled. His name was Jim Cormier, his grandfather Jacques came from Quebec as a young man, and his father was Jacques Cormier too, and by Jim's generation the last name was pronounced *Cormeer*, and he was James. Jim was a construction worker, but his physical strength and endurance were unequally complemented by his mind, his spirit, whatever that element is that draws the attention of other men. He was best at the simplest work, and would never be a foreman, or tradesman. Other men, when he worked with them, baffled him. He did not have the touch: could not be entrusted to delegate work, to plan, to oversee, and to handle men. Bricks and mortars and trowels and chalk lines baffled him too, as did planes and levels; yet, when he drank at home every night—they seldom went out after the children arrived—he talked about learning to operate heavy equip-ment.

Rose did not tell me all this at first. She told me the end, the final night, and only in the last forty minutes or so, when I questioned her, did she go farther back, to the beginning. Where I start her story, so I can try to understand how two young people married, with the hope of love, in those days before pandemic divorce ruined the certainty of love, and within six years, when they were still young, still in their twenties, their home had become a horror for their children, for Rose, and yes: for Jim. A place where a boy of five, and girls of four and three, woke, lived, and slept in isolation from the light of a child's life: the curiosity, the questions

347

about birds, appliances, squirrels, and trees and snow and rain, and the first heart-quickening of love for another child, not a sister or brother, but the boy or girl in a sandbox, or on a tricycle at the house down the street. They lived always in darkness, deprived even of childhood fears of ghosts in the shadowed corners of the rooms where they slept, of dreams of vicious and carnivorous monsters. Their young memories and their present consciousness were the tall broad man and his reddening face that shouted and hissed, and his large hands. Rose must have had no place at all, or very little, in their dreams and their wary and apprehensive minds when they were awake. Unless as a wish: I imagine them in their beds, in the moments before sleep, seeing, hoping for Rose to take them in her arms, carry them one by one to the car while the giant slept drunkenly in the bed she shared with him, Rose putting their toys and clothes in the car's trunk, and driving with them far away to a place—What place could they imagine? What place not circumscribed by their apartment's walls whose very colors and hanging pictures and calendar were for them the dark grey of fear and pain? Certainly, too, in those moments before sleep, they must have wished their father gone. Simply gone. The boy must have thought of, wished for, Jim's death. The younger girls, four and three, only that he vanish, leaving no trace of himself in their home in their hearts, not even guilt. Simply to vanish.

Rose was a silent partner. If there is damnation, and a place for the damned, it must be a quiet place, where spirits turn away from each other and stand in solitude and gaze haplessly at eternity. For it must be crowded with the passive: those people whose presence in life was a paradox; for, while occupying space and moving through it and making sounds in it they were obviously present, while in truth they were not: they witnessed evil and lifted neither an arm nor a voice to stop it, as they witnessed joy, and neither sang nor clapped their hands. But so often we understand them too easily, tolerate them too much: they have universality, so we forgive the man who watches injustice, a drowning, a murder, because he reminds us of ourselves, and we share with him the loyal bond of cowardice, whether once or a hundred times we have turned away from another's suffering to save ourselves: our jobs, our public selves, our bones and flesh. And these people are so easy to pity. We know fear as early as we know love, and fear is always with us. I have friends my own age who still cannot say what

348

they believe, except in the most intimate company. Condemning the actively evil man is a simple matter; though we tend not only to forgive but cheer him if he robs banks or Brink's, and outwits authority: those unfortunate policemen, minions whose uniforms and badges and revolvers are, for many of us, a distorted symbol of what we fear: not a fascist state but a Power, a God, who knows all our truths, believes none of our lies, and with that absolute knowledge will both judge, and exact punishment. For we see to it that no one absolutely knows us, so at times the passing blue figure of a policeman walking his beat can stir in us our fear of discovery. We like to see them made into dupes by the outlaw.

But if the outlaw rapes, tortures, gratuitously kills, or if he makes children suffer, we hate him with a purity we seldom feel: our hatred has no roots in prejudice, or self-righteousness, but in horror. He has done something we would never do, something we could not do even if we wished it; our bodies would not obey, would not tear the dress, or lift and swing the axe, pull the trigger, throw the screaming child across the room. So I hate Jim Cormier, and cannot understand him; cannot with my imagination cross the distance between myself and him, enter his soul and know how it felt to live even five minutes of his life. And I forgive Rose, but as I write I resist that compassion, or perhaps merely empathy, and force myself to think instead of the three children, and Rose living there, knowing what she knew. She was young.

She is Irish: A Callahan till marriage, and she and Jim were Catholics. Devout Catholics, she told me. By that, she did not mean they strived to live in imitation of Christ. She meant they did not practice artificial birth control, but rhythm, and after their third year of marriage they had three children. They left the church then. That is, they stopped attending Sunday Mass and receiving Communion. Do you see? I am not a Catholic, but even I know that they were never truly members of that faith, and so could not have left it. There is too much history, too much philosophy involved, for the matter of faith to rest finally and solely on the use of contraceptives. That was long ago, and now my Catholic friends tell me the priests no longer concern themselves with birth control. But we must live in our own time; Thomas More died for an issue that would have no meaning today. Rose and Jim, though, were not Thomas Mores. They could not see a single act as a renunciation or affirmation of a belief, a way of life.

No. They had neither a religion nor a philosophy; like most people I know their philosophies were simply their accumulated reactions to their daily circumstance, their lives as they lived them from one hour to the next. They were not driven, guided, by either passionate belief, nor strong resolve. And for that I pity them both, as I pity the others who move through life like scraps of paper in the wind.

With contraception they had what they believed were two years of freedom. There had been a time when all three of their children wore diapers, and only the boy could walk, and with him holding her coat or pants, moving so slowly beside her, Rose went daily to the laundromat, pushing two strollers, gripping a paper grocery bag of soiled diapers, with a clean bag folded in her purse. Clorox rested beneath one stroller, a box of soap beneath the other. While she waited for the diapers to wash, the boy walked among the machines, touched them, watched them, and watched the other women who waited. The oldest girl crawled about on the floor. The baby slept in Rose's lap, or nursed in those days when mothers did not expose their breasts, and Rose covered the infant's head, and her breast, with her unbuttoned shirt. The children became hungry, or tired, or restless, and they fussed, and cried, as Rose called to the boy to leave the woman alone, to stop playing with the ash tray, the soap, and she put the diapers in the dryer. And each day she felt that the other women, even those with babies, with crawling and barely walking children, with two or three children, and one pregnant with a third, had about them some grace, some calm, that kept their voices soft, their gestures tender; she watched them with shame, and a deep dislike of herself, but no envy, as if she had tried out for a dance company and on the first day had entered a room of slender professionals in leotards, dancing like cats, while she clumsily moved her heavy body clad in grey sweat clothes. Most of the time she changed the diaper of at least one of the children, and dropped it in the bag, the beginning of tomorrow's load. If the baby slept in her stroller, and the oldest girl and the boy played on the floor, Rose folded the diapers on the table in the laundromat, talking and smoking with the other women. But that was rare: the chance that all three small children could at the same time be peaceful and without need, and so give her peace. Imagine: three of them with bladders and bowels, thirst, hunger, fatigue, and none of them synchronized. Most days

350

she put the hot unfolded diapers in the clean bag, and hurried home.

Finally she cried at dinner one night for a washing machine and a dryer, and Jim stared at her, not with anger, or impatience, and not refusal either: but with the resigned look of a man who knew he could neither refuse it nor pay for it. It was the washing machine; he would buy it with monthly payments, and when he had done that, he would get the dryer. He sank posts in the earth and nailed boards across their tops and stretched clotheslines between them. He said in rain or freezing cold she would have to hang the wet diapers over the backs of chairs. It was all he could do. Until he could get her a dryer. And when he came home on those days of rain or cold, he looked surprised, as if rain and cold in New England were as foreign to him as the diapers that seemed to occupy the house. He removed them from the rod for the shower curtain, and when he had cleaned his work from his body, he hung them again. He took them from the arms and back of his chair and lay them on top of others, on a chair, or the edges of the kitchen table. Then he sat in the chair whose purpose he had restored; he drank beer and gazed at the drying diapers, as if they were not cotton at all, but the whitest of white shades of the dead, come to haunt him, to assault him, an inch at a time, a foot, until they won, surrounded him where he stood in some corner of the bedroom, the bathroom, in the last place in his home that was his. His *querencia:* his cool or blood-smelling sand, the only spot in the bull ring where he wanted to stand and defend, to lower his head and wait.

He struck the boy first, before contraception, and the freedom and new life it promised, as money does. Rose was in the kitchen, chopping onions, now and then turning her face to wipe, with the back of her wrist, the tears from her eyes. The youngest girl was asleep; the older one crawled between and around Rose's legs. The boy was three. She had nearly finished the onions and could put them in the skillet and stop crying, when she heard the slap, and knew what it was in that instant before the boy cried: a different cry: in it she heard not only startled fear, but a new sound: a wail of betrayal, of pain from the heart. Wiping her hands on her apron, she went quickly to the living room, into that long and loudening cry, as if the boy, with each moment of deeper recognition, raised his voice until it howled. He stood in front of his seated father.

351

Before she reached him, he looked at her, as though without hearing footsteps or seeing her from the corner of his blurred wet vision, he knew she was there. She was his mother. Yet when he turned his face to her, it was not with appeal: above his small reddened cheeks he looked into her eyes; and in his, as tears ran from them, was that look whose sound she had heard in the kitchen. Betrayal. Accusing her of it, and without anger, but dismay. In her heart she felt something fall between herself and her son, like a glass wall, or a space that spanned only a few paces, yet was infinite, and she could never cross it again. Now his voice had attained the howl, and though his cheeks were wet, his eyes were dry now; or anyway tearless, for they looked wet and bright as pools that could reflect her face. The baby was awake, crying in her crib. Rose looked from her son's eyes to her husband's. They were dark, and simpler than the boy's: in them she saw only the ebb of his fury: anger, and a resolve to preserve and defend it.

"I told him not to," he said.

"Not to what?"

"Climbing on my legs. Look." He pointed to a dark wet spot on the carpet. "He spilled the beer."

She stared at the spot. She could not take her eyes from it. The baby was crying and the muscles of her legs tried to move toward that sound. Then she realized her son was silent. She felt him watching her, and she would not look at him.

"It's nothing to cry about," Jim said.

"You *slapped* him."

"Not *him*. You."

"Me? That's onions."

She wiped her hands on her apron, brushed her eyes with the back of her wrist.

"Jesus," she said. She looked at her son. She had to look away from those eyes. Then she saw the oldest girl: she had come to the doorway, and was standing on the threshold, her thumb in her mouth; above her small closed fist and nose, her frightened eyes stared, and she looked as though she were trying not to cry. But, if she was, there could be only one reason for a child so young: she was afraid for her voice to leave her, to enter the room, where now Rose could feel her children's fear as tangibly as a cold draft blown through a cracked window pane. Her legs, her hips, strained toward the baby's cry for food, a dry diaper, for whatever acts of

352

love they need when they wake, and even more when they wake before they are ready, when screams smash the shell of their sleep. "Jesus," she said, and hurried out of the room where the pain in her son's heart had pierced her own, and her little girl's fearful silence pierced it again; or slashed it, for she felt as she bent over the crib that she was no longer whole, that her height and breadth and depth were in pieces that somehow held together, did not separate and drop to the floor, through it, into the earth itself.

"I should have hit him with the skillet," she said to me, so many years later, after she had told me the end and I had drawn from her the beginning, in the last half hour of talk.

She could not hit him that night. With the heavy iron skillet, with its hot oil waiting for the onions. For by then something had flowed away from Rose, something of her spirit simply wafting willy-nilly out of her body, out of the apartment, and it never came back, not even with the diaphragm. Perhaps it began to leave her at the laundromat, or in bed at night, at the long day's end not too tired for lust, for rutting, but too tired for an evening of desire that began with dinner and crested and fell and crested again through the hours as they lay close and naked in bed, from early in the night until finally they slept. On the car seat of courtship she had dreamed of this, and in the first year of marriage she lived the dream: joined him in the shower and made love with him, still damp, before they went to the dinner kept warm on the stove, then back to the bed's tossed sheets to lie in the dark, smoking, talking, touching, and they made love again; and, later again, until they could only lie side by side waiting for their breathing to slow, before they slept. Now at the tired ends of days they took release from each other, and she anxiously slept, waiting for a baby to cry.

Or perhaps it left her between the shelves of a supermarket. His pay day was Thursday, and by then the refrigerator and cupboard were nearly empty. She shopped on Friday. Unless a neighbor could watch the children. Rose shopped at night, when Jim was home; they ate early and she hurried to the store to shop before it closed. Later, months after he slapped the boy, she believed his rage had started then, alone in the house with them, changing the baby and putting her in the crib while the other girl and boy spat and flung food from their highchairs where she had left them, in her race with time to fill a cart with food Jim could afford: she looked at the price of everything she took from a shelf. She did not

353

believe, later, that he struck them on those nights. But there must have been rage, the frightening voice of it; for he was tired, and confused, and overwhelmed by three small people with wills of their own, and no control over the needs of their bodies and their spirits. Certainly he must have yelled; maybe he squeezed an arm, or slapped a rump. When she returned with the groceries, the apartment was quiet: the children slept, and he sat in the kitchen, with the light out, drinking beer. A light from the living room behind him and around a corner showed her his silhouette: large and silent, a cigarette glowing at his mouth, a beer bottle rising to it. Then he would turn on the light and put down his beer and walk past her, to the old car, to carry in the rest of the groceries.

When finally two of the children could walk, Rose went to the supermarket during the day, the boy and girl walking beside her, behind her, away from her voice whose desperate pitch embarrassed her, as though its sound were a sign to the other women with children that she was incompetent, unworthy to be numbered among them. The boy and girl took from shelves cookies, crackers, cereal boxes, cans of vegetables and fruit, sometimes to play with them, but at other times to bring to her, where holding the cart they pulled themselves up on the balls of their feet and dropped in the box or the can. Still she scolded them, jerked the can or box from the cart, brought it back to its proper place; and when she did this, her heart sank as though pulled by a sigh deeper into her body. For she saw. She saw that when the children played with these things whose colors or shapes drew them, so they wanted to sit on the floor and hold or turn in their hands the box or can, they were simply being children whom she could patiently teach, if patience were still an element in her spirit. And that when they brought things to her, to put into the cart, repeating the motions of their mother, they were joining, without fully knowing it, the struggle of the family, and without knowing the struggle that was their parents' lives. Their hearts, though, must have expected praise; or at least an affectionate voice, a gentle hand, to show that their mother did not need what they had brought her. If only there were time: one extra hour of grocery shopping to spend in this gentle instruction. Or if she had strength to steal the hour anyway, despite the wet and tired and staring baby in the cart. But she could not: she scolded, and jerked from the cart or their hands the things they had brought, and the boy became quiet, the girl sucked her thumb and held Rose's pants as the four of them moved with the cart between the long shelves. The baby fussed, with that unceasing low cry that was not truly crying: only the wordless sounds of fatigue. Rose recognized it, understood it, for by now she had learned the awful lesson of fatigue, which as a young girl she had never felt. She knew that it was worse than the flu, whose enforced rest at least left you the capacity to care for someone else, to mutter words of love; but that, healthy, you could be so tired that all you wanted was to lie down, alone, shut off from everyone. And you would snap at your husband, or your children, if they entered the room, probed the solace of your complete surrender to silence and the mattresss that seductively held your body. So she understood the baby's helpless sounds for *I want to lie in my crib and put my thumb in my mouth and hold Raggedy Ann's dirty old apron and sleep*. The apron was long removed from the doll, and the baby would not sleep without its presence in her hand. Rose understood this, but could not soothe the baby. She could not have soothed her anyway; only sleep could. But Rose could not try, with hugs, with petting, with her softened voice. She was young.

Perhaps her knowledge of her own failures dulled her ears and eyes to Jim after he first struck the boy, and on that night lost for the rest of his life any paternal control he may have exerted in the past over his hands, finally his fists. Because more and more now he spanked them: with a chill Rose tried to deny, a resonant quiver up through her body, she remembered that her parents had spanked her too. That all, or probably all, parents spanked their children. And usually it was the father, the man of the house, the authority and judge, and enforcer of rules and discipline the children would need when they reached their teens. But now, too, he held them by the shoulders, and shook their small bodies, the children sometimes wailing, sometimes frighteningly silent, until it seemed their heads would fly across the room then roll to rest on the floor,while he shook a body whose neck had snapped in two like a dried branch. He slapped their faces, and sometimes he punched the boy, who was four, then five, with his fist. They were not bad children; not disobedient; certainly they were not loud. When Jim yelled and shook them, or slapped or punched, they had done no more than they had in the supermarket, where her voice, her snatching from their hands, betrayed her to the other women. So maybe that kept her silent.

But there was more: she could no longer feel love, or what she had believed it to be. On the few nights when she and Jim could afford both a sitter and a night club, they did not dance. They sat drinking, their talk desultory: about household chores, about Jim's work, pushing wheelbarrows, swinging a sledge hammer, thrusting a spade into the earth or a pile of gravel or sand. They listened to the music, watched the band, even drummed their fingers on the table dampened by the bottoms of their glasses they emptied like thirsty people drinking water; but they thirsted for a time they had lost. Or not even that: for respite from their time now, and their knowledge that, from one day to the next, year after year, their lives would not change. Each day would be like the one they had lived before last night's sleep; and tomorrow was a certain and already draining repetition of today. They did not decide to sit rather than dance. They simply did not dance. They sat and drank and watched the band and the dancing couples, as if their reason for dancing had been stolen from them while their eyes had been jointly focused on something else.

She could no longer feel love. She ate too much and smoked too much and drank too much coffee, so all day she felt either lethargic from eating or stimulated by coffee and cigarettes, and she could not recall her body as it had once been, only a few years ago, when she was dating Jim, and had played softball and volleyball, had danced, and had run into the ocean to swim beyond the breakers. The ocean was a half hour away from her home, yet she had not seen it in six years. Rather than love, she felt that she and Jim only worked together, exhausted, toward a nebulous end, as if they were digging a large hole, wide as a house, deeper than a well. Side by side they dug, and threw the dirt up and out of the hole, pausing now and then to look at each other, to wait while their breathing slowed, and to feel in those kindred moments something of why they labored, of why they had begun it so long ago—not in years, not long at all—with their dancing and lovemaking and finally marriage: to pause and look at each other's flushed and sweating faces with as much love as they could feel before they commenced again to dig deeper, away from the light above them.

On a summer night in that last year, Jim threw the boy across the living room. Rose was washing the dishes after dinner. Jim was watching television, and the boy, five now, was playing on the floor between Jim and the set. He was on the floor with his sisters and

356

wooden blocks and toy cars and trucks. He seldom spoke directly to his father anymore; seldom spoke at all to anyone but his sisters. The girls were too young, or hopeful, or were still in love. They spoke to Jim, sat on his lap, hugged his legs, and when he hugged them, lifted them in the air, talked with affection and laughter, their faces showed a happiness without memory. And when he yelled at them or shook or spanked them, or slapped their faces, their memory failed them again, and they were startled, frightened, and Rose could sense their spirits weeping beneath the sounds of their crying. But they kept turning to him, with open arms, and believing faces.

"Little flowers," she said to me. "They were like little flowers in the sun. They never could remember the frost."

Not the boy, though. But that night his game with his sisters absorbed him, and for a short while—nearly an hour—he was a child in a home. He forgot. Several times his father told him and the girls to be quiet or play in another room. Then for a while, a long while for playing children, they were quiet: perhaps five minutes, perhaps ten. Each time their voices rose, Jim's command for quiet was abrupt, and each time it was louder. At the kitchen sink Rose's muscles tensed, told her it was coming, and she must go to the living room now, take the children and their blocks and cars and trucks to the boy's bedroom. But she breathed deeply and rubbed a dish with a sponge. When she finished, she would go down to the basement of the apartment building, descend past the two floors of families and single people whose only sounds were music from radios, voices from television, and sometimes children loudly playing and once in a while a quarrel between a husband and wife. She would go into the damp basement and take the clothes from the washing machine, put them in the dryer that now Jim was paying for with monthly installments. Then she heard his voice again, and was certain it was coming, but could not follow the urging of her muscles. She sponged another dish. Then her hands came out of the dish water with a glass: it had been a jelly jar, humanly smiling animals were on it, and flowers, and her children liked to drink from it, looked for it first when they were thirsty, and only if it was dirty in the sink would they settle for an ordinary glass for their water, their juice, or Kool-Aid or milk. She washed it slowly, and was for those moments removed; she was oblivious of the living room, the children's voices rising again to the peak that

357

would bring either Jim's voice or his body from his chair. Her hands moved gently on the glass. She could have been washing one of her babies. Her heart had long ago ceased its signals to her; it lay dormant in despair beyond sorrow; standing at the sink, in a silence of her own making, lightly rubbing the glass with the sponge, and her fingers and palms, she did not know she was crying until the tears reached her lips, salted her tongue.

With their wooden blocks, the children were building a village, and a bridge leading out of it to the country: the open spaces of the living room carpet, and the chairs and couch that were distant mountains. More adept with his hands, and more absorbed too in the work, the boy often stood to adjust a block on a roof, or the bridge. Each time he stood between his father and the television screen, heard the quick command, and moved out of the way. They had no slanted blocks, so the bridge had to end with two sheer walls; the boy wanted to build ramps at either end, for the cars and trucks to use, and he had only rectangles and squares to work with. He stood to look down at the bridge. His father spoke. He heard the voice, but a few seconds passed before it penetrated his concentration, and spread through him. It was too late. What he heard next were not words, or a roar, but a sustained guttural cry, a sound that could be either anguish or rage. Then his father's hands were on him: on him and squeezing his left thigh and left bicep so tightly that he opened his mouth to cry out in pain. But he did not. For then he was above his father's head, above the floor and his sisters, high above the room itself and near the ceiling he glimpsed; and he felt his father's grip and weight shifting and saw the wall across the room, the wall above the couch, so that when finally he made a sound it was of terror, and it came from him in a high scream he heard as he hurtled across the room, seeing always the wall, and hearing his scream, as though his flight were pro-longed by the horror of what he saw and heard. Then he struck it. He heard that, and the bone in his right forearm snap, and he fell to the couch. Now he cried with pain, staring at the swollen flesh where the bone tried to protrude, staring with astonishment and grief at this part of his body. Nothing in his body had ever broken before. He touched the flesh, the bone beneath it. He was crying as, in his memory, he had never cried before, and he not only did not try to stop, as he always had, with pride, with anger; but he wanted to cry this deeply, his body shuddering with it, doubling at his waist with it, until he attained oblivion, invisibility, death.

Somehow he knew his childhood had ended. In his pain, he felt relief too: now on this couch his life would end.

He saw through tears but more strongly felt his sisters standing before him, touching him, crying. The he heard his mother. She was screaming. And in rage. At his father. He had never heard her do that, but still her scream did not come to him as a saving trumpet. He did not want to live to see revenge. Not even victory. Then he heard his father slap her. Through his crying he listened then for her silence. But her voice grew, its volume filled the world. Still he felt nothing of hope, of vengeance; he had left that world, and lived now for what he hoped and believed would be only a very short time. He was beginning to feel the pain in his head and back and shoulders, his elbows and neck. He knew he would only have to linger a while in this pain, until his heart left him, as though disgorged by tears, and went wherever hearts went. A sister's hand held his, and he squeezed it.

When he was above his father's head, the boy had not seen Rose. But she was there, behind Jim, behind the lifted boy, and she had cried out too, and moved: as Jim regained his balance from throwing the boy, she turned him, her hand jerking his shoulder, and when she could see his face she pounded it with her fists. She was yelling, and the yell was words, but she did not know what they were. She hit him until he pushed her back, hard, so she nearly fell. She looked at his face, the cheeks reddened by her blows, saw a trickle of blood from his lower lip, and charged it; swinging at the blood, the lip. He slapped her so hard that she was sitting on the floor, with no memory of falling, and holding and shaking her stunned and buzzing head. She stood, yelling words again that she could not hear, as if their utterance had been so long coming, from whatever depth in her, that her mind could not even record them as they rushed through her lips. She went past Jim, pushing his belly, and he fell backward into his chair. She paused to look at that. Her breath was deep and fast, and he sat glaring, his breathing hard too, and she neither knew nor cared whether he had desisted or was preparing himself for more. At the bottom of her vision, she saw his beer bottle on the floor beside the chair. She snatched it up, by its neck, beer hissing onto her arm and breast, and in one motion she turned away from Jim and flung the bottle smashing through the television screen. He was up and yelling behind her, but she was crouched over the boy.

She felt again what she felt in the kitchen, in the silence she had

359

made for herself while she bathed the glass. Behind and above her was the sound of Jim's fury; yet she stroked the boy's face: his forehead, the tears beneath his eyes; she touched the girls too, their hair, their wet faces; and she heard her voice: soft and soothing, so soft and soothing that she even believed the peace it promised. Then she saw, beneath the boy's hand, the swollen flesh; gently she lifted his hand, then was on her feet. She stood into Jim's presence again: his voice behind her, the feel of his large body inches from her back. Then he gripped her hair, at the back of her head, and she shook her head but still he held on.

"His *arm's* broken."

She ran from him, felt hair pulling from her scalp, heard it, and ran to her bedroom for her purse but not a blanket, not from the bed where she slept with Jim; for that she went to the boy's, and pulled his thin summer blanket from his bed, and ran back to the living room. Where she stopped. Jim stood at the couch, not looking at the boy, or the girls, but at the doorway where now she stood holding the blanket. He was waiting for her.

"You crazy fucking bitch."

"*What?*"

"The fucking TV. Who's going to buy one? You? You fucking cunt. You've never had a fucking job in your life."

It was madness. She was looking at madness, and it calmed her. She had nothing to say to it. She went to the couch, opening the blanket to wrap around the boy.

"It's the only fucking peace I've *got*."

She heard him, but it was like overhearing someone else, in another apartment, another life. She crouched and was working the blanket under the boy's body when a fist knocked loudly on the door. She did not pause, or look up. More knocking, then a voice in the hall: "Hey! Everybody all right in there?"

"Get the fuck away from my door."

"You tell me everybody's all right."

"Get the fuck *away*."

"I want to hear the woman. And the kid."

"You want me to throw you down the fucking stairs?"

"I'm calling the cops."

"Fuck you."

She had the boy in her arms now. He was crying still, and as she carried him past Jim, she kissed his cheeks, his eyes. Then Jim was

360

beside her. He opened the door, swung it back for them. She did not realize until weeks later that he was frightened. His voice was low: "Tell them he fell."

She did not answer. She went out and down the stairs, past apartments; in one of them someone was phoning the police. At the bottom of the stairs she stopped short of the door, to shift the boy's weight in her arms, to free a hand for the knob. Then an old woman stepped out of her apartment, into the hall, and said: "I'll get it."

An old woman with white hair and a face that knew everything, not only tonight, but the years before this too, yet the face was neither stern nor kind; it looked at Rose with some tolerant recognition of evil, of madness, of despair, like a warrior who has seen and done too much to condemn, or even try to judge; can only nod in assent at what he sees. The woman opened the door and held it, and Rose went out, across the small lawn to the car parked on the road. There were only two other cars at the curb; then she remembered that it was Saturday, and had been hot, and before noon she had heard most of the tenants, separately leaving for beaches or picnic grounds. They would be driving home now, or stopping to eat. The sun had just set, but most windows of the tenements on the street were dark. She stopped at the passenger door, started to shift the weeping boy's weight, then the old woman was beside her, trying the door, asking for the key. Rose's purse hung from her wrist. The woman's hands went into it, moved in there, came out with the ring of keys, held them up toward the streetlight, and found the one for the car. She opened the door, and Rose leaned in and lay the boy on the front seat. She turned to thank the woman but she was already at the front door of the building, a square back and short body topped by hair like cotton.

Rose gently closed the car door, holding it, making certain it did not touch the boy before she pushed it into place. She ran to the driver's side, and got in, and put the key in the ignition slot. But she could not turn it. She sat in the boy's crying, poised in the moment of action the car had become. But she could not start it.

"Jimmy," she said. "Jimmy, listen. Just hang on. I'll be right back. I can't leave the girls. Do you hear me?"

His face, profiled on the seat, nodded.

"I've got to get them."

She pushed open the door, left the car, closed the door, the keys in her hand, not out of habit this time; no, she clung to them as she might to a tiny weapon, her last chance to be saved. She was running to the building when she saw the flames at her windows, a flare of them where an instant before there had been only lamp-light. Her legs now, her body, were weightless as the wind. She heard the girls screaming. Then the door opened and Jim ran out of it, collided with her, and she fell on her back as he stumbled and side-stepped and tried to regain balance and speed and go around her. Her left hand grabbed his left ankle. Then she turned with his pulling, his weight, and on her stomach now, she held his ankle with her right hand too, and pulled it back and up. He fell. She dived onto his back, saw and smelled the gasoline can in his hand, and in her mind she saw him going down to the basement for it, and back up the stairs. She twisted it away from his fingers on the handle, and kneeled with his back between her legs, and as he lifted his head and shoulders and tried to stand, she raised the can high with both hands and brought it down, leaning with it, into it, as it struck his skull. For a moment he was still, his face in the grass. Then he began to struggle again, and said into the earth: "Over now. All over."

She hit him three more times, the sounds hollow, metallic. Then he was still, save for the rise and fall of his back. Beneath his other hand she saw his car keys. She scooped them from the grass and stood and threw them across the lawn, whirling now into the screams of the girls, and windows of fire. She ran up the stairs. The white-haired woman was on the second floor landing. Rose passed her, felt her following, and the others: she did not know how many, nor who they were. She only heard them behind her. No one passed her. She was at the door, trying to turn the knob, while her left arm and hand pressed hot wood.

"I called the fire department," a man said, behind her in the hall.

"So did we," a woman said.

Rose was calling to the girls to open the door.

"They can't," another man said. "That's where the fire is." Then he said: "Fuck this," and pulled her away from the door where she was turning the knob back and forth and calling through the wood to the screams from the rear of the apartment, their bedroom. She was about to spring back to the door but stopped: the man faced it then stepped away. She knew his name, or had known it; she could

362

not say it. He lived on the second floor; it was his wife who had said *So did we*. He stepped twice toward the door, then kicked, his leg horizontal, the bottom of his shoe striking the door, and it swung open, through the flames that filled the threshold and climbed the doorjambs. The man leaped backward, his forearms covering his face, while Rose yelled to the girls: We're coming, we're coming. The man lowered his head and sprinted forward. Or it would have been a sprint. Certainly he believed that, believed he would run through fire to the girls and get them out. But in his third stride his legs stopped, so suddenly and autonomously that he nearly fell forward into the fire. Then he backed up.

"They'll have a net," he said. He was panting. "We'll get them to jump. We'll get them to a window, and get them to jump."

A man behind Rose was holding her. She had not known it till now. Nor did she know she had been straining forward. The man tightly held her biceps. He was talking to her and now she heard that too, and was also aware that people were moving away, slowly but away, down the hall toward the stairs. He was saying: "You can't. All you'll do is get yourself killed."

Then she was out of his hands, as though his fingers were those of a child, and with her breath held and her arms shielding her face, and her head down, she was in motion, through the flames and into the burning living room. She did not feel the fire, but even as she ran through the living room, dodging flames, running through them, she knew that very soon she would. It meant no more to her than knowing that she was getting wet in a sudden rain. The girls were standing on the older one's bed, at the far side of the room, holding each other, screaming, and watching their door and the hall beyond it where the fire would come. She filled the door, their vision, then was at the bed and they were crying: Mommy! Mommy! She did not speak. She did not touch them either. She pulled the blanket from under them, and they fell onto the bed. Running again she grabbed the blanket from the younger girl's bed, and went into the hall where there was smoke but not fire yet, and across it to the bathroom where she turned on the shower and held the blanket under the spray. They soaked heavily in her hands. She held her breath leaving the bathroom and exhaled in the girls' room. They were standing again, holding each other. Now she spoke to them. Again, as when she had crouched with them in front of Jimmy, her voice somehow came softly from

363

her. It was unhurried, calm, soothing: she could have been helping them put on snowsuits. They stopped screaming, even crying; they only sniffled and gasped, as she wound a blanket around each of them, covering their feet and heads too, then lifted them, pressing one to each breast. Then she stopped talking, stopped telling them that very soon, before they even knew it, they would be safe outside. She turned and ran through smoke in the hall, and into the living room. She did not try to dodge flames: if they were in front of her, she spun and ran backward through them, hugging the girls against each other, so nothing of their bodies would protrude past her back, her sides; then spun and ran forward again, fearful of an image that entered her mind though in an instant she expelled it: that she would fall with them, into fire. She ran backward through the door, and her back hit the wall. She bounced off it; there was fire in the hall now, moving at her ankles, and she ran, leaping, and when she reached the stairs she smelled the scorched blankets that steamed around the girls in her arms. She smelled her burned hair, sensed that it was burning still, crackling flames on her head. It could wait. She could wait. She was running down the stairs, and the fire was behind her, above her, and she felt she could run with her girls all night. Then she was on the lawn, and arms took the girls, and a man wrestled her to the ground and rolled with her, rolled over and over on the grass. When she stood someone was telling her an ambulance would— But she picked up her girls, unwrapped now, and looked at their faces: pale with terror, with shock, yes; but no burns. She carried them to the car.

"*No*," she heard. It was a man's voice, but one she did not know. Not for a few moments, as she lay the girls side by side on the back seat. Then she knew it was Jim. She was startled, as though she had not seen him for ten years. She ran around the car, got behind the wheel, reached over Jimmy who was silent now, and she thought unconscious until she saw his eyes staring at the dashboard, his teeth gritting against his pain. Leaning over his face, she pushed down the latch on his side. Then she locked her door. It was a two-door car and they were safe now and they were going to the hospital. She started the engine.

Jim was at her window, a raging face, but a desperate one too, as though standing outside he was locked in a room without air. Then he was motion, on her left, to her front, and he stood at the middle

364

of the car, slapped his hands onto the hood, and pushed. He bulged: his arms and chest and reddened face. With all his strength he pushed, and she felt the car rock backward. She turned on the headlights. The car rocked forward as he eased his pushing, and drew breath. Then he pushed again, leaning, so all she could see of him were his face, his shoulders, his arms. The car rocked back and stopped. She pushed the accelerator pedal to the floor, waited two or three seconds in which she either did not breathe or held what breath she had, and watched his face above the sound of the racing engine. Then, in one quick motion, she lifted her foot from the clutch pedal. He was gone as she felt the bumper and grill leap through his resistance. She stopped and looked in the rear view mirror; she saw the backs of the girls' heads, their long hair; they were kneeling on the seat, looking quietly out the back window. He lay on his back. Rose turned her wheels to the right, as though to back into a parking space, shifted to reverse, and this time without racing the engine, she slowly drove. She did not look through the rear window; she looked straight ahead, at the street, the tenements, the darkening sky. Only the rear tires rolled over him, then struck the curb. She straightened the front wheels and drove forward again. The car bumped over him. She stopped, shifted gears, and backed up; the bump, then the tires hitting the curb. She was still driving back and forth over his body, while beyond her closed windows people shouted or stared, when the sirens broke the summer sky: the higher wail of the police called by the neighbor, and the lower and louder one of the fire engine.

She was in the hospital, and by the time she got out, her three brothers and two sisters had found money for bail. Her parents were dead. Waiting for the trial, she lived with a married sister; there were children in the house, and Rose shied away from them. Her court-appointed lawyer called it justifiable homicide, and the jury agreed. Long before the trial, before she even left the hospital, she had lost the children. The last time she saw them was that night in the car, when finally she took them away: the boy lying on the front seat, his left cheek resting on it as he stared. He did not move while she drove back and forth over his father. She still does not know whether he knew then, or learned it from his sisters. And the two girls kneeling, their breasts leaning on the back of the seat, watching their father appear, then vanish as a

365

bump beneath them. They all went to the same foster home. She did not know where it was.

"Thanks for the drinks," she said, and patted my hand. "Next time you're broke, let me know."

"I will."

She adjusted the blue scarf over her hair, knotted it under her face, buttoned her coat and put on her gloves. She stepped away from the bar, and walked around and between people. I ordered a beer, and watched her go out the door. I paid and tipped Steve, then left the bottle and glass with my coat and hat on the bar, and moved through the crowd. I stepped outside and watched her, a half block away now. She was walking carefully in the lightly falling snow, her head down, watching the sidewalk, and I remembered her eyes when she talked about slipping on ice. But what had she been sharing with me? Age? Death? I don't think so. I believe it was the unexpected: chance, and its indiscriminate testing of the our bodies, our wills, our spirits. She was walking toward the bridge over the Merrimack. It is a long bridge, and crossing it in that open air she would be cold. I was shivering. She was at the bridge now, her silhouette diminishing as she walked on it. I watched until she disappeared.

I had asked her if she had tried to find her children, had tried an appeal to get them back. She did not deserve them, she said. And after the testimony of her neighbors, she knew she had little hope anyway. She should have hit him with the skillet, she said; the first time he slapped the boy. I said nothing. As I have written, we have talked often since then, but we do not mention her history, and she does not ask for mine, though I know she guesses some of it. All of this is blurred; nothing stands out with purity. By talking to social workers, her neighbors condemned her to lose her children; talking in the courtroom they helped save her from conviction.

I imagine again those men long ago, sitting among mosquitoes in a room, or sleeping on the fouled sheets. Certainly each of them hoped that it was not the mosquito biting his arm, or the bed he slept on, that would end his life. So he hoped for the men in the other room to die. Unless he hoped that it was neither sheets nor mosquitoes, but then he would be hoping for the experiment to fail, for yellow fever to flourish. And he had volunteered to stop it. Perhaps though, among those men, there was one, or even more, who hoped that he alone would die, and his death would be a discovery for all.

366

The boy from Chicago and Rose were volunteers too. I hope that by now the man from Chicago has succeeded at something—love, work—that has allowed him to outgrow the shame of failure. I have often imagined him returning home a week early that summer, to a mother, to a father; and having to watch his father's face as the boy told him he had failed because he was weak. A trifling incident in a whole lifetime, you may say. Not true. It could have changed him forever, his life with other men, with women, with daughters, and especially sons. We like to believe that in this last half of the century, we know and are untouched by everything; yet it takes only a very small jolt, at the right time, to knock us off balance for the rest of our lives. Maybe—and I hope so—the boy learned what his body and will could do: some occurrence he did not have time to consider, something that made him act before he knew he was in action.

Like Rose. Who volunteered to marry; even, to a degree, to practice rhythm, for her Catholic beliefs were not strong and deep, else she could not have so easily turned away from them after the third child, or even early in that pregnancy. So the life she chose slowly turned on her, pressed against her from all sides, invisible, motionless, but with the force of wind she could not breast. She stood at the sink, holding the children's glass. But *then*—and now finally I know why I write this, and what does stand out with purity: she reentered motherhood, and the unity we all must gain against human suffering. This is why I did not answer, at the bar, when she told me she did not deserve the children. For I believe she did, and does. She redeemed herself, with action, and with less than thirty minutes of it. But she could not see that, and still cannot. She sees herself in the laundromat, the supermarket, listlessly drunk in a night club where only her fingers on the table moved to the music. I see her young and strong and swift, wrapping the soaked blankets around her little girls, and hugging them to her, and running and spinning and running through the living room, on that summer night when she was touched and blessed by flames.

LYRICS FOR PUERTO RICAN SALSA AND THREE SONEOS BY REQUEST

by ANA LYDIA VEGA

translated by Mark McCaffrey

THERE'S A HOLY FEAST DAY FEVER of fine asses on De Diego Street. Round in their super-look panties, arresting in tube-skirt profile, insurgent under their fascist girdles, abysmal, Olympian, nuclear, they furrow the sidewalks of Rio Piedras like invincible national airships.

More intense than a Colombia buzz, more persevering than Somoza, He tracks Her through the snaking river of derrieres. He is as faithful as a Holy Week procession with his hey little fox litany, his you're fine, you're lookin' good, those pants dress you up nice, that's a lush woman, man, packed to load limit, all that meat and me livin' on slim pickins.

And in fact She is a good looker. Brassiere showing through, Bermuda triangle traced with every jiggle of her spike heels. On the other hand, he would settle for a broomstick in a baseball jersey.

Sssssay, fine asssss woman. He comes undone in sensual hissing as he leans his mug perilously close to the technicolor curls of his prey. She then kicks in the secondaries and, with her rear end in overdrive, momentarily removes her virtue to safety.

But the salsa chef wants his Christmas ham and turns on his relentless street song: what a chassis, baby, a walkin' pound cake, raw material, a sure enough hunk of woman, what legs, if I were rain I'd fall on you.

The siege goes on for two biblical days. Two days of dogged pursuit and unnerving ad lib. Two long days of hey, delicious, hey honeycakes, I could light you up, she's an animal that woman, I'm all yours, for you I'd even work, who are you staying in deep-freeze for, man-killer?

On the third day, directly in front of the Pitusa Five and Ten, and with the spicy noontime sizzle of sofrito in the air, the victim takes a deep breath, pivots spectacularly on her precarious heels and slam dunks one.

"Whenever you're ready."

Thrown from his mount, the rider does an emotional head-over-heels. Ready nevertheless to risk it all for his national virility, he alights on his feet and blurts out in telling formality, "as you wish."

At this point she solemnly takes over. A metallic, red '69 Ford Torino sits in the parking lot at the Plaza del Mercado. They get in. They take off. The radio howls a senile bolero. She drives with one hand on the steering wheel and the other on the window, with a couldn't-care-less air about her. He begins violently to wish for a seaside bachelor's pad, a kind of discotheque/slaughterhouse where he could process the grade-A prime that life sometimes drops in one's lap like free food stamps. But unemployment fuels no dreams and he is kicking himself, thinking if I had known about this ahead of time I'd have hit up Papo Quisqueya for his room, Papo is blood, he's Santo Domingo soul, a high-steppin' no-jive street sultan and we're thick with our chicks. Damn, he says to himself, giving up. Then, sporting his best soap opera smile, he attempts to sound natural giving directions.

"Head for Piñones."

But she one-ups him again, taking instead the Caguas Highway as if it were a golden thigh of Kentucky Fried Chicken.

The motel entrance lies hidden in the shrubbery. Guerrilla warfare surroundings. The Torino slides vaseline-like up the narrow entranceway. The clerk nods from a coy distance, gazing coolly ahead like a horse with blinders. The car squeezes into the garage. She gets out. He tries to open the door without unlocking it, a herculean task. At last he steps out in the name of Homo Sapiens.

The key is shoved all the way into the lock and they penetrate the entrance to the room. She turns on the light. It is a merciless neon, a revealer of pimples and blackheads. He jumps at the sight of the open black hand sticking out through the pay window. He remembers the interplanetary void in his wallet. An agonizing and secular moment at the end of which She deposits five pesos in the black hand, which closes up like a hurt oyster and disappears, only to reappear again instantly. Godfather-like gravel voice:

"It's seven. Two more."

She sighs, rummages through her purse, takes out lipstick, compact, mascara, Kleenex, base, shadow, pen, perfume, black lace bikini panties, Tampax, deodorant, toothbrush, torrid romance and two pesos which she chucks at the insatiable hand like so many bones. He feels the socio-historical compulsion to remark:

"It's tough on the street, eh?"

From the bathroom comes the rushing sound of an open faucet. The room feels like a closet. Mirrors, though, everywhere. Half-sized single bed. Sheets clean but punished with wear. Zero pillows. Red light overhead. He like freaks at the thought of all the people that must have blushed under the loud red lights, all the horny Puerto Rican thrills spilled out in that room, the orgies the mirror must have witnessed, the bouncing the bed has taken. He parks his thoughts at the Plaza Convalescencia, aptly named for the hosts of sickies who get their daily cure there, oh, Convalescencia, where the cool stroll of the street lizards is a tribal rite. It is his turn now, and it won't be campaign rhetoric he's spouting. He stands before the group, walking back and forth, rising and falling on his epic mount: She was harder than a mafioso's heart, bro'. I just looked at her and she turned into jelly right there. I took her to a motel, man. They hit you for seven pesos now just to blast a cap.

She comes out of the bathroom. Her goddess complex not undeserved. Not a stitch on her. An awesome Indian queen. Brother, there was more ass on her than you could put up on a movie screen.

"Don't you intend to take your clothes off," thunders Guabancex from the pre-Columbian heights of El Yunque.

He turns to the task at hand. Off comes the undershirt. Off

370

comes the belt. Down come the pants. She lies back, the better to grasp you. At last his underwear drops with the metallic weight of a chastity belt. Remote-controlled from the bed, a projectile closes the strip-tease act. He catches it and—oh, must we not blush—it is a condescending condom and an indisposable one at that.

In the Pine-Sol-saturated bathroom the stud ram engages nature. He wants to go into this in full warrior splendor. Retroactive cerebral functions are no help. Cracks spied through barely open doorways: zip. Social science teacher in black panties: zip. Gringo female sunning her Family Size tits on a terrace: zip. A couple feeling each other up inside and out in the back row at the Paradise Theater: zip. Stampeding women rubbed against and desired on the streets and freely deflowered in his mind; recall of memorized pages of Mexican porno rags; incomparable Playboy centerfolds, rewind, replay; the old hot and heavy war lingo: nail me, negrito; devastate me, daddy, melt me down, big man. But . . . zip. There's not a witch doctor alive who can raise this dead body up.

She is calling him. In vain Clark Kent seeks the Emergency Exit. His Superman suit is at the cleaner's.

From within a Marlboro smoke cloud she is saying her final prayers. It's all up to luck now, you might say, and she is on the threshold of life's own phenomenal cleansing ritual. Since Hector's wedding with that shit-eating white baby doll from Condado, having a hymen is a crime that drags her down. Seven years in a playboy dentist's hip pocket. Seven years filling cavities and scraping tartar. Seven years staring down gaping throats, breathing septic tank breath for a wink or a limp pass or a Tinkerbell tease or a hollow hope. But today the convent lets go. Today the vows of chastity take the tomato pickers' flight out. She changes the channel and tunes in to the cheap deal destiny has dealt her for this date: a plump little cork of a man, stiff-comb Afro, bandana-red T-shirt and battle-weary jeans. Truly light years away from her glittering, dental assistant dreams. But truly, too, the historic moment has come, is banging down the door like a drunken husband, and it's getting later all the time and she already missed the big ride once; there was Viet Nam and there was emigration and that left rationing in between, and statehood is for the poor, and you jog or you get fat though after all it's not the gun that counts but the shot it fires. So there it is, the whole thing, scientifically programmed right down to the radio that will drown out her vestal cries. And then back to society sans tasseled debutante gown, and let the impenetrable veil of anonymity forever swallow up her portable emergency mate.

Suddenly, there is a wrenching scream. She rushes to the bathroom. He is straddled and half-bent over the bidet, pale as a gringo in February. When He sees her he falls to the floor, epileptically writhing and moaning as if possessed. Dawning realization that She may have gotten herself involved with a junkie, an actual, hard-core dope addict. When the moaning reaches all but a death rattle, She asks if perhaps it wouldn't be wise to call the motel clerk. As if by magic, his wailing ceases. He straightens up, maternally cooing and soothing his hurt tummy.

"I've got a stomach ache," he says, giving her his mangy-dog-looking-at-kennelmaster look.

Soneo I

First aid. Mouth-to-mouth resuscitation. Caressing the crisis-stricken belly, She breaks into a full-blown rap on historical materialism and classless society. Vigorous dictatorship-of-proletariat rubdown. Party Program hallelujah chorus. First on a small, then a medium, then a large scale, He experiences a gradual strengthening of his long-napping consciousness. They unite. Intoning the Fifth International in emotional unison, they bring their infrastructures to shuddering excitation. Nature answers the call of the mobilized masses and the act is dialectically consummated.

Soneo II

Heavyduty confrontation: Her on Him. She sits him down on the bed, sitting cross-legged next to him. Inspiringly fluent, dazzlingly lucid, She tears a millenium of oppression to shreds; all those centuries of ironing, comrade, and all that forced kitchen work. She gets carried away in her own eloquence, using her brassiere as an ashtray while emphatically demanding genital equality. Caught in the implacable spotlight of reason, He confesses, repents, firmly resolves to mend his ways and fervently implores communion with her. Their emotions stirred, they join hands and unite in a long, egalitarian kiss, inserting exactly the same amount of tongue into their respective bucal cavities. Nature answers the unisex call and the act is equitably consummated.

372

Soneo III

She gets dressed. He is still holding out in the bathroom. She throws his clothes to him. They split from the motel without a word to each other. When the metallic red '69 Ford stops at De Diego Street to unload its cargo, the holiday of rideable rear ends is still in full cinematic swing. Intense as a Colombian buzz, as persevering as Somoza and as shameless as the Shah, He falls basely back into it. And He's a rogue combing the streets again, a part of the endless daybreak litany that says bless my soul, brown Sally, my but you do move, baby, say, what do you eat to stay so healthy, those are some lamb chops, man, God bless rice and beans, a prime cut I'd say, Momma, watch out if I catch you . . .

JOHNNIERUTH

by BECKY BIRTHA

SUMMERTIME. Nighttime. Talk about steam heat. This whole city get like the bathroom when somebody in there taking a shower with the door shut. Nights like that, can't nobody sleep. Everybody be outside, sitting on they steps or else dragging half they furniture out on the sidewalk—kitchen chairs, card tables—even bringing TVs outside.

Womenfolks, mostly. All the grown women around my way look just the same. They all big—stout. They got big bosoms and big hips and fat legs, and they always wearing runover house-shoes, and them shapeless, flowered numbers with the buttons down the front. Cept on Sunday. Sunday morning they all turn into glamour girls, in them big hats and long gloves, with they skinny high heels and they skinny selves in them tight girdles—wouldn't nobody ever know what they look like the rest of the time.

When I was a little kid I didn't wanna grow up, cause I never wanted to look like them ladies. I heard Miz Jenkins down the street one time say she don't mind being fat cause that way her husband don't get so jealous. She say it's more than one way to keep a man. Me, I don't have me no intentions of keeping no man. I never understood why they was in so much demand anyway, when it seem like all a woman can depend on em for is making sure she keep on having babies.

We got enough children in my neighborhood. In the summertime, even the little kids allowed to stay up till eleven or twelve o'clock at night—playing in the street and hollering and carrying

374

on—don't never seem to get tired. Don't nobody care, long as they don't fight.

Me—I don't hang around no front steps no more. Hot nights like that, I get out my ten speed and I be gone.

That's what I like to do more than anything else in the whole world. Feel that wind in my face keeping me cool as a air conditioner, shooting along like a snowball. My bike light as a kite. I can really get up some speed.

All the guys around my way got ten speed bikes. Some of the girls got em too, but they don't ride em at night. They pedal around during the day, but at nighttime they just hang around out front, watching babies and running they mouth. I didn't get my Peugeot to be no conversation piece.

My mama don't like me to ride at night. I tried to point out to her that she ain't never said nothing to my brothers, and Vincent a year younger than me. (And Langston two years older, in case "old" is the problem.) She say, "That's different, Johnnieruth. You're a girl." Now I wanna know how is anybody gonna know that. I'm skinny as a knifeblade turned sideways, and all I ever wear is blue jeans and a Wrangler jacket. But if I bring that up, she liable to get started in on how come I can't be more of a young lady, and fourteen is old enough to start taking more pride in my appearance, and she gonna be ashamed to admit I'm her daughter.

I just tell her that my bike be moving so fast can't nobody hardly see me, and couldn't catch me if they did. Mama complain to her friends how I'm wild and she can't do nothing with me. She know I'm gonna do what I want no matter what she say. But she know I ain't getting in no trouble, neither.

Like some of the boys I know stole they bikes, but I didn't do nothing like that. I'd been saving my money ever since I can remember, every time I could get a nickel or a dime outta anybody.

When I was a little kid, it was hard to get money. Seem like the only time they ever give you any was on Sunday morning, and then you had to put it in the offering. I used to hate to do that. In fact, I used to hate everything about Sunday morning. I had to wear all them ruffly dresses—that shiny slippery stuff in the wintertime that got to make a noise every time you move your ass a inch on them hard old benches. And that scratchy starchy stuff in the summertime with all them scratchy crinolines. Had to carry a pocketbook and wear them shiny shoes. And the church we went to was all the way

375

over on Summit Avenue, so the whole damn neighborhood could get a good look. At least all the other kids'd be dressed the same way. The boys think they slick cause they get to wear pants, but they still got to wear a white shirt and a tie; and them dumb hats they wear can't hide them baldheaded haircuts, cause they got to take the hats off in church.

There was one Sunday when I musta been around eight. I remember it was before my sister Corletta was born, cause right around then was when I put my foot down about the whole sanctimonious routine. Anyway, I was dragging my feet along Twenty-fifth Street in back of Mama and Vincent and them, when I spied this lady. I only seen her that one time, but I still remember just how she look. She don't look like nobody I ever seen before. I *know* she don't live around here. She real skinny. But she ain't no real young woman, either. She could be old as my mama. She ain't nobody's mama—I'm sure. And she ain't wearing Sunday clothes. She got on blue jeans and a man's blue working shirt, with the tail hanging out. She got patches on her blue jeans, and she still got her chin stuck out like she some kinda African royalty. She ain't carrying no shiny pocketbook. It don't look like she care if she got any money or not, or who know it, if she don't. She ain't wearing no house-shoes, or stockings or high heels neither.

Mama always speak to everybody, but when she pass by this lady she make like she ain't even seen her. But I get me a real good look, and the lady stare right back at me. She got a funny look on her face, almost like she think she know me from some place. After she pass on by, I had to turn around to get another look, even though Mama say that ain't polite. And you know what? She was turning around, too, looking back at me. And she give me a great big smile.

I didn't know too much in them days, but that's when I first got to thinking about how it's got to be different ways to be, from the way people be around my way. It's got to be places where it don't matter to nobody if you all dressed up on Sunday morning or you ain't. That's how come I started saving money. So, when I got enough, I could go away to some place like that.

Afterwhile I begun to see there wasn't no point in waiting around for handouts, and I started thinking of ways to earn my own money. I used to be running errands all the time—mailing letters for old Grandma Whittaker and picking up cigarettes and newspapers up the corner for everybody. After I got bigger, I started washing cars in the summer, and shoveling people sidewalk in the wintertime. Now I got me a newspaper route. Ain't never been no girl around here with no paper route, but I guess everybody got it figured out by now that I ain't gonna be like nobody else.

The reason I got me my Peugeot was so I could start to explore. I figured I better start looking around right now, so when I'm grown, I'll know exactly where I wanna go. So I ride around every chance I get.

Last summer, I used to ride with the boys a lot. Sometimes eight or ten of us'd just go cruising around the streets together. All of a sudden my mama decide she don't want me to do that no more. She say I'm too old to be spending so much time with boys. (That's what they tell you half the time, and the other half the time they worried cause you ain't interested in spending more time with boys. Don't make much sense.) She want me to have some girl friends, but I never seem to fit in with none of the things the girls doing. I used to think I fit in more with the boys.

But I seen how Mama might be right, for once. I didn't like the way the boys was starting to talk about girls sometimes. Talking about what some girl be like from the neck on down, and talking all up underneath somebody clothes and all. Even though I wasn't really friends with none of the girls, I still didn't like it. So now I mostly just ride around by myself. And Mama don't like that neither—you just can't please her.

This boy that live around the corner on North Street, Kenny Henderson, started asking me one time if I don't ever be lonely, cause he always see me by myself. He say don't I ever think I'd like to have me somebody special to go places with and stuff. Like I'd pick him if I did! Made me wanna laugh in his face. I do be lonely, a lotta times, but I don't tell nobody. And I ain't met nobody yet that I'd really rather be with than be by myself. But I will someday. When I find that special place where everybody different, I'm gonna find somebody there I can be friends with. And it ain't gonna be no dumb boy.

I found me one place already, that I like to go to a whole lot. It ain't even really that far away—by bike—but it's on the other side of the Avenue. So I don't tell Mama and them I go there, cause they like to think I'm right around the neighborhood someplace. But this neighborhood too dull for me. All the houses look just the same— no porches, no yards, no trees—not even no parks around here.

Every block look so much like every other block it hurt your eyes to look at, afterwhile. So I ride across Summit Avenue and go down that big steep hill there, and then make a sharp right at the bottom and cross the bridge over the train tracks. Then I head on out the boulevard—that's the nicest part, with all them big trees making a tunnel over the top, and lightning bugs shining in the bushes. At the end of the boulevard you get to this place call the Plaza.

It's something like a little park—the sidewalks is all bricks and they got flowers planted all over the place. The same kind my mama grow in that painted-up tire she got out from masquerading like a garden decoration—only seem like they smell sweeter here. It's a big high fountain right in the middle, and all the streetlights is the real old-fashion kind. That Plaza is about the prettiest place I ever been.

Sometimes something going on there. Like a orchestra playing music or some man or lady singing. One time they had a show with some girls doing some kinda foreign dances. They look like they were around my age. They all had on these fancy costumes, with different color ribbons all down they back. I wouldn't wear nothing like that, but it looked real pretty when they was dancing.

I got me a special bench in one corner where I like to sit, cause I can see just about everything, but wouldn't nobody know I was there. I like to sit still and think, and I like to watch people. A lotta people be coming there at night—to look at the shows and stuff, or just to hang out and cool off. All different kinda people.

This one night when I was sitting over in that corner where I always be at, there was this lady standing right near my bench. She mostly had her back turned to me and she didn't know I was there, but I could see her real good. She had on this shiny purple shirt and about a million silver bracelets. I kinda liked the way she look. Sorta exotic, like she maybe come from California or one of the islands. I mean she had class—standing there posing with her arms folded. She walk away a little bit. Then turn around and walk back again. Like she waiting for somebody.

Then I spotted this dude coming over. I spied him all the way cross the Plaza. Looking real fine. Got on a three piece suit. One of them little caps sitting on a angle. Look like leather. He coming straight over to this lady I'm watching and then she seen him too and she start to smile, but she don't move till he get right up next to her. And then I'm gonna look away, cause I can't stand to watch

378

nobody hugging and kissing on each other, but all of a sudden I see it ain't no dude at all. It's another lady.

Now I can't stop looking. They smiling at each other like they ain't seen one another in ten years. Then the one in the purple shirt look around real quick—but she don't look just behind her—and sorta pull the other one right back into the corner where I'm sitting at, and then they put they arms around each other and kiss—for a whole long time. Now I really know I oughtta turn away, but I can't. And I know they gonna see me when they finally open they eyes. And they do.

They both kinda gasp and back up, like I'm the monster that just rose up outta the deep. And then I guess they can see I'm only a girl, and they look at one another—and start to laugh! Then they just turn around and start to walk away like it wasn't nothing at all. But right before they gone, they both look around again, and see I still ain't got my eye muscles and my jaw muscles working right again yet. And the one lady wink at me. And the other one say, "Catch you later."

I can't stop staring at they backs, all the way across the Plaza. And then, all of a sudden, I feel like I got to be doing something, got to be moving.

I wheel on outta the Plaza and I'm just concentrating on getting up my speed. Cause I can't figure out what to think. Them two women kissing and then, when they get caught, just laughing about it. And here I'm laughing too, for no reason at all. I'm sailing down the boulevard laughing like a lunatic, and then I'm singing at the top of my lungs. And climbing that big old hill up to Summit Avenue is just as easy as being on a escalator.

LAWNS

by MONA SIMPSON

I STEAL. I've stolen books and money and even letters. Letters are great. I can't tell you the feeling, walking down the street with twenty dollars in my purse, stolen earrings in my pocket. I don't get caught. That's the amazing thing. You're out on the sidewalk, other people all around, shopping, walking, and you've got it. You're out of the store, you've done this thing you're not supposed to do, but no one stops you. At first it's a rush. Like you're even for everything you didn't get before. But then you're left alone, no one even notices you. Nothing changes.

I work in the mailroom of my dormitory, Saturday mornings. I sort mail, put the letters in these long narrow cubbyholes. The insides of mailboxes. It's cool there when I stick in my arm.

I've stolen cash—these crisp, crackling, brand new twenty-dollar bills the fathers and grandmothers send, sealed up in sheets of wax paper. Once I got a fifty. I've stolen presents, too. I got a sweater and a football. I didn't want the football, but after the package was messed up on the mail table, I had no choice, I had to take the whole thing in my daypack and throw it out on the other side of campus. I found a covered garbage can. It was miles away. Brand new football.

Mostly, what I take are cookies. No evidence. They're edible. I can spot the coffee cans of chocolate chip. You can smell it right through the wrapping. A cool smell, like the inside of a pantry. Sometimes I eat straight through a can during just my shift.

Tampering with the United States mail is a Federal Crime, I know. Listen, let me tell you, I know. I got a summons in my

380

mailbox to go to the Employment Office next Wednesday. Sure I'm scared.

The University cops want to talk to me. Great. They think, suspect is the word they use, that one of us is throwing out mail instead of sorting it. Wonder who? Us is the others. I'm not the only sorter. I just work Saturdays, mail comes, you know, six days a week in this country. They'll never guess it's me.

They say this in the letter, they think it's out of LAZINESS. Wanting to hurry up and get done, not spend the time. But I don't hurry. I'm really patient on Saturday mornings. I leave my dorm early, while Lauren's still asleep, I open the mailroom—it's this heavy door and I have my own key. When I get there, two bags are already on the table, sagging, waiting for me. Two old ladies. One's packages, one's mail. There's a small key opens the bank of doors, the little boxes from the inside. Through the glass part of every mail slot, I can see. The astroturf field across the street over the parking lot, it's this light green. I watch the sky go from black to grey to blue while I'm there. Some days just stay foggy. Those are the best. I bring a cup of coffee in with me from the vending machine—don't want to wake Lauren up—and I get there at like seven-thirty or eight o'clock. I don't mind it then, my whole dorm's asleep. When I walk out it's as quiet as a football game day. It's eleven or twelve when you know everyone's up and walking that it gets bad being down there. That's why I start early. But I don't rush.

Once you open a letter, you can't just put it in a mailbox. The person's gonna say something. So I stash them in my pack and throw them out. Just people I know. Susan Brown, I open, Annie Larsen, Larry Helprin. All the popular kids from my high school. These are kids who drove places together, took vacations, they all ski, they went to the prom in one big group. At morning nutri- tion—nutrition, it's your break at ten o'clock for donuts and stuff. California State law, you have to have it.

They used to meet outside on the far end of the math patio, all in one group. Some of them smoked. I've seen them look at each other, concerned at ten in the morning. One touched the inside of another's wrist, like grown-ups in trouble.

And now I know. Everything I thought those three years, worst years of my life, turns out to be true. The ones here get letters. Keri's at Santa Cruz, Lilly's in San Diego, Kevin's at Harvard and

Beth's at Stanford. And like from families, their letters talk about problems. They're each other's main lives. You always knew, looking at them in high school, they weren't just kids who had fun. They cared. They cared about things.

They're all worried about Lilly now. Larry and Annie are flying down to talk her into staying at school.

I saw Glenn the day I came to Berkeley. I was all unpacked and I was standing there leaning into the window of my father's car, saying "Smile, Dad, jeez, at least try, would you?" He was crying because he was leaving. I'm thinking oh, my god, some of these other kids, carrying in their trunks and backpacks are gonna see him, and then finally, he drives away and I was sad. That was the moment I was waiting for, him gone and me alone and there it was and I was sad. I took a walk through campus and I'd been walking for almost an hour and then I see Glenn, coming down on a little hill by the infirmary, riding on one of those lawn mowers you sit on, with grass flying out of the side and he's smiling. Not at me but just smiling. Clouds and sky behind his hair, half of Tamalpais gone in fog. He was wearing this bright orange vest and I thought, fall's coming.

I saw him that night again in our dorm cafeteria. This's the first time I've been in love. I worry. I'm a bad person, but Glenn's the perfect guy, I mean for me at least, and he thinks he loves me and I've got to keep him from finding out about me. I'll die before I'll tell him. Glenn, OK, Glenn. He looks like Mick Jagger, but sweet, ten times sweeter. He looks like he's about ten years old. His father's a doctor over at UC Med. Gynecological surgeon.

First time we got together, a whole bunch of us were in Glenn's room drinking beer, Glenn and his roommate collect beer cans, they have them stacked up, we're watching TV and finally everybody else leaves. There's nothing on but those grey lines and Glenn turns over on his bed and asks me if I'd rub his back.

I couldn't believe this was happening to me. In high school, I was always ending up with the wrong guys, never the one I wanted. But I wanted it to be Glenn and I knew it was going to happen, I knew I didn't have to do anything. I just had to stay there. It would happen. I was sitting on his rear end, rubbing his back, going under his shirt with my hands. His back felt so good, it was smooth and warm, like cement around a pool.

All of a sudden, I was worried about my breath and what I

smelled like. When I turned fourteen or fifteen, my father told me once that I didn't smell good. I slugged him when he said that and didn't talk to him for days, not that I cared about what I smelled like with my father. He was happy, though, kind of, that he could hurt me. That was the last time, though, I'll tell you.

Glenn's face was down in the pillow. I tried to sniff myself but I couldn't tell anything. And it went all right anyway.

I don't open Glenn's letters but I touch them. I hold them and smell them—none of his mail has any smell.

He doesn't get many letters. His parents live across the Bay in Marin County, they don't write. He gets letters from his grandmother in Michigan, plain, even handwriting on regular envelopes, a sticker with her return address printed on it, Rural Route #3, Guns Street. See, I got it memorized.

And he gets letters from Diane, Di, they call her. High school girlfriend. Has a pushy mother, wants her to be a scientist, but she already got a C in Chem 1A. I got an A+, not to brag. He never slept with her, though, she wouldn't, she's still a virgin down in San Diego. With Lilly. Maybe they even know each other.

Glenn and Di were popular kids in their high school. Redwood High. Now I'm one because of Glenn, popular. Because I'm his girlfriend, I know that's why. Not 'cause of me. I just know, OK, I'm not going to start fooling myself now. Please.

Her letters I hold up to the light, they've got florescent lights in there. She's supposed to be blonde, you know, and pretty. Quiet. The soft type. And the envelopes. She writes on these sheer cream-colored envelopes and they get transparent and I can see her writing underneath, but not enough to read what it says, it's like those hockey lines painted under layers of ice.

I run my tongue along the place where his grandmother sealed the letter. A sharp, sweet gummy taste. Once I cut my tongue. That's what keeps me going to the bottom of the bag, I'm always wondering if there'll be a letter for Glenn. He doesn't get one every week. It's like a treasure. Cracker Jack prize. But I'd never open Glenn's mail. I kiss all four corners where his fingers will touch, opening it, before I put it in his box. Sometimes I hold them up and blow on it.

I brought home cookies for Lauren and me. Just a present. We'll eat 'em or Glenn'll eat 'em. I'll throw them out for all I care.

They're chocolate chip with pecans. This was one good mother. A lucky can. I brought us coffee, too. I *bought* it.

Yeah, OK, so I'm in trouble. Wednesday, at ten-thirty, I got this notice I was supposed to appear. I had a class, Chem 1C, pre-med staple. Your critical thing. I never missed it before. I told Glenn I had a doctor's appointment.

OK, so I skip it anyway and I walk into this room and there's these two other guys, all work in the mailroom doing what I do, sorting. And we all sit there on chairs on this green carpet. I was staring at everybody's shoes. And there's a cop. University cop, I don't know what's the difference. He had this sagging, pear-shaped body. Like what my dad would have if he were fat, but he's not, he's thin. He walks slowly on the carpeting, his fingers hooked in his belt loops. I was watching his hips.

Anyway, he's accusing us all and he's trying to get one of us to admit we did it. No way.

"I hope one of you will come to me and tell the truth. Not a one of you knows anything about this? Come on, now."

I shake my head no and stare down at the three pairs of shoes. He says they're not going to do anything to the person who did it, right, wanna make a bet, they say they just want to know, but they'll take it back as soon as you tell them.

I don't care why I don't believe him. I know one thing for sure and that's they're not going to do anything to me as long as I say, NO, I didn't do it. That's what I said, no, I didn't do it, I don't know a thing about it. I just can't imagine where those missing packages could have gone, how letters got into garbage cans. Awful. I just don't know.

The cop had a map with Xs on it every place they found mail. The garbage cans. He said there was a group of students trying to get an investigation. People's girlfriends sent cookies that never got here. Letters were missing. Money. These students put up xeroxed posters on bulletin boards showing a garbage can stuffed with letters.

Why should I tell them, so they can throw me in jail? And kick me out of school? Four-point-oh average and I'm going to let them kick me out of school? They're sitting there telling us it's a felony. A Federal Crime. No way, I'm gonna go to medical school.

This tall, skinny guy with a blonde mustache, Wallabees, looks kind of like a rabbit, he defended us. He's another sorter, works Monday/Wednesdays.

"We all do our jobs," he says. "None of us would do that." The rabbity guy looks at me and the other girl, for support. So we're going to stick together. The other girl, a dark blonde, chewing her lip, nodded. I loved that rabbity guy that second. I nodded too.

The cop looked down. Wide hips in the coffee-with-milk-colored pants. He sighed. I looked up at the rabbity guy. They let us all go.

I'm just going to keep saying no, not me, didn't do it and I just won't do it again. That's all. Won't do it anymore. So, this is Glenn's last chance for homemade cookies. I'm sure as hell not going to bake any.

I signed the form, said I didn't do it, I'm OK now. I'm safe. It turned out OK after all, it always does. I always think something terrible's going to happen and it doesn't. I'm lucky.

I'm afraid of cops. I was walking, just a little while ago, today, down Telegraph with Glenn, and these two policemen, not the one I'd met, other policemen, were coming in our direction. I started sweating a lot. I was sure until they passed us, I was sure it was all over, they were there for me. I always think that. But at the same time, I know it's just my imagination. I mean, I'm a four-point-oh student, I'm a nice girl just walking down the street with my boyfriend.

We were on our way to get Happy Burgers. When we turned the corner, about a block past the cops, I looked at Glenn and I was flooded with like this feeling. It was raining a little and we were by People's Park. The trees were blowing and I was looking at all those little gardens coming up, held together with stakes and white string.

I wanted to say something to Glenn, give him something. I wanted to tell him something about me.

"I'm bad in bed," that's what I said, I just blurted it out like that. He just kind of looked at me, he was nervous, he just giggled. He didn't know what to say, I guess, but he sort of slung his arm around me and I was so grateful and then we went in. He paid for my Happy Burger, I usually don't let him pay for me, but I did and it was the best goddamn hamburger I've ever eaten.

I want to tell him things.

I lie all the time, always have, but I keep track of each lie I've ever told Glenn and I'm always thinking of the things I can't tell him.

Glenn was a screwed up kid, kind of. He used to go in his

backyard, his parents were inside the house I guess, and he'd find this big stick and start twirling around with it. He'd dance, he called it dancing, until if you came up and clapped in front of him, he wouldn't see you. He'd spin around with that stick until he fell down dead on the grass, unconscious, he said he did it to see the sky break up in pieces and spin. He did it sometimes with a tire swing, too. He told me when he was spinning like that, it felt like he was just hearing the earth spinning, that it really went that fast all the time but we just don't feel it. When he was twelve years old or something, his parents took him in the city to a clinic t'see a psychologist. And then he stopped. See, maybe I should go to a psychologist. I'd get better, too. He told me about that in bed one night. The ground feels so good when you fall, he said to me. I loved him for that.

"Does anything feel that good now?" I said.

"Sex sometimes. Maybe dancing."

Know what else he told me that night? He said, right before we went to sleep, he wasn't looking at me, he said he'd been thinking what would happen if I died, he said he thought how he'd be at my funeral, all my family and my friends from high school and my little brother would all be around at the front and he'd be at the edge in the cemetery, nobody'd even know who he was.

I was in that crack, breathing the air between the bed and the wall. Cold and dusty. Yeah, we're having sex. I don't know. It's good. Sweet. He says he loves me. I have to remind myself. I talk to myself in my head while we're doing it. I have to say, it's OK, this is just Glenn, this is who I want it to be and it's just like rubbing next to someone. It's just like pushing two hands together, so there's no air in between.

I cry sometimes with Glenn, I'm so grateful.

My mother called and woke me up this morning. Ms. I'm-going-to-be-perfect. Ms. anything-wrong-is-your-own-fault. Ms. if-any-thing-bad-happens-you're-a-fool.

She says if she has time, she MIGHT come up and see my dorm room in the next few weeks. Help me organize my wardrobe, she says. She didn't bring me up here, my dad did. I wanted Danny to come along, I love Danny.

But my mother has NO pity. She thinks she's got the answers. She's the one who's a lawyer, she's the one who went back to law school and stayed up late nights studying while she still made our lunch boxes. With gourmet cheese. She's proud of it, she tells you. She loves my dad, I guess. She thinks we're like this great family and she sits there at the dinner table bragging about us, to us. She xeroxed my grade card first quarter with my Chemistry A+ so she's got it in her office and she's got the copy up on the refrigerator at home. She's sitting there telling all her friends that and I'm thinking, you don't know it, but I'm not one of you.

These people across the street from us. Little girl, Sarah, eight years old. Maybe seven. Her dad, he worked for the army, some kind of researcher, he decides he wants to get a sex-change operation. And he goes and does it, over at Stanford. My mom goes out, takes the dog for a walk, right. The mother CONFIDES in her. Says the thing she regrets most is she wants to have more children. The little girl, Sarah, eight years old, looks up at my mom and says, "Daddy's going to be an aunt."

Now that's sad, I think that's really sad. My mom thinks it's a good dinner table story, proving how much better we are than them. Yeah, I remember exactly what she said that night. "That's all Sarah's mother's got to worry about now, is that she wants another child. Meanwhile, Daddy's becoming an aunt."

She should know about me.

So my dad comes to visit for the weekend. Glenn's dad came to speak at UC one night, he took Glenn out to dinner to a nice place, Glenn was glad to see him. Yeah, well. My dad. Comes to the dorm. Skulks around. This guy's a BUSINESSMAN, in a three-piece suit, and he acts inferior to the eighteen-year-old freshmen coming in the lobby. My dad. Makes me sick right now thinking of him standing there in the lobby and everybody seeing him. He was probably looking at the kids and looking jealous. Just standing there. Why? Don't ask me why, he's the one that's forty-two years old.

So he's standing there, nervous, probably sucking his hand, that's what he does when he's nervous, I'm always telling him not to. Finally, somebody takes him to my room. I'm not there, Lauren's gone, and he waits for I don't know how long.

When I come in he's standing with his back to the door looking out the window. I see him and right away I know it's him and I have this urge to tip-toe away and he'll never see me.

My pink sweater, a nice sweater, a sweater I wore a lot in high school was over my chair, hanging on the back of it and my father's got one hand on the sweater shoulder and he's like rubbing the other hand down an empty arm. He looks up at me, already scared and grateful when I walk into the room. I feel like smashing him with a baseball bat. Why can't he just stand up straight?

I drop my books on the bed and stand there while he hugs me.

"Hi, Daddy, what are you doing here?"

"I wanted to see you." He sits in my chair now, his legs crossed and big, too big for this room, and he's still fingering the arm of my pink sweater. "I missed you so I got away for the weekend," he says. "I have a room up here at the Claremont Hotel."

So he's here for the weekend. He's just sitting in my dorm room and I have to figure out what to do with him. He's not going to do anything. He'd just sit here. And Lauren's coming back soon so I've got to get him out. It's Friday afternoon and the weekend's shot. OK, so I'll go with him. I'll go with him and get it over with.

But I'm not going to miss my date with Glenn Saturday night. No way. I'd die before I'd cancel that. It's bad enough missing dinner in the cafeteria tonight. Friday's eggplant, my favorite, and Friday nights are usually easy, music on the stereos all down the hall. We usually work, but work slow and talk and then we all meet in Glenn's room around ten.

"Come, sit on my lap, honey." My dad like pulls me down and starts bouncing me. BOUNCING ME. I stand up. "OK, we can go somewhere tonight and tomorrow morning, but I have to be back for tomorrow night. I've got plans with people. And I've got to study, too."

"You can bring your books back to the hotel," he says. "I'm supposed to be at a convention in San Francisco, but I wanted to see you. I have work, too, we can call room service and both just work."

"I still have to be back by four tomorrow."

"All right."

"OK, just a minute." And he sat there in my chair while I called Glenn and told him I wouldn't be here for dinner. I pulled the phone out into the hall, it only stretches so far, and whispered. "Yeah, my father's here," I said, "he's got a conference in San Francisco. He just came by."

Glenn lowered his voice, sweet, and said, "Sounds fun."

My dad sat there, hunched over in my chair, while I changed my

388

shirt and put on deodorant. I put a nightgown in my shoulder pack and my toothbrush and I took my chem book and we left. I knew I wouldn't be back for a whole day. I was trying to calm myself thinking, well, it's only one day, that's nothing in my life. The halls were empty, it was five o'clock, five-ten, everyone was down at dinner.

We walk outside and the cafeteria lights are on and I see everyone moving around with their trays. Then my dad picks up my hand.

I yank it out. "Dad," I say, really mean.

"Honey, I'm your father." His voice trails off. "Other girls hold their fathers' hands." It was dark enough for the lights to be on in the cafeteria, but it wasn't really dark out yet. The sky was blue. On the tennis courts on top of the garage, two Chinese guys were playing. I heard that thonk-pong and it sounded so carefree and I just wanted to be them. I'd have even given up Glenn, Glenn-that-I-love-more-than-anything, at that second, I would have given everything up just to be someone else, someone new. I got into the car and slammed the door shut and turned up the heat.

"Should we just go to the hotel and do our work? We can get a nice dinner in the room."

"I'd rather go out," I said, looking down at my hands. He went where I told him. I said the name of the restaurant and gave directions. Chez Panisse and we ordered the most expensive stuff. Appetizers and two desserts just for me. A hundred and twenty bucks for the two of us.

OK, this hotel room.

So, my dad's got the Bridal Suite. He claimed that was all they had. Fat chance. Two-hundred-eighty room hotel and all they've got left is this deal with the canopy bed, no way. It's in the tower, you can almost see it from the dorm. Makes me sick. From the bathroom, there's this window, shaped like an arch, and it looks over all of Berkeley. You can see the bridge lights. As soon as we got there, I locked myself in the bathroom, I was so mad about that canopy bed. I took a long bath and washed my hair. They had little soaps wrapped up there, shampoo, may as well use them, he's paying for it. It's this deep old bathtub and wind was coming in from outside and I felt like that window was just open, no glass, just a hole cut out in the stone.

389

I was thinking of when I was little and what they taught us in catechism. I thought a soul was inside your chest, this long horizontal triangle with rounded edges, made out of some kind of white fog, some kind of gas or vapor. I could be pregnant. I soaped myself all up and rinsed off with cold water. I'm lucky I never got pregnant, really lucky.

Other kids my age, Lauren, everybody, I know things they don't know. I know more for my age. Too much. Like I'm not a virgin. Lots of people are, you'd be surprised. I know about a lot things being wrong and unfair, all kinds of stuff. It's like seeing a UFO, if I ever saw something like that, I'd never tell, I'd wish I'd never seen it.

My dad knocks on the door.

"What do you want?"

"Let me just come in and talk to you while you're in there."

"I'm done, I'll be right out. Just a minute." I took a long time towelling. No hurry, believe me. So I got into bed, with my nightgown on and wet already from my hair. I turned away. Breathed against the wall. "Night."

My father hooks my hair over my ear and touches my shoulder. "Tired?"

I shrug.

"You really have to go back tomorrow? We could go to Marin or to the beach. Anything."

I hugged my knees up under my nightgown. "You should go to your conference, Dad."

I wake up in the middle of the night, I feel something's going on, and sure enough, my dad's down there, he's got my nightgown worked up to like a frill around my neck and my legs hooked over his shoulders.

"Dad, stop it."

"I just wanted to make you feel good," he says and looks up at me. "What's wrong? Don't you love me anymore?"

I never really told anybody. It's not exactly the kind of thing you can bring up over lunch. "So, I'm sleeping with my father. Oh, and let's split a dessert." Right.

I don't know, other people think my dad's handsome. They say he is. My mother thinks so, you should see her traipsing around the balcony when she gets in her romantic moods, which, on her professional lawyer schedule, are about once a year, thank god. It's pathetic. He thinks she's repulsive, though. I don't know that, that's what I think. But he loves me, that's for sure.

So next day, Saturday—that rabbity guy, Paul's his name, he did my shift for me—we go downtown and I got him to buy me this suit. Three hundred dollars from Saks. Oh, and I got shoes. So I stayed later with him because of the clothes, and I was a little happy because I thought at least now I'd have something good to wear with Glenn. My dad and I got brownie sundaes at Sweet Dreams and I got home by five. He was crying when he dropped me off.

"Don't cry, Dad. Please," I said. Jesus, how can you not hate someone who's always begging from you.

Lauren had Poly Styrene on the stereo and a candle lit in our room. I was never so glad to be home.

"Hey," Lauren said. She was on her bed, with her legs propped up on the wall. She'd just shaved. She was rubbing in cream.

I flopped down on my bed. "Ohhhh," I said, grabbing the sides of the mattress.

"Hey, can you keep a secret about what I did today?" Lauren said. "I went to that therapist, up at Cowell."

"You have the greatest legs," I said, quiet. "Why don't you ever wear skirts?"

She stopped what she was doing and stood up. "You think they're good? I don't like the way they look, except in jeans." She looked down at them. "They're crooked, see?" She shook her head. "I don't want to think about it."

Then she went to her dresser and started rolling a joint. "Want some?"

"A little."

She lit up, lay back on her bed and held her arm out for me to come take the joint.

"So, she was this really great woman. Warm, kind of chubby. She knew instantly what kind of man Brent was." Lauren snapped her fingers. "Like that." Brent was the pool man Lauren had an affair with, home in LA.

I'm back in the room maybe an hour, putting on mascara, my jeans are on the bed pressed, and the phone rings and it's my dad and I say, "Listen, just leave me alone."

"You don't care about me anymore."

391

"I just saw you. I have nothing to say. We just saw each other."

"What are you doing tonight?"

"Going out."

"Who are you seeing?"

"Glenn."

He sighs. "So you really like him, huh?"

"Yeah, I do and you should be glad. You should be glad I have a boyfriend." I pull the cord out into the hall and sit down on the floor there. There's this long pause.

"We're not going to end up together, are we?"

I felt like all the air's knocked out of me. I looked out the window and everything looked dead and still. The parked cars. The trees with pink toilet paper strung between the branches. The church all closed up across the street.

"No, we won't, Daddy."

He was crying. "I know, I know."

I hung up the phone and went back and sat in the hall. I'm scared, too. I don't know what'll happen.

I don't know. It's been going on I guess as long as I can remember. I mean, not the sex, but my father. When I was a little kid, tiny little kid, my dad came in before bed and said his prayers with me. He kneeled down by my bed and I was on my back. PRAYERS. He'd lift up my pajama top and put his hands on my breast. Little fried eggs, he said. One time with his tongue. Then one night, he pulled down the elastic of my pajama pants. He did it for an hour and then I came. Don't believe anything they ever tell you about kids not coming. That first time was the biggest I ever had and I didn't even know what it was then. It just kept going and going as if he was breaking me through layers and layers of glass and I felt like I'd slipped and let go and I didn't have myself anymore, he had me, and once I'd slipped like that I'd never be the same again.

We had this sprinkler in our back lawn, Danny and me used to run through it in summer and my dad'd be outside, working on the grass or the hedge or something and he'd squirt us with the hose. I used to wear a bathing suit bottom, no top—we were this modern family, our parents walked around the house naked after showers and then Danny and I ended up both being these modest kids, can't stand anyone to see us even in our underwear, I always dress

392

facing the closet, Lauren teases me. We'd run through the sprinkler and my dad would come up and pat my bottom and the way he
put his hand on my thigh, I felt like Danny could tell it was
different than the way he touched him, I was like something he
owned.

First time when I was nine, I remember, Dad and me were in
the shower together. My mom might have even been in the house,
they did that kind of stuff, it was supposed to be OK. Anyway,
we're in the shower and I remember this look my dad had. Like he
was daring me, knowing he knew more than I did. We're both
under the shower. The water pasted his hair down on his head and
he looked younger and weird. "Touch it. Don't be afraid of it," he
says. And he grabs my thighs on the outside and pulls me close to
him, pulling on my fat.

He waited till I was twelve to really do it. I don't know if you can
call it rape, I was a good sport. The creepy thing is I know how it
felt for him, I could see it on his face when he did it. He thought he
was getting away with something. We were supposed to go hiking
but right away that morning when we got into the car, he knew he
was going to do it. He couldn't wait to get going. I said I didn't feel
good, I had a cold, I wanted to stay home, but he made me go
anyway and we hiked two miles and he set up the tent. He told me
to take my clothes off and I undressed just like that, standing there
in the woods. He's the one who was nervous and got us into the
tent. I looked old for twelve, small but old. And right there on the
ground, he spread my legs open and pulled my feet up and fucked
me. I bled. I couldn't even breathe the tent was so small. He could
have done anything. He could have killed me, he had me alone on
this mountain.

I think about that sometimes when I'm alone with Glenn in my
bed. It's so easy to hurt people. They just lie there and let you have
them. I could reach out and choke Glenn to death, he'd be so
shocked, he wouldn't stop me. You can just take what you want.

My dad thought he was getting away with something but he
didn't. He was the one that fell in love, not me. And after that day,
when we were back in the car, I was the one giving orders. From
then on, I got what I wanted. He spent about twice as much money
on me as on Danny and everyone knew it, Danny and my mom,
too. How do you think I got good clothes and a good bike and a

good stereo? My dad's not rich, you know. And I'm the one who got to go away to college even though it killed him. Says it's the saddest thing that ever happened in his life, me going away and leaving him. But when I was a little kid that day, he wasn't in love with me, not like he is now.

Only thing I'm sad about isn't either of my parents, it's Danny. Leaving Danny alone there with them. He used to send Danny out of the house. My mom'd be at work on a Saturday afternoon or something or even in the morning and my dad would kick my little brother out of his own house. Go out and play, Danny. Why doncha catch some rays. And Danny just went and got his glove and baseball from the closet and he'd go and throw it against the house, against the outside wall, in the driveway. I'd be in my room, I'd be like dead, I'd be wood, telling myself this doesn't count, no one has to know, I'll say I'm still a virgin, it's not really happening to me, I'm dead, I'm blank, I'm just letting time stop and pass, and then I'd hear the sock of the ball in the mitt and the slam of the screen door and I knew it was true, it was really happening.

Glenn's the one I want to tell. I can't ever tell Glenn.

I called my mom. Pay phone, collect, hour long call. I don't know, I got real mad last night and I just told her. I thought when I came here, it'd just go away. But it's not going away. It makes me weird with Glenn. In the morning, with Glenn, when it's time to get up, I can't get up. I cry.

I knew it'd be bad. Poor Danny. Well, my mom says she might leave our dad. She cried for an hour, no jokes, on the phone.

How could he DO this to me, she kept yelping. To her. Everything's always to her.

But then she called an hour later, she'd talked to a psychiatrist already, she's kicked Dad out, and she arrives, just arrives here at Berkeley. But she was good. She says she's on my side, she'll help me, I don't know, I felt OK. She stayed in a hotel and she wanted to know if I wanted to stay there with her but I said no, I'd see her more in a week or something, I just wanted to go back to my dorm. She found this group. She says, just in San Jose, there's hundreds of families like ours, yeah, great, that's what I said. But there's groups. She's going to a group of other thick-o mothers like her, these wives who didn't catch on. She wanted me to go to a group of girls, yeah, molested girls, that's what they call them, but I said no, I have friends here already, she can do what she wants.

I talked to my dad, too, that's the sad thing, he feels like he's lost me and he wants to die and I don't know, he doesn't know what he's doing. He called in the middle of the night.

"Just tell me one thing, honey. Please tell me the truth. When did you stop?"

"Dad."

"Because I remember once you said I was the only person who ever understood you."

"I was ten years old."

"OK, OK. I'm sorry."

He didn't want to get off the phone. "You know, I love you, honey. I always will."

"Yeah, well."

My mom's got him lined up for a psychiatrist, too, she says he's lucky she's not sending him to jail. I *am* a lawyer, she keeps saying, as if we could forget. She'd pay for me to go to a shrink now, too, but I said no, forget it.

It's over. Glenn and I are, over. I feel like my dad's lost me everything. I sort of want to die now. I'm telling you I feel terrible. I told Glenn and that's it, it's over. I can't believe it either. Lauren says she's going to hit him.

I told him and we're not seeing each other anymore. Nope. He said he wanted to just think about everything for a few days. He said it had nothing to do with my father but he'd been feeling a little too settled lately. He said we don't have fun anymore, it's always so serious. That was Monday. So every meal after that, I sat with Lauren in the cafeteria and he's there on the other side, messing around with the guys. He sure didn't look like he was in any kind of agony. Wednesday, I saw Glenn over by the window in this food fight, slipping off his chair and I couldn't stand it, I got up and left and went to our room.

But I went and said I wanted to talk to Glenn that night, I didn't even have any dinner, and he said he wanted to be friends. He looked at me funny and I haven't heard from him. It's, I don't know, seven days, eight.

I know there are other guys. I live in a dorm full of them, or half-full of them. Half girls. But I keep thinking of Glenn 'cause of happiness, that's what makes me want to hang onto him.

There was this one morning when we woke up in his room, it was light out already, white light all over the room. We were sticky and warm, the sheet was all tangled. His roommate, this little blonde boy, was still sleeping. I watched his eyes open and he smiled and then he went down the hall to take a shower. Glenn was hugging me and it was nothing unusual, nothing special. We didn't screw. We were just there. We kissed, but slow, the way it is when your mouth is still bad from sleep.

I was happy that morning. I didn't have to do anything. We got dressed, went to breakfast, I don't know. Took a walk. He had to go to work at a certain time and I had that sleepy feeling from waking up with the sun on my head and he said he didn't want to say good-bye to me. There was that pang. One of those looks like as if at that second, we both felt the same way.

I shrugged. I could afford to be casual then. We didn't say good-bye. I walked with him to the shed by the Eucalyptus Grove. That's where they keep all the gardening tools, the rakes, the hoes, the mowers, big bags of grass seed slumped against the wall. It smelled like hay in there. Glenn changed into his uniform and we went to the North Side, up in front of the Chancellor's manor, that thick perfect grass. And Glenn gave me a ride on the lawn mower, on the handlebars. It was bouncing over these little bumps in the lawn and I was hanging onto the handlebars, laughing. I couldn't see Glenn but I knew he was there behind me. I looked around at the buildings and the lawns, there's a fountain there, and one dog was drinking from it.

See, I can't help but remember things like that. Even now, I'd rather find some way, even though he's not asking for it, to forgive Glenn. I'd rather have it work out with him, because I want more days like that. I wish I could have a whole life like that. But I guess nobody does, not just me.

I saw him in the mailroom yesterday, we're both just standing there, each opening our little boxes, getting our mail—neither of us had any—I was hurt but I wanted to reach out and touch his face. He has this hard chin, it's pointy and all bone. Lauren says she wants to hit him.

I mean, I think of him spinning around in his backyard and that's why I love him and he should understand. I go over it all and think

I should have just looked at him and said I can't believe you're doing this to me. Right there in the mailroom. Now when I think that, I think maybe if I'd said that, in those words, maybe it would be different.

But then I think of my father—he feels like there was a time when we had fun, when we were happy together. I mean, I can remember being in my little bed with Dad and maybe cracking jokes, maybe laughing, but he probably never heard Danny's baseball in his mitt the way I did or I don't know. I remember late in the afternoon, wearing my dad's navy blue sweatshirt with a hood and riding bikes with him and Danny down to the diamond.

But that's over. I don't know if I'm sorry it happened. I mean I am, but it happened, that's all. It's just one of the things that happened to me in my life. But I would never go back, never. And what hurts so much is that maybe that's what Glenn is thinking about me.

I told Lauren last night. I had to. She kept asking me what happened with Glenn. She was so good, you couldn't believe it, she was great. We were talking late and this morning we drove down to go to House of Pancakes for breakfast, get something good instead of watery eggs for a change. And on the way, Lauren's driving, she just skids to a stop on this street, in front of this elementary school. "Come on," she says. It's early, but there's already people inside the windows.

We hooked our fingers in the metal fence. You know, one of those aluminum fences around a playground. There were pigeons standing on the painted game circles. Then a bell rang and all these kids came out, yelling, spilling into groups. This was a poor school, mostly black kids, Mexican kids, all in bright colors. There's a Nabisco factory nearby and the whole air smelled like blueberry muffins.

The girls were jumproping and the boys were shoving and running and hanging onto the monkey bars. Lauren pinched her fingers on the back of my neck and pushed my head against the fence.

"Eight years old. Look at them. They're eight years old. One of their fathers is sleeping with one of those girls. Look at her. Do you blame her? Can you blame her? Because if you can forgive her you can forgive yourself."

397

"I'll kill him," I said.

"And I'll kill Glenn," Lauren says.

So we went and got pancakes. And drank coffee until it was time for class.

I saw Glenn yesterday. It was so weird after all this time. I just had lunch with Lauren. We picked up tickets for Talking Heads and I wanted to get back to the lab before class and I'm walking along and Glenn was working, you know, on the lawn in front of the Mobi Building. He was still gorgeous. I was just going to walk, but he yelled over at me.

"Hey, Jenny."

"Hi, Glenn."

He congratulated me, he heard about the NSF thing. We stood there. He has another girlfriend now. I don't know, when I looked at him and stood there by the lawnmower, it's chugging away, I felt the same as I always used to, that I loved him and all that, but he might just be one of those things you can't have. Like I should have been for my father and look at him now. Oh, I think he's better, they're all better, but I'm gone, he'll never have me again.

I'm glad they're there and I'm here, but it's strange, I feel more alone now. Glenn looked down at the little pile of grass by the lawnmower and said, "Well, Kid, take care of yourself," and I said, "You too, bye," and started walking.

So, you know what's bad, though, I started taking stuff again. Little stuff from the mailroom. No packages and not people I know anymore.

But I take one letter a Saturday, I make it just one and someone I don't know. And I keep 'em and burn 'em with a match in the bathroom sink and wash the ashes down the drain. I wait until the end of the shift. I always expect it to be something exciting. The two so far were just everyday letters, just mundane, so that's all that's new, I-had-a-porkchop-for-dinner letters.

But something happened today. I was in the middle, three-quarters way down the bag, still looking, I hadn't picked my letter for the day, I'm being really stern, I really mean just one, no more, and there's this little white envelope addressed to me. I sit there, trembling with it in my hand. It's the first one I've gotten all year. It was my name and address, typed out, and I just stared at it. There's no address. I got so nervous, I thought maybe it was from

Glenn, of course. I wanted it to be from Glenn so bad, but then I knew it couldn't be, he's got that new girlfriend now, so I threw it in the garbage can right there, one of those with the swinging metal door and then I finished my shift. My hands were sweating, I smudged the writing on one of the envelopes.

So all the letters are in boxes, I clean off the table, fold the bags up neat and close the door, ready to go. And then I thought, I don't have to keep looking at the garbage can, I'm allowed to take it back, that's my letter. And I fished it out, the thing practically lopped my arm off. And I had it and I held it a few minutes, wondering who it was from. Then I put it in my mailbox so I can go like everybody else and get mail.